What Doesn't Kill You

What Doesn't Kill You

Laura E. James

Book 3 – Chesil Beach

Compelling, emotional, hard-hitting novels!

Copyright © 2017 Laura E. James

Published 2017 by Choc Lit Limited
Penrose House, Crawley Drive, Camberley, Surrey GU15 2AB, UK
www.choc-lit.com

A CIP catalogue record for this book is available
from the British Library

ISBN 978-1-78189-346-3

Printed and bound by Clays Ltd

*To the brave women and men who
risk their lives to save ours*

Acknowledgements

By way of a change, I thought I'd put my
family first, because I'm very much aware that
when I'm in writing mode, it's not a position
my husband and children often see.

Thank you for your continued support,
enthusiasm and love to:

Alex, for always celebrating the small successes with
me, for the restorative hugs and for making me laugh;
to Eleanor, for sharing your amazing insight, for
asking all the right questions, and for your willingness
to talk books at any hour of the day; to Garry, for
working hard, never complaining about my late
nights, and for the thousand cups of coffee delivered
to my desk. And for living this book with me.

The Romaniacs, my writing sisters, who have the
ability to pick me up, brush me down and set me
in the right direction. They also make me laugh.
Lots. The Romaniacs are Celia J Anderson, Jan
Brigden, Sue Fortin, Debbie Fuller-White, Catherine
Miller, Vanessa Savage, Lucie Wheeler, and me.

The experts; Katherine, Elaine, and Neil, and
the hard-working, selfless heroes who devote
themselves to keeping us safe. Thank you for your
advice, your patience and diligence in answering
all my questions. Any mistakes are mine.

My friends who talk through plotlines with me, bring chocolate to the house and keep my children occupied during the holidays when I'm in the edits cave – you're fabulous and I thank you for your understanding. And for the chocolate. It is an essential ingredient in writing.

For the continued support from members of the Romantic Novelists' Association, Off The Cuff, and Littoralis.

The readers, reviewers and bloggers for investing your time and energy into books and getting the word out there.

And thank you to the entire team at Choc Lit including the Choc Lit Tasting Panel (Kirsty M, Claire W, Karen M, Lizzy D, Linda W, Sigi, Sharon M, Kate A and Cindy T).

xxx

Chapter One

Griff

The white horses of the English Channel were charging head first into the obelisk of Pulpit Rock, their remains spewing onto the cliff tops of Portland Bill, then receding, threatening to drag the winter tourists and spectators into the rough water below.

The wild spray reached as far as the toes of Griff Hendry's boots as, under the gaze of the red and white striped lighthouse, he stood firm. His instinct was to keep vigil over the families and photo-opportunists gripped by the sight of the huge breakers – people like him, restless and eager to engage with the outside world following the festivities of New Year. It made no difference he was off-duty; his experience as a coastguard and his years of living in West Dorset meant he knew the risk; nature was sometimes a beast – raw, savage, and powerful. She was to be admired, but with reverence. Much like love.

Both could drown you without warning.

He pulled his ranger's coat tighter as he signalled to a man with two small boys to retreat from the brink of the cliff. The wind was gaining strength, and the desperate waves were grasping at the land. One violent gust and the sea would snatch the weakest person away.

'Get back,' Griff shouted. 'You're too close to the edge.'

As he returned his attention to the water, he saw the worst possible scenario unfolding. A massive swell was heading directly for the Bill. And directly for the children.

'Move!' he yelled, covering the distance between him and the boys in seconds. He turned away from the onslaught, propelled the older child to the man, and grabbed the toddler. He thrust them forward, crashed on to the grass, and arched over the young boy, protecting him from the briny storm. He remained there until the noise of shifting shingle ceased, then he brushed the startled lad's fringe from his eyes, and gave a smile of reassurance. 'Okay?'

The boy stared.

Griff pushed away from the ground, wiped his wet hands along his thighs, and helped his ward to his feet. Crouching at the boy's level, he checked him over. 'Are you hurt?' Silence. 'No broken bones?' Still no reply. 'Can you lift your arms like this?' Griff raised his hands over his head, made a play of losing his balance, and launched himself onto his backside. The resulting squelch and Griff's exaggerated call of 'Oh, man!' produced the desired response; the boy's fixed expression broke with a chuckle.

Having risen to his full height, Griff turned to the father. 'He's a little stunned, and his back is soaked, but he'll be fine.' He handed the lad over and accepted the nod of thanks the equally wet man offered. 'It's as dangerous as it is beautiful here,' said Griff. 'More so on days like this. Best to keep safe.'

As he waved to the departing father and boys, his thoughts turned to his own family. He'd kept a close vigil over them, but the undercurrents were far more subtle than in any ocean. From riding high on wave after wave of ecstasy, his relationship with Evie had sunk without trace.

And Griff hadn't seen it coming.

He needed Evie to talk, to tell him what the problem was so he could fix it, but communication was limited. Her usual reply was a shrug, or a silent diversion, and the more he pushed, the further she withdrew. The death blow came when Griff finally forced the issue with a question. A foolish, instantly-regretted question. 'Is it because of someone else?'

Evie, her green eyes fading to a silky grey, turned away and breathed her word into life. 'Yes.'

It was after that she asked Griff to leave.

The fact it had been a week before Christmas – the week before the third anniversary of the day they met – proved to Griff the extent of Evie's distress. Had she been thinking straight, she'd have put the children first, and she'd have kept the family together for the holidays at the very least.

There had to be more to the situation than she was letting on.

Griff raised his collar. Where had it all gone wrong?

The fortnight he'd already spent apart from her felt like a lifetime. Together for three years and married for just half that, the end was hard to accept.

'I should be here with you, and Tess and Dylan,' he said, the squall whisking his words out to sea. 'And Ozzy.' He'd lost count of the number of times he'd turned to call his dog to heel. Walking the Bill wasn't the same without the lumbering beast hurtling around, making Dylan squeal. Or without Evie's hand to hold. He even missed Tess's teenage objections to taking some exercise.

As the icy January spray whipped Griff's cheek, he stepped back, stiffness in his ankle eliciting a sharp intake of breath. He flexed his foot, releasing the old memory seizing his bones.

At sixteen, he'd jumped from Pulpit Rock.

It was that jump that broke his ankle.

It was that day he lost his best friend to the undersea rocks.

Twenty-four years on, and Griff hadn't forgiven himself for allowing it to happen.

And he wouldn't forgive himself if he lost Evie.

He raked his fingers through his hair and flicked the glacial drips to the ground. He'd grown tired of battling the gale for his hood, but his resolve to fight for his wife, his family, the life he loved, was greater than ever.

'All right?' The landlady of the Harbour Inn paused at Griff's table. 'Can I get you a fresh coffee? That must be stone cold.' She nodded at his mug.

Griff nudged it across the dark varnish. 'No, thanks. I'm done. I should get going. I want to take Ozzy for his walk while the rain's holding off.'

'Good luck with that. I've never known weather like it. How's your dad managing?' The landlady claimed the cup and hooked it on her finger. 'He's in Burton Bradstock, isn't he? There's been dreadful flooding there.'

Griff sighed. 'There's been terrible flooding everywhere. This place survived, though.' He scanned the pub. 'Good to see the storm shutters work.'

The Harbour Inn, a ten-minute drive from Portland Bill, was situated a path's width from Chesil Beach. Griff, with one leg resting on the bench and the other tucked beneath, was sitting by a window, peering at beachcombers searching for treasure in the flotsam and jetsam washed or, in recent days, thrown ashore.

'The only drips that breached our defences were those from last night's stag party.' The woman's eyes widened. 'It's a wonder they didn't get swept out to sea.'

Griff hummed in response as he gazed across to the horizon. 'It's been wild. Strong winds and a spring tide.'

'Have you seen the dead cow?' The landlady leaned against the table, and it pushed into Griff's thigh. He swung round and planted his feet on the floor. 'How on earth did it end up on the pebbles?'

'Probably fell off a cliff, or was washed into a river.' Griff shrugged. 'There are dolphins too. And birds. It breaks my heart.' Several times already, he'd walked the stretch of Chesil the recent bout of storms had affected most. 'I'm shocked at the amount of debris.' It was as if the sea had finally got sick of all the dumped waste and vomited it onto the shore. 'It's us. Humans. We've contaminated the ocean. Poisoned nature. And she's had enough. She's throwing it back.' He reached into his coat pocket and pulled out his phone. 'I've seen reports on social media about a washing machine. I'll show you.' He checked his mobile, grimaced at the lack of messages, and touched the application headed *EweSpeak*. After a few seconds of searching, he positioned the screen for the landlady to see. 'Someone's posted a picture of it.'

'How the ...' Bewildered, the woman raised her empty hand to the air, sighed, and returned to the bar.

Griff swept his thumb over the image, vanquishing the washing machine to the ether. He cast an eye to his messages again, and returned the phone to sleep mode. Still no word from Evie.

He toyed with the wild thought that was waving the red rag behind his eyes – that Evie *was* with another man – then he chastised himself. She was a busy woman. She'd only contact him if there was something wrong with the children or Ozzy. She didn't bother him with news of his father unless it was urgent.

It was no less than Griff expected. Evie was either at his dad's or at the baby and toddler group with Dylan, supporting all the new mums. *She couldn't help herself*. Griff flinched at the thought. It was harsh, but accurate. But it was also why Evie had become his father's carer. That, and Logan's damnation of all care firms in England and Wales.

'You're a stubborn man, Dad,' Griff muttered as he left the pub.

His coat had dried in the hour he'd spent inside, but his

jeans, still damp and clingy, pulled tight against his thighs as he walked along the shore. It was unpleasant, and it was cold, especially with the cutting wind slicing through the denim, but he gritted his teeth, and continued the uncomfortable journey to his car.

As he neared a small group of people, each armed with grey litter pickers and black bin liners, he saluted. 'You're doing a great job,' he said, entering the busy circle of workers.

'Watch out. Here comes the only Welsh Highlander in the village.' A spritely man with silver hair and a twinkle in his eyes put his bag on the stones, straightened his back, and gave Griff an appreciative pat on his shoulder. 'Thanks for your help with this yesterday.'

'Hey, no problem, Frank.' Griff poked a foot at a tangle of frayed and twisted turquoise fishing net. 'I bet Olivia's making great use of this.'

Frank chuckled. 'You know Olivia. Never one to miss an opportunity.'

Griff looked over to the buildings bordering the beach. Olivia's shop, painted summer-sky blue, was a hive of activity. Children, wrapped in winter coats, hats and scarves, with driftwood, deformed lumps of plastic, and assorted tattered rope in their mittened hands, were disappearing inside, and then bursting out carrying overflowing cups and treat-laden plates. 'Squash and biscuits in exchange for sea treasure?'

'My darling lady's been supplying the volunteers with food and drink all day. Tea, coffee, cake, soup. She's kept us going.' Frank blew onto his hands and rubbed them together. 'And she's putting the money she makes from this terrible mess straight back into our conservation fund.'

Griff wasn't surprised. Olivia DeVere was generous with both her time and money. It was a mystery how Chiswell

Craft Centre remained a viable business. 'She'll make some wonderful art from this. Tell her I'll call by in the week. Perhaps she can enlighten me as to the workings of a teenager's mind.'

'I'm sure she can. She's taught a few in her time.' The older man retrieved his bin bag and returned to work. 'But you've nothing to worry about with your Tess. She was here earlier. She grafted for two hours.'

'Really?' Tess was a stroppy, bold, defiant fifteen-year-old. She only emerged from her room on a Saturday if there was something in it for her. Evie said all teenagers were the same. Her advice hadn't helped. Griff wasn't stepfather to *all* teenagers. 'I trust she behaved.'

'Impeccably. You've a good one, there. She has your passion for the sea.'

The last statement drew Griff up short. Tess never expressed an interest in anything he did. She took every opportunity to mock his beliefs and belittle his pursuits. *But she loves the sea.* It was a start. Common ground they could walk together. Three years Griff had known her. Finally he was having a positive effect. *Never give up, Hendry.* He grinned.

'Right. I have to go before the storm kicks off and the road's closed again. Don't get cold out here, old man.' Scuffing the stones as he turned, Griff laughed and waved goodbye.

Climbing into his Land Rover, he pinched the damp jeans away from his skin, settled into his seat, and set course for Abbotsbury. Ozzy would be waiting for him at the cottage. He could rely on a warm welcome from his faithful dog. It was more than he expected from Evie. Chances were she was at his father's house. She often took Dylan to visit on a Saturday, in addition to her thrice-daily duty calls. Hopefully, the road to Burton Bradstock was passable, and neither she nor Logan was stranded. The odds increased in extreme weather.

On the last occasion when the road flooded, leaving Logan cut off for several hours, Evie suggested they all might like to live together. Neither Griff nor his father responded well to that. Thankfully, she accepted their apologies, and their well-rehearsed explanation that living together would put extreme pressure on their already-strained relationship.

It was a partial truth. Griff and Logan didn't get along, but what was never revealed to Evie was the sense of betrayal Griff had lived with since the loss of his mother. He'd had six years of trying to understand why his father didn't fight for her. Six years of trying to make peace with what happened.

'I wish I had Evie's accepting nature,' Griff said, halting his car at a give way sign. 'But I can't forget what you did, Dad. Mum was the love of your life, the woman of your dreams ...' He released his grip on the steering wheel, flexed his fingers, and rotated his watch so the face was visible. *Bloody thing, always rolling under.* Three-twenty. Not as late as he thought. The dark skies were misleading.

Checking the way was clear, he pushed down the accelerator and started the final few miles home.

Evie was the woman of Griff's dreams – warm-hearted, compassionate, sexy. She only had to breathe and he was turned on. He used to tell her that, and her ever-changing eyes would dazzle like cut emeralds, but in recent weeks, any suggestions of intimacy made her frown, agitating her eyes in to the stormy grey of the winter sea.

Griff squared his shoulders, and locked his elbows. It was a mistake thinking of sex when he and Evie weren't having any – hadn't had any for weeks – not even the hot, fast, in-between-family-dramas sex they'd previously enjoyed, and they'd had a lot of that because with not enough hours in the day, or lockable rooms in the house, speed was of the essence.

Maybe that was the issue – their love life was nothing more than speed dating between the sheets. But if that was the case, why hadn't Evie told him she was unhappy? Why shut him out? She could talk to him about anything.

Griff stabbed at the window button and breathed in the cool, wet air.

That wasn't right. She couldn't talk to him about his father. He'd cut her off rather than risk his resentment and anger towards the man spilling into their world.

'I love you for wanting to fix things,' he'd say to her, 'and I care about my dad, but we don't get along. Not all fathers and sons do.' Then he'd kiss her, and change the subject, leaving her to believe the rift was a result of too much testosterone in one family. He was maintaining the illusion he'd created when they'd first met. It was simpler and less painful than revealing the whole truth.

'Bloody fool, Hendry.' He thumped the steering wheel as it occurred to him he was now a father to a son himself. Evie was bound to worry the same thing would happen between him and Dylan. That would account for her quiet but persistent requests for Griff to visit Logan, to set aside their differences and get on. To prove he was capable of being in the same room as another Hendry male.

Griff had declined every time.

'Is that what this is about?' he said, trying to see things from his wife's perspective. If it was, she probably felt snubbed, ignored, and anxious for the future, but what did Griff know? These were mere theories. 'I need you to talk, Evie,' he said, glancing at his reflection in the rear-view mirror. 'And I need to listen. Be a better husband. And a better son.'

His first promise would be a joy to fulfil. The second, more of a trial.

The country road, with all its dips and peaks, took him safely into Abbotsbury, past two pubs, and round to a busy back street. With cars parked along one side, and buildings the other, the road was narrow, but navigable, and to Griff, always interesting. Unlike the generic town flat in which he was now living – having moved out of the family home a fortnight ago – no two properties were the same, their single connection being the beautiful golden stone from which they were constructed. Roofs were thatched or tiled, apart from the row of disturbing corrugated asbestos-topped garages, and there was an eclectic mix of craft studios, shops and houses.

The cottage came into view as Griff reached the allotments, as did Evie's old, battered, and totally unreliable red Mini, abandoned on the gravel drive. Griff hadn't expected to find his wife home – he'd expected to take Ozzy for his walk while the house was otherwise empty, but perhaps it was the perfect time to confront Evie. Their time apart had provided them both with space to think. If she missed him as intensely as he missed her …

He squeezed his Land Rover next to her car.

'Evie?' he called as he opened the front door. 'We need to talk.' He dropped his keys on the phone table, hung his coat on the reclaimed tree root stand, and headed for the kitchen.

There she was, her shoulders hunched, and the waves of her red hair trickling onto the large, oval table. She remained still and silent.

In the far corner, snuffling and fidgeting on a large pet bed, an Old English Sheepdog released a short, sharp bark.

'Hey, Ozzy. We'll play later.' The dog snapped his jaws together in response. 'Good boy.' Griff signalled for him to settle, waited for his instruction to be obeyed, and then turned to Evie. His promise to listen started now. 'Hard

10

day?' He crouched beside her. 'Has my father been difficult?' Leaning in to see her reaction, he caught the gentle scent of baby powder drifting around her. 'Dylan okay?' He pulled out a chair, settled himself, and crossed his ankles.

'Dylan's fine.' Evie raised her head. 'I thought you were here to walk Ozzy.'

'I will.' Griff narrowed his eyes. 'But don't you think we should talk? I hate all of this conflict. I hate being apart from you. I miss my family.' He hooked his feet around the chair legs and cast his gaze around the kitchen. Everything was in its place. Work shifts permitting, he'd been back every day for the last two weeks to walk Ozzy, and put Dylan to bed, and he had yet to see evidence of another man. Evie had invented the reason she'd abandoned their marriage, and Griff needed to know why.

His eyes were drawn back to her as she swept her hair behind her ears, adjusted the collar on her polo neck, and joined her hands together.

'Logan is never difficult,' she said.

'What?'

'You asked if your father's being difficult. I'm telling you he's not. He's had a tough few days and needs someone with him.' Her lips pinched together and the blood diffused into her cheeks. 'He asked after you. I told him you were working.'

A prickle swept across the back of Griff's neck at the lie. He flicked it away and directed his attention to his watch. It was face down again. 'Can wrists lose weight?'

He melted at Evie's touch, as she teased the watch into position. It sent a whole different kind of prickle through him.

'Sorry.' She tucked her hands away and stared at the floor.

Griff adjusted his position, swept his fingers through his

hair, and loosened his shirt from his back. Sexual tension was constricting his thoughts. Hell, it was constricting everything. He leaned his elbows on his knees, rested his forehead on his interlocking fists, and breathed out to the count of five. When he looked up, Evie was standing by the sink.

'Logan would love to have you and Dylan there together. Three generations of Hendry men in one room. You could go in the morning. Take Ozzy, too.'

The shaggy-coated, grey and white dog sat upright at the mention of his name.

'The four of you could go for a drive.'

Ozzy yapped.

'Not now, boy.' Evie shook her head to reinforce her words. 'I can spend some mother-daughter time with Tess. We can cook a roast. You could bring Logan here, and we'll sit down to lunch as a family. I'll take him home after tea.'

Griff hesitated while he considered what the correct response should be. He very much doubted his father would be happy to see him, and he could imagine Tess's reaction to being asked to help with Sunday lunch. No. This was Evie asking him to demonstrate he could remain civil in Logan's company. She'd said it herself; *Three generations of Hendry men in one room.*

'Family dinner?' He chewed over the idea. 'Dad doesn't know, does he? About our ...' Griff searched for the term. 'Separation. You've not told him, have you?'

Evie fiddled with the cuff of her jumper, poking its fake button in and out of its fake slit. 'I haven't told anyone. Have you?'

Griff shook his head. In the days when he believed his dad was a superhero, his parents were the epitome of perfect coupledom, and until a few weeks ago, Griff was happily matching his father's example of a good husband.

Or so he thought. He had no desire to lose face by telling Logan the marriage had faltered. That would be admitting defeat. Griff never admitted defeat. Not without a fight. Worse still, he had no real, definitive explanation for the split. His assumptions about Evie's emotional needs were guesswork. All he could hope was that by showing willing with his dad, her door to communication would open and the talking would begin.

'Okay,' he said. 'I'll take Dylan to see him tomorrow and we'll come back for lunch.' He rose from his chair, tapped his thigh to bring Ozzy to heel, and headed into the hall. As he unravelled the dog lead from the coat stand, he caught one of Tess's much-loved black hats. It landed on the floor with a soft thump. He retrieved it, brushed it down and returned it to its peg.

Evie hovered in the kitchen doorway, her hair tucked into the left side of her neck, loose wisps kissing the soft skin Griff's lips knew so well. No longer permitted to go there, he refocused and set his attention on Ozzy, clipping the lead to the collar. From under his brow, he saw Evie fold her arms and rest against the wooden surround.

'What about Tess? It's not right to expect her to lie,' he said.

'I'll speak with Tess. Explain we don't want to worry Logan.' Evie's head bobbed very slightly up and down as if convincing herself it was the right thing to do. 'It's a necessary lie. She'll understand.'

Griff mirrored his wife. His nod was as imperceptible as hers. If he was right about her need for a deeper connection, their relationship could be fixed. She wasn't the only one craving intimacy. As much as he enjoyed the drive-by-sex, he missed the quiet moments with her even more – the midnight raids on the fridge when they'd sneak downstairs for a snack; singing along to the radio as they washed the dishes; his arm wrapped around her as they walked along the beach – simple pleasures that were ailing under the demands of work, children and an aging parent. Assuming he and Evie were heading in the same direction, surely it was only a matter of time before they were back together, and what his dad didn't know couldn't hurt him. A necessary lie.

He ruffled Ozzy's ears. 'I agree. It's for the best. Until we work out what we're doing.'

Evie stood erect from the doorframe. 'We're not *doing* anything, Griff. I just can't be with you.'

Chapter Two

Evie

The words caught in Evie's throat. She no more wanted to speak them than she knew Griff wanted to hear them. His pain was obvious. It destroyed the glimmer of hope she'd seen in the molten bronze of his eyes.

She wanted to reach out, pull him to her breast and comfort him. She wanted to sing to him, whisper words of reassurance, and tell him everything would be okay. But she couldn't. She couldn't tell him anything. Wouldn't tell him anything. The less he knew the better.

With a forced swallow, a slow, protracted blink, and a moment to collect her thoughts, she reminded herself of the reason her marriage was now in jeopardy.

Logan.

He'd asked something so huge of her, she was struggling to know what to do, and she'd given her word she wouldn't discuss it with Griff. She had no intention of going back on that. She didn't want Griff to know herself.

The last thing she wanted was to come between the two men in her life.

'I think you should go,' she said, sliding past her husband to access the living room. 'I'll make sure I'm out of your way when you bring Ozzy back.'

The self-imposed serenity didn't last long. With her legs no longer supporting her, she lurched towards the sofa and collapsed into its obliging cushions. Before she had a chance to draw breath, Griff was kneeling at her feet, concern stretched across his face, his defined laughter lines as miserable as the situation. His head was inches away. It would be so easy to tangle her fingers in his hair and direct his mouth to hers.

'We can work this out,' Griff said, bringing Evie's fantasy to an end. 'But you need to talk to me.'

That was all Evie wanted – to be with the man she loved, in the bosom of her family. No complications, no secrets, no guilt. But Logan's cry for help had changed all that. It had set Evie on a course impossible to navigate.

She steeled herself. 'I have nothing to say that you'd want to hear.'

Griff edged away and slumped against the coffee table.

'I don't believe that,' he said, after a moment's thorny silence. 'Like I don't believe there's another man. Why do you feel the need to lie?'

'I've not lied,' she said, keeping her thoughts chained to the back of her mind. 'When you asked if it's because of someone else, I gave an honest reply.' If he'd asked if she was in love with someone else … Well … Thank goodness he'd kept his question simple.

She looked on as Griff planted the heels of his hands onto the table, extended his legs, and pumped his body up into a seated position. His biceps strained against the white cotton of his shirt, and his chest expanded, forcing the buttons to the furthest extreme of the holes. She'd seen him exercise with that move at the gym.

He brushed his fringe to the side. He'd let his hair grow longer than usual. Evie liked it – the gentle waves gave his face a boyish youthfulness she'd not been party to. Griff would turn forty soon. They'd met in their thirties, on Christmas Day. It was three years ago, at the harbour swim. She was dressed as an angel. He was virtually naked. He'd rushed to save her then.

'You'll lose your halo,' he'd said as they stood ready to jump into the water.

'I lost that a long time ago,' she'd replied as he feathered his fingers along the edges of her wings.

'It's freezing in there. You don't have to do this.'

'I do. My daughter's the other side of the harbour. She's waited for what to her must be an eternity.'

'She'll understand.'

Evie laughed. 'She's twelve, it's ten o'clock on Christmas morning, and I've raised her from the dead, insisting she be here. Besides, I've promised my sponsorship money to the hospice. I volunteer there.'

Griff inched back, appearing to assess Evie. 'You're swimming for the hospice?' He paused as if debating whether or not to add more to his statement, then continued anyway. 'So am I. They helped my mum a few years ago. It's a fantastic cause. And it's great that you work there. A true angel.'

Evie felt the heat of embarrassment rise through her core to her face. 'It's nothing. I like to help. And I get back far more than I could ever give.'

'Sounds like you're definitely diving in, then.' He shook his head and sighed. 'There's absolutely nothing I can do to save you from taking the plunge?'

His cheeky grin and his confident pose made Evie laugh. 'I was beyond saving the second I saw your Santa Speedos,' she said.

Griff's voice dragged a reluctant Evie back into the present. 'Where did you meet?'

'It's not important.'

'Does he come here?'

Her husband's agitation was building. Evie knew the signs. His foot was sending a rhythmic thud through the carpet, his jaw was stern, and he'd developed a sheen to his forehead that he wiped with the back of his hand. Griff was a straight talker and he expected straight answers. And she loved that about him. She loved that he had no hidden agendas; that what she saw was what she got.

That's how she knew the truth would finish him. And his relationship with Logan.

'He's been here, yes.' She curled her legs onto the sofa, and locked her arms around her knees, a position she'd seen her daughter take on many occasions.

'I still don't believe you.' Griff cuffed his forehead and inhaled noisily. 'Has Tess met him? Dylan?'

It seemed to Evie there was little point replying when her answers failed to satisfy. 'You should take Ozzy for his walk,' she said, hoping to bring an end to the interrogation.

At the mention of his name, the dog barrelled into the room.

'Later,' said Griff, repairing to an armchair. He called Ozzy to him, and patted for him to lie at his feet. Once the dog was settled, Griff looked at Evie. 'Have you slept with this mystery man?' His eyes narrowed, and the grooves emphasising his mouth deepened.

'Don't do this.'

'Don't do what? Try and save our marriage? Save you?'

'Not everyone wants saving,' Evie said. That was the sad truth; a fact with which she had to come to terms.

'Everyone's worth saving.'

Evie raised a hand. 'You're not listening to me. I said not everyone *wants* saving.'

Especially not by their son.

Chapter Three

Tess

I wish I was dead. No. That's not right. Not dead, but not here. I wish the smelly, gum-chewing, dirty sod who worked his hand up my thigh, and all the smart-mouthed prats at the back of the bus poking fun at me, suffer some intolerable, skin-splitting disease. Especially the girl from my sports class at school. She's got it in for me, constantly digging and winding me up. Thought I'd be free of her on a Saturday. I hope their heads explode, and bleed red into their hair, then I'd call *them* Ginger Pubes, or Copper Knob – payback for years of tugging at my clothes and calling me Ginger Minge.

They're banging on the window as the bus pulls away. I show them my middle finger, and mouth 'swivel'.

I'm in a foul mood again. I was okay when I was on Portland. Even the journey there was bearable. I went to help clear up the storm mess on Chesil Beach. Frank, from the craft shop, was in charge. He's got an American grandson, Rick. Lives in Hope Cove Castle. He was helping for a while. He's cool. He uses that word *a lot*. I might borrow it for a week. He was trying to chat up this girl, Stephanie, but she was more interested in me and my piercings, especially my nose stud. I got it done to annoy Griff, or Gruff as I like to call him. Not to his face – that would upset Mum. She's pretty broadminded when it comes to fashion – she let me have the eyebrow ring and all the piercings down my ear, but she'd have said no to a nose stud. That's why I didn't ask. Meant to be sixteen or have parental consent. Like I was going to wait until October.

I think the fact I have the other piercings is the reason I wasn't asked for age ID. I already look sixteen, if not older. Besides, the place where I had it done is only interested in making money.

It's a pain taking them all out for school.

Stephanie has two earrings in each lobe. I wonder if French schools are more liberal? Stephanie's French. Comes from Dijon. Reckons she's moving to Chiswell in the spring. Chiswell! From the Eiffel Tower, to Chesil Beach. I didn't ask why. I assume it's to do with her parents' work. Her dad's a marine scientist. I think her mum's in the catering business. Stephanie says we should become friends. I'd like to be friends. There's something about her. She fascinates me. She's dark. And moody. Different. It's weird, but there's definitely something between us. Don't know what. Not felt it before.

Lost souls finding our way, maybe.

I'm different. Ginger hair does that to a person. Mum calls it 'red', or 'flame'. I call it what it is. Ginger, with two hard 'g's. G i n G e r. Rhymes with sinGer. Something else I never want to be. Mum's tried to get me to join the school choir. I'd hate that, but I think if she wants to sing, she should. I told her so. Gruff has too. It was a while ago, but I remember exactly what he said because it made me cringe with embarrassment. He said he could get out his old guitar and he and Mum could make sweet music together.

I'm squirming now just thinking about it.

Nothing came of it, though. Mum says she's too busy to take time out.

I throw my rucksack across my back, admire the bruised purpleness of my Doc Martens, and head for home. I need Mum to be in, and Dylan to be asleep. As half-brothers go, he's okay. Cute. I don't mind looking after him from time to time, but I never want a baby of my own. I would like to have Mum to myself though. Not for long. I know she's got a lot on. I want to tell her about the beach, and Stephanie, and ask her if what I'm feeling is *normal*. I guess if I can take an instant dislike to someone, there's no reason why I can't have an instant connection.

I won't mention the idiots on the bus. Or the middle-aged fart who touched me up. A shudder travels from my neck to my stomach. When the bus is crowded, girls are fair game.

Dirty bastards.

My wilful DMs take me past the garages with the asbestos roofs and I celebrate the fact Gruff hates them – both my boots and the buildings.

He rattles on about asbestos being a silent killer.

I think stepfathers are silent killers.

I fight hard to keep my individuality alive. If Gruff had his way, we'd all be in uniform, standing to attention every time he entered a room. Thinks everything should be done his way, as and when he says.

Belligerence boils in my gut. One day ...

It's just as well he's buggered off out of it.

I look ahead to our cottage.

His car's on the drive, next to Mum's Mini.

I can only pray they're not making up. Not naked and sprawled across the living room floor.

I don't know why we had to move here. It's so far from civilisation. I jangle the keys while I decide whether or not to go in. If he's slobbering all over Mum, I'll throw up. I put my ear to the white door, but the only noise I hear is the tapping of my earrings hitting the wood. Gruff says we're not allowed plastic windows or doors because his cottage is a listed building. Apparently it's full of character. If character means woodworm, a weather map of black, cloudy dots on the bathroom floor, and a howling gale causing my curtains to do some crazy, freaking dance, then yeah, his cottage is the Mickey Mouse of the village.

The wind's slicing through me. Mum says it blows down from the fields behind.

Might as well go in.

I slip the key in the hole, but the door's unlocked, and I decide at that moment not to announce my presence. If I'm quiet, and if I head straight to my room, no one will know I'm home.

As I close the door I hold down the handle, releasing it only as the metalwork is lined up. I untie my laces, pull off my boots and creep upstairs. Thankfully, I've mastered an almost Ninja-like technique to silently open and close Dylan's safety gates. There are three: two covering the stairs and one across Dylan's door. His cell is first on the landing. I poke my head in to check on him. He's awake, but his left thumb is firmly plugged in his mouth. He's settled, and he hasn't seen me, so I back out and head further along the corridor, past Mum's *little piece of sanctuary*, past the bathroom – thank God there's a sound barrier between our bedrooms – and into mine. I shut my door, and step over the loose edge of the carpet – there's a creaky floorboard below and it cracks like thunder if I step on it.

I lick my first two fingers on my right hand and use them to wipe off the splash of salty seawater from the toe of my left boot. I bought these myself. Took me weeks to save up.

The fact my cupboard door squeaks irritates me, so I use speed to open it, working on the theory the sound will be shortened and not draw attention to me. I put my boots away and hang my rucksack on an inside hook. It's not worth closing the door.

Pulling my curtains shut, I fold back my duvet, and lie down. The curtains taunt me. I swear they're sticking two fingers up. I turn and face the wall, yank the cover to my chin, and think about Dylan lying in his toddler bed stress-free and loved, and I send him positive thoughts. I want him to be loved. I want him to grow up with good memories. As much as Gruff frustrates me, he seems to be a pretty decent dad to Dylan. He's coming by when he's not working to tuck him in.

I don't know why Mum asked him to leave. I hope he hasn't hurt her. It must have taken all her courage to face the world after her years trapped in hell with Dad. To this day, I'm in awe of her capacity to trust, but I worry that she sees too much good in people, and they take advantage of her. Her kind nature leads her into complicated situations and she can't see a way out. I'm convinced she'll crack one day and go berserk. You can't keep all of that crap inside. It has to come out somehow. I know.

I stare at the shadows on the wall, something I've done since I was tiny, in every house we've lived in. It's habit now, rather than distraction.

It's so quiet.

I don't like it. Silence makes me nervous. Silence means something's happened.

My mind's racing now. I see blood-spattered images of a massacre in the kitchen – Ozzy dead in his corner, Gruff clutching at his chest, the handle of a silver knife poking through his pale fingers, and Mum, wiping her stained hands on her jumper. Staring. Silent.

That would be a way out.

I've thought about it as a way out. I had a plan when I was ten, because when you're ten there's very little you can do to make things better. You're not big or strong, and no one cares about what you have to say, and when your mum spends her nights crying and her days as far away from the house as she can get, you need a plan.

But I can't think about this stuff now. I have to go and investigate the silence.

Dylan's still watching the ceiling. I don't know what he sees, but it occupies him for hours. As my foot hits the first step, Ozzy barks, and I let out a huge breath. That's two survivors plus me. By the time I'm in the hallway, I hear Gruff's voice – he's saying something about Mum being wrong. As I push open the living room door, she tells Gruff to hush. He's scowling, but the minute our eyes meet, his expression lifts.

'Hi,' he says, running his hands up and down the arms of his chair. 'Good day?'

'Tess!' Mum rises to greet me and enfolds me in her arms. I don't take in her scent in case she smells of him. Masculine smells make me gag. 'You must be frozen. Hot chocolate?'

She guides me towards the kitchen and plonks me on a chair. I check for bloodstains, but it's perfectly clean.

'Griff could have brought you back from Portland if you'd said you were going.' She turns away and messes about with the kettle. I don't actually want a drink, but say nothing. Mum has to help. It makes her feel useful. Loved.

'Everything all right?' I watch her shoulders. They're a dead giveaway. They stiffen, and I notice they run parallel with the bottom line of the wall cupboards. I shoot up from my chair and wrap myself around her. 'What's he done? What's that bastard man done?' I check to see if Gruff's left the living room, but the hallway is empty.

Mum reels, spinning within my hold. 'Nothing,' she says. 'He's done nothing.' As she reaches the end of her statement her words lose power, and her body sags. She's caught between the worktop and me. If I let go, she'll fall.

I will never let her fall.

She regains her strength, and her spine hardens against my fingers. Her voice remains soft. 'He's a good man, Tess, and whatever happens, you must remember that. Promise?' She frees an arm, and tips my chin up. I raise my eyes to meet hers. 'Promise?' She's more insistent this time.

I nod. It's the best I can do under the circumstances. I want to give her my word – I'm desperate to give her my word – but my experience of men has taught me to never think well of them. Any of them. Except Logan. And Frank from Portland. But they're much older than the men I mean. And they've never invaded my personal space.

As I consider this, Mum hugs me, kisses my forehead, and releases me.

'Sit down, and let me make you that chocolate,' she says. 'I need to ask you something.'

I'm instantly on guard, second-guessing her question. I tug my sleeves down and hold the cuffs in my palms. I hide as much of my skin as possible. She mustn't see.

'Go on,' I say, keeping a cool exterior, while my conscience burns a hole in my gut. 'Ask.'

She makes fast work of the drink, and puts it on the table, pulling up a chair next to me. She retrieves her mobile from her back pocket and lays it next to my mug, then sits, and fiddles with the ribbed hem of her jumper, pushing it flat each time it rolls up.

'Can we get this over with?' I weave my arms around the back of the chair, and link my hands together. She can't see them there. She mustn't see them. I keep a close watch on her line of sight. So far, she's looking inwards. This isn't about me. Thank God. Really. Mum has enough to deal with, she doesn't need grief from me. And what I do, I don't do for attention. It's not a cry for help—

'Logan's coming for lunch tomorrow. At least, that's the plan.'

My inner vision shuts down. It's like someone's slammed the lid on a telescope. For a second I saw everything clearly, then bang! It's dark again. 'Logan's coming to dinner? Cool. It'll be good to see him.' I mean it. I am genuinely fond of him. Sure he's old and frail, which as far as I'm concerned makes him safe, but there's nothing wrong with his brain. He's as sharp as my new razor blade. 'Does he know about you and Griff?'

Mum shakes her head, and the colour rises in her cheeks. A blush starts in the stomach. If she wasn't wearing her polo neck, I'd have seen the flush rise from her throat to her face. I must have learned that in biology. Or perhaps it was from one of those TV documentaries.

She fidgets in her seat. 'That's what I wanted to ask you. Are you okay with not saying anything?'

'Do you think it will upset Logan if he knows?'

'Very much so. And he'll worry that I'll stop caring for him, or that he won't be able to see you or Dylan. It won't be for long.'

With my arms still tucked out of sight, I smile, to show Mum I'm okay with keeping quiet. I understand why we're not telling Logan. I know when to keep a secret.

I'm good at keeping secrets.

Very good.

We both jump as Mum's phone blares out the red alert tone. It's Logan's text call. Mum sighs.

'You should get that,' I say, knowing how much Logan relies on her.

'He'll ring if it's urgent.'

She resists picking up her mobile, but her eyes flick back and forth. She needs to know what Logan wants. She's trying to ignore it for my benefit, but I'd prefer she just looked at the bloody thing.

'So,' she starts, flipping the phone onto its front, 'good day?'

My arms are tingling. Pins and needles. I unhook my fingers and fold my hands into my lap. She's not watching, so it's okay. 'I helped Frank for a while. It was pretty disgusting, actually, but we cleared tonnes of rubbish. And Olivia made us all bacon toasties.'

'Was that American lad there?'

I think there's a beginning of a smile on Mum's face, but I could be wrong. It could be a grimace. It's hard to tell. Her mouth's got out of the habit lately. 'Rick? Yeah. He told me about his dad. Said he was a film star. I guess it could be true. They live in that big castle overlooking the cliffs.' I check Mum's expression. There was no smile. 'There was this French girl, Stephanie. Her family's moving to Portland soon.'

She looks up and nods, but it's not at me. She's looking beyond me. I turn and see Gruff lurking in the hallway. He calls Ozzy to him.

'I'll be gone an hour,' Gruff says.

Like I care.

Mum's phone rattles across the table as the siren blares out its reminder there's a text from Logan. Sick of it sending my heart into overdrive, I snag the stupid thing and open the message. It doesn't make sense. 'Here.' I pass it to Mum, who reads it, drains to an impossible shade of white, and heads for the front door.

'Will you look after Dylan, please?' she calls to me.

'What is it?' Gruff catches Mum's arm as she dives past. 'Is it Dad?'

He knows it's Logan. We all know it's Logan.

'Should I come?' Gruff asks.

Mum yanks herself free and glares at Gruff. 'No.' Then more gently, as if she's thought of something, 'No. He's asked for me.'

Dylan joins in from upstairs and Gruff doesn't know where to look. If the situation wasn't so strained, I'd find it funny. Dylan's not crying, he's just making us aware he wants in on the action. He probably heard Gruff's voice. 'I'll go,' I say, glad of an excuse to hide away.

'No. It's all right. I'll go.' Gruff waves for me to sit back down. 'I'd like to see him.'

Mum shakes her head, snatches her keys from the bowl by the front door, and leaves without a further word.

'You saw the text. What did it say?' Gruff holds onto the handrail, ready to launch himself up the stairs two by two. That's how he does it – he never walks. When I'm in my room, I can always tell it's him coming. I wonder if it's to do with his job where every second is vital, then decide it's because he's a plank.

'Tess. What did my father want?'

I review the message in my head, and it still doesn't make sense, so I see no harm in telling him. 'It said, "It's now."'

Chapter Four

'Come on.' The never ready, always unreliable Mini was going nowhere. Evie turned the key for the third time, provoking nothing more than a bray. 'No, no, no!' She whacked the dash with both hands, slammed the gearstick into neutral, and yanked the keys from the ignition. *Why now?* Now. A small word with such devastating consequences. 'Not now,' she said. '*Not now.*'

She'd have to take Griff's car and count on him not using it in the next few hours. The visit to Logan's house was going to take some time. There was going to be a lot of talking. She'd had a few weeks to consider his proposal, but it had been impossible to come to a decision.

When she needed to get things straight in her head, her first port of call was always Griff. He had a way of seeing the world that put problems into perspective, but Logan was very clear; no one else was to know, especially not Griff. Evie was in agreement – the consequences of discussing Logan's request would not only send Griff into a downward spiral, but would point an accusing finger at Evie the second Logan passed away. Any hint she was connected with his death, and she'd be thrown in prison.

She'd googled the terms euthanasia, voluntary euthanasia, assisted dying, assisted suicide – the last one applied to Logan – none were legal in the UK.

'It's madness,' she said, scrambling out of her Mini. 'Why me?' That was desperation asking the question. Evie knew the answer. She understood where Logan was coming from and he saw that. 'It's such a mess.'

After a month of hiding her thoughts from Griff, the burden of the secret weighed her down to a point she thought she would never hold her head up again.

She couldn't look Griff in the eye.

It was then Evie, upset and wracked with guilt, asked him to leave. Blinded by constant tears of distress, she'd failed to register it was the week before Christmas.

But she didn't have time now to reflect. She swooped indoors, swapped her keys for Griff's, and took off in his old, blue Land Rover.

It was a huge car to handle. Simple for a man of Griff's stature and muscular frame, but for slender, slight Evie, it could have been a juggernaut for all the control she had. By the time she was out of Abbotsbury, she was fighting the wheel and fighting the tears.

She blinked away the moisture building in her eyes and concentrated on the road ahead. It was a ten-minute drive, that was all. She just needed to keep calm for ten minutes. Arrive in one piece.

As she was repeating the mantra, a hare bolted from the roadside hedge and ran straight across Evie's path. Evie banged her foot hard on the brake, then lunged forward as the car halted. Winded and shocked, she took a moment to gather her wits before glancing to the side. Had she hit the hare? There was no blood on the tarmac, that had to be a good sign. Cautiously, she pulled back the handle and inched open the door expecting to hear horrific squeals of pain. 'Please God. Please, please, please. Don't let me have hit it.' She stepped onto the road and, through half-closed eyes, checked the front of the vehicle. Nothing. Braver, she got down on her knees and peered under the car. Still nothing. No dents, no limbs. No suicidal hare. She scanned the bushes either side of the road, then, rising to her feet, walked to the rear of the car. Absolutely nothing. Zero.

As she returned to the driver's seat it crossed her mind she'd imagined the whole incident. She knew the nasty games stress played. She'd been an unwilling and unwitting participant in the past, but it seemed a new round had commenced, and Logan was the games master, setting unfair rules and ensuring the advantage was his.

She shook her head and reminded herself how reliant Logan was on her; a fact which had not escaped Griff's notice, although he was of the opinion his father was asking too much of her. Evie had her reasons for refuting this, none of which she could explain to Griff. He'd see for himself tomorrow. If Logan was still with them.

With a renewed sense of urgency, she fired up the engine and pulled away.

The recent high winds and torrential downpours had made rivers of the roads, but Griff's car dealt with the flooded lanes of the Bride Valley with ease, and despite not having complete control, Evie was relieved she didn't have to keep stopping to let the engine dry out. Her Mini had suffered earlier, driving through the temporary fords, and it had taken her almost an hour to travel the seven miles home from Logan's.

She reached her destination within minutes in the Land Rover. She parked roadside, dashed across the pavement to Logan's house and frantically fingered Griff's large set of keys, trying to establish which of the bunch unlocked the front door. After three failed attempts, she gained access.

'Logan?' No answer. 'Logan?' She shoved the keys in her pocket, pushed the door shut and hurried into the room to her left. Logan was slouched in his armchair, his head lolled to one side, a selection of bottles on the nest of tables beside him. Evie froze. Ever since the day she had become his carer, this was the moment she had dreaded. She accepted she was the one most likely to find him like this, but it wrenched at her gut. She had to face the possibility every single day, every single time she walked into that house.

Month-by-month, one year to the next, Logan's physical needs had eaten into her life with Griff, the time she spent with Tess and Dylan, and the space to do something for herself. In the time she'd known the Hendrys, she'd calculated she'd spent almost as many waking hours with Logan as she had her own family. But she wasn't resentful. She wanted to help. His arthritis was no longer under control and every day brought him pain and distress. Evie was keen to do whatever she could to increase his quality of life.

She stared at his chest, waiting for it to inflate. She'd done it a thousand times with Dylan, late at night, watching for signs of life, not knowing if he was sleeping peacefully or lost to the world.

With a phlegmy snort, and a roll of his head, Logan opened his eyes. Their blue intensity found its way to Evie. 'What took you so bloody long?'

His Scottish accent appeared when he swore. Times of pure emotion often brought it to its roundest, fullest extent. Other than that, it came and went with the tide, or so it seemed to Evie.

She released a heavy sigh and crossed the room. 'You scared the living daylights out of me. I thought you'd—'

'Done something stupid? That's what you were going to say.' He flinched as he slowly repositioned himself. 'No Griff, I trust?'

'No. He's looking after Dylan.' Evie studied the contents of the small table before gathering the empty bottles – two miniature Bell's and one special edition Famous Grouse. The lids must have been loose for Logan to open them. 'Have you been partying without me?' She thought her comment would lighten the atmosphere, but Logan growled and turned away.

'I had a Scotch. What of it? I'd like to say it's the only pleasure I've left, but that's a lie. I have no pleasures. Have you any idea what it's like to be stuck in a body that won't do as it's told?'

Evie bit down on her lip, took the empties to the kitchen and returned with a small glass of water, handing it to Logan. 'I'm not judging you.'

'Why not? I judge you.'

That was true. 'I'm here to help.'

'No matter what that entails?' He raised a shaky hand to his mouth, slurping at the water in the glass. 'If ever I needed your help, it's now.' He indicated for Evie to free him of the drink. 'You haven't told Griff, have you? He mustn't know. No one must. If you do this thing for me, you can't tell a living soul.'

Evie set the glass down, and crouched at Logan's feet. His hooded eyes sought hers. 'It's not something I wish to broadcast,' she said. 'What with it being unlawful.'

'But is it something you've thought about?'

'Oh, yes.' Almost exclusively. 'I want to help you, but I don't think you realise how big a deal this is. Have you considered how I feel about it?'

Logan sneered and waved for Evie to distance herself. 'You should be relieved. It will free you from this ... this burden.' He cast his eyes down his frail body before refocusing on Evie. 'The sooner I'm gone, the better. For all of us.'

Evie removed herself to the sofa, and perched on the arm. She fought hard to prevent the tears from falling, but still they came. 'Please don't say that,' she whispered, dabbing a finger across her cheeks.

'Why not? It's the truth. I'm an encumbrance. I'm a ... what's the word Tess uses? A time-suck.' He took in a quivering breath, and dragged a trembling hand across his chin. 'I can't even shave.'

Evie dived forward, taking his fingers in hers. 'I don't mind doing that for you.'

'You don't do it right.'

'I'll take you into Bridport, to that barber's shop – have old Tom do a proper job. Have a day out. We could do it on Monday.'

With the effort showing on his puckered brow, Logan twisted his fingers free, scrubbed them against his thigh, and glared at them, as if they were his worst enemy. 'You don't get it. I'm sick of relying on others.'

Evie reached into her pocket and tugged at a tissue. It ripped on its way out, leaving her with a ragged corner between her thumb and finger.

'Over there.' Logan directed her to the understairs cupboard. 'You'll have to open a new box.'

She knew where he kept the tissues. She knew Logan's house as well as her own, but she played along, thanking him, leaving him as king of his castle. She opened the door, switched on the light, and through blurred vision, studied the shelving unit. It was filled with music cassettes, videos of old films, the telephone directory, shopping catalogues, and two tissue boxes. Having reached for the nearest one, she tore off the top panel and yanked out a tissue. She wiped her eyes, blew her nose, and took a second tissue, stuffing it up her sleeve, then allowed herself a moment to settle before facing Logan.

'I lost my father at a young age,' she said as she exited the cupboard. 'I never even knew my granddad.' She put the tissues on Logan's side table, and her used one in her pocket, before stroking the soft, grey hair growing around Logan's ear. It was fairer here, more like ash than the charcoal on top. He moved his head away. So typical of him.

Evie resumed her seat on the sofa. 'You're seventy-four. That's the new fifty these days.' She attempted to raise a smile, but suspected it looked more like a sympathetic grimace. 'Dylan and Tess will grow up without a granddad. Have you thought of that?'

'Of course I have,' Logan grumbled. 'I've thought of everything. The time, the place. The means. I have all the drugs I need. I've been saving them for the last few months. Missing one here and there. Stowing them away. They're locked in that red cash tin in my bedside drawer.'

So that was what was in there. Evie had seen it often enough, going in and out of the drawer, fetching things for Logan. 'You've been saving them for months?'

Logan produced a laugh which gnawed at Evie's insides. In spite of his fragility, and in spite of his vulnerability, he had the strength to reduce an adult to a child.

'Yes. Months. Did you think it was something I decided on a whim?' He shook his head. 'You've no idea what I've been through. How'd you think all of this makes me feel?' He waved a wonky arm, which he couldn't straighten, in front of his face. 'I've gone from being a carer to being cared for. I looked after Marilyn in her last few weeks. I wasn't as useless then as I am now. I did everything for her – I fed her, bathed her, dressed her, brushed her teeth.' He halted and closed his eyes.

The pain was palpable. It stretched its tendrils out, wrapped them around Evie's throat, and choked her. 'Logan ... Please ...'

'Listen to me, Evie.' He opened his eyes; they were crystal clear, determined and very much in the present. 'I had to clean my wife the same way I cleaned my soiled son when he was a baby. Where's the dignity in that? I understand now, but at the time, I thought I was doing right by her. She begged me to let her go, but it went against every fibre in my body. I'd spent too many years as a surgeon – I'd vowed to do everything in my power to save people, but I've learned not everyone wants saving.'

That was exactly what Evie had told Griff less than two hours ago, and here she was debating the point with the very man she knew wanted to die.

'If Tess had a boyfriend, Evie, imagine him having to do all those private, personal things for you, because that's what it's like for me. You're my daughter-in-law, and it's only a matter of time before you'll have to attend to my intimate needs. It's not right. For either of us.' He dropped his gaze, and lowered his head. 'I won't let it get to that stage, d'you hear?' His soft Highland timbre belied the harsh reality of his words. 'How would you feel? Think about it.'

Evie had spent weeks thinking of nothing else.

Logan continued. 'I've sat here day after day, month after month, thinking about my own death. Planning my *demise*. Coming up with ways to ensure I succeed. And I've had no one to talk it over with. I had to reach the decision on my own. Do you know what it's like to have no one to discuss things with?'

Having been sworn to secrecy over his request, and knowing how much the disclosure would hurt Griff, Evie could empathise. It was lonely. It was torture. 'You could have talked to me.' It was all she had to offer.

'And you'd have insisted I see sense, like you have today.'

Evie fiddled with the tissue tucked inside her cuff, until finally, she yanked it free. For want of keeping her hands occupied, and as an excuse to avoid looking at Logan, she spread the thin paper over her legs, folded it in half, then folded it again, into a quarter of its original size. 'You might have reached a different conclusion,' she said.

'There is no other conclusion.'

Heaving another leaden sigh, Evie left the safety of the tissue and the couch, and approached Logan. 'I've signed your Advance Decision papers.' Another fact she had to keep from Griff. 'I've lodged copies with your GP and solicitor, isn't that enough?' One more reason she couldn't look her husband in the eye. 'Your needs and wants are in black and white. Everyone's clear about how you wish to ...' She trailed off, unable to say the word.

'Die,' Logan supplied. 'But that doesn't help me *now*. That's only any good when I'm at death's door. I don't want to get that far. I want to go while I still have the sanity to choose and the power to do something about it.' He reached for the seat's remote control, took several attempts to press down its button, and huffed with obvious annoyance while the chair reared up. 'I can't even storm out of a room in frustration.' He held an arm out for Evie to take. 'Help me stomp out of here, will you? And then, when we get to the kitchen, throw a bowl on the floor on my behalf.'

As she clasped his elbow to secure him, he placed his hand on her arm and gave her a very gentle, very affectionate pat. It caught Evie by surprise and she stooped to look at him. His thin, straight lips had parted, and the skin around his mouth wrinkled. He was smiling.

'Got to keep your sense of humour, even in the darkest hours,' he said, leaning into her.

She took his weight easily, what there was of it – the scales read six stone this morning when they'd eventually managed to get him to stand on them without hanging onto the towel rail for support. Evie suggested they ask for a dietician's appointment, but Logan refused. Food held no flavour for him these days. He made Evie promise not to bother the hospital, and she agreed on the condition he tried to eat little and often, believing that was the key to encouraging the return of his appetite.

'Have you had anything since lunch?' she asked, taking small, steady steps, letting Logan set the pace.

'Apart from Scotch? I had some Turkish Delight. Three pieces. Would you like to try it?'

They shuffled into the kitchen, where Logan pointed to a white paper bag next to a silver toaster. 'My next-door neighbour gave it to me. I quite like it. That doesn't mean I want more bags of the stuff, though.'

Evie saw him glance at her.

'There's a bowl in that cupboard you can smash,' he said, his slack grin making another appearance. 'Now, let's see how my birds are doing.' He hobbled to his right and rested against the sink. The window in front looked out onto his small back garden, half of which was laid with Portland stone slabs, the other with lawn. Shrubs bordered the grass, and the low level back fence had lost its fight with the wild ivy growing over from the fields behind. It resembled army fatigues, with several shades of green and brown merging with the black shadows.

'Their feeder's empty,' Logan said, his words clipped with irritation.

'I filled it this morning.' Evie peered through the glass – the glass she had cleaned after serving Logan breakfast. 'I'll top it up in a minute.'

'I'm all right here. Go and do it now, while it's fresh in your mind. And maybe you can peel that dead ivy off the fence, too. It'll give you time to reach your decision.'

Every time Evie succeeded in removing a stubborn vein of ivy she waved it at Logan, and then threw it on the grass. She really didn't mind doing a spot of gardening for him, but it wasn't why she'd driven like a maniac to get there. She'd hurtled down the B-something-or-other and hit an imaginary hare to stop him from doing ... yes ... *something stupid.* Naturally, she was relieved he was still in one piece and able to stand watch over her, but she had to get home. To the rest of her family.

As she kneaded her back, now aching from the awkward position she'd adopted, her mobile vibrated. She wiped her hand on her coat, fished the phone out of her back pocket, and accepted the call. It was Tess.

'Mum? Will you be back soon?'

Evie checked her watch, surprised at how quickly the last hour and a half had passed. 'I won't be long. I'll make Logan his tea and get him ready for bed, and then I'll be on my way.' Hopefully that would prevent her having to return later. 'Everything all right?' No reason it shouldn't be with Griff there.

'Not really,' Tess said. 'Dylan's been sick, and I'm feeling weird, all wobbly and hot. Reckon we've caught a bug. Griff said his staff were dropping like flies with one.'

More keen than ever to return home, Evie scraped the strands of ivy into a pile and kicked it to the edge of the lawn. 'Get a glass of water and put yourself to bed. In fact, fetch the plastic bowl from the airing cupboard too. Just in case. I'll be home in twenty.' The silence told Evie there was a problem with her suggestion. 'Trust me, you'll feel better for lying down.'

'I can't. I told you, Dylan's not well.'

'Griff can take care of him. He knows what to do.'

'He's gone.'

'To take Ozzy out?'

'No, to work. About an hour ago. Another officer called in sick. He took your Mini. Said he'll be back later. Mum, I have to go, I think I'm going to be sick.'

The line went dead.

Chapter Five

Having completed his maritime safety information broadcast, and the hand-over to the night watch, Griff reclaimed his personal items from his locker and made his way out of the building. Before slipping his mobile into his hip pocket, he checked for messages. 'Evie,' he muttered, shaking his head. She had the audacity to ask why he always put work first, when she was the one who'd dropped everything to go to his dad.

He thumbed in a functional, non-combative reply: *The Operations Officer was taken ill. I'm leaving now. Back soon.*

He wanted to type *home*, but the cottage he'd lived in ten years prior to meeting Evie was already beginning to feel more like a place to visit than somewhere to stay. The ironic thing was the flat he was now in wasn't home either. It was a shell, with basic furnishings that didn't meet his basic needs, but it was a stopgap, just until he'd sorted everything out with Evie.

She'd told him she didn't want saving, as if what he did for a living was banal and pointless. There was a chance she said it knowing it would hurt, but that wasn't her style. Evie was compassionate and self-sacrificing, often ... no, always putting others first. Helping was as much her nature as it was Griff's, they just came at it from different angles. Two sides of the same coin, his father would say.

Griff unlocked the Mini and wedged himself behind the wheel. He assumed Evie took his car to negotiate the floods – it had taken gentle and expert handling of the Mini to get it from Abbotsbury to Weymouth. He'd filled it up as well, to save Evie the job. In the past, she'd found that a romantic gesture.

'It shows me how much you care,' she'd said.

His short shift at work had been unusually quiet compared to recent weeks. The record rainfall and high winds had battered most of Britain, with Portland taking the brunt in Dorset. Perhaps people had finally got the message it was safer to stay at home. Or perhaps the novelty of nine metre waves had worn off. Griff had seen enough to last a lifetime.

As he headed for the cottage, his mind wandered back to his dad and the lunch Evie had organised. It was destined to be a circus, with Evie the ringmaster, Griff the slapstick clown, and poor Tess, expected to jump through hoops. It wasn't right. Logan was stronger than Evie gave him credit for. He could take the truth.

'Bad idea,' Griff said, disappointed with his lack of clear thought. His problems with Evie were private. Besides, what would his father say? He'd be disillusioned and upset that his son couldn't keep a marriage together, and pity from Logan was not welcome.

The notion was powerful enough to ensure Griff's silence.

After a further ten-minute drive, he parked the car next to his Land Rover and prepared himself for putting Dylan to bed. That meant assuming a relaxed stance, putting on a smile and pretending there was nothing wrong with life.

He opened the door and immediately swapped Evie's keys for his.

There was an eerie silence to the cottage – an unfamiliar stillness. 'Hello?' Ozzy trotted out from the kitchen and nuzzled Griff's legs. 'All right, boy? Where is everyone?'

The pounding of footsteps across the landing, the horrendous coughing and retching echoing around the bathroom, and Evie's voice, speaking in hushed, comforting tones, answered his question.

The commotion disturbed Ozzy and he trudged back to the kitchen.

Griff kicked off his shoes and ran upstairs, taking them two by two as he always did. He stopped outside Dylan's room and waited. Evie and Tess, the daughter enveloped in her mother's arms, disappeared into the far bedroom. Neither saw Griff. Acknowledging Evie had everything in hand, he released the safety gate to Dylan's room, and stepped through. There was his boy, fast asleep, arms signifying his surrender, his head turned to the yellow beam channelling its way in from the landing. Griff pushed the door to, and giving his eyes time to adjust to the shadows, leaned over Dylan's bed. He'd missed putting him down tonight.

He brushed the fine, feathery fringe from Dylan's forehead and laid the back of his hand on his cheek. 'You're boiling,' he said. The heat Dylan was radiating shocked him. He pulled back the blankets, undid the metal poppers of Dylan's sleepsuit, and freed him of the garment. Dylan's eyelids flickered, his dark lashes fluttering, tiny black quills against his hot, pink skin. 'It's okay,' Griff murmured. 'You keep sleeping.'

Without warning, Dylan's arms and legs stiffened, his eyes burst open, and a look of sheer terror projected from deep within. He was fixed on Griff, no recognition, no smile. No breath.

'Shit.' Griff thumped at the light switch, the brilliance illuminating a curtain of blue drawing up from Dylan's chin. Securing the small, rigid body in his hands, Griff lifted his son from the bed and placed him on the floor, the smell of hot skin assaulting Griff's nostrils and the thick, unpalatable air, coating his tongue. His teeth set on edge as he swallowed. 'Dylan? Dylan?' No response. He tapped his son's shoulders, hoping for a reaction. Still nothing. 'Come on,' he muttered. 'Come on!'

A gust of air swirled round him as Evie landed beside him.

'Dylan!' She crumpled to the floor and seized her child's hand, her slim form casting a shadow over him. 'What's happening?'

Griff could hear the tears, the strain in Evie's voice, and as desperate as he was to offer physical comfort, Dylan was his priority. 'He'll be all right,' he said. 'I'm with him.'

Evie's silhouette retreated, giving Griff the light and space he required. He put two fingers under Dylan's chin, a hand on his forehead, and gently tipped the toddler's head back. With his ear an inch from his son's mouth, he listened, watching Dylan's chest.

No gush, no rise. No sign of life.

Never before had Griff been faced with the horror of losing his own child. Never before had a second lasted an eternity.

Years of experience, a career of saving others, awards for bravery – nothing, absolutely *nothing* prepared Griff for this. A cool hand brushed his arm.

'Griff?'

He risked a glance at Evie. At that moment she appeared barely bigger than Dylan. Her green eyes, now grey rainclouds threatening a deluge, were pleading with Griff, needing him to step up. Her sheer intensity powered through him, inducing his instinct to kick in.

He was back.

'It's okay,' he said. 'But I need you to call an ambulance.'

Evie didn't move.

Without looking at her, Griff repeated the instruction, adopting an assertive tone. 'Now.'

He didn't know if it was the increased volume of his voice, or Evie's plea of help into her mobile that entered their son's consciousness, but a huge gasp filled Griff's ear.

It was the sweetest sound.

Dylan's chest rose and fell with a life-affirming rhythm.

'Are you through to the paramedics?'

Evie nodded.

Now working swiftly, Griff put his ear to Dylan's mouth, listened, and watched his child's chest. The regular pattern that greeted him was completely at odds with his own fast-paced, shallow breaths. 'Good boy,' Griff said, rising to his knees. He took Dylan's nearest arm, laid it out to the side, and reached for his furthest hand. He brought it across the tiny body, and placed the palm under the boy's cheek. Lifting the toddler's scrawny leg, Griff faltered. His son's calf was less than half the size of Griff's arm. So small. So helpless. 'Come on, Hendry. You've trained your whole life for moments like this.'

He shouldered away a tear threatening to obscure his vision, and completed the manoeuvre, rolling Dylan onto his side. Keeping a constant watch on him, he spoke to Evie. 'Tell them Dylan's breathing and he's in the recovery position.'

She relayed the information.

'Now, unlock the front door, and wait for the ambulance.' He looked at Evie. The storm had broken and her face was soaked. 'He's okay, I promise.' Griff managed a smile and a nod, and encouraged Evie on her way.

The contrast of the hypnotic calm against the chaos of the last few minutes left Griff uneasy. Every rescue left him this way. His brain would process it as normal, allowing his body to absorb the shock.

But this wasn't normal. This was his son. His son, who for one second too long, he thought was dying.

'I will never let that happen,' he said, his jaw clamped with tension. 'You, your sister, your mum, you're my world, and I'll move heaven and earth to protect you.' He stared down at Dylan, whose colour had returned. 'I'll do whatever it takes to keep you safe. I'm not losing anyone else.'

The paramedics suggested Dylan had suffered a febrile convulsion, brought on by a spike in his temperature, and the hospital confirmed this was likely to be the case, but they were keeping Dylan in for observation. The bed the ward sister offered Griff was comfortable enough, and it was alongside Dylan's bed, but sleep was not on the agenda. Griff had promised Evie he'd watch over their son. Perched on the edge of the mattress, he was sticking to his word.

'Everything okay, Mr Hendry?' A nurse, dressed in white, stepped into the room and took Dylan's wrist between her fingers and thumb.

'It will be, once I get my little lad home.' Griff tried to generate a smile, but wiped away the evidence of his poor attempt as he dragged a hand over his face. 'I thought I'd lost him.'

'The paramedics said you had everything in hand by the time they reached you. A real pro.' The nurse tucked Dylan's arm by his side and looked at Griff. 'Don't be too hard on yourself. Seizures are frightening.'

Griff took up position next to the bed and leaned his elbows on the top of the raised safety bar. 'You're not kidding.' He gazed at Dylan. 'I'd have done a deal with the devil at that moment. Take me, not my son.'

'I would have, too.' The nurse recorded something on a handheld unit and slipped it in to her pocket. 'Technology,' she said as if explaining its use. 'No more clipboards at the ends of beds.'

'He's going to be okay, isn't he?' Griff rose from his stoop. 'I mean, there'll be no lasting damage?'

'He might have some confusion for a day or two, but that's all. Nothing to worry about.' The nurse cast one final look over Dylan. 'He's a lucky boy to have you on his side. Our children are very precious.' Then she left the room as quietly as she'd entered.

'Life *is* precious,' Griff said, repairing to a wooden-armed, padded chair on the other side of the bed. 'And fleeting.' The harsh reality of losing his best friend at sixteen had brought that home to him.

It was inevitable he'd think of Kieran – he'd been like a brother to him, best man material. They'd been friends for eight years, from high-pitched gigglers to strapping youths, travelling the tremulous path to manhood together. *Young adulthood*, Griff corrected.

They'd met within a week of the Hendrys moving to Dorset. Logan had relocated a number of times in his life, working his way through medical school and surgical training. Eventually, he took a paid position in Wales, where he qualified as a surgeon. There he'd met and fallen in love with Marilyn, married, and cradled his son in his arms for the first time. The Hendrys moved when Logan accepted a senior medical appointment in a Dorset hospital. They sold their Welsh chocolate box of a cottage, left Logan's adopted homeland, and settled in a small English village on the South-West coast. It was renowned for its green telephone box, two pubs, and a school with three classes. That's where Griff first encountered Kieran. That's where their mums helped out once a week, listening to the children read aloud.

Griff could picture the two women, their skirt-covered knees almost reaching their chins as they huddled on the pint-sized chairs, their index fingers skimming across the page. They became close, like Griff and Kieran. So did Kieran's dad and Logan – the men often met at one of the pubs on a Friday night. Firm family friends.

The only one without somebody was Kieran's sister, Imogen. She was five years younger than the boys, not even at school when Griff first moved to Weymouth. He remembered how much she adored her big brother – proper hero-worship, despite Kieran's constant teasing.

Griff could picture her too – short, always in red corduroy dungarees and orange wellies. And he could recall how she was forever hanging on to his coattails.

She hadn't held on to them at Kieran's funeral service. She'd hardly even looked at Griff. And while no one directly blamed him for Kieran's death, no one said it wasn't his fault.

From that point on, despite Griff's best efforts to keep a brotherly eye on Imogen, the families drifted apart. Not even their mums spoke to one another.

The twenty-four-year-old memory was as vivid now as it was then.

'Pack it in, Hendry,' Griff said, smoothing his hands along the polished arms of the chair. 'You're tired and emotional. And it's a rubbish combination.' He rubbed his sore, stinging eyes, then examined his fingers, half expecting to find cactus needles embedded in their tips. 'Man, I could use some sleep.' Reclining further, he rested his head on the high back, tuned into the ebb and flow of Dylan's breath, and fixed his eyes on the slumbering boy. 'But I'm not letting you out of my sight.' A succession of yawns and a much-needed stretch distorted Griff's words. 'One minute like this,' he said, 'then I'll text your mum.'

Chapter Six

Tess

Poor Dylan. I hope he's okay. Mum's pretty shaken up by the whole affair. I want to sit with her, but the minute I'm vertical, I throw up. She wasn't looking so good herself last night. I expect it's the shock. Or this bug.

Google told me what a febrile seizure is. Scary to witness, but usually harmless. From what Mum said, it sounds like Griff did all the right things.

He deserves to be called Griff. Just for today.

I wonder how long they'll be at the hospital. I told Mum she should go. I could see she wanted to – even when she was in my room, her head wasn't. She and Griff must have been at the front door when I heard him promise he'd stay with Dylan. His voice was low. It reassured Mum. Even I found it soothing. That's how I know I'm ill. I'm developing a tolerance for Griff. What a crappy bug.

Poor Dylan.

If I had the energy to open my eyes, I'd read the time. It must be getting on for six. Perhaps I should prop myself up a bit. No. Even turning over is stirring my stomach. I'll stay still.

'Hey.'

Mum's crept in. The bed dips at my feet. She's perched on the end.

'I'm awake,' I grumble.

'Have you managed any sleep?'

'A little. You?'

'A little.'

'Heard from Griff?'

48

There's a silence, and I'm compelled to open my eyes. How is it possible for a room in darkness to spin? I catch a glimpse of Mum's profile, a golden aura surrounding her. It's ghostly, and fuzzy, and doing weird things to my gut, so I shut my eyes and hold out my hand. There's sufficient light from the landing for her to see what I'm doing, but not enough to see my arms. Her icy fingers wrap around my sticky palm.

'You're still very warm,' she says. 'Have you had any water?'

'I have, but I got rid of it ten minutes later.'

'It's important you keep drinking. Every little drop helps. I don't want you in hospital as well.'

She fidgets and my bed rocks. It's not good. It reminds me of when I went on a ferry crossing to France. We were with Dad. It was rough. Everyone was heaving and puking, the toilets were blocked, and the stench made it a thousand times worse. I'd never seen a person turn green. I thought it was an expression, but it really happens. I think I must be a pistachio colour right now.

My head rolls to the right and Mum's breath cools my face. She's sharing my pillow. She's curled up next to me.

'Would you like to climb in?' I ask, folding back my corner of the duvet.

'I'm good, thanks.'

It's been a while since we snuggled together. We used to do this all the time when I was younger. We were safe when we were together.

I pull Mum to me. 'Don't catch this bug.'

'Don't be fooled by my size. I've the constitution of an ox.' She releases a short, quiet laugh and the burst tickles my nose. It's not a real laugh. It's not like the ones I hear when she's in her bedroom with Griff. I cringe when the noise filters out from their room because I know what they're doing, but he makes her laugh, and that's so different to what I'd hear when Dad was around.

I never know what to do when Mum cries.

'Griff sent a text five minutes ago,' she says, reminding me I'd asked the question. 'Dylan's had a good night, his temperature is normal and he's waiting for breakfast. They're going to make their own way back so I can stay with you.'

I swear the bed just levitated. Our combined worry was weighing it down.

'They're hoping to come home once the doctor's been round.'

She brushes her fingers over my cheek, and turns the edge of my duvet down. I notice she said the word *home* and included Griff in the sentence. Is he coming home, or is he bringing Dylan home? I'm not sure I should ask. I'm not sure it's my business any more. Something's happened between them to drive them apart, but I don't know what. I have to believe that Mum would tell me if Griff put her at risk. She said he was one of the good guys, and I think he probably is. Despite my knee-jerk reaction yesterday, I can't imagine he would hurt Mum, not intentionally. Not with his fists. He's all about rescues and white knights and galloping steeds, and I want to trust him, but people change. Or lead you on. Or deceive you. I know it happens. I've seen it. I've felt it.

'This is nice,' Mum says, my thoughts carried away on her wave. 'We'll have Dylan with us next time.'

'He wriggles too much,' I say, although the idea pleases me. After what I heard about his seizure, wriggling is good. 'You can have him next to you.'

Mum's silent. She's thinking. She does a lot of that. Not one for talking. I understand. I'm the same when it comes to hard stuff – stuff I know will upset her or make her feel bad. Stuff best kept to myself. She's had plenty to deal with in her lifetime and me adding to it would be selfish. And anyway, it's down to me to handle these things. I'm nearly sixteen. Another few months and I'll be legally old enough to have sex. Not that I want to go there. My mind has drifted into murky territory so I brighten it by visualising Stephanie. 'Did I tell you I met a girl yesterday?'

'The French girl?'

Mum remembered.

'Yeah. Stephanie.' Her name is easy to say – it falls from my mouth – a breeze, a waterfall. 'She's pretty cool.' It's a good word. No wonder Rick likes using it.

'Is she the same age as you?'

'Seventeen, maybe.' She never told me. If she's older, I can't see her wanting to hang out with a fifteen-year-old. 'Speaks great English. Cute accent.'

'Cute?'

My pillow evens out and my hip sinks lower. I'm guessing Mum's leaning on her elbow. 'Yeah. Cute.' I chance opening my eyes in the hope the room stays static. Everything is in focus and perfectly still. Dawning daylight from the window is mixing with the yellow glow from outside my door, and Mum is studying me. I shove my arms under the cover. 'What's wrong with cute?'

She gives this funny one-shouldered shrug and adopts an innocent expression. 'Nothing.'

'Good.'

'I think the French accent is sexy.'

Sexy? Cute? Now I'm not sure. Did I mean sexy? I blunder on. 'Don't let Griff hear you say that.'

Her lips twitch. Another almost-smile.

'The Welsh accent is sexier than all others. That goes without saying.'

I mull this over for a minute. Griff does have a hint of an

accent, but you have to know what you're listening for to hear it. Mum's clearly tuned into it. 'So you don't consider Griff cute?'

She lifts her brow like she used to when I exaggerated the truth. It's saying, '*Really?*' Now I'm smiling. Mine's a proper one.

'Tell me about Stephanie,' she says, rolling on to her back and gazing at the ceiling.

My smile remains, fed by Mum's interest, and prolonged by the image in my head. 'She's a little taller than me, dark hair, brown eyes. Bangles. Lots of bangles. On both wrists. I'd tell you who she looks like, but I've never seen anyone like her.'

'She's made quite an impression. Is it because she's foreign?'

I'm picking up a strange vibe from Mum, and it's stopping me from answering. I've got this weird feeling her question is loaded and my reply will spring the trap. I don't like it. 'She's just cool.' I resort to Rick's word and decide it's not a good time to talk about emotions and love and *stuff*.

And this isn't even the hard stuff.

At least it wasn't until a second ago.

Mum's turned to face me. 'You know you can talk to me about anything, don't you?'

But I can't. I can't tell her about the movies in my head, the whispering voices urging me to release the pressure, the adrenalin forcing me to harm over and over again. I can't speak the words. If I let them out, I'm scared they'll freeze right in front of me, and everyone will read them, everyone will know. It'll confirm what they already think. They'll say I'm crazy, sad, a loose cannon. They'll accuse me of attention-seeking, which is crap. I get noticed just for being ginger. Worse than that, they'll blame Mum, and this is not her fault.

I dig my arms into the mattress. 'I know.'

'Anytime.'

I wish she'd look away now. And I wish she wouldn't make promises she has to break, because it hurts her as much as me. 'I'm fine.'

Her eyes have narrowed, but she doesn't speak.

'Honestly, Mum. There's nothing to report.'

She sits up, spreads her arms wide and invites me in for a hug. I can't accept. My curtains aren't thick enough to prevent the advancing daylight from exposing me. I play it down. 'You're all right,' I say. 'I'll hug you when I'm clean.'

'A bit of guck doesn't put me off.'

She grabs the top of my duvet.

'Mum. Don't.'

Chapter Seven

Evie dropped the cover and bumped herself to the end of the bed. 'I've seen you naked thousands of times.'

'When I was a child. Things have *changed*.'

'We've both changed. You wait until you're my age. Believe me, you've nothing to be embarrassed about.' If she could make Tess laugh, she might loosen up and tell her the real problem. 'You're spring, and I'm autumn.'

'I'm a sensitive teenager and you've had two children. You left your dignity at the maternity unit. Remember?'

'I lost it before then.'

'Mum!'

'All right. I'm going.' Evie slid her feet into her slippers, and pushed herself up from the bed. 'I'm glad you're feeling better.' Concerned her good wishes weren't clear enough, she added, 'From your sick bug.' She patted Tess's covered legs and padded out of the room.

Tess *had* changed. No longer was she the tiny spot of a girl, in flashing trainers and pink dresses, clutching Old Ted to her flat chest – she was a young woman, with purple Doc Martens, artistic piercings, and feminine curves. She was her own person, and Evie, with all her running around caring for Logan, fretting over Griff, and looking after Dylan, had missed her charming little duckling transform into the beautiful swan.

Guilt came with a nasty, bitter taste.

Evie collected her phone from her bedside table, sighed at the empty message screen, and wandered downstairs. Surely Dylan would be home soon.

Ozzy greeted her in the hall.

'Hello, my boy. I can feed you, but you'll have to wait for your walk.'

As she entered the kitchen and opened the blind, her eye was drawn to a glass container on the windowsill. It was as transparent and empty as she felt, the irony being, this was her Happiness jar.

She unscrewed the lid, pulled out the solitary piece of paper, and unfolded it, sighing at the memory it prompted. She read the words again: *We all sat down for New Year's Day dinner – Griff, Tess, Dylan and me.*

For the children's sake, Evie and Griff had managed to set aside their problems for a few testing hours, and eat together as a family – as if Logan had never asked Evie to help him. As if Griff had never left.

She returned the paper to the jar. There should have been a handful of slips for company, but there'd been nothing positive to write about. And if Evie had scribbled a few lines each day, they would have been trivial or fake. Forced.

There was certainly nothing to add since yesterday.

Her mobile rang, startling her from her thoughts. 'Is Dylan okay?' She knew it was Griff. In a moment of humour, she'd programmed Elton John's 'Someone Saved My Life Tonight' as his call tone. Appropriate, under the circumstances.

'Dylan's fine,' he said. 'We both are. The doctor does his round at eight, so we'll be here another hour or so. How's Tess?'

'She seems a little better.' Evie was touched by Griff's concern. 'She just needs to get some sleep.'

'Her and me both.'

'You sound tired.' Evie lodged the phone between her ear and shoulder before screwing the lid back onto the jar. There was no point leaving it open. Until she'd seen for herself that Dylan was well, she had no reason to add another note. 'You didn't rest?'

'No.'

Griff's succinct reply prompted her into returning the phone to her hand.

'I was watching over Dylan,' he said. 'Did you sleep?'

'No. Not a wink.' A tired hum of acceptance travelled the line. 'We can catch up later.'

'What about the family lunch?'

'Your dad can't come here. I can't risk him catching this bug.'

'*We* can't risk him catching this bug.'

As much as Griff was a man of responsibility, it was strange to hear him stake a claim in his father's care.

'So, you'll cancel lunch?'

He was definitely pushing for an answer.

'I'll cancel the family lunch,' Evie said, 'but Logan still needs help.' That was the next problem. Talk about divided loyalties. Somehow in the next hour she had to be confident Tess was well enough to be left alone, get to Logan's and help him prepare for the day, and then be home to take care of Dylan. She held her forehead in her hand. The day had barely started and she was already stressed. And hot. Not sleeping was taking its toll.

She removed her palm and blew onto it, but it remained clammy. 'You could go.'

He wouldn't, but Evie had to try. At some point the two men had to put their differences behind them. Things needed to be resolved before it was too late.

If Griff saw how poorly his father was it might stir him into taking action, but not telling him about Logan's rapid decline was another of the old man's stipulations.

'Yes, it would be good to make peace before I go,' Logan had said. 'But if Griff comes to see me, it has to be because he wants to, not because he's duty-bound or driven by guilt.'

Evie was in an impossible situation.

If anyone could talk Logan round, it was his headstrong son.

A lengthy silence preceded Griff's reply. 'He needs you, not me.'

With no energy to argue, Evie responded with a muted, 'You're wrong. I'll see you when you get back.' She ended the call, giving Griff no chance to reply, and laid the phone on the table. Had she any fight left, she'd have knocked both men's heads together. Both needed to see sense. Both needed to understand one another. They were more alike than either wanted to admit – assertive, strong-willed, wanting to stay in control of the world around them. Make the big decisions alone. If only they'd work together. If only they'd see what a formidable force they'd be.

And had they come together, her marriage wouldn't be in pieces.

She turned as Tess shuffled into the kitchen. 'I'm not sure you should be up.' She ushered her into a chair and studied her pale features. Tess didn't have much colour when she was well – it was a little frightening to see her so white. The dark circles under her deep-set eyes were adding to the overall effect. 'Can I get you anything? Toast? A cup of tea?'

Tess declined. 'I'm okay. I might get myself something later. Is Griff on his way back?'

Overriding Tess's plan, Evie filled the kettle and slipped a slice of bread into the toaster. 'They're waiting to be discharged, but that won't happen until the doctor's been round.' She checked the clock above the kitchen door. 'Another hour or so, probably longer. You know what hospitals are like.'

'Poor little feller.' Tess glanced at Evie. 'Poor you.'

'I'm all right,' said Evie, putting Ozzy's breakfast in his corner. 'But I'll be happier when they're home and I can see Dylan for myself.'

'It must have been scary, though?'

Evie had spent most of the night awake reliving the moment she thought her son had died. She was certain the image of his small body, lifeless on the floor of his bedroom would stay with her forever. She was building quite an album of pictures like that.

What happened to Dylan terrified her, and she never wanted to go through that again, but he was okay, and that was the thought she had to cling to. She waved away Tess's question with far more buoyancy than she felt, and turned her attention to tea making.

'I want you to have this and then you're to go back to bed.' She stirred sugar into one of the mugs and passed it to Tess. 'Don't pull a face. The sweetness will do you good. And so will this.' With a feigned flourish, she tossed the hot toast onto a plate, applied a thin smear of butter to the slice, and dabbed a few blobs of Marmite over one half. 'It used to be digestive biscuits in my day.' She presented the dish to Tess and gestured for her to start eating.

'Aren't you having anything?'

'I had something earlier.' Evie dismissed the lie and busied herself with her own drink. Her appetite would return eventually.

'You've got to eat, Mum. Don't think I haven't noticed. Ever since your bust-up with Griff you haven't sat down for a meal.'

Evie's chest contracted. The last thing she wanted was for Tess to worry, but she was testing the theory that what Tess didn't know wouldn't hurt her.

The theory was proven wrong. In the last few seconds it had become apparent Evie was yet to give her daughter a convincing reason as to why Griff had left. She was yet to produce a reason Griff would accept. But she couldn't tell them. She'd given Logan her word.

She sipped at her tea. 'Things will sort themselves out.' She approached the table and sat next to Tess. 'I promise.'

Tess gave a gentle shake of her head. 'Things don't sort themselves out, you know that.' She moved a hand from under the table and seemed to go to place it on top of Evie's, but at the last minute, pulled her dressing gown sleeve down and retracted her arm. 'I thought you were through with hiding from the truth.'

'I'm not hiding from the truth. I'm not hiding from anything.' Evie swiped up her mobile and stared at the screen, hoping there'd be a message or an alert – something to send the conversation in a different direction. She jumped as it vibrated in her hand and Logan's siren sounded. 'He's wondering where I am,' she said, grimacing at Tess. 'I thought maybe I could nip there and back before Griff brought Dylan home, but I can't leave you on your own. Not when you're so unwell.'

'I'm okay,' said Tess. 'I'm feeling much more with it.'

Without replying to either Tess or Logan, Evie muted the phone and slid it onto the table. It had done its job in taking the attention away from her. 'Would you like me to wash your hair?'

The look of *seriously?* Tess supplied encouraged a faint smile to play on Evie's lips. 'I'll take that as a no,' she said. 'You used to love me washing your hair.'

'Yeah. When I was three. Anyway, it's my turn to look after you.'

Kind, sweet Tess. 'It's not about turns, my beautiful girl.' Evie witnessed the scarlet rush to Tess's face at the release of the word, 'beautiful'. 'We need to look after each other.' There'd been enough role reversal in the past. 'Including

Dylan. You'll need to look out for each other. I know there's a big age gap between you, but I never wanted you to be an only child. That was never my choice. I *always* wanted you to have someone who'll be there for you when I'm gone.'

'Mum.' Tess flicked her head to the side and refused to look at Evie.

'What? I'm not immortal. None of us are. What's that saying about bleeding?'

'"If you prick us, do we not bleed?"' Tess sighed and settled her eyes on Evie. 'It's Shakespeare.'

'It's true. And I knew you'd know it.' She held Tess's gaze. 'Beautiful and intelligent.' Tess wouldn't accept the compliment, but it wasn't going to stop Evie reinforcing the point. She remembered what it was to be a teenager. Especially one whose hair colour made her stand out from the crowd. What she didn't get was why Tess insisted on emphasising her individuality. A smokescreen? She found herself considering the possibilities instead of concentrating on the conversation in hand, when the rumble of her phone brought her back. It vibrated its way across the table. 'All I'm saying is, I'm glad you and Dylan have each other.' Evie reached for the mobile, wishing it was a text from Griff, but knowing in her heart it was Logan trying to reach her.

With her free hand, she dragged her fingers across her forehead, attempting to relieve the growing pressure. When that didn't work, she opened her mouth and squeezed the hollow of her cheeks. The action triggered a yawn, and her jaws cracked. She cradled the side of her face in her palm.

Tess nodded towards the phone. 'What you're saying is you're glad I have someone to share the responsibility with when you're old and grey?'

It was a playful remark, which blew oxygen into the room. Evie took a deep breath. 'Life would be simpler if Griff had a brother or sister, but honestly, I don't mind.

Logan's been good to us. Helping him is the least I can do.'

Helping him to live. Not helping him to die. Evie shoved the thought to the back of her mind. She was too exhausted to cover old ground.

'I can go. You know. To Logan's. We get on okay.' Tess was already out of her chair and heading for the hall. 'I'll go as soon as I'm dressed. I can cycle.'

Evie rose and held out her hand for Tess to take. She didn't, but she'd acknowledged the gesture and she'd wandered back into the kitchen.

'God knew what he was doing when he sent you.' Evie reached for Tess and pulled her into a hug. 'I must've done something right to have a wonderful daughter like you in my life.'

The moment passed in silence until Tess pushed herself away. 'We'll get through this,' she said. 'We always do. But you have to learn to ask for help.'

'I promise I'll ask,' said Evie. 'But that won't be today. You need to go back to bed. I'll see to Logan once Dylan's home. Griff can stay while I'm out.'

'I don't need babysitting. I'm fine. Logan's going to keep calling until you answer.' Tess swung round and pointed to the clock. 'You could be there and back in less than an hour, home in time for Dylan's arrival.'

With many reasons for keeping her visit to Logan short, Evie was tempted. She'd have to go back later, but the minute lunch was postponed she'd known that. It was going to be a three-trip, maybe four-trip day, so it wouldn't hurt to make this morning's a quick one. She rested a hand on Tess's shoulder and spun her round. 'Are you sure?' She checked her eyes. The circles were more grey than black now, almost matching her raincloud irises, but her skin was still pallid. 'No,' Evie said. 'You're my priority.'

'Bloody hell, Mother! Will you just go! I'm fine. More than capable of looking after myself. I'll go to bed and stay there until you get back.'

'No. Logan can wait.'

'Logan can't wait. He can't even get out of bed by himself. He'll need a pee.'

Evie raised her palms in submission. 'Okay. I'll go. But I want to see you in bed first, with a glass of water on your cabinet. And you best still be there when I get back.' She waved her index finger in mock reproach. 'And don't swear.'

As Evie parked up, she knocked back the cuff of her coat and squinted at her watch. It wasn't quite eight. If she worked in an efficient manner and refused to be drawn on Logan's moral dilemma, she'd be home in less than thirty minutes.

Evie had battled with her own moral dilemma for the duration of the journey. Tess was her child, and despite the fifteen-year-old dismissing her, Evie's conscience was waging war, reminding her how awful and frightening it was to be alone and sick, with no one to hold your hair back as you leaned over the toilet.

Without warning, a vivid and terrifying memory seized her and held her to ransom. She clutched the steering wheel, and held her breath. Her heart was thrashing against her ribcage, her lungs were desperate to deflate and her nerves were making her entire body judder. As she gave in to her lungs' demands, she gasped for air, coughing as the cold reality of day hit the back of her throat.

He could have been right there with her – Neil – alcohol on his breath, yanking at her ponytail, swearing and calling her *useless*, *pathetic*; yelling at her to stop puking; threatening to do her, *'there and then'*, if she didn't stand up. He did once. While Evie vomited.

She closed her eyes and allowed the scene to play out. It was enough to make her sick, *there and then*.

'Give it up,' she whispered. 'Set it free.' She eased open her eyes, listened to the sounds of the world outside, and brought herself back to the empty vehicle. He wasn't right there with her, but sometimes ... *sometimes* she could smell him – cardamom, amber – expensive aftershave she could no longer bear. Sometimes she could hear his intimidating, insistent commands to do as he said – vile, disgusting things. And sometimes she could taste the stale mint of the gum he would push into her mouth with his tongue.

He wasn't there; he couldn't be there; but he would never leave.

Evie chanced a glimpse of herself in the rear-view mirror and accepted the mess staring back. A brush and a band would tidy her hair, but she didn't tie it back these days.

She didn't need a visual reminder of Neil's cruel method of controlling her.

Pulling her around by her ponytail had been a favourite pastime of his.

She appreciated the sense of freedom leaving her hair down produced.

With her nerves under control, she clambered out of the car and hurried to Logan's door, aware time was marching on. She thrust the key in the hole and let herself in.

'Morning, Logan. Sorry I'm late.'

No answer. This had become the norm in recent days. It didn't help with Evie's nerves. She needed to hear a response from him. 'I'm coming upstairs,' she called. 'Are you decent?' Still nothing. Was *this* it? Was *this* the moment she'd been dreading for the past few months?

She waited outside Logan's bedroom, her hands clasped, her knuckles kneading her mouth. What if he was dead? What if he'd managed to ... No. He said himself he couldn't open the pill containers. He was sleeping, that was all. He wasn't dead. He couldn't be. No one should die alone.

A dim glow from the bathroom window cast Evie's small shadow onto Logan's door, and she stood, transfixed on the shape.

This could be the moment she was released from Logan's impossible proposition.

Horrified she'd permitted such a callous thought to run loose, she scolded herself. She didn't wish anyone dead.

Except Neil MacDonald. And that wish had been granted.

She grasped the brass handle and edged her way into the room.

'Logan, my love, it's me, Evie.' As her eyes adjusted to the gloom she saw Logan slumped against his headboard, his chin tucked to his chest and his arms hanging by his sides. She drew back the hefty velvet curtains, filling the room with positive, faith-restoring light, and examined him further. As shallow as it was, there was air passing between his lips. There were also splashes of sick on the blanket concealing his lower half. Logan's mobile was spattered with the same. 'Oh, Logan.'

The old man opened his eyes. 'I called you,' he said, his voice not much more than a whisper. 'I called you and you didn't answer.' A tear tipped over the brink of his lashes and pooled in the deep trench above his cheekbone. Another, and then another, until the tiny salt lake could hold no more and water flooded his face.

Evie cradled his head to her bosom, offering apologies and hushes for comfort. She gave no excuses, no reasons for her negligence regardless of its origin. They wouldn't help Logan, and right now that was all she wanted to do. 'You're not to worry, do you hear? It's only sick. I get worse at home. It's nothing I can't handle.'

With those words, Logan's body went into spasm, inconsolable sobs accompanying every one. Evie softened her hold and stooped to see him, but he refused to expose his face.

'Don't,' he said. 'Don't look at me.'

'Logan. It's fine.'

His head rocked from side-to-side. 'It's not fine. It'll never be fine. Never.' He jerked free from Evie's hold, scrunched his eyes shut and clenched his jaws together. 'Can't you smell it?' The words were forced through his teeth. 'Can't you smell the shit?'

Chapter Eight

Griff

As the taxi pulled up next to the cottage, Griff hugged Dylan close to his chest. They'd spent the journey from the hospital snuggled together, both strapped behind one safety belt. In the chaos of yesterday's emergency, taking a car seat in the ambulance had been the last thing on Griff's mind.

'We're home, little feller.' He reached into his pocket, tugged out a crumpled note and knocked on the panel separating the passengers from the driver. 'Cheers, mate. Is that enough?'

The man in the front seat took the money from Griff, waved his thanks and reset his meter.

Griff shuffled forward, yanked at the handle and shoved open the door. 'Good to be home.' He hitched Dylan higher to his shoulder and stepped onto the path, using his hip to knock the door shut. 'Let's get you in.'

As he spoke, Griff glanced along the driveway. His lump of a Land Rover was still there, but Evie's Mini was missing. 'Looks like your mum's out.' He rubbed Dylan's back and kissed the top of his head. 'I thought she'd be here to greet us.' He revised his statement. 'You. I thought she'd be here to greet *you.*'

The house was still and quiet, the only sign of life being Ozzy's tail sweeping away at a small area of kitchen floor. He'd have to wait. Dylan needed changing. The white sleepsuit the hospital had lent him was a little snug, but since he'd arrived there in nothing other than a nappy, there was no complaint to make.

Conscious of his son's lack of movement, Griff tucked in his chin and looked at him. The boy's tiny rosebud mouth was parted and his dark, button eyes were closed.

A deep, satisfying sigh, which Griff not only heard but experienced as Dylan's body expanded within his arms, broke the anxious pause. His baby's breath was followed by his own. 'It's going to take some time before I stop watching you,' he said. 'Can't go through another day like yesterday.'

But he was in no position to keep his promise, not the way things were right now, and that hurt.

With his precious cargo in his arms, Griff forwent his usual two by two ascension to the landing, and took one step at a time, his footfall making little sound. He crept into Dylan's room, laid him on the changing table and undid the poppers of the sleepsuit, easing his son's relaxed limbs out of the sleeves and legs. He changed Dylan's nappy without disturbing him, slipped him into a pair of pyjamas, and transferred him to his bed.

Griff kneeled at his side, keeping guard.

If Evie allowed it, he'd be doing that for all of them – watching over them. They were his family; his responsibility. His loved ones.

With his arms resting on the hard, wooden edge of the bed frame, Griff clenched his fists together and supported his head with them. He was so damned tired.

'You're home.'

The voice startled him into answering, but he stayed hunched over. 'We've been back a few minutes. Where were you?'

'In bed.'

The belligerent tone forced Griff to look up, and he realised his mistake.

'Sorry, Tess. I thought you were your mum.' He attempted an apologetic smile. 'You sound alike.'

'She was hoping to be here. She must have got delayed.'

Griff straightened up and stretched out his arms, tensing and relaxing his muscles to get his stiff, night-in-a-chair joints working again. 'She's at my dad's, isn't she?'

Tess nodded. 'She was going to wait, but we weren't sure what time the hospital would release you. And Logan kept calling.' She peered at the bed. 'How's Dylan?'

'He'll be fine. Sleep's the best cure.' Griff glanced at Tess. She looked as rough as he felt. 'How are you?'

Tess sauntered across to the nursing chair and collapsed into it – an unusual move on her behalf, suggesting she was willing to engage in conversation.

'Tired, mainly,' she said, rocking the chair back and forth. 'I told Mum I was okay. She didn't want to leave me here, but I could see she was worried about Logan.'

Griff gave Dylan another check before leaving his side. He leaned against a set of white drawers a few feet away from Tess. If he encroached on her personal space, he knew she'd edge away. To keep Tess near, he needed to keep his distance. One day he'd find out why. It had something to do with Evie's first husband, that much he knew, but neither Evie nor Tess had discussed their past in detail, and he wasn't about to press for information now. He propped the heels of his hands on the dresser, crossed his ankles and stifled a yawn. 'Tired just about covers it. Can I get you anything?'

The chair came to a halt. 'I'm good, thanks. Mum made sure I was sorted.'

'I wasn't suggesting she hadn't.' The stare Griff was getting wasn't the harshest he'd received from Tess, but it left him in no doubt his offer of help had insulted her. Teenagers. They were all the same. In his days as a Coastguard Rescue Officer he'd risked his life for a selection of scowls, scorns and mutterings of, 'I didn't need your help.' Par for the course.

He'd been like that once. So had Kieran.

The arrogance of youth was a dangerous thing.

'I can't fight with you, Tess. Not today.' From the corner of his eye, Griff saw Tess shrug, rise from the chair and slouch her way to the door.

'I wasn't looking for a fight.'

'What was with the stare?'

'Bloody hell, Griff.' Tess slammed her hand onto the wall and glowered at him. 'That wasn't a stare.'

'Don't swear.'

Tess's jaw set firm, her eyes narrowed and her glare pinned Griff to the drawers. 'This is the stare.' She paused, clearly allowing Griff time to appreciate its power. 'And I'll bloody swear if I want to. You don't get to tell me what to do. You are not my ...'

Griff was immediately on alert, and he stood erect in anticipation of Tess's attack. He could count on one hand the number of times she'd used the father–daughter beating against him, but each lashing cut deeper to the bone than the last. He wanted to be a father to her, but Tess was right: it was something he could never be, no matter how much he felt it in his heart.

To his surprise, Tess closed Dylan's safety gate and retreated onto the landing.

'We're both sleep-deprived,' she said. 'And I don't have the energy for some weird Griff Hendry version of the Battle of Trafalgar.'

That was something. Neither did Griff. The likelihood was Tess would sink him without a trace. He waited to see what she did next, breathing a little easier now the warning light had gone to amber, and was surprised to hear her voice echo from downstairs.

'Believe it or not, I think what you did for Dylan was pretty cool.'

After a bout of fitful dreams and sudden, waking jerks that jolted the chair, Griff conceded defeat, rose to his full height and ventured to the window. Surely Evie was home now.

The empty space on the gravel indicated not.

'This needs to be sorted.' For too long Evie had been at the beck and call of Logan. Even before the rift in their marriage, the differing approaches towards the old man's care had created tension between Griff and Evie. Her compassion was one of the reasons Griff loved her, but she had to learn when to say no. Logan did need help, that fact was not in dispute, but he was taking advantage of Evie, and it wasn't on.

Griff was of a mind to employ an outside care firm and present it as a fait accompli, but that would get him nowhere, except out through the door of both houses.

A heavy sigh did nothing to relieve the weight of his concerns. 'I don't know what to do.' His words, deadened by the glass, were aimed at Dylan. 'Promise you'll always be straight with me, son. Always tell me the truth. Even if it's to tell me I'm too difficult to live with.' He turned, hoping his child's innocent features would fill him with renewed optimism and faith.

The half-size bed was empty.

Griff pushed past the open gate, ran to the top of the stairs and lunged for the wooden support. 'Tess! Where's Dylan?'

The living room door opened a crack and Tess poked her head round. 'He's in here. Why the panic?'

Relaxing his grip, Griff slid his hand down the bannister. 'Nothing. My fault. I was expecting to see him in his bed, that's all. Is he okay?' He jogged down the stairs, ensured the lower gate was secure, and waited for Tess to clear the way into the lounge.

'Of course he's okay. He's playing.' She stepped back and pointed to Dylan, who was busy crawling in between two piles of books. 'He woke up, so I brought him down.'

Griff surveyed the scene. His son fell onto his bottom, swished his hands through the hardbacks and picked up one with a picture on it of a bright red fire engine. A whispered 'nee-nar' accompanied his smiling face.

'I didn't hear him,' Griff said. 'Sorry.'

Tess clambered over a mountain of plastic cars and giant building blocks and settled on the sofa. 'I left you to sleep.'

'I was sleeping?' It hadn't felt like it.

'Yeah. You were twitching. Like Ozzy does when he's dreaming.'

'Ozzy!' The dog hadn't been walked in hours. 'I need to get him out. He'll need a pee.'

Tess snorted. 'That's what I said to Mum about Logan. Don't worry. Ozzy's fine. I took him out. We had fun, didn't we, Dylan?'

The toddler waved at Tess and then returned to his book, scoring the words with his index finger.

'You took Dylan and Ozzy out?' This was a new practice in the Hendry household. 'I didn't think I was sleeping that heavily,' said Griff. Or that long. Certainly not long enough for his family to alter their habits. The speed with which life was changing was disconcerting, and the fact it was happening without him was unnerving, *but*, more important than that, Tess had done something for *him*. And it wasn't an empty gesture. She was still recovering from the effects of the sick bug, but she'd taken on Griff's responsibilities so he could rest. It was a touching, caring and selfless act, and one that injected hope into his soul. 'Thank you, Tess,' he said. 'I mean it.'

Chapter Nine

Evie

Logan had insisted on being dressed and helped on and then off his stairlift, so he could access his living room. Nothing Evie said convinced him he was better off in bed.

'Don't you think I've suffered enough indignities this morning?' he'd said. 'I'm not spending the day stuck in this godforsaken room. It's the beginning of the end.'

And so, after an hour of personal cleaning, sheet changing, whispered reassurances that everything was all right and shouts of, 'This is why I want to go', and, 'I don't want to be a burden', Evie and Logan were seated in separate chairs, in silence.

Evie gave consideration to Logan's declaration. If this was the beginning of the end, how far away was the finish line? Her father-in-law was seventy-four. Granted, he wasn't a young man, and this morning's trauma had aged him, but people lived full lives well into their eighties.

She sneaked a glance at him. He was staring at the blank TV. There was something of Griff about him – the squareness of the chin and an intensity behind the eyes – other than that, she wouldn't have picked either of them out of a line-up as related. Their personalities were the clue. Both were confident, protective and spoke from the hip. Both would risk everything to make a difference and leave a lasting memory. And both needed to be in control of their own life.

Or death, in Logan's case.

'You will help me, won't you?' Logan's gaze remained rooted to the TV. 'You're the only one I can ask. The only one who will see it through.'

'I signed your Advance Decision, and I've promised to

see that through. Isn't that enough?' Evie cocked her head, waiting for a reply. An answer wasn't forthcoming. 'There are other ways, Logan. You must see that?'

Logan turned, his hooded, blue eyes the most animated part of his body, striking the inharmonious chords in Evie's conscience.

'Don't, Logan. This isn't fair.'

'And this is?' With the physical strain extending across his face, Logan raised an arm a couple of inches and half turned his palm to the ceiling. With his body tremoring, his shoulders dropped and his hand thumped down onto his lap. 'These were surgeon's hands. They saved lives. I saved lives. Surely I have the right to decide when to die?'

'You're disabled, Logan. With rheumatoid arthritis.' Evie left her seat and made her way to the kitchen. The room was closing in on her. 'You're not in imminent danger of dying.'

'Don't you walk away.' Logan's voice had gained strength. 'Get back here and let this play out. It's what I have to do. I don't have the luxury of taking off when the heat is on.'

Scolded and instantly remorseful, Evie returned to the living room. 'I'm sorry. What I said was unforgivable.' She perched on the pale oak coffee table. Although sympathetic towards his situation, she had to consider the gravity of the consequences. 'You must know what you're asking is against the law. It's assisted suicide.' There. She'd said it. But the jolt of speaking it out loud was greater on her than Logan, with graphic visuals of her weeping children invading her head. That was where it was heading, though. Ultimately. The death of their granddad and the incarceration of their mother. Unless Evie could talk Logan round. 'There are other options. Other means of help.'

Logan shook his head and closed his eyes. 'I've told you before. I don't want *other* help.'

He'd objected to the idea on numerous occasions, and

Evie had backed him up. She understood Logan not wanting strangers in his house, turning up late in the morning to get him out of bed, or early in the evening to put him back in. He argued he would be at their mercy, *and* they'd have total access to his house, coming and going as they pleased, perhaps even when he was out with Evie.

'You wouldn't like it,' he'd said to her. 'You'd have to hide everything away each time you went out.'

Evie could see his point.

'In fact,' he continued, 'you couldn't leave anything out at any time, day or night. I don't want strangers looking at my bank statements. How would I know what they were up to once I was *put* to bed?'

'There are decent firms out there,' she'd replied. 'But I hear what you're saying.'

'I trust you, Evie. And I know you're not on the take. You're a capable, caring woman, with the energy of a power station, and I appreciate what you do for me. I can never thank you enough, and I promise, the moment I become a burden, the second my body holds me prisoner, I will find my own solution.'

At the time, Evie hadn't considered suicide as the solution, but finding Logan as she had that morning – having to clean him, dress him and tell him it would be all right – brought home everything he'd said about the loss of dignity.

But *suicide*?

She was still shocked that she was contemplating his plea. She should have said no from the get-go. No, like she'd told Dylan when he'd played too rough with a boy at the toddler group. No, the word she'd used on Ozzy when he'd jumped up at the kitchen counter. No, the reply she should have given when Griff asked if there was someone else … At times it came to her freely, but never when someone needed or wanted something from her.

Although not at ease with the idea, she felt less conflicted by the Advance Decision. It was a document outlining the care Logan wished to receive in his final days – no tubes, no assisted breathing, no resuscitation. It was daunting stuff, but it wasn't about him taking his life, it was about Logan being allowed to let go. There was a subtle difference and one Evie could live with.

She could try to talk him round. Ask him to look beyond the present. Explain the demands and pressures she was facing. Tell him how much she needed to be at home for Tess and Dylan, both at crucial stages of their lives. Tess was in her exam year and Dylan needed to socialise with his peers – get to know the children with whom he'd be attending pre-school.

Perhaps she should let Logan know what a strain it had put on her and Griff's marriage.

Strain was too generous a word. Fractured was nearer the mark. She'd made the damage done to her marriage sound like a sprain to a muscle, as if a few weeks of rest would set it right, but with the constant beating it was taking, and with nothing to support it, a complete break was inevitable.

Would any of this make a difference to Logan?

Evie shook her head in reply to her question. He was an intelligent, protective, wilful man, who would use those reasons to fuel his fire. He'd say his continued existence would only serve to perpetuate the problems and that by taking him out of the equation his family could return to being a happy, strong and solid unit.

Somehow she had to convince him life was worth living and put a positive spin on the carer situation. Find a way to show him trained staff could improve his quality of life. And hers.

'You're not a burden,' she said, waiting for him to open his eyes before she continued. 'It's an honour spending time with you.' She hesitated, not wanting to add a 'but', knowing the word would take away the importance of the preceding sentiment. 'I miss being with you as your daughter-in-law, the mother to your grandchildren, the wife to your son. With a little extra help, we can get that back.' He'd be Logan the granddad and the father, not Logan the patient. Evie longed to see those sides of him again. He called her his daughter-in-law, but she felt more like his warden. 'We'd spend time together as a family.'

No reaction.

Evie tried another angle. 'You'd have an expert looking after your medical needs. We both know I'm not much good beyond sticky plasters and antiseptic.'

That provoked a twitch of an eyebrow, but nothing more.

She had one last argument; one she was uncomfortable with using, but it would elicit a response.

There'd been a definite shift in their dynamics today, one which neither could ignore.

Logan, the patriarch, the man whose intelligence and courage saved lives, and whose authority and influence had brought an entire hospital to its knees until it addressed its mortality rates, had been reduced to the level of a baby. Everything Evie had done for him that morning, she was to repeat later with Dylan.

This was the catalyst for the renewed cries for help.

'You wouldn't have to face me cleaning and dressing you,' she said, clutching her hands to her breast.

'The fact anyone has to clean and dress me is enough,' Logan said, his voice adopting a soft quality.

It sent a shiver from Evie's chest to her stomach.

He called her to him and she kneeled at his feet. His bony, twisted fingers stretched out for hers. She held them, gently.

'I used to be like Griff,' he said. 'Full of life. Strong. Virile. I took care of my family. I loved Marilyn and Griff with every cell in my body. Everything I did was for them. Always the provider. Always the strong one holding it together. And I've never asked for anything in return. I've never asked anything of anyone. Not until now. I'm asking you for help, Evie, that's all. Help me move on to the next life, where Marilyn waits and where there's no more pain. No more sitting in my own waste. No more … fear.' A fragile hand pulled away from hers and stroked her hair. 'You don't even need to be here when I do it. I just want to make sure I'm not left in limbo. Do you understand what I'm saying?'

She wasn't sure she did. She looked up expecting to find Logan crippled with pure emotion, but instead was rocked by his steely glare and sheer determination. His thin lips were set hard in a perfect line. He appeared calm, focused and resolute.

'I'm going to do it, Evie, with or without you.' His hand withdrew from her head. 'You're not the only one who can find other methods.'

Logan's indomitable expression had stayed with Evie from the second she'd seen his face, to the moment she stepped into the cottage, and now the result of driving home blind, the worry of Logan's threat, and the shock of Dylan's seizure was hitting her. All she wanted was to see her baby boy, check in on Tess, and take shelter in Griff's arms.

As she shut the door and glanced into the kitchen, she saw Griff, his shirt pulled tight across his back, huddled in Ozzy's corner. She could hear Dylan singing away, repeating the words, 'Good dog,' to an indistinct tune. Relief and sadness brought her to a standstill and she allowed herself a moment to work out which emotion had the strongest hold. Relief was the first to let go.

Griff peered over his shoulder. His jaw was set firm, his mouth, reminiscent of Logan's, was as straight as the horizon, and his eyes were directed at Evie's. Where his were warm with autumn colours and Logan's were a cool Arctic blue, both pairs were asking Evie the same question: Why won't you help me?

He nodded, then returned his attention to the scene in front of him.

'I'm sorry I wasn't here when you got home.' Evie ventured into the kitchen, stopping after she'd stepped over the threshold. 'I planned to be, but ...' Excuses, reasons – whatever name she gave to them – weren't going to help. 'How's Dylan?' She edged a little nearer, circumnavigating the table. 'He looks his usual self.'

The toddler scrambled to his feet and trotted across to Evie. 'Mummy!'

She lifted him from under his arms, kissed him several times and held him tight to her chest, taking strength from his display of unconditional love. *If only children ruled the world* ... She laid a cheek on top of his head, his mop of thick hair providing a downy cushion. 'You had us worried, Dylan. I thought you were—' She pulled herself up, stopping short of saying, 'dying', but the thought alone was enough to trigger the tears. They fell onto the soft feathers of her baby's head, turning spots of his hair from brown to black. She smoothed them away, wishing her pain was as easily eradicated. She changed her gaze from Dylan's head to the back of Griff's. 'You must be exhausted.'

'He is.' Griff remained facing away.

'I meant you.' Evie kept her tone gentle. 'Have you had any sleep?'

Griff's head moved from side-to-side. 'Not enough.'

'Can I get you anything? A bite to eat?'

It seemed so inadequate after everything he'd done for Dylan, but it was all she could permit herself to offer. What she wanted to do and what was appropriate under the circumstances were two entirely different things.

Dylan's weight shifted and he nestled into her. 'I'm going to put Dylan down and then I'll be back,' she said. 'Let me make you some lunch. Please.'

Before she left the kitchen, she saw Griff shrug, and took it as acceptance of her proposal. His indifferent gesture was an indication of how unhealthy their relationship had become. Griff was a communicator; a talker; the man who encouraged Evie to open up, express herself, speak out when she had something on her mind. To see him answer in such an apathetic way, and to know it was her actions that had brought him to it, delivered despondent tears to her eyes, a ball of wretchedness to her gut, and a familiar sense of isolation she thought she'd buried with Neil.

If Griff and Logan would just talk ...

It was a pointless wish and one that wouldn't change the fact Evie had no one to blame but herself.

Things had got out of hand and she owed Griff an explanation, but until she'd sorted out the mess in her head and reached a decision about Logan, she'd have to continue on her treacherous course. The journey had to come to an end at some point.

As she settled Dylan into his bed she heard footsteps pad across the landing, followed by a door clicking shut and a squeak of a floorboard, indicating Tess had not been in her bedroom. She too deserved an explanation, but she'd never asked for one. Not even when her father was around. She accepted Evie's actions without question and, like Dylan, her love was unconditional. 'She doesn't need to know,' Evie said, brushing a finger against Dylan's cheek. 'Not yet. I'll protect you both for as long as I can.'

She'd promised Tess that no matter what, she and Dylan would be her number one priority, but Evie had allowed all the stuff with Logan to sabotage her efforts. It wasn't good enough. Her children would only ever have one mum.

Logan could have any carer he chose. 'Your granddad's right about one thing,' she whispered. 'It's time for change.'

Having looked in on her daughter, Evie returned to the kitchen. She took her seat at the opposite end of the table to Griff. 'Tess has flopped on her bed. She says she's fine, but she's so pale normally it's hard to tell if her colour's returned.' Evie's attempt at humour had no impact on Griff's fixed expression. 'It's a nasty bug.'

Griff's eyes, already narrow through sheer tiredness, became arrow slits, and his lips, so tight and thin, blanched and almost disappeared. 'What was so urgent with my dad that you had to shoot off?'

'I wasn't going to go until you were home, but he kept trying to reach me.' Evie pushed her chair away from the table. 'I was concerned something awful had happened to him.'

'But he's okay?' Griff gripped the edge of the table with both hands. His fingernails were as white as his lips.

'That's a matter of opinion,' Evie said, turning to sit side-saddle. 'He's as well as can be expected.'

She stared at the kettle. Griff's skewed reflection in the curve of the shiny chrome stared back. His face loomed large, out of proportion to his body. It was an unpleasant, distorted vision of him, and one Evie didn't wish to see, so she switched her view and studied the white handle of the fridge. She could see Griff in her peripheral vision, but at least there were no details glaring back at her from the plastic door grip. 'Logan needs help,' she said.

'Morning, noon and bloody night. He's taking you for a ride.' Griff scraped a hand through his hair. It was what Evie called his *frustration* tell. 'You're too soft,' he said. 'You need to start saying no. Take back the control.'

Even though Griff had lowered his voice, the words reverberated through Evie. *Take back the control.* 'It isn't about that,' she said. 'It's about compassion and love. He's family and he needs us.'

'No, no, no.' Griff was back to clutching the table. 'Dylan needs you. Tess needs you. Our family needs you.' He fell silent, compelling Evie to look at him. He left his chair, approached her and lifted her chin. 'I need you.'

That simple connection sent a commotion of confused sensations around Evie. When Griff traced the outline of her face with the back of his hand, she disappeared into a moment of time when making love with her husband didn't involve a conscious decision.

Life was simpler before Logan made it all about death.

She put a hand to Griff's chest to prevent him leaning in further. He stopped, but didn't pull away.

'You don't need me, though, do you?' It was as if an on-switch was flicked behind his eyes. An understanding had occurred, but of what was anyone's guess.

Evie opted to remain silent, letting Griff reach his own conclusions.

He stood upright, nodded, and retreated to the rear door, unlocking it and allowing Ozzy into the garden.

'My father designed this.' Griff waved a hand at the outside space. 'Before I knew you. It was the summer of Mum's chemo. She had one cycle of treatment to go. Dad would bring her to the house, set her up in one of the padded recliners just here ...' He gestured towards the doormat. 'And he'd work on the garden. Just things he could manage, you know, weeding, pruning. I did the donkey work.' Griff ran his fingers along the doorframe.

Evie banished an image from her mind of her and Griff having sex against the door he was now caressing. It had only been the once, but had she known it was a place of such precious memories ...

'Towards the end of summer, I came home to find Mum

and Dad sitting on the newly-stained decking.' He pointed to the far end of the property. 'It was bare wood when I left for my shift. Dad must have worked like a Trojan. He said Mum slept for the best part of the day, so he knuckled down and got on with it.' He paused. 'Dad said it was something he had control over. I remember the way he looked at Mum, and her weak smile she gave in reply. She was pallid grey, and her skin had aged ten years in the last twelve months. Then Dad brought me indoors, sat me down where you are now and told me Mum's cancer had spread further than originally thought.'

Griff turned in Evie's direction. He was chewing his lip, a reaction she'd seen enough times to recognise he was struggling with emotion.

After a huge expansion of his chest, he continued with his story. 'Dad said Mum had chosen to stop her treatment. She wanted to live whatever life she had left experiencing reality. She wanted clarity. She wanted to know she'd heard the blackbird's morning song and not imagined it through a drug-induced haze. She wanted ...' Griff hooked a foot round the leg of a chair, reeled it in and collapsed onto it, his arms limp at his sides. 'She wanted to know when she was dying.' He cuffed his nose and then resumed his slumped position.

This was a part of Griff's life of which Evie knew little. He rarely spoke of his mother, but it was obvious to Evie from the day they met that Marilyn's loss had affected him on many levels – levels he'd never invited Evie to explore. She could only assume the dreadful situation they now found themselves in had provided Griff with a need to reach out.

She considered reaching out herself, to show him how much she loved him, explain why she couldn't be with him right now; tell him the whole story about Logan. It was a revelation to learn how Marilyn and Logan's paths were so parallel. Marilyn's decision to stop treatment must have had a profound effect on Logan, influencing his thoughts on the right to die. Put in the same situation, watching a loved one suffer with constant pain, and witnessing their agonising deterioration, Evie could see how one would question quantity over quality. It wasn't that part of Logan's request she struggled with.

'I didn't realise Marilyn had stopped the chemo,' she said. 'What did Logan think about that?'

Griff's mouth twitched. 'He supported Mum. I couldn't believe it. He was a surgeon. He saved lives. He wasn't a man who gave up just because things got difficult.' Griff slapped his hands down on the table, then gave his palm a firm rub. 'We argued. I mean, *proper* argued. We'd always clashed heads, often disagreed, you know?' His brow creased as he appeared to study his hand. 'This was different. This was important. This was about my mum wanting … *wanting* to die.'

His gaze levelled with Evie's but his sight appeared to be searching through the devastation behind his eyes.

'Who *wants* to die? Life is precious. It's worth fighting for.' With a long, onerous blink, he released a slow breath. 'I lost my best mate at sixteen. Kieran. It was a pointless, tragic death.'

There was a microscopic shake of his head that Evie would have missed had she not been observing Griff so closely. Understanding the importance of what was being shared, she waited to hear more.

'A group of us decided to spend the day over at The Bill. Girls and boys. They were talking about tombstoning, jumping feet first from a cliff into the sea. It's so dangerous. I'd always found reasons to not go, but we were there, on the spot, on Pulpit Rock, and Kieran didn't want to leave.'

Evie extended a hand across the table. She was too far away to make a connection, but she wanted Griff to know she was reaching out, even if the gesture was literal.

'I told him not to do it. I pulled him back, but everyone was cheering and whistling and showing off, and he shoved me away. Next thing I knew, he was hurtling through the air, heading for the sea.' Griff flexed his ankle.

It was another small movement Evie noticed.

'When I looked over the ledge, he wasn't there. The boys who'd tombstoned before him had surfaced within seconds, so where the hell was he? I counted to ten, praying he was horsing around, hoping I'd hear him whooping and laughing, but by then the girls were screaming and the lads were shouting for help. I couldn't believe what was happening.'

He looked at Evie. 'He'd gone. Vanished. And somebody needed to find him.'

'You jumped in after him?' Evie identified with the feeling of helplessness and the desire to act, but what a terrifying experience this would have been for a young lad.

Griff nodded. 'But I caught my foot on some rocks under the surface – rocks we couldn't see from up high. The pain was excruciating. I heard myself cry out, but I had no sense of actually doing it. The waves were knocking me about, the cold had hit my system, and I'd lost my bearings. The last thing I remembered was thinking it's all my fault.' He tipped back his head and stared at the ceiling. 'I'm told the coastguard arrived within minutes of the call going out.'

'And they got you to safety quickly?'

His eyes returned to Evie. 'So the others said. I was unconscious.'

'Do you know what happened to Kieran?' Evie steadied herself, waiting for the reply.

'I guess he must've hit the same rocks. Went straight under. He just ... disappeared. The coastguard found his body washed up further along the shore.'

'Oh, Griff, I'm so sorry.' What else could Evie add?

There were no words meaningful enough to express the sorrow and anguish she felt for Griff. She could show him by enclosing him in her arms, but she'd given up the right to hold him.

Griff cleared his throat and continued. 'From that point on I vowed to do everything in my power to save lives. I finally understood my father's relentless pursuit in doing the same.'

The loss of his young friend was the start of Griff's road to adulthood. It explained his unremitting motivation and dedication to saving lives, and Evie loved him for that, but as sad and as devastating as it was, Kieran's death was an accident. Marilyn's wasn't. Not when it came to the crunch. The woman had maintained control of what was left of her destiny and had chosen to live her final days in peace.

It concerned Evie that Griff couldn't see that. He was a man who valued self-ownership. The only conclusion she could reach was that Kieran's death and Griff's belief he was to blame for it had clouded, possibly even blindfolded Griff's judgement. He needed someone to take his hand and show him the way.

She'd given up that right, too, but she had to try.

She stood and took a tentative step towards him. 'It was different with Marilyn,' she began. 'When it came to your mum—'

'Dad let her down. He was a hypocrite. He set aside everything he believed in. He abandoned his faith in science, in progress, and in the possibility the smallest change could turn things around.' Griff's lip curled in obvious disapproval. 'He'd let me down, too. He couldn't be bothered to fight for Mum. He was taking the easy way out.'

Evie recoiled and retook her seat. It was clear Griff wasn't ready to be led from the fog.

'I remember standing here, on the threshold,' he said, pointing at the door, 'staring at Mum, thinking how she'd never turned her back on us, when Dad put his hand on my shoulder and said letting her go wasn't what he wanted either. He'd always thought of Mum as immortal. They'd built their lives around him going first. Then he explained how ill the chemotherapy made her, and how that had influenced her decision. It was what she wanted. According to him, I'd only seen her on good days and that particular day was the best she'd been all week. I was shaken to the core.'

'So you started to come round to their way of thinking?'

Evie's question scored her an iron-laden scowl, which was quickly replaced with an expression of hurt.

'You don't know me at all.' Griff left his chair, and patted his leg, gaining Ozzy's attention. 'It made me realise we should be doing more to help Mum, not less. Not *nothing*.'

Flinching at the pile-driven stomps Griff took towards the front door, Evie shifted in her seat and watched as her husband reached the coat stand. He snatched at Ozzy's lead, lassoing Tess's hat in the process, sending it skimming across the polished floorboards.

'Not again.' Griff stretched for the beanie and hoopla-ed it onto the hook. 'When I told Dad I'd help, that I wouldn't sit by and watch my mother die, that I'd do whatever it took to show her the value of her life and how much better we were with her in the world, he shook his head and told me it wasn't for me to get involved. It was between a husband and wife, and together they'd made their peace. Nothing I could say or do would change their minds, and if all I was going to do was challenge their decision, then it was best I kept away. They didn't need me.' He attached the lead to Ozzy. 'Just like you don't.'

As Griff opened the door, Evie sprung to her feet,

desperate to speak, but cautious of the words to use. She needed Griff, but the past fifteen minutes had told her more about the man she loved than she'd learned in the last three years. And now she understood the reasons behind his and Logan's rift, she was convinced the father-son bond would be ripped to shreds should Griff find out about Logan's request. This was a far worse mess than she'd anticipated. For every day she delayed giving Logan an answer, she moved further away from the man she adored; the man who'd rescued her and shown her the beauty of true love.

'Griff ...' She wavered, her conscience quashing her impulse to confess. Logan was relying on her discretion and compassion, but that extended to Griff, too. If she told him what was going on, it would be the end of them. All of them. She just needed a little more time to sort things out. There was a chance Griff never needed to know. 'I'm sorry,' she said, bowing her head. 'I don't know what else to say.'

She should have said I love you, I want you home, I didn't mean for any of this to happen, but she'd travelled too far down Logan's path to see a way back.

'The truth would be good.' Griff's expectant silence was filled with a yap from Ozzy. 'In the car, boy, you're coming home with me.' He followed the dog onto the gravel, and stopped beside his vehicle. 'I'll collect his things tomorrow when I see Dylan. It's probably best that you and I don't cross paths. I'll wait in the Land Rover until you leave for Dad's.' He paused. 'Because you will. Helping him somehow validates you as a person. It shouldn't.' Griff scuffed his foot through the golden stones leaving an arc of bare soil. 'I love you for who you are, not what you do.'

He threw his hand up in what Evie considered a gesture of resignation, bundled Ozzy into the back of the car, and took his seat in the front.

Without a second glance he drove away.

Chapter Ten

Tess

I was in my bedroom when Mum got home. She'd just put Dylan down for a nap when she came in to see me. She looked wrecked. Her hair was scruffy and tangled, and her sleeves were shoved up to her elbow. She has thin wrists. She has a thin everything. She can take or leave food and I know she won't bother eating now. She'll say it's too late, or she had something at Logan's.

Her eyes are dull, like they've been smeared with wax that nobody's polished off. I wonder what it will take to make them bright again. She has the most amazing glint. They really do shine like emeralds. Griff says that to her. I've heard him. He sounds genuine, which is more than I could say about my father. The only time he was genuine was when he followed through with a threat.

My dad was not a man I looked up to. Not a decent role model.

I'm pleased Dylan has Griff. A boy needs his father.

I told Mum I'll go round to Logan's tonight, but she's forbidden me from seeing him. She's using my sickness as the reason, saying Logan's been ill. Me going won't make any difference to the old man's health. I pointed this out to Mum, but she didn't agree.

'He's a private, proud man, Tess. He hates the thought of anyone looking after him, even me, but we've reached an ... understanding.'

She'd struggled to find that word – understanding. She glanced at the floor as she said it. I do that when I'm hiding something. I thought she was going to say she and Logan had reached an impasse. That wouldn't surprise me. He's bloody stubborn, but I like that about him. If he says he's going to do something, you can guarantee he'll do it.

Griff's like that, too.

Mum gave me her weird smile – the one that means things aren't right at the moment, but they will be. That look rarely delivers on its promise, that's how I know Mum's not all right. I've seen that smile too many times. Not so much since she's been with Griff, but often with my dad.

We don't talk about him. My dad. Mum and I made a pact to keep our past between us. What I can say is he didn't hurt me, not physically, but he wasn't a nice man. Not a good man. He's been gone four, five years, but I can see him very clearly in my head. He's a big, thuggish man. Tall. Huge hands, especially when they're scrunched into fists. He has blond hair that's short like a soldier's, and he wears size thirteen boots, with steel toecaps. He works as an architect. Well, he did, until he got the sack for drinking on the job. He punched his manager. Instant dismissal. Word soon got out and none of the local firms would employ him. He was a loose cannon.

Mum thanks God we're free of him. I don't think we are. I'm a reminder of everything he's done to us.

I hate the fact part of him exists in me.

I wish I could remove it. Him.

Griff's gone, but before Mum got back, he and Dylan were in the kitchen, messing about with Ozzy. The kid was chuckling, but Griff was quiet. And he had the face of a pig off to slaughter. I watched him for a few seconds. It's not often I get a chance to study him, but he was so caught up in thought, he was oblivious to me.

I'm not in the habit of thinking about Griff's moods, but I can't shift the feeling he's scared of something. I'll assume it's to do with Dylan's seizure, although, I know he doesn't like seeing Mum upset any more than I do.

My dad used to do his damnedest to upset her, and he'd laugh at her suffering. I expected Griff to be the same, but he's not.

Keen to check on Mum, I step onto the landing and head for the stairs, but I halt as I become aware she's in her room, crying. I hate that sound. I hate it with a vengeance. It stirs up intense emotions and visions of the years of torment and torture he, my father, put her through. The sound rips my insides out, exposing my darkest secret.

Her quiet sobs awaken my urge to cut.

No child, regardless of their age, wants to hear their mother weeping.

As I near her door, I'm deciding whether or not I should go in and comfort her. I'm hoping the moment will carry me through, because right now I want to run to my room, take my blade and score my skin, because ... *because* that hurts less than the crushing pain in my head.

Chapter Eleven

Evie

While Logan was in the bathroom, Evie collected a duster from the airing cupboard, and wiped the top of his golden-pine tallboy. On it was a photo of her and Griff on their wedding day. Evie picked it up, and moved to under the ceiling bulb.

Griff was so handsome in his tails, and so happy, his square jaw set in a permanent smile, a six-month-old Dylan nestled on his shoulder. Evie was happy, too. Her new life had begun. She was safe, secure and madly in love.

She sighed as she cast her eyes over the image of Tess. She looked stunning in a deep green, shot silk dress. Even then she was emerging into a young lady. Her body was taking on the curves and fullness of a woman. 'I'm missing you grow up,' Evie whispered as she trailed her finger over the picture.

'I'm ready.' Logan's voice cruised along the landing.

'Coming.' Evie replaced the photo, returned the duster to the cupboard and scurried to the bathroom. Opening the door, she took Logan's dressing gown from the hook and opened it up, ready to help him put it on.

'I don't need that,' he said, indicating for Evie to move away. 'I'm going straight to bed.'

Evie folded the gown over her arm, stepped aside, and held out a hand for Logan. 'I've set the recorder for that film you wanted to watch, and I've put the nuts out for the birds.' Logan liked regular updates. 'Once you're settled, I'll make us both a drink.'

Together, they ambled back to the bedroom, their joint

efforts concentrated on reaching the bed in one piece. With the duvet already folded back, Logan was able to sit down and slide his feet in. Evie passed him the adjustable bed's remote control, and Logan pressed one of the black rocker switches.

Nothing happened.

'Bed's not working,' he said, handing the remote to Evie. 'Must be the batteries.'

'But I changed them three days ago.' Evie tried the button for herself, and the head end of the bed began to rise. 'Perhaps it was just a bit sticky.' She kept her thumb down until Logan gave her the nod to stop.

'Don't patronise me, Evie. You changed the batteries because it wouldn't work. If it's still not working, it's because I've lost the ability to hold down the bloody button.'

As much as it upset Evie to agree, she was in no position to argue. She'd put new batteries in twice this month already – she'd even replaced the rectangular one under the bed. And she'd seen Logan struggling with remotes and buttons a lot recently. He'd try first with one thumb, then with two, both hands quivering under the strain of pressing down the switch. Even the toggle on his stairlift was proving difficult.

The loss of power had nothing to do with the Duracells.

Logan sunk into his pillow and closed his eyes. 'Would you put the foot up, please?'

Evie obliged, again stopping at Logan's mark. 'Perhaps we can find a touch remote. I can search online or ask at the disability shop.'

'No point.'

Placing the unit next to Logan, Evie retreated, and took a seat in a white wicker chair by the window. 'And there's no point because …'

'Because there's no point.' Logan's eyes opened, and he

zoomed in on Evie. 'Why can't you accept I don't want to be here?'

'I get it, really, I do. I've had times in my life when I was convinced the world would be better off without me, but things change.'

'I don't want change.'

And that was where they were different. Even at her lowest point, Evie had clung to the belief things would move on, that Neil would love and not resent Tess, that he'd drink less, that he'd disappear – anything, because one alteration could lead to another, and then another, and then another. In that respect, she was very like Griff. He believed change could have saved his mother.

'Why have you never told me about your wife?' Evie reclined and crossed her legs. She was in for either a long chat or a long silence.

'What was I meant to tell you?' Logan closed his eyes again.

'About how she stopped her treatment. How that made Griff feel.'

'So he's told you.' Once more Logan's eyes opened and he locked onto Evie. 'Then I expect you to understand why I want to go.'

'Okay, but I also understand why Griff doesn't visit. He thinks you gave up on his mum.'

'I know what he thinks, but I don't have the energy or the patience to baby him along. The choice was not his to make. Marilyn was my wife and I supported her until the bitter end.' Logan's face contained all the rage a younger man would store in his fist. 'And this is why I don't want him knowing my plans. He'll make it impossible for me to go quietly. The fewer people who know, the better.'

He was talking as if Evie had agreed to assist him. She folded her arms. 'Hang on. I've not said I'm going to help you.' She absorbed the glare of defiance aimed at her and used its energy to awaken a latent rebelliousness within. 'Right this moment I'm inclined to tell Griff everything. This *secret* has ruined my marriage. I've not told you before because I thought I was sparing you further distress, but I don't think it would make any difference to you. I hate lying to Griff, and I can't look him in the eye. He doesn't understand where we went wrong.'

Evie jumped to her feet and paced the width of the bedroom. 'I've even hinted there's another man. He doesn't know it's a seventy-four-year-old with a death wish.' She was aware Logan was tracking her moves. 'He's not living with us. It's not right. I love him. He's my husband, although for how much longer is anyone's guess. I shouldn't keep secrets from him. What you're asking of me is too much. I will not be responsible for another person's death.'

Decision made. That was something for the Happiness jar.

Dizzy from her outburst, and exhausted by weeks of constant conflict, Evie sunk onto the edge of Logan's bed. 'I'm sorry. I should have given you an answer a long time ago. I'll continue to care for you, but if you go through with your plan, and I find you, I will call an ambulance. I won't help you die.' She put a hand on Logan's arm. 'I hope you understand. And I hope you don't think any less of me.'

Logan's eyes hadn't left Evie for a second. 'You'll respect my wishes written in my directive?'

'The directive your son knows nothing about?' It was bound to be a bone of contention between her and Griff, but one Evie felt he would come to accept, given time and a thorough explanation of its workings. 'Yes, of course. I've signed it, haven't I?'

'Even though Griff would hate the idea?'

'It's my name and number they'll call when the time

comes.' It was the only compromise she was prepared to make. She didn't want Logan to suffer at the end, however it came about. With his no resuscitation instruction, if she did find him stranded after a failed suicide attempt, there was a chance his Advance Decision would provide him safe passage to the next world, anyway. She could live with that.

'Then that is the best I can hope for.' Logan unrolled the top of the duvet until it was under his chin. 'And I'm sorry for the trouble I've caused. Things will improve once I've gone. In the meantime, I'll consider what you've said about employing someone else.' With that, he turned his head to the side, closed his eyes, and waved Evie off. 'Turn the lamp off on your way out.'

Chapter Twelve

January's leaving the way it arrived – grey, fierce and short-tempered.

I'm in the kitchen, looking through the window over the sink. The bushes opposite keep lurching, like they're threatening to get me. If they weren't home to half the wildlife of Weymouth, I'd have taken a pair of shears to them. No, that's harsh. They're providing shelter and a splash of colour on a rotten and stormy day. I just don't like the shadows they're casting.

From the corner of my eye I can see a glass container sitting on the terracotta-tiled sill. It's Mum's Happiness jar, and it has two measly slips of paper languishing at the bottom. To the inexperienced, they could be dead, decaying moths. It's sad. I pray it's not a reflection of her life. She deserves so much more. She deserves a greenhouse filled with happiness, Crystal Palace even, not an old, empty jam jar.

I'm tempted to add my own positive notes. I imagine writing them out.

One: I fought and beat the last urge to cut.

Two: I've left a message on a self-harm forum.

Three: I received a reply.

They're all true and worthy of going in the jar.

About a year ago, maybe eighteen months, certainly a while after I first cut, I found this self-harm website. I've dropped in from time to time, and lurked in the background, but only recently plucked up the courage to post a message. I gave an account of when I started cutting.

Hi. I'm fifteen and I've been self-harming for two years.

It was a lame opening, but I went on to explain that, when I was thirteen, there was this boy in the year above at school who kept asking me to go out with him. I knocked him back every time, but he kept hounding me, said he had a soft spot for redheads, and in February, he sent me a Valentine's card. I'd not had one before.

Mum was seeing Griff by this point – I didn't mention any names on the forum – and despite my misgivings, he made her happy. They'd just had Dylan. I was forced to accept that some men, and therefore some boys, were okay.

I agreed to go out with the fourteen-year-old.

We'd meet in town and mess about in the video game shop, or hunt for two-pence pieces in the machines at the arcades. He'd buy me a sausage roll, or a burger, or a bar of chocolate. Sometimes we were alone and sometimes we'd hang about with his mates.

He kissed me. A lot. Especially in front of his gang. I was indifferent. I didn't dislike kissing, but it didn't set my world alight. It was an experience.

Then one day, he pushed it too far. I didn't like where he put his hand, and when he refused to take it away, I brought my knee up and belted him in the balls. Then I ran.

I got a shit-load of grief from his mates at school, calling me a prick teaser, the camp vamp, redhead-head-deader. Even the girls joined in.

That's when I started self-harming. I had so much crap clogging my brain, and so much pressure, I needed a way to get it out. I was so angry. I ran home, locked myself in the bathroom and started pulling at my hair. Then, in the mirror, I saw Mum's razor on the side of the bath. She must have changed the blade and forgotten to throw the old one away. Purely on impulse, I picked it up and ... well, like I said, that's when I started. I wish I hadn't.

The next time my head was set to explode, I did it again. Then again. And again.

No one knows I do it.

The person on the website who replied knows, but she's in the same boat. Besides, we have usernames, so we're incognito. The only info I have on her is that she lives in Manchester.

She's given me some ideas on how to distract myself when the urge to cut is strong, like drawing or origami, and told me to make sure my equipment is sterile, which I do, and always have clean bandages available. She called it harm minimisation.

She also said if I want to stop and I have someone I trust, I should tell them. I could write it all down first, get it clear in my head, and then choose a time to talk, when there'd be no interruptions.

Having the support of her best friend has given Manchester Girl the strength to confront her demons. They go to counselling together. She's been clean for two months.

I'm pleased for her, but confronting demons is a hell of a big step.

She's waiting for my reply.

I'm not going to add anything to Mum's jar. My notes wouldn't be beautiful butterflies of happiness; they'd be clues to my secret addiction. If it is an addiction.

I've read a few personal accounts on the website from teens. Most say they wish they'd never started because now they can't stop and they live in this vicious circle of guilt, distress, release, guilt, distress, release. I suppose it could be to do with the adrenalin rush, but I don't know. I'm no doctor and I'm a long way off truly understanding my behaviour. I am recognising the triggers, though, and if I can avoid them, there's a chance I'll stay clean like the girl in Manchester.

Mum crying is a trigger. She's called out in her sleep a number of times since Griff left. Nothing distinct, more a yelp than a word. It's chilling in the darkness of night. I always check on her. Sometimes I sit with her until she's settled. She doesn't know, and I don't tell her.

She shouted out Dad's name last night.

That properly freaked me out. I haven't heard her do that since Griff's been on the scene.

So, at two in the morning, I was drawing stars. Six sheets of them. Worst representation of the solar system I've ever seen, but I've kept the pictures, because they kept me from cutting.

I've hidden them in the back of my wardrobe.

Perhaps I should get those glow-in-the-dark stars and stick them to the ceiling. I could arrange them into constellations and learn them off by heart. That would give me something other than shadows to fixate on at night. Might suggest Mum has some, too.

If I'm honest, all she really needs is Griff.

And I never thought I'd say it, but I miss him, too.

Chapter Thirteen

Griff

February was a mean month. The meanest of the entire year. Not hard or difficult. Mean.

Griff shut down the car engine, checked in the rear-view mirror to see Ozzy licking the condensation off the back window, and then braced himself for the wild walk ahead.

'I don't want you going in the sea today, Ozzy. Do you hear?'

Rubbing the glass with his sleeve, Griff peered through the makeshift portal. Apart from the washed-up debris strewn across the stones, and a luminous pink speck in the distance, Chesil was empty. 'All hiding in the pub,' Griff murmured.

The storms and high tides, though abating, weren't ready to quit; the chilling easterlies attacked any skin Griff was careless enough to leave exposed, and work was punishing and unforgiving.

Two lives had been lost at sea; both local fishermen from the same crew. It hadn't happened on Griff's watch, but every loss was personal. He knew the family of the fishermen – they were much-loved Weymouth folk, always first to put their hands in their pockets for the RNLI, always involved in fund-raising committees, always in the newspaper praising the work and courage of the rescue services. The town would pull together for them. The memorial service would be well attended.

Thorough searches for both men were executed, but neither body was found. Those deaths were the worst. There was no closure. No physical entity over which to grieve.

Griff was comforting his mother when she died.

In her few remaining days in the hospice, he spent as much time with her as his shifts and Logan's presence allowed. Both men had agreed the tension between them needed to remain outside Marilyn's room. For Griff that meant waiting in the communal area until Logan had left the building. He wasn't avoiding the problem; he was reducing the risk of it being compounded by an outburst of emotion.

Much like he was doing with Evie.

They'd crossed paths a handful of times since he'd taken Ozzy away, each occasion awkward and stilted. It was as if Evie was a ghost, the way she passed by Griff in the cottage – a brush of a cobweb, an unsettling breeze, as she drifted from one room to another. No eye contact, no touching.

In some ways, he was grieving right now – grieving for the loss of his marriage, the loss of Evie's love.

Griff flicked the wipers on and tracked the blades as they swished at the rain and salty spray.

It rained the day his mother died. He remembered thinking how fitting the wretched weather was as he held her hand, and brushed her hair. He said his goodbyes as her last rattle of breath shook his resolve not to cry.

The hospital called Logan back in, but he arrived a minute too late, frustrated and shocked, demanding answers from Griff, expecting him to relate every second of the last half an hour in explicit detail, questioning why he hadn't been notified of Marilyn's sudden deterioration. Unable to speak, Griff removed himself to the back of the room and watched the nurses prepare his mother's body for her next journey. Their solemnity and dignified manner brought calm to the room, and they spoke to Marilyn in soothing tones. The words didn't matter to Griff, it was their humanity that touched him. And quietened Logan.

When it was time to go, he gave a final squeeze to his mother's hand and placed a gentle kiss on her cheek. He stood side-by-side with his father as the porters wheeled her body along the sterile corridor to the waiting morgue.

She never liked the cold.

Griff wrapped his ranger's coat over his knees and considered reviving the engine. It was bitter out there. It was biting in the car.

Ozzy snuffled as a Labrador hurtled down the beach, a flying stick following close behind. Griff waited, assuming the animal's owner was bringing up the rear. A vibrant, pink smudge, brightening the landscape, scuttled past his fogged-up window. 'Mad dogs and Englishmen,' he muttered, thinking the song clearly applied to women too. 'And not just in the midday sun. Reckon it could snow.' Ozzy's tail whacked against the inside of the Land Rover with a rhythmic pat-pat-pat, and Griff turned to him. 'We'll go out in a minute, mate.'

By the time he faced forward, the cerise rain mac and black wellingtons were heading for the foot of the cliffs, the Labrador long gone.

'I've seen it snow over the sea. Only once, but it was worth the frostbite. It was down in the cove – where those beach huts are. The cove with the steep steps you hate.' Griff wasn't that fond of them himself. They'd left him and Ozzy panting on numerous occasions.

'It was Easter, late March, early April, fourteen, fifteen years ago.' He glanced in the mirror. Ozzy's nose was pressed up against the window, and his tail wagged in and out of view. 'I'd gone down there with Imogen, Kieran's sister. I've told you about Kieran.'

Griff shifted his gaze to the sea. 'I hadn't spoken with Imogen since Kieran's funeral. I tried. I called by the Joliffe house the next day and the day after, but was turned away by her mum, and told in no uncertain terms to stop hounding the poor girl. The family were grieving and I should respect that. My being there was upsetting and I wasn't to bother them again. It hit me hard. I wanted to be there for Imogen, look out for her, take responsibility for what had happened. I owed Kieran that.'

The Land Rover rocked as Ozzy, yapping and pacing in the confined space of its boot, displayed his eagerness to hit the beach.

'All right. I'll cut it short,' Griff said. 'Ten years later, having kept my distance, I heard Imogen was having a party for her twenty-first. I gatecrashed. Not the most mature way of gaining her attention, but it worked. I tell you what, Ozzy, she has a death stare to match Tess's. Anyway, she agreed to hear me out and met me the next day at the cove. It was one of Kieran's favourite places. Just as Imogen and I reached the waves, the air changed and there was a sudden flurry of snow. It instantly disappeared into the water. Of course it would, but I found it fascinating to watch. I was mesmerised. There was this sheet of snow stretching from the sky to the sea, and because it left no evidence of its arrival, it was like a net curtain was hanging from the clouds. The flurry stopped as abruptly as it began, and when I turned to speak to Imogen she was at the top of the steps. By the time I got back to the car, she'd gone, along with my chance to make amends. She'd led me on, letting me think there was a chance she'd forgive me.'

Ozzy ramped up the barking.

'Okay.' Griff clambered out of the car, crunched his way to its rear and set the excitable dog free. 'It was odd seeing her again. She wasn't the stroppy, skinny girl who'd followed Kieran and me everywhere. She'd grown into a young woman. It suited her.' Griff paused. 'I just wish she'd have let me help her. Especially later, when her mum died.'

He reflected on a newspaper report he'd read from a few years back.

'She was killed in a car accident,' he said as Ozzy barked at him to play. 'All I wanted was to offer Imogen comfort and support, but the *Echo* said the Joliffes had left the area years before the accident and they were living in Somerset. I didn't know.' He'd assumed his local paper had deemed Mrs Joliffe's death newsworthy on the basis of the family's Dorset connection and their tragic history. 'All I could do was send a wreath and a card to the crematorium.' The details of the funeral service had been listed in Mrs Joliffe's obituary. 'It was a pitiful attempt to let Imogen know I was thinking of her, but turning up out of the blue at the cremation would've been wrong. She didn't get in touch. It was clear she still wanted nothing to do with me.'

He sighed and drummed his fingers on the car roof, inciting himself into action. 'I met Evie shortly after and confined thoughts of Imogen to the back of my mind.' As he slammed the door shut, Ozzy charged to meet the white horses head on. 'Don't go in the water,' Griff yelled.

Too late. The Old English Sheepdog had all four paws firmly sunk into the Old English Channel, and he was challenging Griff to join him.

'Are you daring me to come in?' Griff laughed. 'You're a nutter. And you're good for me, Ozzy. I'm glad I have you.' The words dragged the smile from Griff's lips, taking with it his temporary delight.

The night before, while Griff was putting Dylan to bed, Tess had mentioned Ozzy, remarking how quiet it was without him lumbering through the cottage. She hadn't said she missed him, in the same way she hadn't added anything about life being different without Griff at home, but he hadn't expected her to. The only times she verbalised her feelings was when she was upset or angry. He took it on the chin. She was a teenager, after all. And no doubt hormonal. Not that he'd had much experience in that field. It was Evie's area of expertise. He'd promised to guide Dylan through the Y chromosome milestones, although with no man in the house, the poor boy would only ever know how to pee sitting down.

If this was how it was going to be, even in the short term, there had to be a structure put in place. Dylan and Tess needed stability, and it was important to Griff they both knew he was there for them. With all the will in the world, he knew Tess would never take him at his word, but if she needed his help or a place she could go to be alone, he'd sort it. He could start by asking her if she'd like to walk Ozzy at the weekends; invite her and Dylan to stay at the flat once in a while – Griff would sleep on the sofa, Tess could have the bed and Dylan could use the travel cot that was gathering dust in the cottage attic. They could go out for a burger.

The idea brought a sliver of light to Griff's dull day. Making plans was good. Positive. A signifier he was moving on.

The light dimmed.

Griff didn't want to move on. Not without Evie, and not without getting to the bottom of why she'd thrown their marriage overboard. Moving on without her was as good as giving up.

Ozzy plunged further into the water. He was a large, strong dog, capable of holding his own, but the waves were gathering power. 'Hey, boy. Back to dry land before you disappear.' Griff followed his instruction with a whistle.

If only rectifying his marriage was as simple. He was drifting in an ocean of unknowns with no one to throw him a lifeline. He'd been out at sea too long, and with only himself to rely on, it was time to swim ashore.

'Jeez, Ozzy,' Griff said as the shaggy, soggy dog careered towards him. 'My life's full of clichés.'

Moving on, acceptance, pushing forward, they all equated to the same thing – giving up, and despite his self-deprecation, surrendering was not part of Griff's make up.

He squared his shoulders, filled his lungs with the cold, clarifying air, and advanced along the beach, a sense of purpose building with each stride.

'We're going to see Olivia,' he said to Ozzy. 'Come on.' He rattled the lead and the dog came to heel. 'We'll stop by for a cup of tea and, with a bit of luck, Olivia will dish out a serving of her sage advice.'

Griff had taken to Olivia DeVere the first day they'd met. She was the wise woman of Portland. He was relaxed in her company, able to talk about any subject, general or personal, without embarrassment or fear of judgement. Her outlook on life was not dissimilar to his. She cared deeply about the environment, believed the best things in life were free, and refused to buckle when the odds were stacked against her. In fact, Griff thought, those times were the ones she revealed the full extent of her strength and determination.

He smiled. She'd told him her daughter-in-law had called her indomitable. It was a great word. It summed Olivia up to a tee.

Aware of a presence either side of his legs, Griff looked down. Ozzy was in his usual position to Griff's left, but to his right, with a stick in its mouth, was a Labrador, trotting with an air of triumph.

Griff stopped, crouched and received a lick to his ear from Ozzy. 'Thanks, mate.' He scuffed the slobber off with his shoulder. 'Who's this, then?' He reached for the silver disc on the Labrador's collar and angled it to read the name. 'Honey.' He scratched the top of her head. 'All right, girl? Where's your owner?'

He was certain this was the dog who'd sprinted towards the cliffs earlier.

Starting at the rocks below Hope Cove Castle, where he'd last seen the woman, Griff scanned the length of the beach. Other than a dozen cars parked outside the Harbour Inn, the place was empty. Not soulless. Just empty.

Puzzled, Griff gave both dogs a firm pat on their sides. 'Definitely saw someone with you, Honey. The woman in pink.'

He checked the flipside of Honey's disc to find a crudely etched mobile number. Fishing his phone from his back pocket, he keyed in the digits and listened, not to the dialling tone, but to the surrounding noise. If Honey's owner was nearby, there was a chance Griff would hear her phone. He strained to single out a mechanical tune, but the thunderous wind and the rattle of the pebbles as they were seduced back into the icy depths of the sea made it impossible.

When the phone requested he left a message after the beep, he cast his concern and vexation down the line.

'My name's Hendry. I have Honey. If I don't see you by the rocks in the next five minutes, I'm taking her—' The phone went dead mid-sentence, and Griff checked the signal. That too was dead. 'Man!' His voicemail sounded more like a ransom demand than a rescue mission. 'Where the hell is your owner?'

He headed for the car, hopeful that retracing his steps would jog his memory – perhaps he'd seen more than his eyes had led him to believe. He was more hopeful Honey would pick up the woman's scent.

Sitting in the driver's seat, with his door open and his eyes trained on the rocks, Griff ran through the sequence of events that resulted in the Labrador flying past the window. He tried to visualise the figure that had followed the dog. Definitely female. Petite. What was her hair like? No hair on show. She was using the hood of her shocking pink rain mac.

He raised a hand to a halt position. 'There was a black flower on the back of her coat. A poppy.' If she had fallen, at least she'd be easy to spot. 'Purple waterproofs,' he muttered, 'with the black boots.' He hadn't consciously tracked her, but the more he delved into his subconscious, the more the scene played out. She'd disappeared over the rocks in the direction of Preacher Cove, chasing after Honey. A section of the path had collapsed in recent weeks following the storms, but the cove was still accessible if trodden with care. It was a worry. It was possible the woman had slipped and fallen, twisted her ankle or knocked herself unconscious.

Griff leapt out of the car, slammed the door shut, and sprinted to the end of the beach, the dogs galloping behind. The white Portland boulders hampered his progress, but he wasn't about to give up. He clambered over the first, battling with two excitable dogs for adequate footholds, but when he lost traction on the second rock, thanks to Ozzy using Griff's hand for purchase, the situation became intolerable.

Honey was more interested in snapping at the sea spray than sniffing for a trail, and Ozzy was yo-yoing back and forth like an overgrown puppy.

An alternative course of action was required, before all three of them ended up stranded and broken on the rocks.

With no signal to his mobile, Griff needed to call backup from a landline.

Shepherding the dogs back onto the pebbles, the pack made their way to Chiswell Craft Centre and piled into Olivia's shop. The door and the howling gale attacked the bell, and it rang with fury.

'Everything all right?' With her ankle-length skirt flapping against the edge of the display shelves, Olivia approached the dogs and bent to stroke Honey. 'Are you sure now is the right time to adopt a second one?'

'I've not adopted her,' Griff said. 'I'm trying to find her owner. There's a chance she's gone over near Preacher's Cove.' He instructed Ozzy to sit. 'I need to use your phone.' A forceful gust rattled the shop. 'Scratch that. Call the coastguard, tell them a woman, five-foot-four, in a pink raincoat with a black poppy on the back, is suspected missing on the path to the cove. I'm going back there. She's been gone long enough.' He opened the door, sending the bell into another frenzy. 'Can I leave the dogs with you?' Seeing Olivia nod, he turned to run out of the shop, and collided with a fast-moving pink creature half his width.

Undeterred, the woman shoved Griff from her path and ran straight at Honey.

'There you are!' She cradled the dog's neck, kissed the top of its head and ran a cursory check over the body and legs. 'Oh, Honey. I was so worried. I thought something awful had happened to you.'

'Shut the door, Griff, will you? The wind's tangling my dreamcatchers.' Olivia stretched up to steady her feathery sales goods.

Griff pushed the door shut. The pink creature still had her back to him, the black poppy on full display. Nice to know he'd not imagined it. 'Glad you're safe. Nearly had the coastguard searching for you. What do you think you were doing, tackling the path to Preacher's Cove on a day like this?'

'Excuse me?' The woman's tone and the sudden stiffening of her shoulders said more than her words.

Griff caught sight of Olivia pulling a *you're for it* face and he shook his head. He wanted to see who had been careless enough to try and walk a dog in a known danger spot. He stared at the back of the hooded figure. 'You put yourself at risk. Not only that, but if we'd called out the coastguard, you'd have put them and others at risk.' With the warmth of being inside and the heat of irritation rising, Griff ripped open his coat and threw it off. As it landed on the floor, Ozzy nuzzled it, stomped on it and settled down, clearly preferring his master's soft coat to Olivia's hard floor. 'It was irresponsible.'

'Irresponsible? Who the hell do you think you are?' The woman sprung up, reeled on the spot and glared at Griff. A look of astonishment replaced the scowl. It was short-lived. The woman's mouth went from a perfect circle to a tight and hard rectangle. 'Should have known,' she said, releasing her hold of Honey. 'You just can't keep out of my business can you?'

The Labrador took advantage of her new freedom and joined Ozzy on Griff's coat.

Olivia, amusement plucking at her lips, settled on the shop's counter, crossed her ankles and leaned forward. 'You two know each other?'

'Hard to tell. My eyes haven't recovered from the garish pink of the coat.' Griff blinked several times for effect.

'And I've never recovered from the way you gatecrashed my twenty-first birthday, you arrogant arsehole.'

'Oh, Griff. You didn't?' Olivia's legs were swinging, and with every backward sway her heels clonked at the veneer of the counter. 'That's not very gallant.'

Griff glanced at Olivia, acknowledged her reprimand, and then directed a stare at the pink, hooded figure. He'd only bulldozed his way into one party, and that was Imogen Joliffe's. He ducked his head to see under the brim of the hood. A pair of bright, too-blue eyes glowered back. Imogen's eyes were always too blue. Had Griff not known her since she was a scrap of a girl, he'd have sworn she wore contact lenses.

He pulled at his collar. 'Efficient heating in here, Olivia.' Still trying to determine the stranger's identity, his peripheral vision caught Olivia waving a hand, a second before she spoke.

'That's your conscience providing the heat, not my boiler,' she said.

As always, Olivia had assessed the situation with alarming accuracy. Her no-nonsense, straight-talking approach appealed to Griff. The sixty- ... seventy-year-old woman was never afraid to speak her mind, and she was in control of her own destiny – a quality Griff respected and one to which he responded well.

He opened the top two buttons of his shirt and considered his current predicament. He wasn't about to reveal he'd been speaking of Imogen today – that would suggest he thought of her often. He conceded he frequently remembered her brother and then, by association, Imogen, but to blurt out he'd mentioned her in passing to the dog ... He regarded the two animals. They were snuggled side-by-side, as comfortable as an old married couple. Honey's tail quivered in a tiny wag of contentment. It really was a dog's life. If only Griff's was as simple.

Returning his attention to Imogen, if indeed it was she hiding in the pink monstrosity, Griff decided it was more than a coincidence she'd shown up. Somewhere in his subconscious he must have known it was her as she'd run past the Land Rover, and that was the reason she'd come to mind.

The woman folded down her hood, and fluffed her hair free from her coat. Long and blonde, it tumbled the length of her body, coming to rest at her hips. Her perfectly-made-up face, with cheeks as rosy as her rain mac, was exposed in the full light of the grey day.

Years had passed since Griff had last seen Imogen, but

there was no mistaking the look of loathing levelled at him – it was identical to the one he'd received from her when he'd crashed her party; the same her mother had used the last time he'd called at the Joliffe's house. 'Imogen.' He raised a brow in salutation. 'What are you doing here?'

'What do you think you were doing kidnapping my dog?' She pointed at Honey.

'You got my phone message, then.'

'What phone message?' Imogen reached into her coat pocket, retrieved her mobile, and checked the screen. 'Looks like I missed a voicemail,' she muttered, preparing to play it back.

Resigned to the moment, Griff waited in silence as Imogen listened to her phone. Her eyebrow's relayed her feelings in a clear and concise manner.

She swiped her thumb across the bottom of the display. 'What was next? Honey's whisker in the post? A ransom note?'

'I—'

'Uh! I haven't finished. Where do you get off stealing my dog? Is this another clumsy attempt to get me alone, so you can explain yourself? Plead forgiveness? There was no party to crash, so you thought you'd stalk me on the beach and *take my dog*.'

Griff winced at the rise in pitch and incredulity, but Imogen was in full flow.

'You can't keep doing this to me … It's like … It's like you have an uncontrollable surge of conscience every ten years.'

'It was fourteen years this time. And I didn't stalk you. You came to the beach.'

'Griff. Hush.' Olivia hopped down from the counter and approached Imogen. 'Having a conscience is a positive attribute, young lady. Losing your temper is not.' She took hold of the woman's free hand. 'I'm Olivia DeVere, proprietor of Chiswell Craft Centre.'

Peace was instant and a welcome relief to Griff.

'Imogen Joliffe. I'm sorry. I didn't mean to upset you.'

'I'm not upset.' Olivia patted Imogen's arm. 'But I want to share something with you. In my experience, shouting doesn't get you heard, especially where men are concerned.' She leaned in closer. 'It's just noise to them.' Peering over her shoulder, she then addressed Griff. 'Isn't that right?'

'It depends.' He was going to expand on his answer, but Olivia waded in again.

'Whatever this is ...' she wafted the air around her '... it's none of my business. But if you want to keep history from repeating itself, you need to deal with the present, and unless you're in a hurry to get swept away outside, here and now seems like an excellent place to start. Face the storm inside, or deal with the one brewing over the Channel. I'll go and put the kettle on and fetch a bowl of water for the dogs.'

Olivia disappeared through a door to the rear of the shop.

'She's an ex-school teacher.' Despite welcoming the silence, Griff deemed an explanation of Olivia's behaviour necessary. To the uninitiated, at least. 'I take it you've not been in here before?'

'No reason to.' Imogen scanned the four walls of the interior. 'Looks like a tourist tat shop.' She flicked the dreamcatcher dangling above her head. 'I'm only here now because I caught you bringing Honey in.'

'Caught? I was making sure she was safe so I could search for you.'

'I was right behind you, screaming my head off and, as usual, you ignored me, and carried on doing your own thing.'

The woman may have advanced in years, but her petulance and hot-headedness hadn't improved. Age suited her looks, though.

'I didn't hear you,' Griff said, making his way to the shop counter. 'If I had, I wouldn't be standing here now, taking your insults on the chin. I'd be having a pleasant chat with Olivia, and admiring her skilful work.' Tat, indeed. Olivia would have something to say about that.

He pulled a tall stool out from behind the desk and offered it to Imogen. She folded her arms in response. 'Olivia makes most of this herself.' He sat down.

'I can tell.'

'You're very rude. My teenage daughter has better manners.'

'Do you know what, Griff? I've seen enough in the papers over the years to know you're the *perfect hero*. I don't need to know the details of your perfect life, too.'

Interesting. Imogen had been keeping tabs on him, although it was a few months ago the local press last deemed him newsworthy, and he doubted the Somerset papers would have run the story. Imogen must have read it on the internet. Griff's life had changed considerably since then, and not all of it for the better. 'It's hardly perfect.' That slipped out. He glanced at Imogen to gauge her reaction. To his dismay, his statement appeared to have spiked her curiosity.

She tilted her head to the side. 'Some would say that's karma.'

'Some would say I've spoken out of turn. My mistake.'

'Is that how you get by in life? You reason your way through your titanic cock-ups by thinking that admitting to them will bring forgiveness?' Imogen marched across the shop floor, and confronted Griff face-on. 'Is that how you live with yourself? Is that how you deal with Kieran's death?'

The attack, along with the first mention of his friend's name knocked Griff sideways. He took a moment to recover before countering. 'Until you agree to talk to me about it, I can't *deal* with Kieran's death. And I don't believe you can, either.' He studied her, keeping his eyes locked on hers, giving her nowhere to go but straight back to him.

She retaliated instantly. 'He was my brother. Of course I'll never deal with it. I've carried it around for twenty-four years and not a day has passed when I haven't thought about him. It destroyed my parents.' There was a shift in her body language as her entire frame went from rigid to defeated. 'You know about Mum?'

Griff hopped from the stool and carried it across to Imogen. 'Sit. I insist.' He wasn't happy at the speed with which her rosy cheeks had blanched. She hitched herself up and issued a nod of thanks before lowering her head. Griff continued. 'I tried to contact you as soon as I heard. I sent a wreath to the crematorium.' Imogen must have known that. 'And a card.' He watched her shoulders rise and drop.

'I didn't want anything from you. Or your family.' Another draw of air. 'You know what happened?'

Griff crouched at the foot of the stool, inclining his head to see Imogen. 'It was a car accident.'

'No.' Imogen looked at Griff. Her eyes had lost none of their colour. 'It was no accident.'

Chapter Fourteen

Evie

The uneasy ceasefire between Evie and Logan did little to reassure her of his supposed change of heart. It was almost a month since she'd exposed every distressing detail of the state of her marriage, and although he'd promised to give serious thought to receiving outside care, nothing had happened.

He'd not even looked through the brochures Evie had supplied.

She picked up the pile from the coffee table and held them out. 'All three companies were recommended,' she said, hoping to spike Logan's interest.

'And what does Griff think about it?' Using both thumbs, Logan pressed a button on the grey remote on his lap. The foot of his armchair extended out, lifting his legs level to his hips. He winced.

Evie perched on the corner of the table and filtered off the top booklet. 'I haven't consulted him. This has to be your decision.'

Logan stretched out a shaky hand, indicating for Evie to place the book on his lap. She obliged, despite recent experience teaching her this meant nothing. That particular brochure had spent many quiet, untouched hours in Logan's company. Dylan had shown more interest in it on their last visit, fascinated by its glossy cover.

'You need your glasses.' She wasn't falling for that excuse again. 'Are they upstairs?'

'They're in the kitchen. They were filthy. I tried washing them. Made no difference. I have no push. I couldn't satisfy an itch on a bloody flea.'

His grumble was understandable. To have so little strength that he couldn't wipe the lenses on his spectacles was upsetting. For Logan, it must have been frustrating – soul-destroying to a man of his intelligence, whose professional life had depended on faultless dexterity and pin-point accuracy.

Evie returned the remaining books to the coffee table, gave Logan's knee a gentle rub, and excused herself from the room. 'Tea?'

She filled the kettle to the max line, bedded it in its cradle and flicked the switch down. The only hot drinks Logan had were those made by visitors. His mealtimes were at others' mercy, too, as were his rising and retiring times.

Others? There were no others. There was Evie.

She continued to think on the problem as she picked up the spectacles from the draining board. Her life was similar. The needs and wants of a toddler and, to a large degree, Logan dictated her coming and going.

As she pulled out a soft cloth from the under-sink cupboard, she chided herself. That was an uncharitable and mean-spirited thought. Her life was nothing like Logan's. At any given moment she could stand up and walk away. Not that she would, but having the ability ... having the choice ... gave her a sense of independence. And often guilt.

She eased up on herself. Feelings of guilt were normal at times like this. She'd read that somewhere. Or maybe someone had said it to her on the one occasion she attended a carers meeting. She'd not gone again due to her commitments. Irony at its best.

With the lenses buffed, she held the glasses up to the window and gave them a final inspection. One of the nosepieces had worked loose – most likely the reason Logan had given up on them. It didn't require a lot of pressure to snap the pad into position, but more than he could manage.

He was an expert at pressuring Evie, however. Twenty-four-seven. Evie, whose plan to return to work once Dylan was at pre-school was scrapped; Evie, who carried on regardless of sickness or incapacity; Evie, whose marriage had suffered such intense strain she was certain it was no longer bent, but snapped in two.

There had to be a better way to live life than this. For all of them.

Having made the tea, she returned to the living room and handed Logan his mug and glasses. Her reward was an irritable sigh and a begrudging thanks.

'Perhaps we could trial the care companies,' she said, taking a seat on the sofa. 'I could come in at the same time and observe. Just until we've trained the person up.' She endeavoured to smile, but Logan's tut stunted its growth.

'What good will that do?' he said. 'They won't fall out of line with you spying on them.'

'That's the point.' It sounded to Evie as if Logan wanted the carer to foul up. 'I promise I won't leave you with anyone who makes you feel uncomfortable. There are excellent firms out there, with honest, caring workers. If it takes another month, we'll find someone you can get along with. Someone you can trust.'

What was another month to Evie – another month living apart from her husband, another month withholding the truth from him, another month of watching him move beyond her reach, when to Logan it was potentially the difference between life and death?

Given time, understanding and infinite forgiveness, most things could be fixed. A person's demise wasn't one of them.

Evie put her mug on the floor and leaned forward. 'I know this is difficult for you.'

'But?'

There was no *but*.

'Logan, I love you as I did my own father—'

'Did you pay someone off to look after him?' Logan's hand wobbled with the force of his words and a teardrop of tea worked its way down the outside of his mug.

'No.' Rather than attending to the spillage, Evie stared at the stain the hot liquid had left behind. 'That was hurtful.' She lowered her gaze to the ground. 'You know I lost him when I was young.' Swiping her cup into her hand, she leapt to her feet and forced herself to count to five, remembering Logan was in pain and how it affected him. 'I don't feel good about any of this,' she said. 'I just can't manage it any more.'

'You'll manage,' he said, struggling to wave his mug at her. 'And I don't want any of *this*.' He brushed the care company brochure onto the floor. 'This is your idea. My way is much simpler, and since I'm such a liability to you and your family, I suggest you reconsider my proposal.' He closed his eyes and turned his head; his way of bringing the conversation to an end.

Undeterred, Evie set her mug on the table, retrieved the book and reinstated it on Logan's lap. His obstinacy would be the death of him. With that disquieting thought triggering a sequence of images in her mind, ending in Logan, cold and grey, with an empty pill bottle fixed in one hand and a cloudy brandy glass in the other, Evie was convinced she'd made the right decision. She could never help Logan in the way he'd asked. He was family and she loved him. Regardless of the guilt or the frustration, she was stupid to think she would ever agree to anything other than caring for him.

She'd lost Griff, but there was no way she was about to lose Logan.

'Your option is no longer under consideration,' she said, keeping her voice steady. 'I thought I'd made that clear.'

Logan's head turned, and his eyelids slowly parted. 'Final answer?'

'I understand why you asked me … I even get why we can't discuss it with Griff, but I won't take responsibility for your death, and that's what you're asking of me.' She dropped to her knees and seized Logan's hands. 'You have so much to live for. Dylan. Tess. They need you in their lives. And what about Griff? Can you truly give up on him?'

'You have.'

Evie snatched away her hands, sending the carer brochure to the floor once more. She knocked it under the coffee table, wishing she'd never discussed her marital problems with Logan. 'I haven't given up on him. I love him, but how do you expect me to look him in the eye when I'm keeping this huge, life-changing secret from him?'

'So, tell him.' Logan's shoulders lifted in a pathetic shrug. 'Makes no difference now. I'll have to find another accomplice. I have to say I'm disappointed in you, Evie. I thought you'd see me right. I thought you were courageous and compassionate. I didn't have you down for a selfish coward.'

'How can you say that?' Evie scuffed across the carpet, away from Logan, hoping the physical distance would give her space to think.

'Don't bother counting to five,' he said. 'And don't convince yourself I'm only saying these things because I'm in pain. I'm always in bloody pain. Stand up and give as good as you get. For once in your life, fight for your beliefs.'

Evie put up a hand and shook her head. 'I'm not doing this, Logan.' She was well aware he was goading her into a fight, searching for a way to release his anger at her refusal to help. Refusal to help? She helped him all the time – more often than she did Tess – and she would continue to do so if it meant he lived until the point God or the Grim Reaper or whoever the hell it was made the call.

She hauled herself onto the sofa, combed her fingers through her hair and allowed a moment to pass before speaking. 'I could no more help you die than I could my children.'

Logan's silence screamed danger to Evie.

His intent was implicit: he would find another way.

Or, as he'd said, another accomplice.

Chapter Fifteen

Griff

With Ozzy and Honey settled on the craft centre floor, Olivia busying herself in her stockroom, and Imogen silent and cradling a mug of coffee in her hands, Griff was using the time to process everything he'd learned in the past half an hour.

He'd believed Mrs Joliffe's death had been a terrible, unfortunate accident, but Imogen was telling him something different.

'When did you realise what had happened?' Griff placed the hot drink Olivia had supplied on the counter.

'Killed herself, you mean?'

There was no venom behind the words, more a sad acceptance of the facts. Griff nodded.

'As soon as I heard. We'd had a strange conversation the week before about paying bills on time and tying up loose ends. She insisted on showing me where she kept her paperwork, and gave me the court documents relating to her and Dad's divorce. Said I should read them so I knew exactly why the marriage broke down. I knew why, but she insisted I kept the files.'

'Your parents divorced?'

'It kicked off just before my twenty-first. None of us had come to terms with Kieran's loss, and Mum and Dad had spent years arguing and accusing each other of failing him. The plans I was making for my party seemed to be the catalyst for a series of particularly nasty rows. Mum thought I was callous and unfeeling, celebrating my *special* birthday when Kieran never got to see his.' Imogen ran her finger around the rim of her mug. 'When Dad stood up for me and told her I had the right to live my life, all hell broke loose. They were vicious to one another. I mean, really brutal. Things were said that could never be forgiven. Or forgotten.' She reached into her pocket and pulled out a tissue. 'Dad couldn't take it any more. He upped and left. I haven't seen or heard from him since.'

The tremor in Imogen's voice and the glistening in her eyes forced Griff to look away before the weight of his escalating guilt brought him down.

The sharp blow of her nose and a breath-controlling sigh indicated Imogen was about to continue.

'After the initial shock and upset, once we realised Dad wasn't coming back, we reached this ... *level.*'

Griff raised his head. 'Of understanding?'

'Of life. We weren't happy, far from it, but there were no arguments, no hate, no blaming one another for Kieran's death.'

She stalled at the word, recovered her composure, and gaped at Griff. His neck prickled under the heat of her unspoken accusation. It confirmed what he'd suspected for years. She blamed *him* for her brother's death. Why wouldn't she? He blamed himself.

'I should have gone with my gut,' he said, bowing his head. 'I knew jumping off that rock was idiotic.' He dared himself to look up and connect with Imogen. 'You have every right to hold me responsible.'

Imogen maintained the eye contact, but at that moment Griff struggled to read her. The previous stare she'd issued was packed with resentment and condemnation, but this ... this was something else. This was fluid. Shifting. He waited, watching for clues as to what was going through her head.

After a lengthy and considered pause, she spoke.

'You were always the one to hold back. Reconsider.

Determine the risk. You'd tell Kieran to take my hand when we crossed the road. Do you remember?'

Griff's memory of the gangly eleven-year-old objecting to being yanked onto the pavement came with a smile. 'I remember you swearing like a trooper at him. I was shocked at the language.' The smile was gaining strength. 'But you worshipped him, all the same.'

'I did, and I only repeated what I'd heard. You and Kieran used to swear all the time.'

'Not when you were around, which, as I recall, was all the time. We couldn't go anywhere without you tagging along.' Griff arched his brow.

Imogen set aside her mug and tissue, stepped off the stool and approached the dogs. 'You didn't seem to mind.' She crouched and ran Honey's ear through her fingers. 'Do you know why I didn't want Kieran holding onto me?'

'You were asserting your independence. Breaking free from that whole *baby sister* thing.' Griff joined her at the dogs and gave a sleeping Ozzy a gentle rub of his neck.

'There was a little of that going on, but it wasn't the main reason.' Letting Honey's ear flop back into place, Imogen turned on the balls of her feet towards Ozzy, and stroked him down the length of his back. 'I was hoping you'd give me your hand.'

'To get you across the road?' Griff would have done that.

'No.' Imogen gave a slow shake of her head. 'I wanted to know what it felt like. Whether your skin was rough or smooth. Hot or cold. Was your grip firm and reassuring or teasing and playful? How would you hold me?'

'Seriously?' Griff stopped petting Ozzy, rested his hand on the dog's back and assessed Imogen's admission. If that was what it was. 'You had a crush on me? You were ten, eleven at most.'

'And what? You never fantasised about your English

teacher?' Unembarrassed, Imogen laughed. 'Kieran told me all about it. What was her name?'

Griff brushed Ozzy's fur with his fingertips, as if sweeping Imogen's comment away. 'I don't recall, but fair point. You surprised me, that's all.'

Imogen reached for the counter, grasped its edge, and hauled herself up. 'Don't put yourself down. You were a good-looking boy.' She offered her hand to Griff.

'Were?' He laughed as he accepted Imogen's help to his feet. 'Well?'

'Well what?'

'How's my grip?'

They stood, toe-to-toe, hand-in-hand, Griff clenching his jaws together to suppress his amusement, Imogen committing to the moment with a tight squeeze of his fingers.

'Rough,' she said, turning his hand over in hers. She circled his palm with her thumb. 'They could use some attention.'

'They're worker's hands,' Griff said. 'They weren't like this when I was sixteen.'

Imogen increased the pressure, massaging each of Griff's fingers, lightly pinching and straightening them in turn, taking up his other hand when the first was done. The sensation was so unexpected and intense, it was verging on erotic. He fought the urge to close his eyes.

'Is there no one at home who does this for you?'

Imogen's caresses ceased and Griff regained his focus. 'I can look after myself,' he said, reclaiming his hand.

'I'm sure you can, but life's better shared with people you love.' In one swift move, Imogen was back on the stool, feet on its bar, her head down. 'I have no one.'

With the rapid mood change and the twist in Imogen's words reopening Griff's emotional valve, the guilt flooded his system. If he'd had the courage of his convictions, if he'd stopped Kieran that day, if he'd saved him, Imogen would have her family now.

Logan believed it was pointless living by what-ifs, but it was a shortcoming of Griff's, and one he wasn't afraid to admit. The what-ifs gave him both hindsight and foresight. They made him question his decisions, providing him with the potential to prevent future failure. They gave him the confidence to know his enemy and the conviction to issue orders with authority. They kept his mind sharp, his losses minimal, and proved to him, without a doubt, everything and everyone was worth saving.

What if he'd not vowed to look out for Imogen?

Then she'd be alone.

'You have me,' he said. 'You've always had me.'

'No. I lost you the day Kieran died.'

Griff stepped forward, wanting to comfort Imogen – draw her into his arms – close the gap and put an end to their distance, but he held back. 'I was there, at his funeral. Don't you remember?'

'I remember.' Imogen picked up the tissue she'd left by her mug, and tore at its corners. 'I remember walking into the crematorium to "Stairway to Heaven". I remember the solemn hymns. I remember hating you for what happened to Kieran.'

For a split second, Imogen's expression was that of her eleven-year-old self who'd followed her brother's coffin into the church. She'd caught sight of Griff the moment she'd stepped over the threshold and sent such immense waves of loathing in his direction, it had rocked him and cast him adrift.

He shook the image from his mind. After years without contact, Imogen was there, in front of him, saying all the things he'd been desperate to hear – all the things he'd told himself. Even under the peculiar circumstances that led her to the shop, the time was right. Imogen was prepared to talk, prepared to listen, and perhaps, prepared to accept Griff's friendship.

'I don't expect you to forgive me,' he said. 'I've never forgiven myself. I've spent my life trying to save people and every loss takes me right back to the moment Kieran jumped. I wanted to be there for you, but your parents were clear – I was to have nothing to do with you. I understood. You were a child and they were protecting you, and you'd gone through so much.' He stopped and checked Imogen's face. A vulnerable, isolated and broken woman had replaced the hostile eleven-year-old.

Without further hesitation or question, he gathered her to him, locked his arms around her and held her until Olivia's return to the shop front prompted him to pull away.

'Fence mending or bridge building?' Olivia motioned for Griff to pass over the coffee mugs.

'Aren't they the same thing?' Griff finished the last mouthful of his drink, collected Imogen's cup and passed both vessels to Olivia.

'It depends on your perspective. From where I'm standing, it looks very much like the bridge has been built, tested for stability and crossed.' Facing Griff, Olivia positioned herself between him and Imogen, looked him in the eye, and swiped her free hand from left to right, creating an imaginary divide. 'My mistake. It's lines that are crossed.'

Olivia rarely expressed disapproval; Griff was left in no doubt she thought he'd overstepped the mark.

'It's not like that,' he said, certain an explanation would set her straight. 'I've told you about Kieran, my friend who jumped off Pulpit Rock?'

'The young lad who died?' Olivia's stern expression softened. 'I remember you saying. So tragic.'

'Well, Imogen is Kieran's sister.' Griff gave Imogen's arm

a gentle pat. 'We were talking about Kieran and it's opened up old wounds.'

'They never healed,' Imogen said, her voice trembling. 'It's been a shock running into Griff. I've spent the best part of twenty-four years avoiding him.'

Olivia migrated to the desk. 'That's a long time. How's that worked out for you?'

'Until today, just fine.' Imogen folded her arms.

'I'm not judging you,' Olivia said, 'but for a woman whose dislike of Griff is as obvious as the danger in walking your dog down to Preacher Cove, I was surprised to waltz in and find you in his arms.'

Imogen flicked her head to the side and glared at Olivia, the hostility of which sent barbs up the back of Griff's neck and onto his skull. He knew Olivia was looking out for him, but this unexpected and unnecessary confrontation was one he could live without. 'Please don't worry,' he said, addressing Olivia. 'Imogen's like a sister to me.'

'A sister who's avoided you like the plague and then succumbed to your manly charms?'

'Olivia!' This was so out of character for the older lady. 'She was upset.'

'As Evie would be if she'd found you with a beautiful young thing in your arms.'

'Evie?' Imogen peered beyond Griff, towards the shop door. 'Who's Evie?'

Perplexed with the way the moment was listing out of control, Griff endeavoured to reel it in. 'Can we stop this? I appreciate what you're saying, Olivia, but really, I can look after myself.'

'So you keep saying.'

'You were listening to my conversation with Imogen?'

'I wasn't listening. I heard. The door was open. And what's more, you're doing a terrible job of looking after yourself.'

'Will someone tell me who Evie is?' Imogen climbed down from the stool and approached the window.

Griff rammed his fingers through his hair, called Ozzy to his side, and encouraged Honey to get off his coat. He picked it up and shook it out. 'Thanks for the coffee, Olivia.' Bewildered, he shoved his arms into the sleeves, threw the hood up and seized the door handle. 'Evie's my wife,' he said, heading out into the rain.

The ferocity of the wind and the sheer force of the rain drove Griff and Imogen into joining the would-be beach walkers in the warm and dry Harbour Inn. They struggled to find two seats together. Bagging a small table next to the wood burner, Griff stole a stool from the bar and passed it to Imogen.

'My second of the day,' she said, glancing through the far porthole window.

Griff followed her gaze. Olivia's blue shop stood out against the grey horizon.

With the dogs settled in front of the fire, and drinks on the way, he perched on the table, keeping one foot on the floor. 'Would you prefer to stand?'

Imogen smiled. 'No. The stool is fine, thank you. Just making an observation. Like your friend over there.'

'Olivia's one of the good guys. She was looking out for me. Don't take the things she said personally.'

'Hard not to when she was so rude.'

'Not rude. Direct. There's a difference.' Griff stood as the landlady delivered two full glasses of fruit juice and an oversized packet of crisps. He nodded his thanks. 'And I'm all for being direct.' He popped open the packet and offered the contents to Imogen.

'So you won't mind telling me about Evie?' she said, freeing a large, heart-shaped crisp from the bag and holding it up. 'Is she the love of your life?'

As a customer left his place at the bar, Griff whipped away the vacated stool, and claimed it as his own. He placed it next to Imogen and sat down. 'I met her at the Christmas swim three years ago. Turned out we were both raising money for the hospice.'

Imogen's questioning eyes brought him to an abrupt halt. He shouldn't have mentioned the hospice. It was the wrong time to discuss his mother's death. He pushed on. 'Evie was a new volunteer there.' As he spoke he visualised the moment he first saw Evie – she was dressed as an angel, with a golden halo above her head and a plume of white feathers for wings attached to her back. Her emerald eyes dazzled him and her commitment to a cause so close to his heart touched him.

'We married eighteen months later.' He tipped a handful of crisps into his mouth, providing a brief respite from the conversation. He wanted time to enjoy his memories – memories of when he and Evie found time for romantic dinners, soppy films, late nights and long lie-ins.

There was no stealthy *drive-by sex* in the early days.

Griff dropped the crisp packet onto the table, picked up his glass and downed the juice. He returned it to the table, leaving his hand resting there.

Life was different now. Logan demanded Evie's time. Dylan needed his mum. Tess ... Tess had changed. Since the split, she'd become unsettled – a natural reaction to a family breakdown, Griff accepted that, but he had the notion there was something more affecting her. If he could get to the bottom of it, he would, but he hadn't felt able to ask, and she never turned to him for help. In fact, no one did. Not any more. And no one told him how they were or what they'd been up to, or even asked how he was. Occasionally Evie sent a text if it was too awkward for Griff to visit Dylan, and Tess would make him the odd cup of tea in the evening before he returned to his flat, but other than that, he was surplus to requirements.

'You mentioned you have a daughter.' Imogen nudged his fingers. 'You said she has better manners than me.'

'I may have exaggerated,' said Griff, setting aside his thoughts. 'Tess. She's fifteen. She's Evie's daughter.'

'A ready-made family.'

Griff watched as Imogen traced the outline of his hand. She appeared to be doing it in a moment of absent-mindedness. Her glassy eyes, as blue as Zircon, suggested her mind was somewhere other than in the room. Griff left his hand in situ. 'We made one of our own, as well. Dylan. He was two at Christmas.'

'Dylan? That's a good Welsh name. Not forgotten your roots, then?'

She was back, the energy restored and burning bright.

'So, what keeps you busy?' Griff steered the conversation away from Welsh connections before Imogen asked after his mother. 'Trips abroad?'

Now with her arms steepled, Imogen was supporting her chin on her hands. Her skin was bronzed, and her third finger was devoid of a telltale white stripe where a wedding band could reside.

'Not unless you count Glastonbury as abroad?' She smiled, then lowered her head. 'What made you ask?'

Griff poked at his empty glass. 'You have a healthy glow.'

'Oh, that.' Imogen laughed, reclined and dropped her hands into her lap. 'It's out of a bottle. Much safer that way.'

'True.' Fake or not, a tan suited her. 'Is that where you've been living? Glastonbury?'

'Yes. Once Dad left, and Mum and I reached that level of life I mentioned, we decided to move away. Leave behind the bad memories. Start again.' Imogen stood and pointed at the bar. 'Another juice, or should we have something more adult?'

The offer was tempting. A drink with his best mate's sister was more than Griff had believed possible. The last time that had happened, he'd bought Imogen a can of cream soda. It was her favourite drink back then. 'Nice idea, but I'm driving home after.'

'You need to live a little.' Imogen tutted, deposited the glasses on the bar, and returned to her stool. 'I learned not to be so hard on myself when I was in Glastonbury. I met some really good people. They took me under their wing and opened my mind to a whole alternative way of life.'

'How alternative?'

Imogen's eyes widened. 'Within the law alternative. What do you take me for?' She reached for her bag, which she'd left at the foot of the table. 'Here.' From an opened pocket on the front, Imogen produced a small, white business card and handed it to Griff. 'I came back home to Dorset to set up my own business. I'm a holistic practitioner. I specialise in massage. You should come for a session. It would loosen you up. You could bring Evie.'

'I'm not sure that would work.'

Imogen sighed, put her bag on the table and appeared to be making preparations to leave. 'We were doing so well. We'd even mentioned Kieran without either of us getting defensive.' Climbing back off her stool, she looped her coat from its hook and took up Honey's lead.

Griff clamped his hand down on the bag. 'We are doing well.' He wasn't allowing the new honesty and the open lines of communication to break. Not now. Not after it had taken twenty-four years to establish them. 'I meant I don't think I could persuade Evie to come along.'

Imogen threw on her mac, and glowered at Griff. 'I

was extending the hand of friendship, not suggesting a threesome.'

'It's not that,' Griff said. 'I'd love to see how you've set yourself up.' It gave him comfort to know one area of Imogen's life was working out. 'It's Evie.' He stared at the small, round table. 'We're ...' He searched the mahogany swirls for the right word. All he could see was Evie's face morphing out from the patina. 'I don't know what we are. Giving each other space? Separated?' He rubbed his thumb over the ribbon-like stains masquerading as Evie's hair. 'Estranged?'

He caught sight of Imogen's coat-tail gliding back in his direction and he drew his eyes away from the table. She had retaken her seat.

'How long?'

'A couple of months.'

'Why?'

A half-laugh escaped from Griff. 'I don't know. It was so sudden.'

Imogen pulled her stool tight to the table, her scowl lost its hard edges, and her brow lifted. 'You asked, though? And got no answer?' She nodded as if anticipating Griff's reply. 'I had similar happen to me. I was madly in love with a man I met in Glastonbury. I thought he was serious, thought we were going somewhere, I'd even booked a holiday for us both in Italy, then bam! Roll credits. No explanation, no apology, no last kiss, just goodbye. It's a wicked thing to do to another human being.' Her lips pressed together. 'It's cowardly. You wouldn't do it, would you?'

Griff swished his hand across the table. 'Well, no, but that's not how it happened with Evie.' He wasn't at all comfortable with Imogen comparing his wife to her loser lover. 'Evie's not a coward.'

Imogen shrugged. 'I'm not judging. I'm empathising with

your situation. Letting you know you can talk to me. I'm discreet. Everything you say will remain with me.'

As she leaned back and crossed her legs, her foot brushed against Griff's ankle. The whisper of a connection reminded him why he was with her, and it wasn't to talk through his marital problems.

'I appreciate the offer, I do, but I'm not in the habit of discussing my private life.' He retracted his legs, safeguarding them under his stool. 'There's not much to tell you, anyway.' The truth was he'd not reached any real conclusions as to why he found himself living alone in a cramped flat in the middle of town. 'I have asked Evie why, but she's as elusive as you.' He skimmed his finger through a ring of condensation on the table. 'At least you and I are finally talking.' He stole at look at Imogen. Her head was tilted to the side and a smile was teetering on her lips. Her eyes gave it balance.

'Lord, for your sake, let's hope she comes round sooner than me.' She gave Griff's forearm a squeeze, left her hand there, then adopted a pensive expression. 'Have you told your parents about Evie? Only I find myself wondering about them. Why it is you've not mentioned them.'

Slipping free from Imogen's touch, Griff weaved his fingers together, and rested his arms along his thighs. It seemed there was no avoiding the subject of his mother's death, but he could spare Imogen the details. 'I lost my mum six years ago. Cancer.'

'Oh. Not Marilyn?' Imogen shrunk back, her slight frame almost collapsing in on itself. 'That's a horrible disease. How did you get through it?'

There was a leading question. 'I'm not sure we did.' Griff revised his statement. 'I'm not sure I have. Dad made his peace at the time.'

'And how is Logan?' Imogen flinched; an indication she was expecting more bad news.

'He's still with us.' Griff smiled and rubbed his hands together in an attempt to lighten the mood. 'He's not as mobile as he used to be, but there's nothing wrong with his brain.'

'Still opinionated?' Imogen's spirit returned to the room. 'I remember Logan very clearly. Strong, independent, in charge of his own destiny. He and my dad loved a good old debate. Do you see much of him?'

'Not a great deal.' Griff's stomach tensed at the admission. 'Evie's always asking me to go, and I should, I know, but we'd end up arguing.' He could list a multitude of half-truths for his neglect of Logan – moving out of the marital home, juggling Dylan's care, working extra shifts … but the one that trumped them all – the one Griff kept to himself – was the fear his ingrained sense of betrayal would drive him into hating his own father. Staying away prevented that from happening. 'Not sure I'm up for the confrontation,' he said, leaning forward onto the table.

Imogen matched his posture, enclosing them in an intimate and private bubble. She shimmied her coat off her shoulders and as it fell and draped the stool, a wisp of fresh, sweet orange danced its way up. Griff hadn't noticed it earlier – not even when he'd hugged Imogen. The rain and damp must have stifled it, he reasoned, not to mention the awkwardness of the moment. But it was out there now, free and uninhibited, and injecting him with an unexpected shot of pleasure. Inappropriate as his arousal was, the scent's appeal drew him closer still. 'Nice perfume,' he said, his breath causing the delicate strands of Imogen's hair to billow.

She gathered them up and tucked them behind her ears. 'Does Logan know about you and Evie?'

Brutally yanked back to the topic in hand, Griff refocused. 'I haven't told him,' he said.

'What does that mean?' Imogen narrowed her eyes and inched even nearer.

'It means if he does know, it hasn't come from me. Can you imagine the fallout?'

'What about Evie?' Imogen asked. 'Would she tell Logan? And don't you think it should come from you?'

With the constant firing of questions, Griff's gentle arousal waned, allowing his usual common sense and good judgement room to manoeuvre. 'I don't remember you being this challenging as a child.'

Imogen pulled back her shoulders, and resumed her hands-in-lap pose. 'Oh, I think I was, but as you're well aware, I'm no longer a child.'

The stiffening of her back gave a defined elegance to her slim outline and the positioning of her arms framed her breasts, giving them a prominence that pushed Griff into turning away. He stared into the flames of the wood burner. It was an uncomfortable sensation realising he could feel something sexual for Imogen, however brief or subtle, and there was no excuse for his behaviour.

Exhaling noisily, he reclined, extended his arms to their full length and flexed and tensed new life into them. 'Evie could have told him,' he said, settling his hands on top of his head. 'She spends lots of time there. She's his carer. And yes, it should come from me.'

'Are you likely to run into her at your dad's?'

'That's always a possibility, but she tends to go in at the same times each day –mealtimes, mainly.' Griff cocked his head and looked at Imogen. 'Why d'you ask?'

She was gazing down at the sleeping dogs. 'Just curious.' She paused, raised a hand as if she had something to add, and then shook her head. 'I think it's time my kidnapped dog and I left. I'm glad we managed to talk. Perhaps we can meet again?' She smiled, hopped off her stool and picked up her coat. 'With less drama next time. You made a note of my number.' As she rattled Honey's lead, the dog opened an eye and yawned, clearly planning on not moving anything but her mouth and tail. 'Come on, girl. Time to go.' Imogen attached the lead to the collar, and gave a gentle pull of encouragement. 'She is so stubborn.'

'You could let sleeping dogs lie.' Griff produced his best innocent face.

'Like you've done with your father?' Imogen cast a look over her shoulder. 'If I've learnt anything today, it's that facing difficult situations head-on can produce positive outcomes. If you and I can make progress in burying the hatchet, speaking to your father will be a walk in the park.' She returned to goading Honey into action and when she finally had her up and alert, they headed for the door.

As the freezing gust of wind swept in, it delivered Imogen's parting words.

'I can come with you. If you like.'

Chapter Sixteen

Tess

It's Logan's birthday tomorrow. March twenty-eighth. He's seventy-five. Mum took Dylan and me to see him at the weekend, but I guess when you reach that age, birthday gatherings are more hassle than pleasure. He barely spoke. He thanked me for his card and chocolate orange, and muttered a few words to Mum, but other than that, nothing.

He looks frailer each time we visit. I'm surprised at how quickly he's declined. Mum hasn't mentioned anything particular about his health, but for the last month she's spent more daylight hours with Logan than she has with us.

School was a drag today. I was dealing with the fallout from a nasty incident yesterday. I'm glad to be home. It would've been nice to have Mum here for more than five minutes before she dashed out, issuing instructions as to what to feed Dylan. A two-year-old is hardly up for dinner conversation about GCSEs or exploring why Griff and Mum have fallen out. I snort. Even Mum's not up for discussing that, saying these things happen in marriages. I'm not convinced. She says all these brave things, but I know she's bluffing. It's obvious she's unhappy without Griff.

It's his birthday soon, too. I've bought his card already. It's in the shape of an electric guitar. I saw some with *step-dad* on the front, but I've never given him one like that.

He'll be forty. I suppose that warrants me thinking of him as Griff. That and because he's being a decent father to Dylan. It must be awkward, coming to your own home to visit your son. This cottage was Griff's place long before he met Mum. I can't help feeling it should be us that moves out, not Griff. I don't actually know why anyone has to move out.

I resolve to tackle Mum about it when she comes home.

'Spaghetti, Dylan?' His brown eyes grow large at the 's' word. He loves pasta, especially the messy sort. It's not what Mum's told me to give him, but unlike her, I've got time to make it and time to clear up afterwards. I pull up my sleeves, run the kitchen tap and wash my hands, gritting my teeth as the soap creeps into a new cut on my wrist.

I'd been clean for almost a month, pushing my limits every day. *Just get through the night*, I'd said to myself. *Eat breakfast, walk to the bus stop, make it to the tutor room* – every step taking me further away from the last time I'd self-harmed. I've been avoiding triggers, but yesterday was tough.

Since Griff moved out, our days have started before *Breakfast TV*. With Mum helping Logan first thing every morning, I'm left to sort out myself and Dylan. Yesterday, I was ready to leave for school when Mum returned from Logan's. Her eyes were red. She told me she'd been rubbing them and spouted some rubbish about it being the hay fever season. She's never had hay fever in her life. She asked me if Dylan had been good, and made sure we'd both eaten. I'd made scrambled eggs on toast, which Dylan had wolfed down, and I'd put him back to bed for a snooze. Mum kissed me, thanked me and waved me off. As soon as the front door closed, I heard her cry out.

'Ghetti!' Dylan's hooked himself around my legs, and is yanking at my jeans. I pick him up, wriggle him into his booster seat and pass him a *Noddy* book to occupy him while I sort out the spaghetti. Fibres from my sleeve catch and chafe the extremes of my cut. This one needs a larger covering.

As my fingers root through the medicine box, my mind is searching for a plausible explanation as to how I've hurt my wrist, should anyone notice.

I find some gauze and a stretchy, tube-like bandage, and cobble together a dressing, folding the bandage back on itself. It's secure, and as long as I pull my sleeve down, it's hidden. I bury the inadequate Band Aid in the bin.

Dylan throws his book across the table, making my insides tumble. I was so zoomed in on my arm, so far inside myself, I'd forgotten he was with me. I'm embarrassed, but I'm determined to fight that horrible rise of guilt and shame that begs me to harm. I'm determined not to give in again so soon. 'I can't leave Dylan on his own,' I whisper.

I zap some milk in the microwave, test its temperature and pass it to him. I receive a smile and a staccato 'Ta', for my efforts. It goes a long way to appeasing me, and the urge to cut is weakening. 'Fifteen minutes. Just keep going for fifteen minutes.' It's become my mantra of late.

With the medicine box returned to the cupboard, Dylan placated, and my cut clean and protected, I can carry on making tea. I lift the lid from the pan of boiling water and swear as the steam scorches my skin. There's no damage, but the incident has given me a cover story for my bandage.

I snap the thin, crisp strands of spaghetti in half and shove them into the pan, picking up the splintered pieces that shattered under the pressure of breaking. I'm trying hard not to compare them to my life. The splintering sound and the physical force of the crack vibrating through my fingers discharged an acute degree of tension. I follow it up with a deep breath and a slow release.

I hate the fact I slipped yesterday, but hearing Mum cry out was the start. It reminded me that no matter how old I am, and no matter how hard I try, I can't protect her. There is nothing I can do that will stop her getting hurt. And if I can't help her, who's going to be there to help me?

Then, at school, I had sport.

I have scars. I don't wear them like a badge. I don't want people to see them. I don't want to have to explain myself. What I do is private. And sport is the worst possible lesson for someone like me. Getting changed is like running the gauntlet. I can usually separate myself from the class, find a corner and get into my kit with minimum fuss, as long as I'm swift. The isolation makes me a target, but a few choice words and showing the abuser the finger can have a devastating effect. The colder months are better, as I can wear my sweatshirt, but yesterday, the crafty spring weather did the dirty on me and chucked out the warmest day of the year so far.

The teacher told me to strip down to my polo shirt. I refused. I heard the class bully say, 'The Ginger Whinger's being all weird again.' Then her friends joined in. 'Stressy Tessy', and 'Minging MacDonald.'

I got sent to the changing rooms for telling them to piss off. How unfair is that?

Anyway, I was glad to be out of the spotlight. It meant I could get back into uniform without suspicious eyes glaring at me.

As I dragged my sport's top up and over my head, I heard the *swoosh* of the cloakroom door. I scrambled into my school shirt and turned round to find the bullies' ringleader standing a foot away. Her arms were folded, and she had a sneer plastered on her face. She's bigger than me. She's bigger than most people in the year, to be fair.

'Are you frigid or something?' she said, laughing. 'Only I've heard you never get your tits out. You know, for the boys. And you're always quick to change. You never shower after hockey.' She stepped to the side and looked me up and down. 'No wonder you stink, you filthy cow.'

I did the cuff buttons up and reached for my blazer, unconcerned my front was still exposed. My arms were my priority. Facing away from the girl, I hitched my jacket over my shoulders, and picked up my trousers from the slatted bench.

'I don't know what you're hiding,' she said, lunging towards me, 'but I'm going to find out.'

With her breath hitting my neck, she snatched at my hair, pulling it to the side until the pain made me go with it. She eased up once I was facing her, and she stood there, staring at me.

I couldn't speak. And I was frozen to the spot.

I was five all over again, watching the dominant person take control through violence, knowing that hair pulling led to something worse – something that made my mother cry in agony – something she begged my father not to do. Then, all I could see was him scrambling out of his trousers, out of his pants. Him pinning Mum to the wall, or the door, or the cabinet, shoving her over the bath, the sofa, the table, ripping clothes from her, his whole body banging into her, and her screaming with every single push.

I didn't know what he was doing, but I wanted it to finish. I ran to my bedroom and hid under my duvet. I put my hands over my ears to block out the sounds – the grunts, the yells, the sobs, the slaps – but I heard everything.

And could do nothing.

'Let go,' I said as my vision returned to the changing room.

The girl scoffed as she closed the gap between us even further. 'Why? What are you going to do?'

I did nothing. I did nothing and I said nothing. I was passive, resigned to my fate, and accepting of the consequences. As long as I didn't retaliate, the situation remained manageable.

The girl began to smirk. It started as a twitch on her top lip, but quickly turned into a sneer of disgust. 'I know what you are,' she said, flicking away my hair. 'And it makes me sick to the stomach.'

As she drew back her fist, the life-saving sound of an opening door brought an instant halt to my ordeal.

'You tell anyone about this and I swear, the next time I find you alone ...' The girl shoved herself away, followed up her threat with a murderous glare, and then carried on as if nothing had happened, greeting her cohorts as they piled into the changing room. 'Guess who's not showering,' she said as she stripped to her underwear.

'Ghetti! Pease!' Dylan's banging his plastic beaker on the table trying to get my attention.

'Soon,' I say, wiping my brow with a sheet of kitchen roll. 'Fifteen minutes. Just fifteen minutes more.'

I wanted to tell Mum everything when I'd got home from school yesterday – the intimidation and humiliation I'd suffered at the hands of the school bully, my crazy, confused, mixed-up feelings about my sexuality, my mistrust of men, how I cut myself, how I'd stayed clean for almost a month – everything. But she wasn't in. Griff was, building a train track with Dylan.

But it wasn't Griff I needed.

By the time Mum returned, I'd already resorted to the quickest way I knew of relieving the pressure in my head and the pain in my gut.

And I'd decided Mum didn't need my shit piled on top of her own.

I open a can of bolognaise, knock it into a saucepan and let the heat do its thing. After a few minutes, my stomach acknowledges the comforting smell, and I set the table for two.

Credit where it's due, Griff was sweet yesterday. He

tried to help, but my head was all over the place and I was unreceptive. After he'd told me Mum was at Logan's and not due home for another hour, he asked if anything was wrong, but my urge to cut was so compelling, I waved my response at him, and dashed upstairs to my bedroom.

I didn't expect him to follow me there five minutes later.

It was too late by then. I'd already nabbed the bottle of gin from under the squeaky floorboard, and poured it over the blade. I was slicing into my wrist when Griff knocked. It startled me, causing me to push the metal deeper than I intended.

'Don't come in,' I shouted.

I reached into my drawer, tugged a sanitary towel from its packet, and pressed it against the wound. Not ideal, but with the severity of the cut I needed something more than my cosmetic tissues to soak up the blood. I prayed I wouldn't need stitches.

I sat in silence, hoping to hear Griff's footsteps run down the stairs, but he rapped on the door again.

'It's okay,' he said. 'I'm not coming in, but I'm concerned. You're upset.'

I tried to hone in on his voice, but I wanted to give myself up to the moment. Despite it happening so quickly – the bleeding, the interruption, the desperation to hide my equipment – the release had come, and the rush convinced me I'd done the right thing.

'Tess?'

'Give me a minute,' I said. 'Just another minute.'

'Ghetti? Ta?' Dylan's quiet request touches me and I give his food one final stir.

'It's ready,' I say, smiling and serving up the bolognaise. I sit next to him and hand him his spoon and fork. They have rubber handles and Dylan's chubby fingers can grip them easily. My fork is metal. Like my blade. The one I'd thrown under the floorboard in my haste to prevent Griff finding out my secret.

Once I'd agreed to talk with him, he'd backed off and gone downstairs.

The sanitary towel had done its job, and when I'd stopped bleeding, I'd replaced it with a tissue, letting my sleeve hold it in place. I'd wanted to climb into bed and sleep. I was relaxed, loose, and breathing with ease. Instead, I cleaned myself up, sterilised the blade and buried my tools again.

'Just nipping to the loo,' I shouted down to Griff.

I found a box of plasters in the bathroom cabinet and applied the largest I could find. It didn't cover the length of the cut, but it was better than nothing.

When I reached the living room, Griff was sitting on the sofa. Dylan was snuggled in beside him, and there were two mugs on the small table.

'Made you a coffee,' Griff said, pointing to a red cup.

'Coffee? Mum never lets me drink coffee.' I picked it up and settled in the armchair.

'It's decaf.'

'Figures.'

Smiling, Griff stroked the top of Dylan's head. 'Tough day?'

'No tougher than normal.' Of course I lied. I couldn't explain myself to Griff. 'But thanks for asking.' I meant that. Life was difficult for us all and I appreciated him taking the time to ask. 'What about you? Were you working?'

'Nope. In the middle of my four days off. It has quietened down at work, though. Can't say I'm missing those storms.'

'You're talking literally, right? You mean the actual storms that flooded Portland? Not the ones that tore through the cottage at Christmas?'

He smiled again. The creases around his mouth strengthened his structure. It made him look solid. Reliable.

'I'm talking literally, but granted, the high tides and your mother are formidable forces of nature.'

Dylan popped his thumb in and closed his eyes.

'I don't want you to worry about your mum and me,' Griff said. 'I love her. And I want to be here for you and Dylan. Nothing that happens between Evie and me affects my relationship with you.' He pulled Dylan in tighter, wrapping a muscular arm right round his small body. 'I realise you and I don't always see eye to eye, and I know how protective you are of your mum and how close you are – you had quite a few years when it was just you and her against the world, and I get that – but I'd really like to be a person in your life you can turn to. I'd like to earn your trust, Tess.'

Dylan's giggling at the way the spaghetti keeps slipping off my fork. I act the clown for him with the next three mouthfuls, and then prompt him to finish his portion. 'We'll have custard after,' I say, pushing my bowl away. 'And then it's bath time. Fun for both of us.' I'll have to wear a rubber glove to protect my bandage. 'We can play with the foam letters. I promise to keep the words clean.'

Clean. I'm no longer clean. There's a chance the new cut will produce a thick, ridged scar. I pledge to massage oil into it as soon as it heals over. It's how I manage the after-effects.

Griff's asked if Dylan and I would like to visit at weekends when he's not working. He said we could walk Ozzy and maybe stay over once in a while.

'Your dad wants to take us out for a burger,' I tell Dylan. 'I can't help feeling that's a slippery slope, as Mum would say.'

Fast food restaurants are the hangouts of divorced dads and their children. Divorce is not the answer. Griff told me he loves Mum, and I know she's miserable without him.

'I'm not sure about this love stuff, Dylan. This man and woman thing – I can't see how it can work. We're different species, put on this planet to procreate. Do we need love to do that?' I look at Dylan. The food stains circling his mouth like a racetrack are as brown as his eyes. 'Okay,' I concede. 'You're a cute advert for love, but I don't think it's for me.'

In my experience, love between a man and a woman always ends badly.

Chapter Seventeen

Evie

The small box, gift-wrapped with Evie's usual care, remained on the bedside cabinet, where she'd placed it the day before. She'd come upstairs to collect a warm cardigan for Logan. March was disrespectful of weather lore, deciding to hang on to its lion status. One day warm, the next chilly.

'In like a lion, out like a lamb?' Evie said, first picking up the birthday present, then pulling a grey, woolly jacket from Logan's wardrobe. 'More like in like a lion, tease us with your lamb-like innocence, and then clamp your huge jaws around the month.' She hugged the jacket to her as she returned to the living room.

Logan was huddled in his chair, the green fabric accentuating his pale features. Evie placed the gift on the coffee table, and held out the cardigan. 'Would you like this on, or over your shoulders?'

Logan shuffled forward. 'Just wrap it round.'

Evie obliged, helping Logan settle back. 'Haven't you got a heated pad?' She approached the understairs cupboard and flicked on the light. 'I'm sure we bought a fleecy one for your lap.'

'I don't want it,' Logan said.

His tone wasn't far from one Evie had heard Tess use towards Griff. Petulant.

She exited the cupboard. 'You have to keep warm, Logan. You refuse to turn the heating back on, you're not eating properly, and it's nippy outside. It's no wonder you're cold.'

'I am not a child. I don't need you making decisions for

me. This jumper is enough.' He turned his head and closed his eyes. 'I don't need anything from you, except—'

'You haven't opened your present.' Not wanting to enter the whole assisted suicide debate again, Evie cut him off. 'It's from all of us, and I've not used any sticky tape on the paper. Just a loose ribbon. One small pull and it will unwrap.'

The package contained a box of Logan's favourite and difficult-to-buy mint fondants, a pocket book on 'armchair' gardening, so he could plan his seasonal plants and maintain control over what went on in his garden, and a limited edition of Harper Lee's *To Kill A Mockingbird*, which had cost Evie more money than she was prepared to let on. Certainly more than she could afford.

A gift of hope didn't deserve to be left languishing unseen.

'I told you not to buy me anything.' Logan opened his eyes and stared at Evie. 'It's just more junk for you to clear out when I've gone.'

'Did he open it?' Tess liberated a tangerine from the fruit bowl next to the fridge and dug her thumbnail into the peel. Juice squirted onto her cheek, sending a giggling Dylan running from the room.

'Not by the time I left.' Evie took a tangerine for herself and sat at the table. 'He's never really been one for birthdays, though. I don't know why I expected this year to be any different.'

'Because you love birthdays.' Tess chucked her peel straight into the food recycling bin. 'And because you always think the best of people.' She sucked a segment into her mouth, and pushed out a thread of pith with her tongue. 'Why are oranges so disgusting and difficult to get into?' She wiped her hand on the side of her black jeans.

Evie sent her a disapproving look and nodded towards the sink. 'Wash your hands if they're dirty.'

It was an interesting phrase. To some extent, it was what Evie was trying to do with Logan by getting him to agree to outside care – wash her hands of him. If that was how she saw it, the outside world would see her as a monster. 'Am I wrong to ask for help with Logan?' She gazed at the dimples in the fruit skin as Tess joined her at the table.

'How can you think that? You've done so much for him over the past couple of years. You get up at ridiculous o'clock every morning and go to bed at stupid o'clock every night. You've done more than your fair share.' Tess hesitated as Dylan re-entered the kitchen and held his hand out for some tangerine. She picked off the remaining pith, and passed the almost-complete ball to him. 'I'll help more, Mum. I can go to Logan's after school, and at weekends. I can do his breakfast on Sundays and you can have a lie-in. We're a team. We always have been. You and me against the world.'

Evie smiled. Her beautiful girl's kindness and care had warmed her heart. 'It's a lovely idea, but it's not fair on you. I already leave Dylan with you when you should be out with your friends.'

'Honestly, Mum, I don't mind. And I'm on Easter holidays now.'

'Then you'll have time to study for your exams.'

'They're mocks.'

'Your science one isn't. And mocks need just as much attention as the real thing.'

Tess produced a dramatic huff and a groan, and threw her hands up in a gesture of despair. 'Mum, I'll be fine, but if it worries you, tell Griff it's time he took some responsibility. Logan's his father.'

The indignation in Tess's voice was barely detectable, but it was there. Evie reached a hand across to her, but withdrew as soon as Tess clamped her arms behind her back. 'I married Griff, making Logan part of our family,' Evie said, quietly.

'And Griff has buggered off.'

'Language, Tess.' Evie glanced at Dylan, who, although too young to understand, was old enough to copy. 'It's not as simple as that. It wasn't a case of Griff upping and leaving. Things were difficult between us. We needed space and time away from each other so we could work out what's best. For everyone,' she added.

A troubled look replaced the anger in Tess's eyes, alerting Evie to the thoughts behind. 'He hasn't hurt me,' Evie said. 'He is nothing like your father. I promise.' She saw Tess's shoulders tense and could only imagine how tightly she was clenching her hands together. 'It took me long enough to escape Neil and there's no way I'd expose either of us or Dylan to anything like that again. We're free of men like him. We're free of him.' She tried to foster a smile to reassure her daughter they were stronger now, safe, but it was hard to issue an honest expression when her words were telling lies.

Neil featured more often in her nightmares than she would admit.

His death hadn't brought the closure Evie had prayed for.

'I know you think of him.'

The instant Tess spoke, Evie blinked away Neil's image. 'Do I?'

'Mum! Be honest with me. You used to tell me everything.'

Not everything.

From the moment Tess was born, Evie was so overwhelmed with love she swore she would always protect her. Had she known the promise included safeguarding Tess from Neil, she'd have taken her straight from the hospital and disappeared. No trace. No contact. No problem.

But she hadn't.

Her early relationship with Neil and the first year of their marriage had been perfect. Too perfect, upon reflection, but Evie was naïve then. She assumed that was how it was meant to be. Together all the time. Inseparable, with an insatiable desire for making love. Any time they were alone, Neil would pull her to him, and press himself against her. Always hard. Always ready to take her. Sometimes there and then, sometimes teasing her and keeping her on the cusp for what seemed like eternity. And Evie was always a willing participant. She enjoyed being the centre of Neil's attention. His devotion gave her a sense of security, and he was a skilful lover. Strong. Commanding. Exciting. As long as she kept saying yes, and as long as they were each other's world, they lived a happy life.

The day she took Tess home, things changed.

Neil wanted to know how long he'd have to wait before he and Evie could have sex, but Evie couldn't give a definite answer. She'd requested time to recover, time to adjust to motherhood, and time to get used to her new body, and its new functions. Her response angered Neil, but Evie brushed it aside, putting his behaviour down to the stress and worry of becoming a parent. She assumed the enormity of the situation was hitting home and making him unreasonable.

Three weeks on, and Neil was still demanding sex, making crude attempts to fondle Evie into action, but no matter how hard she tried, she couldn't think of her breasts as objects of sexual pleasure. They were heavy and sore and smothered in a cream the chemist had recommended, held in a maternity bra twenty-four seven, and covered with pads to stop the milk leaking through. They were no longer accessible to Neil to do with as he pleased. No longer a starting point for an orgasm. And there was no way Evie could think of them in that way. Breasts were for feeding and nourishing Tess.

Swigging from a bottle of rum, Neil expressed his unhappiness at the situation, and laid down the law.

'Sex is our foundation,' he'd said. 'It ensures we centre on one another. That we pay attention to each other's wants and needs. It lets us thrash out our frustrations. And don't tell me you don't like it. You get off on what I do to you.' He'd licked his lips, gazed at Evie's engorged breasts and had shaken his head. 'What a waste. Don't think for one minute I'm happy about this. Two months. No more. And no excuses after that. I don't want to hear you're tired, that you've been up all night with the squirt, that you don't have time. You're to make yourself available at my request, and *we will* resume the husband and wife relationship I've worked hard at building and maintaining. And I never want to hear the word *no* again.' He'd adjusted the crotch on his trousers, and he'd emitted a low groan. 'You see how much I want you? I'd have you now if *she* wasn't surgically attached to you.'

He'd walked away and within seconds Evie had heard the bolt to the bathroom door slide into place. He hadn't bothered being quiet, clearly making sure Evie knew what he was doing to himself, and when he had finished.

As time marched on it became apparent Neil blamed Tess for the lack of *intimacy*, as he called it, in his life, displaying obvious signs of resentment towards the baby. He blamed nothing on his ever-increasing intake of alcohol.

'You're always with *her*,' he'd said. 'Pandering to *her* needs. What about me? It's your duty to fulfil *my* needs, too. Show me your love's not all invested in *her*. What has she got that's so special, anyway? The little shit machine.'

It shocked and upset Evie that her love for Tess enraged Neil. He was jealous of the attention Evie gave her. Jealous of the time she spent with her. Jealous of the love and bond between them. And one way or another, he insisted Evie would show him the same depth of love. She would show him the same degree of respect. And if she didn't give it, he would take it, until she remembered how to love him as a husband – wholly and without distraction.

When the atmosphere in the house thickened and stole their breath, and when Neil prowled around from room to room, whispering their names, Evie called him to her. She put herself in the way. She took beatings, verbal abuse and sexual violence to stop him getting to Tess.

As she'd promised at Tess's birth, she protected her. She'd protected her daughter from her own father; a man whose jealousy threatened to tear their world apart.

'I know it's something we don't talk about, but he's in my head. Too much. If he's left me with scars …'

Tess's unfinished sentence dragged Evie away from the horrors of her mind. 'Scars?' she said, giving herself time to catch up with the conversation. 'What scars?'

'Mental scars, Mum.' Tess fidgeted in her seat. 'The sort that never heal because no one can reach them to give them the proper care. I reckon we both have them.'

It was a frank and mature observation, awash with understanding far beyond Tess's fifteen years. Its honesty almost drowned Evie, flooding her heart with sorrow and regret, and deluging her conscience with sudden insecurities and guilt. She'd taken the decision for her and Tess to not speak about Neil; to never discuss what Tess had seen, or what Evie had endured. At the time Tess was young, and it had been the right thing to do, but Evie hadn't considered what the effect would be on her daughter in later years.

Perhaps it was time to talk.

'I have nightmares,' she said. 'About your father.'

'I know.' Tess remained seated, with her arms still linked behind her back. 'I've heard you call out in your sleep.'

Evie dropped her tangerine. 'What have I said?' This

was the part of her life she hadn't shared with Griff. She didn't want her past to alter his perception of her, nor did she want the shouting in her sleep to give her away. 'Have I called his name?'

Tess shook her head. 'And it's only been since Griff left. I don't remember you doing it before.'

Relieved, Evie took in a deep, extended breath. 'That's something,' she said, once more offering her hand to Tess. 'If I decide to tell Griff about Neil, I'd like it to be when I'm awake.' She paused, waiting for Tess to grasp her hand. 'Why won't you take it?' she asked. 'You always used to hold my hand.'

'You're thirty-eight, Mum. I don't need to hold your hand any more.'

'Maybe I need to hold yours, though, if we're going to talk about your father.'

The sigh Tess released caused a disturbance to the loose pith on the table. Her shoulders dropped and she brought her arms to the front. 'I'll take Dylan through to the living room and put a DVD on for him, then we can talk.' She yanked her sleeves down, pushed herself up from her chair and herded Dylan into the hallway.

Evie continued to lament the loss of Tess's childhood. It had been taken from her too early. Even at fifteen she should have been carefree, worrying only about the latest fashion, or which of the three boys who'd asked her out she should date. But Neil had stolen her youth, not by anything he did to her, but by what she saw him do to Evie.

He'd thrown Evie against the basin in the bathroom. He'd grabbed her hair, pulled her head back, and forced his way into her. It had taken all of Evie's concentration and effort to remain silent, allowing no yell or whimper to pass her lips, despite her tears, but Neil was vocal, explicit and loud. When, to her horror, Evie saw Tess standing on the landing witnessing the violence, she prayed the five-year-old would leave before Neil spotted her and headed in her direction.

Evie had rushed to her in her room as soon as she was able; as soon as she could walk without trembling, fearful of what Tess would say, scared of what she would ask. She was petrified as to how she would answer.

Just as she was terrified now of the conversation that lay ahead.

But ten years ago, Tess had said nothing, seeking only the comfort of her mother's arms.

Evie doubted that would suffice now.

'Dylan's watching his *Noddy* collection.' Tess resumed her seat. 'Can't say I'm a fan. He's a little high-pitched and energetic for my liking. Noddy, not Dylan.'

'You never did like him. Noddy, not Dylan.' It wasn't the opener Evie had expected, but she could see how talking about Tess's childhood would lead to Neil. 'You were a *Tweenies* and *Teletubbies* girl, with Barbie films thrown in for good measure.' Evie smiled at the reminiscence. 'You loved *Barbie of Swan Lake* and *Barbie in the Nutcracker*. We used to turn the volume right up when your dad was at work.'

'I used to turn it right up when he was home.'

'You did?' It wasn't a memory Evie could bring forward. 'Your father wouldn't have allowed that. He hated noise.' Neil deemed anything other than sports programmes or action films as noise, and when he was in residence he alone had access to the TV remote. 'I think you're remembering it wrongly.'

'Nope.' Tess rubbed at her wrist.

'Is that scald still giving you pain?' Evie motioned for Tess to show her, but Tess ducked her arms under the table. 'We should get it checked over.'

'No. It's just itchy, Mum. Means it's getting better.' Tess pulled her chair in tight to the table. 'And I'm not remembering the thing about the TV wrong. My memory is in full working order. And I don't just remember, I hear and see things. In high def, too.'

'But you were just a child, Tess. It's easy to get memories muddled. And sometimes we think we've remembered something, but it's a manufactured thought, brought on by seeing a photo or having heard someone relate the story.' Evie stopped the instant she realised what she was saying. 'Sorry. I think that's what's called deflection, or denial. I don't really know. It's some or other psychobabble thing. Avoidance, maybe.' She brushed her hair away from her neck, draping it over her left shoulder. The air was immediately and gratifyingly cooling. 'Please understand how hard this is for me. I'm not convinced talking about our past will help either of us.' She avoided eye contact with her daughter, but could sense her glare.

'I used to turn the sound up when he was home, upstairs, with you,' Tess said, her determination to continue apparent in her firm and steady tone. 'After the first time I saw him ... *at you* ... I'd turn the TV up. So I couldn't hear.'

'The first time?' Evie brought her gaze up to meet Tess's. Her eyes were like lasers, targeted on Evie's conscience. 'The first time?' she repeated, whispering.

'I didn't know what he was doing to you,' Tess continued, 'not at the time, but you were crying, and I thought about the times I cried and why I cried, and I knew you must be hurting. And I didn't like it.' She paused, but Evie and the truth were clearly in her sights. 'Yes. The first time, Mum. I saw him *at you* more than once.'

Chapter Eighteen

Griff

Using his teeth to pull his glove off, Griff reached into his trouser pocket and fished out his keys. 'I can't believe how cold it is,' he said, his fingers numb from the icy wind. 'It was so warm yesterday.' The waist-high, red brick wall separating Logan's house from the path gave no protection from the elements. 'I wish Dad would add a decent porch on instead of this pointless door canopy. If nothing else, it would shelter him from the traffic as he comes and goes.'

It wasn't a heartfelt gripe – it was a few distracted words spoken to conceal Griff's hesitation in entering his father's home. They hadn't seen one another in recent months, and Griff acknowledged that was down to him, but he was convinced he was shielding them both from upsetting and unnecessary grief. Their meetings would end in an almighty row, with Logan exhausted from all the shouting and Griff frustrated and angry at not being heard. It was unhealthy and destructive.

He searched through his bunch of keys and identified Logan's.

Visiting his father was the right thing to do, and it was the only way to put into practice Griff's resolution to be a better son.

It was Imogen who'd pointed out time was not on Logan's side.

'He's not a young man any more,' she'd said, when she and Griff had met for a coffee. 'And I imagine Logan's set in his ways. You say you don't get on because you're too similar, then I say, be different.' She'd made it sound so simple. 'If you want change, Griff, it'll have to come from you. Why don't you visit him on his birthday?'

Griff had berated himself at the time. Evie had made these points in the past, but he hadn't been ready to listen then.

He truly was his father's son.

He was about to unlock Logan's door when, from behind him, Imogen spoke. 'Don't you think you should knock first?'

Griff peered over his shoulder. 'I think Evie goes straight in.'

Imogen pulled a face. 'That's their arrangement, and he expects her at certain times. We've pitched up out of the blue. On his birthday. He could have guests. He could be entertaining.' She splayed her hands out in a *don't you think?* gesture.

'Entertaining? What sort of entertaining?' Griff returned the hand signal, but partnered his with a frown.

'You know. *Entertaining*. A woman. Good grief, Griff. You're hard work.'

Amused by Imogen's exasperation, Griff laughed. 'I take your point, but let's not dwell on it.' He looked back at the door, stepped away and raised his knuckles to the wood.

'There's a doorbell.' Imogen's slim finger appeared in his peripheral vision as she pressed the small brass dome embedded in the doorframe. 'We'll wait a few seconds, then ring again and go in. It's the right thing to do, especially if you want to keep Logan on side. Let's start off on the right foot.'

Griff raised his left knee. 'Right foot. Got it.'

His corny attempt at humour was rewarded with a generous smile from Imogen, followed by a less charitable shove to his elbow. He slammed his foot onto the path to avoid toppling over. 'You're here to make sure I keep both feet on the floor, then?' he said, arching his brow.

'Who bought you a joke book for Christmas?'

'The same person who gave you the book on diplomacy.'

The banter felt good. Familiar. Which in itself was odd because as youths they didn't possess the necessary skills to produce friendly banter. It was mostly requests from Kieran and Griff for Imogen to behave, or bullish commands for her to go away.

He could see her in his mind's eye, in her red corduroy dungarees, hanging off the handle to Kieran's bedroom door, begging to be included in whatever it was she thought teenage lads got up to. She was hanging off Logan's door now, waiting to discover what it was seventy-five-year-olds got up to on their birthday.

At least she'd progressed from the dungarees.

'You look nice,' Griff said. 'The make-up and stuff.' He'd thought that when he'd collected her from her house. Her style worked for her. Her short, cream and cranberry summer-weight dress, whilst a little optimistic for the time of year, showed her figure to its full advantage, including her legs, which Griff considered fit for any catwalk. Who said models had to be Amazonian? Five foot four worked for him.

Evie was shorter, at five foot three, but as far as Griff was concerned she towered over the super-models. She was petite and slim, with everything in proportion, and a mouth that mesmerised him. She could cast all sorts of spells with those lips.

He missed kissing. The intimacy it created between him and Evie was incredible; unique. It started with her eyes. Always the eyes. Green, soft, hot, luring him in. But beyond the heat and sensuality, there was a vulnerability he was yet to understand. Her kisses asked questions, but left Griff in no doubt about the strength of her love or her faith for him. He'd hoped to one day answer those questions.

The muffled barking of Ozzy and Honey drew Griff's attention to his Land Rover parked roadside. As soon as he raised his head, the dogs jumped themselves into a frenzy, tails wagging so fast they became a blur. 'They need to come out,' he said, turning to Imogen, momentarily confused at who he saw. He'd been so deep in thought about Evie he'd forgotten he was no longer with her. He pushed the heels of his hands into his eyes and admonished himself.

'Are you deliberately trying to wind your dad up? Leave the dogs where they are. We'll ask if we can bring them into the house. We mustn't assume it's okay.' Imogen pressed the bell button for the second time. 'That was a funny look you gave me a moment ago.'

'Was it?' Griff didn't feel the need to explain. 'Shall we go in, then?' He slotted the key into the lock, twisted it to the right and nodded for Imogen to turn the handle. 'Dad? It's me.' He entered the hall and slipped off his coat. 'Come in,' he said to Imogen. 'We need to close the door before the warmth escapes.'

Imogen stepped forward and wiped her feet on the doormat. 'What warmth?'

'Yeah. It is a bit chilly in here.' A taster of the icy reception he was expecting? Griff pushed the door shut and offered to take Imogen's coat. She declined.

'I need to acclimatise first.' She ran her fingers along the top of the radiator situated beneath the coat hooks. 'He's not got the heating on. I trust he's okay.'

The same thought occurred to Griff and all his other concerns fell away. 'Dad?' he tried again. 'I've brought someone to see you.'

Still no reply. He puffed out his cheeks, gave a half-shrug and opened the door to the living room. Logan was sitting crumpled and hunched in a green chair, his withered frame half the size Griff remembered. The chair and the television were different, too; both items Logan would have once asked Griff to research before committing to buying. The uneasy sensation of redundancy swept over Griff. First Evie, now his father, proving they could manage without Griff in their lives.

'Pack it in, Hendry,' he said to himself. *Being in control of your destiny is a good thing.* It was how he lived his life. Besides, he and his father hadn't been close for years. Although, that was Griff's call.

'I suppose Evie's told you, then,' Logan said.

'Told me?' Without waiting to be invited, Griff opened the door to its fullest extent, and crossed the threshold. 'She didn't have to tell me, Dad. I remember when your birthday is.' He took a seat on the sofa. 'Happy birthday. I thought I could take you out for a beer to celebrate. How are you?'

'I wasn't talking about my birthday, and if you wanted a truthful answer to your question you'd have been to see me a long time ago.'

Logan raised a shaky, insubstantial hand, infirm and exposed, but it possessed the strength to send a powerful shock straight to Griff's stomach. He'd openly accused Evie of letting Logan take advantage of her kind nature, positive his father was fitter and healthier than he let on. The last time Griff had seen him, Logan was stronger, but that was not the same man seated in the new green chair.

Griff swallowed away the lump forming in his throat and breathed away the gathering mist of guilt. 'Not so good, then.' Aware Imogen had entered the room, Griff signalled for her to join him on the sofa. He didn't often need moral support, but having her there was a comfort. Safety in numbers, he thought.

'Do you remember Imogen Joliffe – Kieran's sister? We bumped into each other a few weeks ago.' He waited for Logan's acknowledgement.

'Of course I do. Is this she?'

Imogen rose from the sofa, used Griff's shoulder for support as she stepped over his feet, and crouched at the side of Logan's chair. 'Happy birthday, Mr Hendry. You haven't changed a bit.' She took his hand and kissed the back of it. 'It's wonderful to see you after all this time.'

'That's what I should be saying to my errant son over there.' Logan greeted Imogen's kiss with a weak smile. 'I'd like to say *you've* not changed a bit, but it's good to see you out of those wretched dungarees.' As the smile grew, it appeared to strengthen Logan's spine. He wriggled back in his chair and lifted his head. 'I see you still like red, though.'

Imogen had defused the bomb Griff was certain his father was ready to deploy.

Now able to relax, he pointed to the huge screen suspended on the wall next to the understairs cupboard. 'New TV? What is it? Sixty, seventy inch? I've been to smaller cinemas.'

It was meant as a joke.

'I don't get out much,' said Logan. 'I don't have visitors, other than Evie and Tess. I can't hold a decent sized book, and I can't get outside to tend to my garden. So what if I have a big TV? I'd say it's my one pleasure in life, but it would be a lie. There are no pleasures in my life. If it wasn't for your wife and daughter, I'd go days without seeing another human. And the TV is six months old.'

Griff flinched as the accusations hit him. He could give any number of reasons as to why he hadn't visited, but it was obvious Logan was in no mood to hear them. Nice to know his father's mind wasn't failing him. Griff put his hands together and sat on the edge of his seat. He'd start with an apology – perhaps that would pave the way to a full and frank discussion whereby he could explain his actions and tell Logan about the separation from Evie. He cleared his throat. 'I'm sorry, Dad. I should've come to see you more often. I should have made an effort to sort out our differences.'

'Six years is a long time to hold a grudge.' Logan worked his hand free from Imogen. 'Would you put the kettle on, please, Imy? I've not had anything to drink since Evie was here at breakfast. I think she said there's chocolate powder in the cupboard if you fancy that. It's what a slip of a girl like you needs on a day like this. I'll have a decaf.'

'Imy.' Imogen laughed as she stood. 'I haven't been called that in a very long time, Mr Hendry.'

'You don't mind, do you? And please call me Logan. We're all adults now.'

Griff pointed the way to the kitchen and looked on as Imogen vanished around the corner.

'I'm not holding a grudge,' he said, once he and Logan were alone. 'And I've seen plenty of you in those six years. You were at my wedding, Dad. You've met Dylan. You've been over for Sunday lunches. You make it sound like I walked away and left you to get on with it.' He detected a slight movement of Logan's shoulders, and matched with the resentment in his father's eyes, it was evident Logan didn't agree. 'I'm not holding a grudge.'

'So you keep saying.' Logan lowered the footrest of his chair, and inch by inch, twisted his body round to face Griff. 'I did the right thing by your mother. She asked for my support and I gave it. She believed in quality, not quantity, and at the time we discussed withdrawing her treatment, she had neither. She was already a terminal patient. She had already lost her dignity in life, and I thought it right she wanted dignity in dying. She deserved it. You have no idea how hard it is to accept help, to allow people to see you at your worst, to wait to be taken to the toilet, to clean up your mess. You're strong and healthy, and you have control over your life. You rely on no one but yourself, and I pray you always will, because this ...' He waved his trembling hand around the room. '... no matter what others do for you, is not living. This is barely even surviving.'

His father's words challenged Griff. He dragged his hand over his chin. He'd heard all of this six years ago and hadn't accepted it then. Everything and everyone was worth saving.

He'd argued at the time that a cure could be found at any given moment, that medical advances were being made in leaps and bounds, that one more treatment could be enough to change the prognosis. He'd fought for his mother's life with as much belief and as much passion as Logan had fought for her release. Griff had understood it was Marilyn's choice, but he had a child's faith in his dad to do the right thing – to encourage Marilyn to live, to keep fighting; to let her know she was wanted. But Logan gave up and gave in, and that was the bitterest pill Griff had ever swallowed. Logan was not the man of Griff's youthful ideals.

The day his mother died, Griff grieved for the loss of both his parents.

He'd learned to love his father differently since then.

'How do you take your coffee, Logan?' Imogen's voice drifted into the living room.

'I'll come and do it.' Glad of a reason to create breathing space between him and his father, Griff jumped up from the sofa and joined Imogen in the kitchen.

She leaned against the counter. 'What did Logan mean about you holding a grudge?'

'Not now.' Eager to hide his shame, Griff opened the fridge and ducked behind its door. 'I can't get over how Dad's deteriorated so quickly. I thought he was putting on Evie, but she really has her work cut out.' He removed the milk carton, stood it next to the kettle, and elbowed shut the fridge door.

A gentle hand was laid on his forearm.

'Hasn't she said anything?'

Squeezing his eyes shut, Griff tried to recall the last few conversations he'd had with his wife. When he next looked at Imogen, she was pouring hot water into three mugs. 'Dad takes his white without sugar, like me.'

'I take it black with one sugar.' Logan's order was received loud and clear.

'He's making a point,' Griff said. 'Proving to me things have changed and I know nothing about them. Make sure you top his cup right up.' He collected a teaspoon from the cutlery drawer, added sugar from a nearby jar, and stirred the coffee until he could no longer feel the sweet grit. 'I wonder if this is why Evie wanted me to visit.' He chucked the spoon into the sink and it landed with a clatter. 'Why didn't she just tell me? She knows I like directness.'

'And you could have taken some of the pressure off her,' Imogen supplied.

'I'd already suggested full-time carers. Admittedly, it was more for my sake than Evie's, but she vetoed it anyway. Wanted to do it all herself. I started to believe she came here to avoid thrashing things out with me, but once we separated ... Well ... I don't know.' He stared through the window, not really acknowledging there was a magpie on the garage roof, but registering its plumage. 'Not everything is black and white, is it?' He nudged Imogen's hot chocolate towards her, and picked up his and Logan's drinks. 'Except our coffees, apparently.'

With Imogen taking the lead, the pair returned to the living room.

'Coffee. Black. One sugar.' Griff attempted to hand Logan the mug, but he was dismissed with a shake of the head.

'It's too full.'

'I thought you liked it to the brim.' On the occasions Griff had made drinks for his father, he'd been sent back to the kitchen to add more water. 'I was saving you the trouble of joking about the vicar coming to tea. That was the phrase, wasn't it?' Griff smiled, trying to lighten a situation that had rapidly gained weight. He glanced at Imogen. 'I think it was in reference to the empty centimetre around the rim looking like a vicar's collar.' Returning to Logan, he said, 'That's right, isn't it?'

Logan mumbled a few unintelligible words into his chest and then lifted his chin. 'It's too full. I'll spill it.'

Had Evie told Griff his father was unable to hold a full cup he'd have probably dismissed it as another of Logan's attention seeking tactics. He'd have asked Evie to help his father by letting him help himself, and to believe she would still be loved if sometimes she said no. A day ago – Jeez – an hour ago, the inability to hold a full cup would have seemed such an inconsequential problem, but now ...

'I'll deal with it.' Imogen rescued the mug from Griff, and left the room.

Griff collapsed onto the sofa, immediately fighting with the cushion he'd squashed. He yanked it out from behind his back and threw it into the chair opposite. 'Stupid thing.' His remark was aimed at the cushion, but meant for himself. If he'd had the courage to face his fears, his and Logan's differences would have been sorted years ago, and this moment, *now*, wouldn't have been a shock to Griff.

For the second time in his life, he had to adjust his perception of his father.

This once powerful man was reduced to a twig, with liver spots dotting his arms, red veins mapping his eyes, and bony fingers barely capable of lifting a glass. In what? Six, nine months? This man's hands were capable of saving lives; of using and manipulating precision equipment; of caring for Marilyn at her very worst; of grasping Griff's palm and congratulating him on the birth of his child. The one photo Griff had of Logan holding Dylan was most likely the last. Imagine never being able to hold your grandchild. Imagine … No. Griff's thoughts were getting out of hand. Control was required. Calm, efficient, orderly control.

'How do you manage when Evie's not here?' It was the right place to start. Assess the current status and move on from there.

'I stay put. I watch TV. My big TV. Until Evie arrives.'

Griff risked a glimpse of his father. 'What about eating and drinking?'

'I wait for Evie.'

'And the toilet?'

'Unless I'm desperate, I wait for Evie.'

With every answer ending in his wife's name, Griff's methodical approach was swiftly sabotaged. His mind filled with pictures of the times he thought Evie was running away; with the hours he'd wasted thinking she'd rather be at Logan's than with him; with all the quiet pleas he'd ignored about visiting his dad; with all the guilt that false accusation, doubt and assumption dispensed.

The juggernaut of emotions jack-knifed, and a convoy of questions backed up in Griff's head, each one shunting into the last. It was a car crash of whats, whys and whens, with piercing screams for help, and alerts and alarms he'd failed to heed. And it made his brow throb.

He massaged his temples with his thumbs. It was a futile attempt to soothe the pain. A temporary fix was not the solution. Healing required time and understanding. He straightened his posture. 'How did things get so difficult so quickly?'

'It only seems that way to you because you've been living life in the fast lane.'

The lane that's jammed up with questions, Griff thought. 'So, how long?'

Without interrupting the conversation, Imogen appeared and placed Logan's coffee in his hands, soundlessly slipping past the green chair to sit next to Griff.

'I had a flare-up just after Dylan was born. It was downhill from then on.' Logan targeted his attention on the mug.

'But we've met since then.' Griff accepted he hadn't been the most attentive son in recent years, but he was certain he'd seen Logan every few months. 'You weren't like this last time.'

'Like what?'

'Well ... Disabled.' The word sat awkwardly on Griff's tongue.

Logan let out a strangled grunt. 'I've been disabled since your mother died.'

A considerable silence filled the room as Logan managed a sip of his drink. 'Thank you, Imy,' he said, resting the mug on his lap. 'It's a good temperature. You added cold water?'

'Just a drop or two, to take the edge off.'

'You're a thoughtful girl.' Using one hand to support the bottom, and the other to pinch at the handle, Logan lifted the mug to his mouth again, and drank until he declared the coffee gone. 'Is your cooking as good as your brewing skills?'

'I pride myself on the fact I've never killed anyone with my food, either by throwing it at them or them eating it.' Imogen laughed. 'That's as good as it gets. I take it you were thirsty.'

Logan motioned towards an empty glass on the small table beside his chair. 'I finished that straight after Evie left this morning. She won't be here for another hour.'

'You could do with a fridge in here,' Imogen said. 'Your own mini bar.'

'Now you're talking.' Logan's face broke from its grimace. 'Evie's never suggested that.'

Griff observed the interaction with interest, thinking how now was not the time for humour, but as his father's face creased into a smile, he was forced to revise his opinion. It was good to see a glimmer of happiness in Logan's eyes.

Relaxing and reclining, Griff gave Imogen the floor. Her performance was greater than his by far.

'Logan,' she said. 'A smile. How lovely. I can see you've not lost any of those handsome Highland features. You always had a smile on your face. It's how I picture you in my mind's eye.'

'You still think about me?' Logan's frown made a reappearance, but it was softened with puzzlement. 'Why?'

Imogen's head tilted as she threaded her fingers together and raised her hands to her mouth. A thoughtful pose, Griff decided.

It was a moment before she spoke.

'You were close to my dad.'

It was a simple enough statement, presented in an uncomplicated manner, yet it was packed with complex and volatile matter. Griff inched closer to his father, and braced himself, aware of the potential explosion.

He'd only broached the subject of Imogen's dad once in the last few weeks, but had rapidly regretted doing so.

Caught somewhere between expecting him to be dead and hoping he was alive, Imogen was yet to grieve for her dad. Years of zero contact had left her in a permanent state of limbo where he was concerned. She told Griff that the moment she laid eyes on her father, she'd hug and throttle him with equal pressure, whether he was on this plane or had transcended or descended to another world.

She'd laughed at the reference to hell, and then, releasing what must have been years of stress, worry and upset, she'd thrown herself at Griff, pressed her face to his chest, and dug her nails into his shoulders. With every convulsion she issued a great, heaving sob that made Griff's heart pump harder and faster. It reminded him of how Evie described the effect Dylan's crying had on her; how he felt when a shout went out at work.

It was a call to action.

His response was to offer Imogen brotherly comfort, a steadying arm, and time for the scenario to play out.

He hadn't expected the kiss. Imogen said it was a simple thank you for him being so kind, but when he suggested a peck to the cheek would have been enough, she dabbed his lips with her fingertips and made no further comment. He chose to believe her. To over-think it and give it significance was dangerous. He wasn't looking for anything from her other than forgiveness and friendship.

The next day he'd taken his jacket to the dry cleaner's to have the tear and mucus stains removed. Handing it over to the shop assistant proved difficult. It felt like betrayal, as if Griff was wiping out all traces of Imogen's pain. Pain for which he was responsible.

'What's wrong with him?' Logan's timely question to Imogen put Griff back in the room, preventing him from delving any deeper into the complexities of betrayal. As if sensing his apprehension, Imogen patted his knee, and laid her hand to rest.

'It's all right,' she whispered. 'I'm in a much better place than before.'

'What did you say?' Logan leaned forward. 'I couldn't hear you.'

'Griff's colour drained at the mention of my dad,' Imogen said. 'The last time we spoke about him, I had a meltdown. I was just reassuring Griff it won't happen again.'

'That's a word our Tess uses. Meltdown. Everybody

seems to have them these days.' There was an air of triumph to Logan's statement. 'Not bad for someone of my age to be *down with the kids*. So, why the drama surrounding your father? Is he dead?'

The house wasn't warm enough to make a penguin sweat, yet the heat from Imogen's palm was seeping through Griff's jeans.

'I don't know,' Imogen said. 'He left some time ago. He and Mum divorced.'

The coolness of her reply belied the story of anxiety her hand was telling. Griff's knee was uncomfortably hot.

Imogen continued. 'Seeing you smile, hearing you talk – it puts me within touching distance of my dad.' She removed her hand and gathered her hair into a ponytail. 'Sounds silly now I've said it out loud.'

'It's not silly.' Logan, his expression now one of contemplation, was studying Griff's face. 'It's how I feel about Marilyn when I see my son.'

Chapter Nineteen

Tess

I'm worried that I've told Mum too much. She's in a state of shock, dead still and silent, and not seeing any further than the back of her eyes. I bet she's going through all the visuals she's stored there. I know I do. It's like a slide show sometimes.

I wish I could climb inside her head and see things from her perspective, then I'd know. Then I'd be able to help.

I wish I could hold her hand and remind her we're in this together, but I can't risk her seeing my scars. One revelation is plenty to keep us in emotional turmoil for the foreseeable future, and I need to have this conversation about Dad. Here it goes.

'Why did it happen? Why did he do it? Was he unhinged? Drunk? Did he tell you it was because he loved you?'

Mum stirs, raising her head and levelling her troubled eyes on mine. 'Why'd you say that? Did he say those things to you?'

Despite the fear in her voice, I can't help but snort. 'He hated me,' I say. 'I learned that early on.'

Her head drops again, like she's lost her backbone. It looks like she's praying. Maybe she is. Maybe she's asking for forgiveness, or the will to vocalise her past. I stoop to check, but her eyes are open and her lips are sealed. 'And that's the problem,' I say. 'You don't talk.'

Her chest fills with air. 'It was a horrible time in our lives, Tess. Why do you want to relive it?'

She's addressing the table. It seems I have to shock her into looking at me. 'I relive it every day.'

That does the trick. I have her full attention.

'What do you see?'

She's surprised me with that question. I expected her to shut me down – to dam and divert the flow, not swish it along. Good. I'm glad. I have lots to say.

'I see him slapping you. Leering at you. Sometimes I hear the door squeak, even though you oil every hinge in the house.'

She brings her hands to her mouth as if preventing herself from responding.

'Sometimes I see him in the bathroom, and I can smell his aftershave.' I can't stop my lip trembling in disgust.

'But he's never been here.' Mum talks through her fingers. 'And Griff wears a different cologne.'

Cologne Mum buys Griff every Christmas to make sure.

'I know, but being in the bathroom is enough.' I pause to blow my nose, hoping to shift the stench lodged there. 'You're there too. Being sick.' We both know what my dad was doing to her, so I don't need to be explicit. 'Nothing stopped him, did it?'

She gags and I rush to retrieve a plastic bowl from under the sink. I put it in front of her, then fetch her a glass of water.

Satisfied Mum's not about to vomit, I continue. 'There are times when I wake in the middle of the night and I think I hear you crying, saying *no*, over and over again. It's so real, I call out for you and when I get no reply, I come into your room. You're fast asleep. In Griff's arms. In reality, it's only since he left you've *actually* cried out. All those other times were … echoes.' It's a good word. It captures how it sounds in my head.

'Echoes.'

Mum repeats my word. I think it resonates with her.

'What else?' she says.

I flick to the next scene in my head. 'You and him in the car, parked outside our house. There's snow, and a dog's howling from somewhere down the street.'

The fingers from her left hand drift towards her throat. 'You saw that?'

'I'm seeing it now.' It was our old Astra. Blue, with alloy wheels. A sport version. Showy. 'The babysitter thought I'd gone to bed, but I was looking out of your bedroom window. I was worried he wouldn't bring you home.'

Mum collapses into the table, and supports her head with her hands. 'Oh, Tess.'

Either she couldn't bring herself to say any more, or the horror of the moment had stolen her voice. It had taken what was left of her colour.

'I was ten, nearly eleven. I thought he was going to kill you.'

They'd pulled up under the street lamp a few feet away from our house. I could see them through the windscreen. As soon as the engine was off, Dad crashed his hands down onto the steering wheel. He was ranting; shouting at Mum. She was shaking her head and holding her hands up to her face, much like she was now. I watched from the first floor, using experience to predict Dad's next move. *Get out of the car*, I said. *Get out of the car, before he grabs your hair*. But Mum just sat there. I remember thinking she must have been frozen with fear. I'd been like that when my maths teacher yelled at me. I'd had to sit there and take it, because I was too scared to move.

Dad rammed his seat back, snatched at Mum's hair and gave it a vicious tug. Her mouth jammed open at the violent jerk. He was still yelling as he crushed her throat with his free hand. *This is it*, I whispered. *He's going to strangle her.* How could I stop him? What could I do? I was just a child. And I was glued to the spot. I was seized by fear, and incapable of moving. Even my scream came to no more than a pathetic whimper. I was in a living nightmare.

At the moment Mum's head started to loll, Dad released her neck and pushed her face into his lap. Her head bounced as her cheek banged against the steering wheel.

Then all was still, except Dad's chest, which was heaving. I couldn't see Mum, just a hunched, dark shadow. Was she dead? Was Dad crying? Was that what he was doing?

And then the black shadow moved, pulled up by the hair, and shoved down by my dad's hands. Up, down. Up, down. Up. Down.

Up.

With her head in view, suspended by her hair, Dad closed his eyes, threw himself against the padded rest, and opened his mouth. He let Mum's head fall.

As soon as she was free, she clambered out of the car, ran to the house, and let herself in.

I ran to my bedroom and hid under my covers.

Shadows and echoes haunt me.

They're haunting now, as Mum uses her cardigan sleeve to wipe away her tears.

'Did you ... Did you realise what was going on?' She stiffens and sits up.

'I knew you were scared. I could see he had his hand around your throat.'

'But did you—' She puts her palms up in the stop position and edits herself.

It doesn't matter. I've already worked out she's asking if I realised he was forcing her to go down on him. 'I had no idea what oral sex was, Mum. Not then. But I could see how frightened you were. I knew he had a furious temper, and I knew he used threats and violence to control people. He made you do things you didn't want to do. He was a bully. He was evil.'

176

I'd thought that about him for years, but it was the first time I'd put it out there. I'm waiting for a reaction, either from Mum or from some greater power. I'm half expecting the ground to break open, a fiery hand to reach out, grab at my leg, and pull me into the burning bowels. Not that I believe in Lucifer. Although I do wonder if a person's energy survives long after their body's rotted. I'm prepared to accept that ghosts exist in that form.

I remember that Mum hasn't answered my question. 'Is that why he did those things? Was it because he was pure evil?'

She swallows, then takes a sip of her water. 'He wasn't always like that.'

That answer implies more than I believe she wanted it to. I don't think she's making excuses for him, and she's not questioning my use of *evil*, so something must have happened to awaken his latent nature. 'What changed?'

Mum takes a breath, as if to answer, and then nothing.

'Don't you ever feel him?' I say. 'Sense him?' I need to know. 'I've carried this stuff in my head for years, because you and I ... we ... made a pact to keep the secret and bury it somewhere inaccessible. But that's never happened. Every time a shadow appears on the wall, every time I hear you cry, every time a man looks at me, I'm back to being that child.' Back to feeling useless and helpless and unworthy of anyone's attention. 'He's in me – in my head, under my skin, in my blood, and I need to try and talk him out, because the alternative will—' It's my turn to leave a sentence hanging. My blade had become Damocles's sword.

'What's the alternative, Tess?' Mum's eyes are wide with suspicion and fright. 'What's the alternative?'

She's jumped off her chair, pulled me to her and has her hands on my face. I'm careful to put my arms around her, out of sight, out of harm's way, and I'm forced to backtrack.

'I don't know. I was being dramatic. I just want us to talk about what happened. And I want to learn about the good stuff, too. It's a relief to hear he wasn't always evil.' I worry I've pushed Mum too far, and I check her eyes. They're full of swell, but the water only magnifies the understanding behind. I push a little further. 'If you can bear to go there, I'll be by your side. And we can get all of this shit out of our heads and give it up to the skies.'

She's kissing my forehead, and her tears transfer to my cheeks. They blend easily with mine. 'You've been mixing with Olivia DeVere,' she says, between breaths.

It's a sunshine moment meant to alleviate the gloom.

'She gives it up to the sea, Mum,' I say, appreciating the break in the clouds. 'Reckon she's got life sussed.'

'Reckon so. Not like us.'

'We'll get there, Mum. I promise.' I mean it. 'But I think we need Griff's help.'

Her sudden breath whistles past my ear.

'You mean tell him?'

'He deserves to know.'

She releases her hold and approaches the patio door at the rear of the kitchen. Her back is to me.

'Is that why you think he's left?'

I can't prevent myself from shrugging even though Mum can't see me. 'I think it could be a reason. Secrets have a way of announcing their presence.' *You should see my arms*, I want to say. 'He's a good man, you've said so yourself, and I've heard how much he makes you laugh, how much he cares for you. You've never shied away from him, or flinched if he's made a sudden move, and I've never heard him shout, or have a go, not in an angry way.' I take a moment to let my words settle. Mum continues to stare at the garden. 'I'm sorry I've given him such a hard time. It was my stupid attempt to protect you.'

'Misguided. Not stupid.'

She's wheeled round and is marching towards me.

'You are not and you never will be stupid.' She nets my hands before I'm able to retract them into my cuffs. I make sure we maintain eye contact. 'You are a bright, intelligent, loving daughter who's seen too much horror in her life, yet in spite of it you've grown into an amazing, wise, incredible young woman.' She encloses my fingers in hers, and I can feel her shaking. 'Okay,' she says. 'We'll talk. First I think I should tell you why Griff left.'

Chapter Twenty

Griff

The energy and joy Ozzy and Honey exuded at being set free to splash in the river was contagious. Other walkers commented at the fun the Old English Sheepdog and the Labrador were having chasing each other into the icy water. Griff nodded and issued polite and civil responses, but he wasn't feeling it himself. He was grateful for Imogen's suggestion that he give the dogs a run, as it gave him the chance to think: he was preoccupied with Logan's admission that seeing him brought Logan closer to Marilyn.

When Imogen had said the same thing about Logan and her father it had sent a shiver down Griff's neck. He'd rubbed his skin, half expecting to find a hair or feather there. When Logan stated his case, another shiver travelled from Griff's skull to his back, but this was more like a spider weaving its thread.

A sticky web of guilt and a telling off from Logan followed.

'Good grief, man. Have you never considered the possibility?' As Logan pressed the rocker switch on the chair controller, he indicated for Imogen to help him stand. 'Did you not think I miss you?'

'Because I look like Mum?'

'No. I miss *you*.' Logan's speech was laboured as his efforts went into leaning forward from the tilted chair. Imogen assisted, placing a hand under his elbow, and the other under his forearm. 'I miss my son.'

Sentimentality wasn't Logan's forte, so to have two confessions on the table within the space of a few seconds put Griff on guard.

'Is everything okay, Dad?'

The soft hum of the chair being returned to its sitting position was the only reply tendered.

'Would you help me into the kitchen, Imy?' Logan shuffled to his left, with Imogen still supporting him under his arm. His slippers scuffed at the carpet fibres. 'I'd like to take a look at the garden. Evie does most of it. She was born with green fingers.'

At the threshold between the living room and the kitchen, the pair came to a halt, and a breathless Logan spoke.

'I don't know why it surprises you, Griff. A father missing his son. You miss Dylan, don't you?'

Imogen peered over her shoulder and raised her brow. 'He knows,' she mouthed.

Mirroring Imogen's expression, Griff inclined his head. 'Yep,' he said, softly. 'So Evie's told you?' He watched as Logan and Imogen continued their course. They vanished from view.

Griff remained seated.

'I'm not talking about Evie, except to Imy about the garden. Your marriage and how you go about it is your business.' Logan's disembodied message was received. 'You miss your son. I miss mine. The fact you remind me of your mother is a bonus and a blessing, because her beautiful face is no longer here for me to gaze upon.'

Griff sat in quiet contemplation for some time before Logan, with Imogen leading the way, returned to the room.

'Garden's ready for April,' Logan said as he was settled into his chair. 'Evie's a natural. How's yours looking? Have you re-stained that decking?'

'The decking?' Griff was used to quick thinking – it was an essential skill in his line of work – but Logan's swift change of subject left Griff streets behind. 'No. I haven't stained the decking. I'm not even living at the cottage at the moment.'

'Like I said, that's not my business.'

Griff lurched forward. 'Yeah. I get your point, Dad. A marriage is between a husband and wife. And I have no right to an opinion about Mum choosing to die.' He froze at Imogen's frosty glare. It was enough to take the heat out of the moment. 'Sorry,' he said. 'It's an emotive subject.' And an aspect of Marilyn's passing he'd refrained from telling Imogen. 'I'll explain later.' She was owed that. 'I believe in fighting for life.'

'No matter how awful it is?' Logan rested his head on the high back of the chair, and closed his eyes. 'You're young, Griff. Fit. You've children to take care of. Death seems a long way off.' His eyes eased open, and he stared at the blank TV. 'I pray you're never put in my position. You'd make the wrong choices. Selfish choices, ultimately, because your view on life is skewed. Not everyone wants saving.'

This, again? 'How many more times do I have to say it? Everyone is *worth* saving.' Griff was on his feet. He'd come here to build bridges, not blow up the remaining foundations. 'Didn't you think Mum was worth saving?' He held his breath.

'Of course I did. But it wasn't about me.' Logan locked eyes with Griff. 'It was about what your mother wanted. I loved her. I let her go. Now you must do the same. With your mum and with Kieran.'

The mention of Kieran's name knocked Griff off-kilter at the same time as sending Imogen to the front window. He checked on her, and as soon as she signalled she was okay, he turned to Logan. 'What's Kieran got to do with this?'

'You can save a thousand lives,' Logan said, 'and a thousand more trying to find peace, but you will never bring Kieran back. Nor your mum. And that is what you have to deal with. That, and the fact there are far worse things in life than death.'

A young, dog-free couple walking hand-in-hand glanced at Griff. He held their stare for a moment, thinking how much life they had extending before them – love, optimism, youth – all things in their favour, and he wished them luck. Genuine, heartfelt luck.

He called Ozzy and Honey to heel and set off towards the road. It wasn't fair leaving Imogen with his father for too long, even if exercising the dogs was her idea. *Even* if she and Logan had hit it off.

She'd certainly made an impression on Logan, and Griff suspected it was mutual. There was a sincere and instant warmth between them, and Imogen was a salve to Logan's coarse manner. She soothed him, and eased his anxieties.

The dogs were still excitable as Griff reached the Land Rover. They were on their leads, straining, and testing Griff to his limits.

'Settle down,' he said, stopping yards from the vehicle. 'I can't have you bouncing around in the back of my car. Ozzy!'

The Old English Sheepdog barked at the call of his name. He jumped up, his lionesque paws thumping Griff's chest, his cold nose snuffling and snorting, and his warm tongue licking his master's cheek.

'All right, boy. I'm sorry. I love you too.' Griff reached into his pocket for two biscuits. 'It's Honey. She gets you all worked up.' He patted the Labrador's head, and addressed her. 'Ozzy's never had a girlfriend. Now, sit nicely and you can each have one of these.' He held up the bone-shaped treats. 'I just need a few minutes of calm before we head back.'

The sight of the reward encouraged both dogs to park their bottoms onto the path, their tails sweeping the dust and dirt into the gutter with speed and efficiency.

'Are there worse things in life than death?' Griff said,

wondering what the purpose was behind Logan's statement. 'What's worse than death? It's the be-all and end-all. The final destination. What could possibly be worse? And why would Dad say that?'

His mind occupied with images of his mother and Kieran, a distracted Griff threw the biscuits down.

Before he had time to register where they'd landed, the leads were yanked from his hand, and a gut-wrenching screech of tyres and a yelp of a dog hit his stomach.

Chapter Twenty-One

Tess

I think Mum's regretting telling me why Griff has moved out. She shouldn't. Stuff makes sense now. I knew she loved him.

You see, this is what *not* talking does. *Not* talking is destructive. It's good that she trusts me. She should. For a while it was just her and me, even when Dad was around, and as I grew older I took on the responsibility of caring for her. Not like she cares for Logan, but making sure she ate regularly, had a chance to rest, had someone to chat with, that sort of thing. She's brilliant at looking after others, but crap at taking care of herself. That's when we became tight. Unbreakable.

She's standing in the doorway. When I get to the top of the road, I'll stop, turn and wave. I always do when I cycle to Logan's.

I've offered to go over, sort out his lunch and tea, and help him get ready for bed. Mum said she'll come over once Griff is with Dylan, but she needs a bit of time to herself. I told her she's to stay at home. Logan and I will manage, and I can get a taxi back. Mum's not keen on me cycling in the dark. She's promised she'll sort stuff out with Griff and this evening is the perfect opportunity – I'll be out of the house and Dylan will be in bed. Not that he's any bother. He's totally involved in his *Noddy* marathon. He didn't disturb Mum or me once while we were talking. We both checked in on him, concerned about the quiet – always a suspicious sign in my experience – but he was happy, sitting on the floor, Enid Blyton books scattered at his feet, and the television lighting his smiling face.

He's going to break a few hearts when he's older.

My face will break mirrors. That's what my dad said. 'It's why you don't have friends,' he'd said. 'People can't bear to look at you. I can't bear to look at you. And don't blame me. I didn't give you that stupid, freaky hair.'

At eight years old, I believed him. At eight years old, I smashed my mirror. At eight years old, my one remaining friend called me a weirdo and stopped coming to the house.

I was ten when I realised Mum no longer had friends, and even her mum, not that we saw much of her, had disappeared off the radar. Dad's family had given up on us, too. I don't recall how or when their visits and phone calls stopped, they must have phased out, but I remember searching that year for Nan and Granddad's Christmas card, and Mum saying it must have been lost in the post. When nothing arrived on my eleventh birthday, I cried. Dad yelled at me for being a pathetic, over-sensitive female. He called me a ginger whinger, and told me to get over it. 'They're not interested in you any more,' he said.

Maybe Dad told his parents the same thing. Who knows what lies he spread about us? I think he must have stopped Mum seeing her friends, too. And goodness knows what happened to her mum.

I imagine this is what happens when a control freak rules your life.

It's pretty shit.

At eleven years old, it dawned on me it was him or us.

As promised, when I reach the T-junction I turn and wave to Mum, and then I'm off. I've a lot to think about on my journey.

A year after Dad died, Mum decided it was time to rebuild her life. We moved from Bournemouth to Weymouth, and when I was settled at school, Mum volunteered at the local hospice – just a few hours, three days a week. I was really proud of her. I am really proud of her. When I asked her about it she said she'd fought too damned hard to get our lives back to let that screwed-up shithead of a man rule from the grave.

It was the first time I'd heard her swear. I was twelve.

That Christmas she met Griff.

It's good she confided in me today and I'm pleased I was able to help, although I have no intention of interfering in her and Griff's marriage. I know more about the split than Griff, which will be awkward if I bump into him, but I've learned when to step back. I'm happy to listen to Mum's problems, and man, she has one huge dilemma to work through, but that's it.

When I said I thought she should explain to Griff, not only about Dad, but about Logan's stuff, too, she turned as white as the onion she was peeling. She was making Dylan spaghetti bolognaise. I didn't mention he'd had it recently. It's his favourite. And Mum makes it from scratch, not out of a can. I wouldn't know where to start, which is what she said about talking to Griff.

The roads are busy today. I make a mental note to take the back streets.

'Where would I begin?' she asked. 'I should have told him when Logan first asked for my help. Griff would still be here if I had.'

I didn't answer. I was thinking the same about my cutting. If I'd told Mum that first time I'd cut, my arms wouldn't look like a page of hashtags. If we'd been open and honest about my dad from the off, I might not get the urge to drag the blade across my skin. And I wouldn't have been talking literally when I said I wanted to cut a person out of my life.

I let go of the right handlebar and give my left arm a gentle rub. It's itchy, but I'm avoiding scratching it, as I'm scared I won't stop.

Logan's being unfair asking Mum to help him, but I understand where he's coming from. A life half-lived is no life. And if I planned to kill myself, I'd want to make sure I didn't cock it up.

Asking Mum was his mistake. I have no idea why he thought she'd agree. Perhaps he's playing on her need to help people. If he is, that's a pretty shit thing to do.

He should have asked me.

It's uphill for a while. I change gear to cope with the incline.

We're not related, Logan and I, not by blood, but we're more alike than we first realised. Don't get me wrong. I don't wish to die. Not now. I might have once, a while ago, when I thought there was no way out for Mum or me, but I dealt with that. No, I just think he and I have the same outlook on life. On death.

I'm not frightened of it or by it. The method concerns me, but when you have control over where and when, you make the how as sweet as possible. Or as bitter.

Almost at journey's end. This is the easy part.

I enjoy the sense of freedom I get when I'm on my bike. I don't ride it around town or anything, just between our house and Logan's, where the idiots from school are less likely to spot me. They'd take the piss, and I'm trying to avoid triggers like upset, conflict, and squeaky doors and floorboards.

That's the real reason I step over the loose board in my bedroom. I kid myself it's to avoid being found, but it's not. Our old bathroom had squeaky boards. Our old bathroom, where I saw Dad go at Mum on more than one occasion.

I'm working really hard on getting clean.

Pulling up outside Logan's house, I loosen my coat. The ride has made me sweat. I lock my bike to an iron drainpipe that runs down the side of Logan's pre-fab garage, and head for the front door. I ring the bell first, because Mum said I should, and trawl in my pocket for the key. It takes me a moment, as I've shoved my gloves in there, but just as I'm about to fit it into the hole, I hear footsteps. They're too fast and clicky to be Logan's.

'You took your time.' A woman's voice.

That's ... odd. Unless Logan's finally agreed to outside care, which would be great as Mum's problems would disappear overnight. She'd have her life back again. For the second time. She'd have Griff. And I could step back. Get off Griff's case, make the effort to be nice to him, let him and Mum get on with their relationship. And maybe ... *maybe* I could do something about mine.

The incident, as I'm calling it, in the school changing rooms, got me thinking. Yeah, it was unpleasant and frightening, and it refreshed the images in my mind of what my dad did to my mum, but I'm over what the stupid teenage witch did to me. In fact, it's made me realise it's not always men who use violence to dominate and control another person. Women are capable of the same behaviour. In the depths of my psyche I know that, but I'd chosen to let the reality sleep. Well, I've had a rude awakening, and I realise I should distrust women as much as I do men.

The fact I don't tells me something.

Love is not about gender.

And that's why Stephanie is still in my head.

She said she was moving to Chiswell in the spring. It's spring now. I wonder if she remembers me. I can picture everything about her. I haven't forgotten one millimetre of her face.

I've got this whirl in my stomach, thinking of her. No boy's had that effect on me, and if I'm completely honest with myself, no boy will. But I'd like to see Stephanie to be sure what I'm feeling is real. If it is, well, I guess I'll have to be straight with her. It's scary stuff, but it's a relief to have got it sussed.

Mum sometimes talks of the time she met Griff as the fog clearing. She says he was the fresh breeze that blew away the mist. It's poetic, isn't it? She says I have a poet's heart. I do like Shakespeare. Well, right now, I'd say Stephanie's the missing x in my equation. Okay, that's more mathematical than poetic, but it's taken me a while to work it all out.

The door's opening. I'm expecting to see an older woman wearing a blue overall, with her greying hair tied back in a ponytail. 'Wow.' I can't help myself.

'Excuse me?' The woman smiled.

'I got the ponytail bit right,' I say, drawing my hand down the back of my head.

'Not following you.'

'Who is it?' Logan's voice interrupts our moment.

The woman folds her arms and leans against the wall. I can tell she's amused. There's a dance going on behind her eyes. They're the blue I'd assumed her overalls to be. That's a compliment, but perhaps it's one to keep to myself.

'I was expecting an old lady, with white hair and healthcare assistant clothes, not a blonde ...' I stop. Her neat, precise eyebrows arch. 'Well, you're younger than I was imagining.'

'Who is it?' Logan, again.

'It's Tess,' I shout. 'Happy birthday.'

'You're Tess?' The blonde woman stands up straight. 'Griff's daughter?'

'Step-daughter,' I say. I want to be clear from the start. 'You know him?'

She holds out her hand. I'm not sure if I'm meant to be shaking it or appreciating its warmth. She closes her fingers around mine and invites me in.

'I'm an old friend of your dad's. We've come to see Logan.'

'Step-dad.'

'Sorry. Step-dad.' She closes the door, still with my hand in hers, and she guides me to the living room. 'You didn't say your granddaughter was so beautiful, Logan.'

'Step ... Doesn't matter.' She's nice. I'm not going to keep picking her up on her mistake.

She releases me and I kiss Logan on the forehead. I've seen him more responsive. I've also seen him fuller-faced. I know girls at school who'd die for cheekbones like his. 'You've lost weight,' I say. I noticed at the weekend, but kept quiet. I didn't want Mum worrying. Today I'm moved to speak.

I'm reminded of an old cat my nan once had. He reached the grand age of twenty before he died. He was scraggy. Hollow. His fur and body had thinned. It's not a good memory.

'I've come to make you some lunch. What do you fancy?' I keep my tone cheerful. 'I can open tins,' I joke, 'and make sandwiches, but only those little tiny triangles with the crusts cut off, and only with cream cheese or Marmite.' I turn to the woman. 'They're Dylan's favourite. He's my baby brother.'

I notice her smile is still hanging around.

'We've already eaten.' Logan pats his stomach. 'Imy put a few things together.'

'Imy?'

'That's me. Imogen Joliffe.'

The blonde woman holds out her hand again, and once more, I find myself in her grip. She sticks to protocol this time, but she's slow to let go. I'm not pulling away either.

This woman is a new and surprising variable to my Stephanie equation. She's intriguing.

'I hope I haven't caused a problem, or messed up your plans. It's just that Logan was hungry, and I was here waiting for Griff to get back ...'

'Get back from where?'

'He's out walking the dogs. We were expecting him home half an hour ago. You've not heard from him, have you?'

Imogen's concern seems genuine. That bothers me. 'How did you say you know him?' I claim the armchair, and Imogen takes the sofa.

'We're old family friends. My brother, Kieran, was Griff's best friend.'

She says it like I should know. 'Okay. So, what? You and Griff have kept in touch?'

Putting her knees together, she sits forward and shakes her head. 'No. Nothing like that. We bumped into one another a few weeks ago. At Chesil. He was doing his knight in shining armour thing, thinking I'd been washed out to sea, but basically, he kidnapped my dog.'

An uncontrollable snort escapes through my nose, but I'm laughing too much to be embarrassed. 'He kidnapped your dog?'

'Honey. She's not been the same since.' Imogen's mouth curves and soft lines appear at the corners of her eyes. 'We're just friends,' she says, a slow blink of reassurance robbing me of her blue brilliance. 'Griff and I.'

'Yeah. I got that.' I consider the reasons for her clarifying her point, and while I realise it's probably so I know she's not out to destroy Mum's marriage, there's that swirling thing going on in my stomach that says she might be sending me other signals.

'Imy's father was a good friend of mine when the kids were younger.' The way Logan speaks of Imogen is the same way I've heard him talk about Mum. There's a lot of affection there. 'I remember this one from her dungarees and welly days.'

'Not that again. Will I never be forgiven for my appalling sense of fashion?' Imogen gives Logan's knee an airy tap. 'I could retaliate, you know, and tell Tess about your jackets with elbow patches, and the summer you wore socks with sandals.'

'No way!' I scream. 'At least I know where Griff gets it from.' We're all laughing now. It's been ages since I saw Logan this relaxed. 'I think you look great,' I say, directing the comment to Imogen. 'But you've a body that would look good in anything.'

'And what about me, young lady?'

Logan's trying to be stern, but his face is too mobile.

'You do all right for a man of seventy-five,' I say, his age bringing me back to the fact it's his birthday. 'So, how's your morning been? Good birthday?'

'Better than expected, thank you. Tiring. It was good to see Griff, though. Perhaps he can give you a lift home when he gets back.' Logan's head lolls onto the high cushion that hangs over the top of his chair, and his eyes close. 'He should have brought the dogs in. Would have been nice to see Ozzy.'

'When he gets back,' Imogen says.

'He's going to be busy *when he gets back*.' I hold up my fingers and put imaginary quote marks around my words. Poor Griff. I think he's in for a telling off. When he gets back.

'Your mum must be a beautiful lady.' Imogen reclines and crosses her legs. Her dress, which is stunning, rides to above her knee. She spreads her arms out along the cushions. It's an open gesture, like she's laying herself bare. 'You certainly don't get your looks from Griff.'

I'm trying to gauge whether or not she's teasing? I don't want to be rude. She's too nice to be at the foul end of my temper. 'That's because he's not my dad,' I say, slowly, hoping I've pitched it correctly. 'But you're right. Mum is gorgeous. My dad was an ugly sod. In all senses of the word.'

She's taken aback by this and she closes up like a flower without sun.

'No. Of course. I'll try harder to get it right. Forgive me?'

I wave it away. 'No problem. I don't expect Griff has told you much about me.' I'll have to change that – give away more of myself, so she'll give something back. I want her to reveal herself. 'My dad died when I was eleven.'

'I'm sorry.' She's clasped one hand on top of the other, across her heart. 'I know what it's like to lose someone close to you.'

'We weren't close.' I'm considering how much I can divulge, remembering that Mum's not even hinted to Griff about our difficult past. I need to be sparing with the detail. 'But, yes, it took a while to get over it.' It's not a lie.

Logan mumbles in his sleep, making my insides thump. I blink. I've been engrossed in Imogen and forgotten he was here. 'Can I ask how old you are?' I've put her in her late twenties, not a lifetime away from my age.

She drops her hands away from her breast, uncrosses her legs and leans forward. Her ponytail tumbles down her back. 'I promise I'm not a threat to your mum. Griff and I are just friends. He's really not my type,' she whispers.

My palms are clammy and my throat is dry. I actually feel a little sick. It's like the time I had to recite Shakespeare's *Sonnet 18* at the school Lit Fest. Sir said it was the worst case of nerves he'd come across in his ten years organising the recitals. 'Did you know Imogen was the name of a Shakespearean heroine?' I say, finding confidence on solid ground.

She's surprised. 'I didn't know that.'

'Yeah,' I continue, finding my rhythm. 'It's from *Cymberline*. It's thought Shakespeare used the name Innogen, but it appeared in a folio edition as Imogen. It's said to be a misprint.' She's staring at me. I've said too much. Revealed even more. 'I like Shakespeare,' I say, aware it sounds like an apology. 'I'm a freak.' My words crash out of my mouth.

Imogen's chest rises, her eyes soften and she rests her face in her palms. 'You're not a freak.'

I dare to hold her gaze, willing her to say more about me. Anything. Because she makes me want to believe in her.

'Griff told me you have an old head on young shoulders. I can see that. It's in your eyes.'

She continues to look at me, and I have to remind myself to swallow and breathe and not to be an idiot.

'I'm thirty-five,' she says.

The breath I've remembered to take is knocked out. 'Thirty-five?' She's over twice my age. I've shocked myself with that truth. She won't be interested in me. I'd got this all wrong. I was still fizzling from the sexual lightning bolt that was Stephanie when I saw Imogen. I've transferred those feelings or something. I'll have to google it later. Whatever it's called, some strange shit's happened in my head. 'You don't look it,' I say, forcing a rapid recovery. I break the intense deadlock and experience an immediate loss. Jeez. My cheeks will be as red as my hair.

'Thanks. Age really is just a number.' Imogen reverts to her open flower position. 'Do you often take care of Logan?'

'If Mum's tied up.'

'What about your homework? Seeing your friends? Your boyfriend. What does he think about the time you spend here?'

It's an interesting question, but I don't read anything into it. It's just women's talk. 'I don't have a boyfriend.' There. Imogen can do with that what she will. 'Or a girlfriend.'

Did I say that out loud? Good grief. That's a first. What is it about Imogen that's making me say these things? I've lost the ability to edit myself.

She dips forward and peers at me from under her brow. 'What just steamrollered through your head?'

'You saw that?' Intriguing and perceptive. 'I was considering how honest I should be.'

'With me?'

I nod and she absorbs the moment and the air around her, drawing me closer.

'How honest would you like to be?'

I want to tell her everything – how my dad hurt my mum, how I hurt myself, how I'm aching inside for something more than I have. Everything. It's madness.

She's left the sofa and is heading for my chair. She's not taken her eyes off me once. I don't know if she's concerned or curious. She's close now, sitting on the arm. I haven't got a clue what's going on. Not with her and not with me. I'm just going to stay still, and count three heartbeats before I answer any questions.

'What's ticking away in that pretty head?'

For a second her fingers brush my temple and I forgive her for substituting intelligent with pretty. One, two, three. I opt to change the subject. 'Are you married?'

She laughs and then apologises. 'Your question was a bit left field. No. I'm not married.'

'And you and Griff are definitely not—'

She hushes me with a finger to my lips. It's taking all my will power to keep my mouth closed.

'I'm not married, I'm not having an affair and I'm not trying to bed Griff. I'm too selfish to share my life with another person.' Imogen removes her finger and lays her head on mine. 'But I do recognise a troubled soul when I see one.' She squeezes me.

We spend a few minutes in silence, and I think about Imogen's assumption that I possess a troubled soul.

I do. As a child I saw violence. I saw my father administer

sex to my mother as punishment and I watched, helpless and powerless.

'You and me are two of a kind. I can feel it.' Imogen gives me another hug. 'My experiences have shaped me. So have yours. We have stories to tell.'

'I've never told mine,' I say. 'Not to anyone.'

I watch Logan's chest, holding my breath until I'm sure he's still taking his. Mum does this with Dylan. She stands over him when he's sleeping and doesn't leave until she's satisfied he's okay. I wonder if she does it with me, and the idea she might know about my scars panics me. Then I comfort myself with the knowledge I'm not a sound sleeper. I doubt Mum would get away with opening the door, let alone sitting on my bed.

Logan's slipped to the side, and I'm worried he'll wake up with a stiff neck. Reluctant as I am to be the one to pull away from the embrace, I need to make him comfortable. 'I have to put a cushion under Logan's head,' I say, leaving the warmth of the chair. It's like having the duvet ripped off in the morning. Cold, shocking, exposing.

'You're lovely with Logan,' Imogen says, waiting for my return. 'You don't begrudge one second of your time with him. I wish I'd been like you.'

'You do?' My frown's so deep I can see my eyebrow ring.

'You understand how fleeting life is. How important it is to show you care. If I'd known at your age what you know ...' She sighs. 'Do you think it would be possible for me to visit Logan on a regular basis? Maybe help out from time to time? Having another pair of hands will take the pressure off you and your mum, and who knows? Maybe we can encourage Griff to pop in more often. Which reminds me.' She checks her watch. 'Where is he?'

We both jump as a phone on the coffee table vibrates and pings.

'We've conjured him up.' Imogen stretches to reach the mobile. She puts it to her ear. 'Griff. We've been wondering where you've got … When?' Imogen's face develops hard lines. 'Is Honey okay?' The lines lessen. 'And you?' She's listening to Griff. 'Sure. I'll get there as soon as I can. No. Your dad's fine. Tess is here. Don't what? Don't tell … Yep. Yep. Understood. And don't worry about Honey. Sort yourself out.'

She leaves the chair, collects her handbag and rushes into the hall.

'Is Griff okay?' I ask, following.

'He's fine.' She attempts a smile, but is preoccupied with putting on her coat. 'I have to go. I have to collect Honey from the vet's.'

'The vet's? What happened?'

'She … she … ripped a claw out. It's nothing. Really.' Imogen's opened the front door and is about to step onto the path. 'Will you say bye to Logan for me? Fingers crossed I'll see you again. It's been nice. Look after yourself.'

She's on her phone again, requesting a taxi, and walking up the road. She could have waited indoors.

I head back to the living room, wondering if I'll see her again.

Chapter Twenty-Two

Griff

'You did everything you could, Mr Hendry. You've given Ozzy the best possible chance.'

They'd find out if that was true in the next few hours.

The gravel crunched beneath the Land Rover's tyres. With the vet's words ringing in his ears, Griff had no recollection of the journey to his cottage, only a sense of how empty the car was. And that he'd arrived. He had to be there for Dylan.

The vet was being kind. Griff knew the patter – he'd recited it a thousand times to Coastguard Rescue Officers distraught at losing a life; to fathers whose sons believed they could tame the sea; to mothers who took their eye off their child for one second. He'd said it to everyone whose desperate attempts to rescue, resuscitate and alter the inevitable outcome had been in vain. They needed to hear they'd done something right because at that moment, swamped with fear and guilt, they thought themselves the most wicked, the most selfish, and the most careless being on the planet. They deserved to know their final act was one of kindness and courage.

As the engine shut down, Griff waited for the familiar thump of Ozzy's tail. Silence.

'Stupid fool,' he muttered. How was the brain able to think one thing one moment and completely reverse it the next? He fastened his hands behind his neck, and winced as his shoulder jarred. It was nothing. An over-stretched muscle from where the dogs had yanked at their leads. He'd experienced worse at the gym.

What a banal thought.

His mind kept flitting between explicit visions of Ozzy, lying in the road motionless, half-hidden under a van, to the ordinary and everyday problems of gym injuries. 'I should be concentrating on Ozzy,' he said. 'Working through what happened. Putting together a plan of action.' He lowered his arms and glanced at his reflection in the rear-view mirror. He should have shaved this morning. 'Man!' He smacked his hands down on the steering wheel, this time ignoring the wrench of his shoulder. He had no time for trivialities. There was too much at stake.

As he opened the door, the arctic wind assaulted his face – fierce, unrelenting daggers stabbing at his eyes already sore from the horrendous rigours of the day. They stung, and they watered, but Griff fought to keep them open. Behind lay images of mud-caked spades, fresh, deep, dark holes, hand-made wooden crosses, and cold, small bodies wrapped in fleecy blankets. Commemorative rosebushes, shrubs of remembrance – a garden graveyard for his pets.

And if he further developed that picture he exposed images of his mum, and her small body swathed in cumbersome, blue blankets, cannulas the size of barrel taps plunged into the backs of her child-sized hands, and the rasping heave of her chest as she gasped her final breath.

Beyond that was a panoramic view of the crematorium, with its vibrant flowers and evergreen wreaths, and a girl in a navy dress and black patent shoes, her too-blue eyes clouded with grief and hostility, staring back.

He'd seen it all earlier, when he'd dared to close his eyes.

Having wiped the wet from his cheek, he inhaled the fresh, biting air, and knocked on the front door. He was greeted with, 'Why didn't you use your key?' as the door opened, followed by, 'Tess is helping your father today, that's why I'm still here.'

Unable to speak, Griff looked beyond Evie. He had nothing prepared. His instinct had driven him home. He was there to take care of Dylan, but he needed to see his family, hold them, and feel their strength; know for himself they were safe.

'Griff? Are you okay?' Evie opened the door to its fullest extent. 'You're as white as the woodwork. Talk to me.'

'Something's happened,' he said. 'There's been an accident.' The words were out. They were dry and husky, but they were out.

'Tess?' Evie's green eyes were wild with terror. 'Please, not Tess. She was on her bike.' Evie made a grab for her keys. 'She went to Logan's. I shouldn't have let her go.'

Griff intercepted, taking the keys from Evie and returning them to the phone table. 'It's not Tess.'

Before he had chance to draw breath, Evie said, 'No. Not Logan?'

Without further hesitation, his hand was seized and, as Evie reversed onto the bottom step, Griff was drawn into the hall, the door closing behind. His head was guided into the soft, sweet spot between Evie's neck and shoulder.

It was a spot he'd visited many times, delivering shivers of delight to Evie, but today it provided him with comfort and security. It was familiar and safe. No secrets lurked there, and no shocks pounced from the hollows. That was Evie all over. Honest and true. There wasn't a deceitful bone in her body, every inch of which, at this moment, was conveying how much she loved and cared for Griff.

Whatever it was that had driven the wedge between them, it wasn't her love for another man any more than she'd fallen out of love with Griff.

His head was clutched tighter as Evie's breath quickened, accompanying the heavy thump of her heart. 'Oh, Griff, I'm so sorry. Logan—'

'It's not my dad.' Griff swapped places with Evie. The open toddler gate clanked against the wall as he dropped to the bottom step. He wrapped his arms around his knees, linked his hands together and said, 'It's Ozzy.'

He watched as dismay followed the immediate relief Evie displayed. Her body was hunched and sunken, but within a beat she was in front of Griff, her cool hands holding his head, her feline eyes hunting his for answers.

Griff cast his gaze to the floor. 'He was hit by a van. He has head trauma. Fractures.' He stopped, desperate to cling to any chance of Ozzy surviving. If Griff didn't vocalise it, it wouldn't happen.

Removing her hands, Evie knelt on the hall floor, swaddled Griff in her arms and cuddled her face into his neck. 'What's going to happen to him?'

'I … The vet … He …' Unable to set the words free, Griff turned his cheek to meet Evie's, the corner of his mouth finding hers.

'It's okay,' she said, her lips feathering his skin. 'It's okay.'

Sheltered from harm and seeking solace from the devastating storms of the day, Griff took refuge in Evie's caresses. She was there for him, providing the protection he needed, and offering the love he so desperately wanted.

Unfurling from his embryonic state, and lifting Evie to her feet, they stumbled and climbed their way to the top of the stairs, kisses sustaining them until they reached the top. As they neared the bedroom, Evie held up a hand, and broke away. Griff's heart plummeted to his stomach.

'One minute,' Evie said, disappearing into Dylan's room.

Catching his breath, Griff pulled his shirt straight and wandered into the master bedroom. It was as he remembered – a private space for him and Evie – and he was relieved to see his absence hadn't led her to remove every last trace of his being. It meant she wanted him there. If he could hold onto that, he could get through the day.

As he smoothed his hand over Evie's side of the bed, he heard her pad into the room. He sat down and waited for her to approach.

'Dylan's sleeping,' she said, pushing the door to. 'With his thumb in. Little mite's had a busy day.' When she reached Griff, she stepped between his knees, put one hand on his shoulder and stroked her other through his hair. 'It suits you longer,' she said, brushing her lips against his ear. 'I like this new look.'

He could not only hear her voice, but feel it too, as the licks and curls of Evie's words trickled their way through his nerves. Every action had a reaction and when she stooped to kiss him, he could hold back no longer.

From being clothed at the end of the bed to lying naked on top of the duvet was a matter of seconds, not minutes. A frantic disrobing followed a deep, drawing kiss from Evie, which as always, had started with the intent in her eyes. The passion and desire they projected were as much a turn on to Griff as the kiss itself.

With the day's ordeals melting in the scorching heat, Griff's focus was on Evie. No longer leaving her to lead the way, he rolled her onto her back, kissed the welcoming pillows of her thighs, and passed his hands over her hips. Her frame was more defined than Griff remembered. It was evident that in the few weeks they'd been apart she'd not eaten properly. Promising to reel in the concern later, he cast the thought adrift and concentrated on becoming acquainted with her new form.

His fingers navigated the curve of her waist, rode the gentle ripples of her stomach, and skimmed the surface of her skin, coming to rest an inch away from her breasts. Her response was to anchor his head in her hands and tousle his hair. With his tongue tasting and teasing his way over her form, Griff charted a course to Evie's mouth, his body settling in the wake, their hips connecting and adopting a gentle rhythm.

Hot breath billowed on his chest as he entered her.

She was warm, soft, and accepting.

Locked inside, he was free.

'Hey.'

Griff's reward for opening his tired eyes was to see Evie sitting next to him, with Dylan in her arms, both content, both looking at him.

'We've brought you a cup of tea.' Evie gestured towards a mug on the bedside table.

'And bitkits.' Dylan waved a Digestive under Griff's nose.

'You might find that one a bit soggy.' Evie smiled as she swept Griff's fringe over. 'I didn't know your plans, so I thought we ought to wake you. And Dylan's desperate to give you a hug.'

Hauling himself into a seated position, Griff patted the space beside him. 'What time is it?'

Dylan scrambled away from Evie, climbed under the duvet, and snuggled up to Griff.

'No crumbs in my bed, young man.' Evie stretched across the bed, pulled out a tissue from under her pillow and laid it across Dylan's lap. 'Crumbs go here, okay?'

''Kay.' Dylan offered the remains of his damp snack to Griff, who pretended to take a huge bite. 'Daddy!' The scream was accompanied with a giggle, which stopped the instant Griff feigned another bite. 'Mine,' Dylan said, crushing the semicircle against his small mouth.

The fallout was tremendous considering how wet the biscuit was.

Evie's face was a picture. 'That's your fault,' she said, poking Griff in the ribs. 'You can clean the bits out.'

He scrunched up the tissue, set it aside and kissed Dylan on the top of his head. 'I'll sort it later.' For now he wanted to enjoy the ordinariness of the situation. Novelty was overrated. And exhausting. All he needed to create the best possible version of normality was for Tess to sneak into her bedroom, avoiding the floorboard Griff couldn't get in to repair, and for Ozzy to …

Ozzy.

'What time did you say it is?' Griff turned the clock radio towards him. 'It's gone seven.' Handing Dylan to Evie, Griff whipped back the cover, bundled together his clothes from the end of the bed, and dressed with alacrity. 'I've got to get back to the vets. I have to see Ozzy.'

Leaving Evie and Dylan standing in the bedroom, Griff raced downstairs, yanked open the front door and got behind the wheel of the Land Rover. 'Stupid, stupid idiot,' he muttered, twisting the key in the ignition.

He'd fallen prey to his own fantasy. Nothing about what had happened was normal. Nothing about his world was ordinary. Ozzy's life hung in the balance, Logan was half the man he used to be, and Griff had made love to his estranged wife.

It was madness.

With no time to check his phone for messages, he pushed the pedal to the floor and skidded off the gravel. The vet was a good fifteen minutes away, but with the traffic in Griff's favour, there was a chance he could make it before she locked the doors for the night.

And there was also a chance he'd already lost Ozzy.

He would never forgive himself if Ozzy died alone.

Chapter Twenty-Three

Evie

For the fifth time since getting out of bed, Evie checked her mobile. It was as devoid of messages as it had been on the four previous occasions. No word from Griff. Nothing since he'd fled from the house last night.

With Dylan taking a nap, and Tess spending a second day on the trot at Logan's, Evie was left kicking her heels. It had been a good two years since she'd spent an evening and the following morning at home. She was used to being busy and not having space in her day for thinking. Space was unsettling.

She'd showered, she'd fed and changed Dylan, and she'd shared a brief exchange with Tess before she'd shot off on her bike; she'd even given the bathroom the once-over, but now there was nothing left to tackle. She was such a whirlwind of activity, she found it difficult to unwind. And she was aware too much quiet in the house would force her to reflect on the events of the night before.

Taking one last peek at her slumbering son, she headed downstairs to the kitchen and considered her options. 'A coffee,' she said. 'And morning TV.' It wasn't the best use of her unexpected time off, but watching programmes about other people's problems would keep her from analysing her own. She nodded, filled the kettle and flipped the switch.

Dylan had the right approach. Wake, eat, play and sleep.

As she waited for the water to boil, her eyes and mind wandered to her Happiness jar.

Yesterday, euphoric from the hopes and dreams her and Griff's lovemaking provided, she'd added a ticket. Not straight away – it hadn't occurred to her until after Dylan had woken and she'd taken him downstairs – but while Griff was still in the house, sleeping. Aware the papers were available for the family to read, she'd kept her comment vague, knowing that come the annual reveal on New Year's Eve, her words would stir a multitude of erotic memories and sensations in her.

Right now, it was her gut stirring. Instinct was writing and sending its own message and questioning whether or not it was an appropriate use of the jar. And whether or not sleeping with Griff at this current time was something to celebrate.

Fully intending to talk to him about Logan as she'd opened the door, Griff's distressed appearance had thrown Evie. Her first response had been to pull him to her and keep him safe. It was instinctive. His vulnerability had struck at Evie's core and her self-imposed rules about the right to hold the man she'd given up were forgotten.

Her next response, having established Tess and Logan were safe, had been to say nothing of Logan's death wish. For a split second she'd thought he'd carried out his threat. It was a shocking moment. The possibility Griff could have been the one to find him slumped and lifeless in his green chair had made Evie want to retch. When Griff announced it was Ozzy who was hurt, and despite a desperate attempt to cover it up, Evie was aware her relief had been palpable. Logan's predicament was foremost in her mind.

She was thankful Griff hadn't picked up on it – if he'd pushed her she'd have been forced into telling him about his father right then and he was already upset and distressed about Ozzy. Thank goodness the speed with which they found themselves in bed diverted them both from that course.

Selecting the decaf from the cupboard, Evie prepared her

drink, stuffed the biscuit barrel under her arm, and headed off for the living room.

Within fifteen minutes she was bored of the ear-splitting woman who'd denied cheating on her boyfriend, and she had zero interest in the results of the promised DNA test of their baby, although she couldn't help worrying what impact the show would have on the child in later years. 'Poor soul,' she muttered, pressing the off button on the remote.

She could imagine how mortified Tess would be – she was a private person, who only shared her thoughts when the situation demanded, or if she was backed into a corner.

It had shocked Evie on two counts when Tess revealed the details of the harrowing scenes she'd witnessed. First, that Tess had seen more than Evie realised, and second, that she was pushing to talk it through.

The car incident was the second most frightening experience in Evie's life, and like Tess, she thought death was imminent. Neil had said he'd kill Evie if she didn't comply with his wishes, and he never made threats he wouldn't follow through.

Her throat constricted.

Tess was right. Neil had left them with far more than painful memories, and the man had been dead four years. Why wouldn't he leave them alone? Revenge? 'Don't be ridiculous.' Evie washed the notion away with a gulp of coffee. 'He engineered his own exit.'

His death was sudden and gory and distressing, and the first most frightening experience in Evie's life.

Her statement to the police noted that she'd found Neil lying on a blood-soaked bed, not breathing, with a deep gash running from the wrist to the elbow of his left forearm. An empty rum bottle was on the floor.

A pair of scissors was later discovered in the folds of

the sheets. Forensics identified one set of fingerprints. Neil's. With his history of drinking, his lack of continuous employment, and Evie's neighbour supporting her claim Neil was unstable and often displayed erratic behaviour, it appeared he'd committed suicide, but with no note present, the coroner returned a verdict of accidental death.

Evie and Tess never spoke about that, either.

While done with the best of intentions, the pact of silence Evie had devised left Neil's echoes and shadows free to roam the dark corridors of both her head and Tess's.

Perhaps Tess had hit upon something. They couldn't flush him out, and blocking him out hadn't worked, so maybe talking him out was the way forward, more so if it helped Tess, and Evie had promised she'd give it a shot.

She hadn't, however, promised she'd discuss their past with Griff. It was a deliberate omission on Evie's part, and one she knew Tess would forgive. She would tell Griff if and when the time was right, and she was confident her daughter would follow her lead.

Breaking the news about Logan was as much as Evie could handle right now, and she was sure it was plenty for Griff to deal with.

Telling him was the right thing to do, though. He needed time to speak with Logan and come to terms with the decision. His mother's had been thrust upon him, and it was unfair to do that to him a second time.

Evie hoped Griff would understand why she'd been unable to talk about Logan's request, and forgive her part in the deceit. She hoped he'd try to understand his father's reasons, and even though he was bound to object, respect them. She prayed her honesty, albeit late, would herald the start of a good phase in their lives.

Together they would move forward, help Logan, and get their marriage back on track.

She closed her eyes as her insides pirouetted. The memory of her and Griff making love last night existed both in her mind and her flesh. It was easy to recall every touch, every kiss, every lost breath.

But as the sensations arced from nerve to nerve, the vision of Griff leaving without a second glance continued to play. As wonderful as it was being with him, and as encouraging as it was for him to have come to her, it was possible he was seeking comfort only from sex, not reconciliation.

Depositing her mug on the coffee table, Evie swapped the remote for her phone. 'He wouldn't,' she said as she swiped the screen.

It was blank.

'Nothing and no one.' She switched to her photos app. The first image was of Dylan, showing off a pair of new shoes; the next, a rare picture of Tess; and the third, a snapshot of Griff with his faithful companion by his side, standing at Portland Bill, looking out at Pulpit Rock. 'He'll be busy with Ozzy,' Evie said, pushing all the contrary evidence to the back of her mind.

Yesterday's events suggested she and Griff had reconciled, but his manner as he'd left the cottage, and the lack of communication since, implied not.

Chapter Twenty-Four

Tess

It's the start of the Easter holidays. Two whole weeks of freedom. No school bus, no sport, and no confrontations in the changing rooms.

I can't wait to leave school. I'm taking my GCSEs next year, but I've already decided to study for A-levels at college. I've heard you get to call the tutors by their first name. And they don't care how you dress, what colour your hair is, or how many piercings you have. Self-expression is encouraged.

Mum thinks it's the right decision.

I've come to Logan's again, to give Mum a break. She rarely has time in the morning to wake up slowly. If I'd thought about it, I could have stayed here last night.

Perhaps I should. I could pack a few clothes, bring my homework. I could be a live-in carer for a few days.

I glance across the room at Logan, who's already installed in his chair. 'Fancy a lodger for a couple of nights?'

He glares at me. 'So I can be spied upon?'

His hostility surprises me, then I realise he thinks I'm talking about a nurse or professional carer. 'I mean me. I'm on holiday. I could stay over. We could order takeaway, watch some films … You could help me study.' I pause. I haven't sold the idea to him yet, but I know what would pull him in. 'You could teach me some gardening stuff. The weather's changed again today. Spring has definitely sprung.'

A flicker of interest transfers from his eyes to his mouth. 'Gardening?'

The old bugger's laughing.

'I know what a lawn mower is,' I say. 'And Mum's had me pruning at home.' I'm not mentioning that I used to think pruning was to do with sitting in the bath too long. Or that I once thought secateurs were part of the Queen's jewels.

'It's a kind offer, Tess, but I don't think my garden or I are up to the challenge.'

I shrug. 'It was just an idea. Let me know if you change your mind.'

'I won't,' he says, staring at me. 'You should be out enjoying yourself with your friends.'

'That's what I said yesterday.' Imogen's come in from the hallway. 'Bathroom's sorted,' she says.

Imogen was here when I arrived. It wasn't a repeat of yesterday's charade, but I was surprised to see her. She, on the other hand, seemed pleased it was me, even though she disappeared upstairs as soon as I took off my coat.

Logan said she phoned last night, after I'd left, asking if she could pop round first thing this morning. Obviously he said yes, which is interesting, because he was expecting Mum. I haven't worked out what's going on yet. 'So are you helping Logan now?'

Imogen's weaving her way past me and Logan.

'I left in such a hurry yesterday, I felt I owed Logan an explanation.' She's gone straight through to the kitchen.

The intrigue I had for this woman has turned into curiosity. 'She could have explained when she phoned,' I say to Logan.

'She did, we had a long chat, and then she offered to come over.'

'But she was here before me, and you were up and dressed.'

'I was. Imy helped.'

Imogen's tinkering about with the kettle. The tap's gushing at full pelt. 'I'll make us all a hot drink and then I'll take a look at the shrubs out the back,' she says, her voice carrying into the living room.

I raise my eyebrow in a theatrical, melodramatic detective kind of way. 'So that's your game. I've been replaced with ...' I pause for effect. 'With someone who can garden.'

Logan knows I'm mucking about.

'You're still chief sandwich maker,' he says. 'I like the crusts cut off.'

Joking aside, I'm wondering how Mum would feel about this. With Imogen helping him, Logan could have called and saved us a visit. Not that I mind. I'm happy to see him. And Imogen. It would have been a bit of a shock for Mum though, finding another woman here. We've not had a chance to talk yet. 'I guess you wanted Mum to meet Imogen.'

'*I'd* like to meet your Mum.' Imogen re-enters the room. She puts Logan's mug on the small table next to his chair. 'Let me know when you're ready to drink it and I'll pass it to you.' There's a lightness to her voice. Her back is to me, but I imagine she's smiling. She's wearing her hair down today. It reaches her hips. She turns and offers me the second mug. 'Hot chocolate?'

I accept and thank her. 'Why do you want to meet my mum?'

'We have a proposition,' Logan says. 'One your mum needs to be comfortable with.'

'And Griff,' Imogen adds as she wafts past me on her way to the sofa. 'But I think he'll be more than happy.'

My attention is flitting from Logan to Imogen and back again. Both are looking at me, nodding. They're including me in their conspiracy. 'Go on.'

Imogen settles into her seat and crosses her legs. She's

wearing skinny blue jeans with a pink, fluffy jumper. Probably cashmere. She's a person with expensive tastes. I can tell.

'It was so lovely seeing Logan yesterday. It brought back a lot of fond memories and gave me a proper sense of time and place. Being here restored a piece of my history I thought lost.' She's circling her finger around the rim of her mug. 'I feel reconnected.'

This is all wonderful, I'm sure, but I haven't got a clue what she's on about. I don't even know what questions to ask. 'Reconnected?' I offer. It's pathetic.

'To my father. To my brother.'

'And to Griff?' My curiosity is morphing at a rapid rate into suspicion.

Imogen has fixed her eyes on me. They are too blue to be real. I decide she must be wearing contact lenses. I'd like red ones. That would totally freak out the bitch at school.

I've distracted myself. I need to concentrate on Imogen and Logan's proposition. 'Sorry,' I say. 'Carry on.'

'I'm going to be honest with you, Tess. I do feel reconnected to Griff. He was an important part of my life, as was Logan, as was Kieran.'

'Kieran?'

'My brother. Griff's best friend.'

I nod, remembering the fleeting reference Imogen made to him yesterday.

'Griff's told you what happened?'

'I don't think Tess knows,' Logan says. 'Griff doesn't talk about his past.'

Nor does Mum. I imagine that's why she and Griff get on. Got on. Hmm. Sparkling gems of wisdom to keep to myself.

'Your mum will know,' I hear Imogen saying. 'He must have told her.'

Irritation is making my arms itch. 'Can't you just tell me?' It has to be easier than all the cloak and dagger stuff.

Imogen's waving a hand through the air. I believe my plea has been dismissed.

'The point is I want to help Logan,' she says. 'We had a long chat on the phone last night and then again here this morning, and I think … *we* think me joining the team would suit us all, you and your mum included.'

Logan asks for Imogen to pass him his cup, and while she does, I take a sip of my hot chocolate. 'You mean you've both agreed you'd become one of Logan's carers?'

'That's right.' Imogen is sitting on the arm of the sofa, next to Logan. 'Now, I know it sounds as if I'm the one doing the favour, but believe me it's completely selfish on my part. It's all about me, honestly.' She watches Logan as he finishes his drink, relieves him of his cup and takes it out to the kitchen.

'You're okay with this?' I direct my question at Logan.

'I am.'

Well, that was succinct. And odd. From what Mum's said in the past and from what Logan's told me himself, he hates the thought of anyone other than Mum or me looking after him. I have to be missing something. 'Why Imogen?' I ask.

Logan calls me to him and I sit on the raised foot of his extended chair. I notice how much room there is for me, another sign his mass is disappearing.

'I realise I've been unreasonable expecting your mum to cope,' he says. 'She has Dylan and you to care for, and you have important school years coming up. You need to be concentrating on your studies, not wasting your time on me.'

That explains the *why now?* but not the *why Imogen?* 'Mum said we'd get help from an agency. She brought you the brochures.'

He winces as he shuffles in his seat and I find myself thinking how awful it must be to live with chronic, physical pain. It's rough living with mental pain.

Logan's chilled hand lands on mine.

'I've known Imy since she was a child. I'm comfortable in her company, I don't need to explain myself to her and it's lovely having someone else to talk to. Another's perspective.'

'Gee. Thanks.'

'Come on. You know I can go a whole week without seeing anyone but your mother. Now, before you get all hotheaded and defensive, I appreciate that's not her fault. She's a good woman and she does her best to keep me *socialised*, but it's difficult for me to leave the house, and I don't always feel like going out. Imy and I get on, we have a lot of memories we can share, and she's prepared to come here.'

'That's right.' Imogen's back in the room and she's taken residence in the armchair. 'And I'm a holistic practitioner – I don't think I told you, Tess. I'm going to help bring balance to Logan's life.'

That's made Logan laugh. 'Good luck,' he says, releasing my hand.

I retreat to the sofa and stuff a cushion behind my back. 'So what does that mean? You're going to revitalise him with a few mixed herbs?'

Imogen's softness has solidified. Her face could literally be set in stone. 'I offer homeopathy as a therapy, yes, but there are others available. I trained in a number of treatments. Do you know what the most powerful healer is?'

'Parsley?' I'm out of my depth. Humour is my life-ring.

I got a snort from Logan.

'The most powerful healer is unconditional love,' Imogen says. My reply has not deterred her.

I can't help feeling the conversation's gone a bit weird. A bit hippy.

'But you weren't far off with parsley.' Imogen's developed a twinkle in her eyes. 'It's great for suppressing garlic breath.'

'Imy tells me we are born with the ability to heal ourselves.' Logan flexes his feet. First the left, then the right. Quite balletic.

'We are. And we are responsible for our own well-being. It's time you took charge of your body, Logan.' Imogen's crunched her hand into a fist. She's gone from hippy to Rocky in less time than it took Stallone to climb the famous stairs in the film.

I can see how her ideas appeal to Logan. It's nasty being a slave to pain. 'Does your stuff work on just the body?' I finish my drink and clunk the mug down on the table.

'No. We treat the person. I must point out though, I work as part of a team. We have different areas of expertise. Mine's therapeutic massage.'

'You sly, old devil.' I wink at Logan. 'Now I get it.'

He says nothing.

Imogen's sitting forward on the chair, ready to speak. Her knees are together, and she's resting her arms along her thighs. It's business-like. I can imagine her interviewing her clients like that. Does she have clients, or are they patients? Clients sounds a bit *card in a phone box*.

'I have colleagues who practice psychotherapy and spiritual counselling, if that's what you're asking.'

Her intense gaze is unnerving. I wouldn't be surprised if she practised hypnotherapy as well. I'm reminded of the snake in *The Jungle Book*, and his spiral eyes enticing Mowgli into his constricting coils. Actually, that's not a good comparison to make, not when Imogen's being so kind in offering her help.

'I don't need any of that head nonsense.' Logan's gruff voice blasts me from the Disney wonderland back to his living room. 'Someone I trust and who believes in my ideals will do me nicely, thank you.'

Ideals? The last Mum told me, Logan's ideals involved a date with death, not that I've seen or heard any evidence over the past two days to suggest he's had enough. He's certainly seemed more settled since Imogen's arrival.

'So, what's the plan?' I ask. 'A meeting with Mum to thrash out the details?' I can see Mum taking it personally. She'll feel pushed out and she'll assume she's done something to upset Logan. I guess her refusal to help him die could upset him, but if that was the case he'd have stopped her coming ages ago. She needs to be given all the positives – time at home with Dylan, occasional days out with me, a chance to repair her properly-screwed-up marriage. If we approach it that way, it could work. 'Is this a business arrangement between you two?' I spread my hands to encompass Logan and Imogen. I'm thinking that could also work. It would be no different to employing a specialist care firm, which Mum was encouraging Logan to do.

'I'm helping because I want to. I thought I explained that.' Imogen's vacated the armchair and she's peering through the window. I join her to see what's so fascinating, but there's only the road and the houses opposite. 'It gives me a valid reason for visiting Logan,' she says, quietly. 'And a chance I might bump in to you.'

Crap. I don't know what to do with that. 'How's your dog?' I ask.

'Honey?' Imogen's grimacing. I can see her reflection in the glass. 'She's fine.'

'Her paw's okay?'

'Her paw? Oh! Her paw.' She flicks the hair off her neck and gathers it in one hand. 'Like I said, she's fine. Thorns don't do that much damage.'

'Thorns? I thought she'd ripped out a claw.'

Imogen lets her hair fall as she turns and walks away. 'Oh, yes. That's right.'

Chapter Twenty-Five

Griff

As soon as his day shift was over, Griff procured his phone from his locker. He rubbed the back of his neck as he stared at the screen. There were four voicemails. Someone was eager to get hold of him. The vet said she'd keep him informed as to Ozzy's condition. If all four messages were from her, that surely meant one thing. 'Not Ozzy,' he whispered. 'I can't lose him, too.'

Griff had broken a host of road traffic laws the night before, attempting to reach the vet's before they closed. He'd made it with minutes to spare. Invited in, he was taken through to the back, where Ozzy was lying on an operating table, his wounds dressed. A drip bag hung from a metal stand, with plastic tubing leading to a front paw. A veterinary nurse stood beside Ozzy, stroking his long body. She issued a nod of respect as Griff approached.

He rubbed his hands together for warmth. Nerves and the low temperature of the room had brought on the cold. 'Chilly,' he said to the nurse.

The nurse remained silent. It was the vet who'd taken Griff to Ozzy who replied. 'We keep it cool. It reduces the risk of infection.' She paused, as if assessing the situation, then stepped nearer to the table. 'It's all right to stroke him, Griff.'

She'd called Griff by his first name. He'd heard and understood its implication. She was preparing him for bad news.

'You stay with him, while I fetch the X-rays.' She exited through a rear door.

'Hey, Ozzy.' Griff forced the words out, using all the steel in his reserves to stabilise his voice. 'I wish I could take you home.' He fell silent. The day before his mum died, he'd promised her he'd take her home so she could water her flowers, see the new plant pot he'd fitted to the front of the house, and watch the latest episodes of *Coronation Street* he'd recorded for her. She hadn't left her beloved home intending to never return. She had clothes laid out for the next day, her mug in the sink ready for washing up, dirty laundry in the wash basket.

A book half-read.

But he wasn't able to keep his promise.

The next time his mum made it home, she was in the back of the hearse.

A distant bark from the on-site kennels broke through the dark memory, stirring Griff. Ozzy didn't flinch. No ear flickered, no tail wagged. If it wasn't for the brightly-coloured dressing highlighting the entry of the IV, it appeared as if he was enjoying a well-earned rest after a trek across Portland Bill.

The vet returned, pinned the X-ray sheets onto a lightboard, and flipped the switch. The panel buzzed into life.

The damage was obvious even to Griff's untrained eye.

'It's not good, I'm afraid. Ozzy's sustained multiple injuries.' The vet pointed to the right hand image detailing Ozzy's pelvis. 'Can you see the fractures?'

Griff nodded.

'There's a chance we could plate and screw, but the damage is extensive, and I'm concerned about the associated risks of surgery. He's not a young dog.' Griff's attention was drawn to the left-hand picture. 'He's suffered head trauma, too, which comes with its own set of problems.' The vet looked across to Ozzy. 'He's no bladder control, either.'

'What's the prognosis?' It was a question Griff didn't want answered. For once, he'd prefer to live with the peace that ignorance supplied.

'As I said, he's not a young dog.'

'But he's healthy.' Griff scraped his fingers through his hair. 'Other than ... You know what I mean. Why shouldn't he recover?'

The vet stationed herself next to Griff. 'We'll know more in the next twenty-four hours. There's nothing you can do for him right now. Perhaps you should go home and get some rest. The nurse will stay with him and we'll keep you updated. We'll call if his condition changes.'

Griff sat with Ozzy for another hour before taking the vet's advice.

After a restless night, and an early morning update from the vet advising no change, Griff considered giving work a miss in favour of spending time with Ozzy. It was short-lived as *Breakfast TV* reminded him it was the start of the Easter holidays. Dorset was waking from its wintry slumber and the promise of brighter, if not consistently warmer weather attracted jet-skiers, kayakers, pleasure yachts, and fun-seekers. It was all hands on deck.

Slamming shut the door to his locker, Griff made his way out of the building and into the narrow street, where the damp night air deepened his grey mood. The sun had gone down nearly an hour ago, but it wasn't pitch-black. The lights from the harbourside bars, busy fish restaurants and orange streetlamps threw shafts of optimism onto the pavement, and golden halos onto the water opposite. Lost in thoughts of Ozzy, they went unappreciated as Griff crossed the road and got into his car.

If he didn't listen to the voicemails, he could believe Ozzy was fine. He could take a calm, steady, law-abiding drive to the vet's and deal with the situation once there. He had fifteen minutes until they closed. Plenty of time.

At the point he decided to hide the phone away, it vibrated.

'Don't want to know,' he said, reaching across to the passenger side of the vehicle. He flicked the latch to the glove box and the lid fell like a drawbridge.

The phone continued to rumble. This was a call, not a text.

Griff manoeuvred back into his seat, sucked in a lungful of air, and readied himself for bad news. He answered the phone. 'Hendry.'

'It's Imogen. Is everything okay? I've been trying to get hold of you all day.'

The relief of hearing a friendly voice loosened the tension responsible for keeping Griff upright. He leaned forward and let the steering wheel take the weight of his head. 'I thought you were the vet calling.'

'That's why I'm ringing. How are things? How are you?'

Griff wrapped his fingers around the wheel and pushed himself up. A young man standing on a yacht moored opposite gave Griff a querying thumbs-up. Griff nodded and waved his thanks, ending the mime show with his own thumb-up. The man returned to his business. 'Not good,' Griff said, responding to Imogen's question. 'I'm on my way to the vet's now.' His reply was greeted with silence. 'Imogen?'

'I'm still here,' she said. 'Is Ozzy going to be okay?'

'I don't know. He's in a bad way.'

'Hasn't your vet been in touch?'

'I've been at work. Not allowed to have my phone on.' He hesitated as a young family walking their Dalmatian passed by his car. 'I've not picked up my messages yet.'

'Don't you think you should?'

He thumped the steering wheel. He had enough on his plate without Imogen nagging him. 'Of course I should,' he said, instantly reining in his frustration. 'I just thought—' He laid his head on the cushioned rest behind. 'Hell. I don't know what I thought. I guess I was putting off the inevitable. I'll phone them and then I'll go down there.' Forewarned was forearmed. 'Please don't let me have missed him.' Griff's throat was tightening with every thought of Ozzy. He swallowed away the rising grief and took in another gulp of air. 'He's got to live, Imogen. If he's still with us, I won't let him die. I'll do whatever it takes – time, money – anything. I'll get him better.' He rubbed his eyes, sore from holding back the tide. 'He'll be running along Chesil Beach in no time.'

'Griff?'

He didn't like the tone of that. If Imogen was going to preach about doing the right thing, the kind thing, or say something stupid like it was time to face facts, he wasn't interested. He'd made his pledge and he wasn't about to give up on Ozzy *or* give him up.

He clamped his mouth shut. To avoid an argument, it was best not to answer.

An exchange of breaths followed.

Eventually, Imogen spoke. 'Would you like me to come with you?'

Grateful Imogen was neither confrontational nor moralistic, Griff stood down. 'That's kind of you, thanks, but there's no need.' He forced a smile, hoping it would shape his words into sounding positive. 'We'll be fine.'

'Okay. By the way, I spent the morning with your dad and Tess.'

'You did?'

'He's asked me to become his carer.'

Too much had happened in the last twenty-four hours for

Griff to process new information. For now it was simpler to accept what he'd heard, file it at the back of his mind and refer to it later. 'That's nice,' he said. 'Is Tess okay?'

'She's fine. She's intending on spending her holidays at your father's. You should come over. She'd like to see you.'

'She would?' A flash of headlamps from a patrolling coastguard vehicle drew Griff's attention to the present, and sharpened his focus on the conversation in hand. Imogen was inviting him to visit his own daughter and father. That wasn't right.

He was about to challenge Imogen, when his phone beeped. 'I've a call coming through,' he said. 'I have to go.' With that, he cut Imogen's call dead and received the incoming one.

'Griff. It's Susan, from the vets. Did you get my messages?'

Panic was an unwelcome and alien sensation to Griff. His neck bristled with heat, his stomach turned in on itself, and his airways narrowed. His head … His head was full of unlit tunnels, buried questions and surfacing words – words that didn't sit still long enough for him to sort into a logical order. 'I've not had a chance to listen to them,' he said. 'Sorry. Ozzy's okay, isn't he?'

His question was answered with a lengthy pause.

'I think it's best we discuss things here,' said the vet. 'How soon can you get to the practice?'

It was another blind, wild drive, with every roll of the trip meter taking Griff closer to his greatest fear.

Although it was a different course to the previous evening's journey, the urgency and desperation were excruciatingly similar.

Today it had been work keeping Griff from Ozzy. Last night it was his selfish need for comfort and forgiveness, and an unexpected, but welcome act of life-affirmation. It hadn't been his intention to sleep with Evie – he was calling in on his son – but when she opened the door, her eyes invited him into her world, and it was familiar, reassuring and accepting.

He flattened the brake pedal to the floor as he registered the view through the windscreen. Traffic was backing up from a signal-controlled junction and the rear end of a people carrier was looming large. Griff swore as his Land Rover came to a whiplash stop inches away. His car illuminated the interior of the one in front, and a pair of saucer eyes stared at him from its rear-view mirror. Griff waved an apologetic hand. 'Take it easy,' he said to himself, rumbling his fingers on the steering wheel. 'Breathe.'

As he reached the head of the queue, a Mini, heading in the opposite direction, drove him back to thoughts of Evie.

He'd left in a hurry last night, but he'd told her he needed to get to the vet's, hadn't he? He hadn't just *dumped* her? That would be unforgivable.

Problem was, it was all a blur. Except the sex. He could remember every last detail of that; the depth of Evie's kisses, the heat of her touch, her hot breath on his chest; her whispered words of love, spoken so quietly, they were somewhere between reality and imagination. She held nothing back. Months of confusion, restraint and separation disappeared as their souls, *their beings* connected again, once more together and whole.

And there was love and meaning in Griff's every move, too. It went without saying. Actions speak louder than words, right? 'You fool, Hendry.'

Broken into its basic components – he'd arrived at the cottage, had sex, given no declarations of love, and left in haste with no further contact – last night could be misconstrued as a wham, bam, thank you ma'am moment.

And Evie would have every right to think that, but it wasn't what Griff had intended and he certainly hadn't set out to hurt Evie.

He rubbed his forehead, pre-empting the arrival of the pain hammering its way through from the back of his neck. 'Please don't think I used you,' he said, ramming the car into gear and pulling away.

With no further delays, the final part of the drive was straightforward. The open road gave Griff's mind the space to consider how to apologise to Evie, and the freedom to wonder why Imogen was working for his father. At all other times, he was occupied with the sickening swirls in his gut caused by anticipating Ozzy's condition.

It was bewildering to think that four months ago Griff was a happy, family man in a stable marriage, receiving the love of an incredible woman, and enjoying walks along Chesil Beach with his old pal, Ozzy. The speed with which solid foundations were washed away astounded him.

It wasn't only the coast that had suffered the storms.

As Griff reversed into a parking space at the vet's, Susan greeted him from the doorway. 'A reception committee,' he muttered, not liking the sense of doom slithering through him.

Now was the time to fight. Griff would do whatever it took to get Ozzy back on his feet. Giving up was not an option.

It was never an option.

Determined and resolute, he locked the car and headed for the building.

The sheer sadness in Susan's eyes knocked him breathless.

Neither party spoke until they were inside and the door was shut.

'You should come through, Griff. We need to talk.' Susan led the way to the back room where Ozzy lay.

There was a different nurse with him than yesterday. 'He's a gorgeous boy,' she said.

Susan advised the nurse it was okay for her to leave, then directed Griff to a chair next to the table. 'Have you had a chance to listen to my phone messages?'

Unable to speak, Griff shook his head.

'Okay.' Susan moved to the other side of the table. 'Well, here it is. Ozzy's not responded to treatment and as sometimes happens in these cases, his condition has worsened. Considerably.' She ran her hands through Ozzy's shaggy grey and white coat. 'The injury to his head is more than he can cope with.'

'What does that mean?' Griff watched the repeated movement of Susan's hand.

'The old boy's shutting down. He's in a coma and I don't believe he's going to wake.'

'A coma?' That was new, a shock, a challenge, but not insurmountable. 'So, he could wake?' Griff cast his eyes over Ozzy. He looked so peaceful. So calm. He was sleeping, that was all. Taking the time he needed to recover.

From his peripheral vision, Griff saw Susan clasp her hands together and raise them to her mouth.

'No. It's not just that,' she said. 'His organs are failing.'

There was no significance in that. Logan had heart failure. He'd had it for years. It hadn't brought about his immediate death. He took pills.

Laughter and muffled voices from people leaving the waiting area joined Griff's internal conversation, upsetting his train of thought. 'What about medication? Surgery?' he said, trying to steal order from the chaos.

Susan shook her head as she swung her hands down to rest in front of her thighs. 'Surgery's not an option, Griff. We need to be realistic. The prognosis isn't good. It's not … hopeful.'

'Unbelievable.' She was just like everyone else. Just like his father. No one stood up for the weak. No one took responsibility. No one was prepared to fight. Leaning his elbows on his side of the table, Griff rested his chin on his fists. 'You're saying do nothing.'

'I'm saying there's nothing further I can do that would alter the expected outcome.'

'Expected outcome?' Upright and alert, Griff glanced from Ozzy to Susan. 'Not guaranteed.'

'There is no magic bullet. At most, Ozzy has days, at worst—'

'No.' Griff rose from the chair, walked around the table and crouched in front of Ozzy's nose. 'You say *days* like it's a sentence. It's not. It's a chance to find other methods, other meds. Things can change in *days*.'

A small, featherweight hand was laid on his shoulder.

'*Days* in his condition is a sentence. He can't fight back. His body can't take any more intrusions and it's not fair to leave him in this state of limbo.' Susan's tone was kind but firm. 'He's lost bowel control now, as well as his bladder, and he's only going to get worse. This isn't living, Griff. I know it's hard. It's heartbreaking, but you need to think about what's best for Ozzy.' She squeezed the top of Griff's arm. 'He's had a long and happy life. He's been well-loved and looked after, but now he needs you to let him go.' She paused, removed her hand and stepped away. 'I'll leave you for a while. Call if you need me.'

As soon as she had gone, Griff rubbed his eyes, sniffed, and cuffed his nose. He ran a finger under Ozzy's soft, warm ear. 'She won't listen to me, boy. She thinks you're a lost cause. Show her you're not. Come on. Wake up, wag that beautiful tail we refused to have docked. Come on, Ozzy. I need you. We need you. You have to come through this.'

The silence and stillness of the room magnified the total

lack of response, and Griff's chest ached. Collecting his chair, he sat at the end of the table and put his head next to Ozzy's. 'This is my fault. You're here because of me.' He wrapped his arms around the dog's neck, pulled himself in tighter, and prayed for a miracle.

His heart contracted at the sound of his mobile. Evie's ringtone reverberated around the room. Hearing her concerned voice carried the risk of breaking Griff, but he had to answer; had to clear up any misunderstandings about the day before; had to tell her about Ozzy.

With a heavy reluctance, he withdrew from his hug, fished the phone out of his pocket and touched the answer icon. 'Hi.' His voice was dry and rasping. He cleared his throat, stood, and looked down on his old pal. 'I'm at the vet's.'

'I thought you must be. Tell me about Ozzy. How is he?' There was an uncertainty and a quiver to Evie's voice which was enough to push Griff over the emotional cliff.

'It's my fault he's here,' he blurted out. 'My fault he's lying on this table, with tubes sticking in him, his leg in plaster, his life in the balance.' A sharp intake of breath accompanied each phrase. 'I threw the biscuits. I wasn't thinking. I threw them and they landed in the road. Evie, it was terrible. Honey – she was okay, but Ozzy ...' He pressed the phone to his ear until the pain became intolerable. 'I had both the dogs with me. I should have been concentrating on them, not on what my dad had said.'

'I don't know who Honey is,' Evie said. 'Tell me about Ozzy.'

Griff heard her, but he couldn't disengage from the scene of the accident. 'He went under a van. Bang! It was so fast, so loud. A woman ran across the road and took hold of Honey and the van driver helped me get Ozzy onto the pavement. He wasn't moving, but he was breathing. I asked the van driver if he had a blanket or a towel we could lift

Ozzy onto. He had a couple of dust sheets in the back of his van so we used them. I tore off scraps to bind the wounds. Ozzy was bleeding. And his leg was twisted and mangled. I wrapped him up. He had to be kept warm, you know? Secure. I was worried shock was going to set in, and that could have killed him. We put him and Honey in the van and brought them here.'

'I meant tell me about Ozzy, now,' Evie said, gently. 'How is he?'

'Now?' Griff's sight returned to the operating table, the jolt of which took his legs from under him, and he collapsed into the chair. 'They think we should let him go.'

'Let him go?' Evie's quiver had developed into a full-blown quake. 'He's not coming home?'

Clutching his head, Griff clenched his jaws together and scrunched his eyes shut.

Death was a bastard. It had taken too many loved ones from him already, and once again it was waving its scythe, taunting him and whispering wicked words of victory in his ear. 'I hate death,' Griff said, restoring his vision. 'I don't care what my father said. I'll fight it all the way.'

'You're not making any sense, Griff. You keep talking about your dad.'

'Yes, because he thinks I'm on some sort of crusade to save lives so I can find peace, but I'm not.'

'Griff—'

'He said it's something I have to deal with, that there are worse things in life than death. Like what? What can possibly be worse than death?' Griff was up again, and marching back and forth, stopping and staring at anatomical posters on the end walls at every turn.

'Griff?' Evie demanded his attention. 'Tell me about Ozzy.' She paused, her sniffs and snuffles distorting down the line. 'Is there really no hope?'

No hope. Two tiny, succinct and powerful words.

Griff quietened down. His moment's respite brought him out of his head and back into the world; the world where it was apparent Evie was crying. 'I'm sorry,' Griff said. 'You love him, too. I shouldn't have laid all that stuff on you.' This wasn't just about Griff; Ozzy was his dog, but for the last three years, he'd been part of the Hendry and MacDonald family. Evie still asked after him, Dylan squealed with delight at seeing him, and Tess's willingness to visit Griff's flat to take Ozzy for a walk showed how much she missed having him around. How could Griff tell the children there was no hope?

'He's in a coma,' he said, choosing words that would lay a path for Evie to follow. 'The vet says he has days at most. She says it's unfair to leave him in limbo; that it isn't living.' He halted as a shiver snaked its way from his skull, down his spine and into his core. He let his arms drop to his side. 'A half-life is worse than death,' he said. 'A life without pleasure or freedom, or a life unable to be lived is worse than death.'

He stared at his dog; his friend; his trusty companion, who could never again romp across the pebbles of Chesil, who'd never bark or yap and snap at the wild spray of the sea at the Bill, get under Griff's feet, lick his face or sit with him in the peaceful evening hours, play chase with the children.

All the things that made Ozzy's life joyous and worth living had been ripped away, and that wasn't going to change. Not in days.

Griff raised the phone to his ear. 'Evie. I understand now. I have to let him go.'

Chapter Twenty-Six

Evie

Evie swished her hand through the warm water in the kitchen sink. Washing the dishes was a mundane job and one that required little attention. It suited her. It was a welcome and normal occupation after yesterday's abnormal and stressful day. Having fed Dylan, and with Tess back home from Logan's and in her bedroom, it gave Evie a chance to settle.

Since lunchtime, she'd dealt with a fractious two-year-old, broken the news about Ozzy to Tess, and then consoled the shocked and silent teen, all the time supressing her own acute sadness. She was good at that. Putting others first was what she did. She'd made it her role in life. When her family needed her, she was there.

Stepping up was easy; natural. It was the backing off she wrestled with.

She wanted to be with Griff last night; be there for him and Ozzy. Say their goodbyes together. Cry together.

'Tess is with your dad,' she'd said. 'And I've not put Dylan to bed yet. We could be with you in twenty minutes.'

'It's no place for Dylan,' Griff said. 'Just hug him a little tighter tonight, will you? And Tess. Make sure they're all right.'

This was a life-changing moment for Griff, and one Evie didn't underestimate – all the more reason for her to be with him, either in person or on the phone. She offered support and kind words, reassurance that he was doing the right thing and reiterated that he didn't have to face the awful moment alone.

'I know,' he said, 'but I don't want you to remember Ozzy the way he is now. Keep the good memories alive. For all of us. And be with the children. They need you more.'

Evie picked up a dirty mug from the side, plunged it into the water and scrubbed at its inside.

To not be needed hurt. To not be needed by Griff, when he'd come to her, upset, seeking comfort and seeking love, was devastating.

As feelings she'd long since drowned bubbled to the surface, she continued cleaning the mug, each rub more vigorous than the last.

She had to have the confidence that Griff hadn't used her; that she wasn't just a convenient object, a handy receptacle for his frustrations; that two nights ago, they'd made love together, not that he'd had sex with her. She had to believe his grief and his distress over Ozzy proved how caring he was; that it wasn't that he didn't need her at all, he just didn't need her at that moment. She had to keep the faith she'd invested in him, and not confuse or merge him with memories of Neil. They were two very different men.

With the last item washed, Evie shook the drips from her hands and crossed the kitchen to Ozzy's corner. His bed hadn't been there for weeks, but it was still his space.

'It's sad.'

Evie looked up to see Tess, with Dylan mounted on her hip, standing in the doorway. 'It is.'

'I keep thinking about Griff and wondering how he is.' Tess stepped into the room and joined Evie in the corner. 'He's lost his best mate. They've been together forever.'

Tess was right. Griff and Ozzy were an item long before the MacDonalds came along.

Evie pulled her children in for a hug. 'Did you know Ozzy's full name is Osrid? It's Welsh,' she said. 'Griff told me on our first date. It means divine counsellor.' The

233

recollection made her smile. 'He said Ozzy was as good as his name. A great listener.'

'Poor Ozzy.' Tess sighed, kissed Dylan on his nose, and brought his head into her neck. 'And your poor dad having to deal with it all,' she said to him. 'What a horrible final memory. Life can be so brutal.'

'It can.' Evie squeezed her daughter and planted a kiss on her cheek. It was a bit of a stretch. 'When did you get taller than me?'

Tess moved away and dispensed her '*Really, Mum?*' look. 'Do you remember not being able to reach the icing sugar for Dylan's birthday cake? His *first* birthday cake? Yes? Well. Since then.'

Where had that time gone? 'I've missed so much, Tess. Even when I'm here, my head's at Logan's, or I'm thinking about Griff. When you were born, I promised to always make you my number one priority.'

'Priorities change. It's all right. Logan and Dylan need you more right now.'

'But it's not all right.' Evie brought her arms close to her body, holding them across her chest. 'Just because you don't make a fuss shouldn't mean you get overlooked.'

Tess hoisted Dylan onto her other hip. 'Despite what you think, you're not Superwoman. When Dylan was born, I knew he'd need your attention. And I understand why Logan's so dependent on you. That's not to say I'd turn down spending time with you.' She smiled. 'I'm saying I get it.' As she spoke, Dylan began to wriggle and show his dissatisfaction at being lodged on the wrong hip. 'He's never liked being held this side. You're a strange boy,' she said, handing him to Evie.

'Let's do something now,' Evie said, a sudden change in speed carrying her through to the hall. 'I'll sort Dylan, you get your coat on and we'll go out.'

The ensuing silence and lack of activity on Tess's part stopped Evie in her tracks. She glanced back at her daughter. 'Not now?'

'I'm heading out. That's what I came down to tell you.' Tess checked the clock above the door and stirred into action. 'And I'm running late. Got to go. Sorry.' On her way out, she grabbed her hat, fluffed Dylan's hair, and kissed Evie. 'I'll be back to help with tea.'

Recovering from the teenage whirlwind, Evie took Dylan into the living room, picked up a *Noddy* book and settled on the sofa. 'It's you, me and Big Ears, then.'

Her attempt to enter her daughter's life had been put on hold. It wasn't a snub, although Evie could understand that – she'd cancelled her plans with Tess left, right and centre in the past to deal with Logan or see to Dylan – it was that Tess's trip out was a far more attractive proposition than spending an afternoon with Evie.

The question was, who was that more attractive proposition?

Chapter Twenty-Seven

Tess

I feel bad at ditching Mum. It's been a tough morning, all things considered. Every time I think of Ozzy, I have to steel myself, and seeing the pain in Mum's eyes stirs up my insides.

It's not only the tears I'm fighting.

When Imogen contacted me asking for us to meet on the seafront, I didn't think twice. It was the distraction I needed, and away from my room, away from the temptation to lift up the floorboard, means I've managed to remain clean.

I've Imogen to thank for that, although I'm not enjoying the breeze blowing in from the Channel. The contrary spring weather's tricked me again. I wish I'd brought my coat.

I use my hand as a peak, shielding my eyes from the glare, and scan Weymouth beach. It's mostly young couples with pushchairs, or the elderly bent over their walking aids. Easter attracts the newly-weds and nearly-deads.

I shouldn't say that. It's disrespectful. Besides, I can see an old man paddling in the sea and another offering his woman an ice cream. They're enjoying themselves, no matter their age or the chilly breeze.

I wonder if Logan would feel differently about life if he got to live a little.

The old bugger refuses to use a wheelchair, and a walk along the Esplanade's a non-starter, but we could take him out for a drive, stop for fish and chips, or tea and Dorset apple cake. There's a lovely café and gardens in Upwey. They have a wishing well. I threw a pound coin in last summer. I thought about all the things I could wish for, like being free of my father, understanding who I am, to stop cutting, but I decided to wish Mum and Dylan long, happy and healthy lives. I should probably go back and top up my pound.

I budge up on the wooden bench, as a woman eating chips sits beside me. They smell good. It doesn't matter I had lunch a short while ago, my stomach still rumbles. She offers me one, but I smile and politely decline. I'm hoping when Imogen gets here we can head for a cosy coffee shop where I can buy a hot chocolate and a pecan and maple twist.

That's something I'd like to do with Logan, but I have no way of transporting him. We could go with Mum, but he complains about getting into her Mini. It's too low and there's not enough room for him. He needs to stretch out to stop his joints from seizing up. We need a bigger car, like Griff's, but I doubt Logan would go out in that. He'd need a leg-up for a start, and extra padding on the seat. The Land Rover's a bit rustic. As Griff says, it's built for practicality, not comfort.

Logan's built for comfort these days.

Still no sign of Imogen. I was surprised to receive a text from her. She got my number from Logan. Says she'd like to get to know me better, especially since we'd be seeing more of each other. She feels we have a connection, and she'd like to explore it further. Explore was her word, not mine. I've not had a chance to tell Mum about her yet, what with Ozzy and then rushing out after lunch. I'll let her know before she goes round tonight.

Imogen suggested meeting by the Clock Tower. It's an easy landmark and it's clear along the pavement at the moment. The Easter fair will be set up at the weekend. It'll be heaving then. I never go. I hate all the sidling past people that goes on, all the up-close-and-personal stuff. Totally outside my comfort zone. Makes me sick with nerves.

I'm nervous now, and pleased I didn't accept the chip

from my bench neighbour, as I can feel my lunch working its way back up my food pipe. My mouth's dry, too, but that could be the wind blowing away the moisture.

A dog's appeared and it's sniffing my boots. It's a Labrador. 'Tess. Hi. Sorry I'm late.'

I divert my eyes from the dog and see Imogen in a lurid pink mac, which is open and flapping like a crazy flamingo. She's standing next to the Clock Tower. Her hair's blowing around her face, and she pulls a strand from her mouth. She's hanging onto the dog.

'This is Honey,' she says. 'I thought we could walk her along the beach. You take the lead.'

In our friendship? In the yomp across the sand? Imogen thrusts the leather strap from her hand to mine, and the dog pulls me into a standing position. I've taken the lead. I mock myself for thinking Imogen meant something else.

'She's lively today. It's the wind. Gets right up her tail.' Imogen laughs, shoves her hands into her pockets, and nods for me to get going. We head for the large sweep of the bay. It's the only place dogs are allowed during the holiday season.

I'm reminded of Ozzy and the raw ache resurfaces. I blame the wind for the tears in my eyes and hand the lead back to Imogen. 'Sorry.'

An arm is threaded through mine. 'Is this about Griff's dog?'

Nodding, I look out to sea. 'Have you heard? We lost him.' I'm pulled so close to Imogen, I can feel her body heat.

'I'm so sorry. I knew things were bad. The other day when we were at Logan's and Griff phoned, he asked me not to worry you with the details. That's why I didn't say anything.'

'And why you lied about Honey?'

We stop, my forward motion coming to an abrupt halt because I'm under Imogen's control.

'I did lie. You're right. I had to think up a reason as to why she needed collecting from the vet's.' She looks at me, pleading for my forgiveness. 'I didn't want you stressing.'

We continue on our course, Honey stopping to sniff at the flowers, the bus shelters, and the steps down to the beach, and we make our way onto the sand.

The nearer we get to the sea, the blowier it's becoming. Imogen sets me and Honey free. I choose not to charge head first into the sea. I shiver at the thought as Honey bounds in and out. I can't separate her splashes from the waves.

'Are you cold?' Imogen offers me her mac.

'You keep it,' I say. 'It'll clash with my hair.'

She smiles, but accepts my reason. 'Your hair's a gorgeous colour.'

I point to my head. 'It's ginger.'

'Yes, it is, and from now on, whenever I see a beautiful redhead, I'll think of you.'

'And that's a good thing?' I'm not seeking compliments. I'm trying to work out where I stand, because I'm no expert when it comes to friendships, but I'm pretty sure you shouldn't flirt with people unless you fancy them or, being cynical, want something from them, and what could Imogen possibly want from me? I have nothing.

'Why so much self-doubt, Tess?' She's folded her arms and she's frowning. 'This is to do with your past, the story you've never told, isn't it?'

The sea's reflecting the bright blue of the sky today, and I notice how Imogen's eyes are doing the same. I'm concerned she'll reflect my thoughts. I turn away and try to pick out Honey from two other Labradors bouncing in and out of the water.

Without warning, I find myself in Imogen's hold again. This time she's taken my hand and is guiding me towards the wall near a small standpipe. I hitch myself up, sit down and lean against the blue and white horizontal railings. They were redecorated two weeks ago. All their cracks and blemishes have been covered with a simple lick of paint.

Imogen joins me on the wall. 'I was a lot like you at your age,' she says. 'I was happiest in my own company or with my mum, because I didn't have to explain myself all the time.'

Her knee is resting against mine. I wish she'd explain what that's about.

'What were you avoiding?' I'm confident in asking this question because it's what I've been doing for years – avoiding speaking out, not admitting who I am, sidestepping the truth.

'I didn't want to talk about the death of my brother.' Imogen's sight is fixed at a spot in the distance. 'He died when I was eleven.'

That's heavy, but I sit in silence, respecting her need to not explain herself. I feel the same about Dad's death. It's nasty having to go through all that vile detail just to satisfy someone's morbid curiosity. I know what happened to Dad, I don't need to enlighten anyone outside of the law.

Imogen's drawing breath. 'I wasn't with Kieran at the time, but my mother told me he died trying to save Griff.'

Woah. Imogen's statement lands a hefty punch. It's left me lying on the floor of the ring. Griff was the man who did the saving, not the other way round. What had he done that he required saving from? And more than that, what was so dangerous Imogen's brother died in the process? Holy shit.

Dizzy from the power of Imogen's verbal blow, I try to remain focused and keep my mouth shut.

She nudges me. 'It's okay. I introduced the subject, you can ask me questions.'

'I don't want to,' I say, realising she's doing exactly what I did to her at Logan's – trying to trade secrets. I had no idea hers would involve Griff, but in doing so, it could compromise my mum, and I'm not putting her in danger.

Imogen looks expectant. She wants me to ask. I don't want to be rude to her, so I'll tread carefully. 'Is this what you and Logan mentioned yesterday? Mum knowing about your brother?'

'Yes.' Imogen leans into me. 'I take it neither Griff nor your mum told you about Kieran.'

'Well, no, but it's not my business, is it?' And I vow to keep it that way. If Mum had wanted me to know, she'd have told me.

Imogen sits up straight. 'No. It wasn't Griff's finest hour.' She's talking about it with such composure, I'm impressed. It's a trait I recognise and connect with. 'He tombstoned off Pulpit Rock and got into trouble,' she continues. 'Kieran jumped in after him, but the sea and the boulders got the better of him.' She's quiet now; thinking. 'Thank God Griff came away with only a broken ankle,' she says, after a moment or two. 'Of course, he blames himself for Kieran's death. It seems he's been trying to put it right from the moment it happened, but you can't remedy something like that.'

I agree with her. Some things we just have to bear. 'I guess that explains his need to save everyone and everything.' I hope that wasn't disrespectful. My mouth's engaged before my brain, and if it wasn't for the stone wall behind my heels, I'd kick myself. 'He's all about saving,' I add, looking at Imogen.

'That's what the newspapers said. He's been quite the local celebrity in the past with his heroic deeds and acts of courage. Did you see the latest piece on him in the *Echo*?'

'Griff's been in the news?' He kept that quiet. I make a mental note to google him. 'I'm sorry about your brother,' I say, realising I haven't yet acknowledged his death. 'I was eleven when my dad died.'

'I remember you saying.'

That's right. I told her on the day we met.

'You said you weren't close,' she continues. 'He was part of your family, though. You must have experienced his loss.'

I experienced many things under my father's regime. His physical loss was not one of them. Not in the way Imogen means.

On the day he died, Dad was demanding Bombay mix of all things. He was drunk, so Mum wasn't going to risk upsetting him. We got in the car and drove to the supermarket, leaving Dad to fester in his own company. When we got home, I saw him at his bedroom window. He was spying on us, timing our trip or something. I helped Mum put the shopping away, washed my hands and then I rushed upstairs to my room, shutting myself in, purposely avoiding him.

'Tess.'

I jumped. Hearing his voice panicked me. He was in my room. When I turned, he was there, on my bed. I couldn't process what I was seeing. Five minutes before, he'd been at his window, sneering down at Mum and me, now he was sprawled top left to bottom right on my bed, one arm across his chest, the other, spewing blood.

'Get your mum,' he said. 'She has to take me seriously now.' The words were gasped out. 'Go! I'm not meant to die.'

Like all the times before, when his actions rooted me to the spot, and froze me with terror, I couldn't move or speak. I couldn't help, even if I'd wanted to.

His last words were, 'Think of your mum.'

And that's what I did. I thought of Mum and how he'd never let her leave. I thought of all the times he'd threatened and abused her, and I thought how in trying to ruin Mum's life, he'd destroyed his own. He was mad, dangerous, and bleeding to death.

As I watched him take his final breath, Mum entered.

After a moment of us both staring at his body, Mum shoved me out through the door and down the stairs to the kitchen, where she made a cup of tea and suggested we should work out what to do next. It was surreal. It was as if nothing bad had happened.

And then reality kicked in.

Mum said, 'You can't be involved, Tess. We'll tell the police we came home, unpacked the shopping and then sat down for half an hour. I'll say it was me who went upstairs and found Neil. All you need to remember is that you stayed in the kitchen, drinking tea and eating biscuits.' She checked the barrel. 'Digestives. Eat one now.' I did. 'Dip it in your tea. Let a few crumbs fall in.' I did that, too. 'Leave your mug on the table.'

'They'll want to know what you were doing in my room, Mum.'

'I was looking for your father.'

'He doesn't go in my room.'

She'd faltered at that.

'Had you checked the other rooms?' I asked, giving her a valid reply.

'Yes. And yours was the last place left. I think he was making a point. Getting to me by hurting you, thinking you'd be the one to find him.'

I actually believed that.

After thirty minutes, Mum called the police.

Through the railings, a dog snuffles at my back, and I'm reminded of where I am and who I'm with. I refrain from speaking the words poised on my lips. No matter what connection Imogen and I have, I mustn't tell her my secret.

I change the course of our conversation. 'I feel Ozzy's loss,' I say. 'But Griff will feel it more.'

'He will.' Imogen launches herself off the wall and invites me to do the same.

'He had to let him go.' I jump down and aim for where I last spotted Honey. The sand is firm and easy to walk on. I'm barely leaving a footprint. My boots make a shallow impression, but it disappears as soon as I take another step.

'Tough call,' Imogen says. 'Especially as Griff's all about saving.' She calls Honey to her, and the dog gallops across the beach. Imogen steps back to absorb the collision. 'He'd *insist* on someone living, even if they didn't want to be here.'

Although I'm concentrating on not being part of Honey's shake and spray act, I'm aware Imogen is weighing me up.

I move out of Honey's way just as she's whirring into action. I'm amazed at how far dogs can eject water from their fur. Imogen's all right. She's wearing a rain mac.

'Are you and Logan close?' she asks, fitting the lead to Honey's collar.

'I don't think of him as my granddad, but we get on.' I'm of the opinion the question is linked to Imogen's comment about Griff saving lives. Logan may well have told her about the directive Mum's signed and I suppose he might have spoken about his desire to die. Imogen's very easy to talk to. There's a way about her that makes people share stuff. I've had to stop myself once or twice already.

She links her arm through mine again, and we march towards the promenade. 'Would you be shocked if I told you Logan's asked me to help him with something?'

'I'll be offended if it's the gardening.' I know where this conversation is leading. A joke won't stop it from happening.

'He's been very honest with me about how he feels living alone, how much he misses Marilyn, and how much of a struggle life is for him, and he's asked if I would help him find a happier place. Do you understand what I'm saying?'

'He wants to die,' I say, plainly. 'I understand that.'

Imogen sighs. 'I'd like to help him, Tess, I really would,

but it goes against my principles. The thing is, and you can't repeat this to anyone, he's put me in a difficult position. I know he's asked your mum and she's refusing to have anything to do with it, and he said he could never ask Griff because he'd vehemently oppose it and it would be the end of their relationship, but what if Logan tries something and messes up? It has to be all or nothing for him. He can't deal with having a sharp mind trapped in a useless body. He needs someone on his side. *By* his side.' She pauses as we climb up the wooden steps, Honey straining to pull ahead. 'Any thoughts?'

My left wrist itches, but I can't scratch it as I'm on as short a leash as Honey. I'm locked to Imogen's arm. 'I have loads of thoughts,' I say. 'But none that would help Logan.' Here's one: If I decided to see his plan through, I wouldn't tell anyone. Not even Mum. It would remain between Logan and me. 'The old bugger's going to have to put up with us looking after him.' I raise a smile and hope it's enough to put an end to this particular subject. 'Can we go to a café now? There are dog-friendly ones over the road.'

Honey's found a patch of sun to lie in and daydream. The crashing and lolloping around she did on the beach has worn her out. It's like being out with Dylan. Crazy madness one minute and flat out the next. I'm enjoying the pecan and maple twist I promised myself, and Imogen is sipping a fruit flavoured tea. Our conversation has moved on from Logan, but I've given my word I wouldn't repeat any of it to anyone. Imogen's obviously made up her mind she can trust me, and I'm flattered.

I'm also warm and comfortable. The coffee shop has large, squishy armchairs.

'I'll have to go soon,' Imogen says, returning her cup to its saucer. 'Will you be at Logan's later?'

A muffled no works its way out through an oversized bite of sweet pastry. I swallow, wipe my mouth and try again. 'Mum's popping round tonight. I'll be looking after Dylan. You?'

'I'm not sure when I'm next there. Logan wants to discuss the new arrangement with your mum first.' She's smiling as she trails her thumb up and down her china cup. 'She sounds like a lovely lady.'

'She is.' I rub the crumbs off my hand and push away the plate. I pull out my phone, search for a photo of the family seated around the table on New Year's Day, and show it to Imogen. Her head tilts and one brow cocks, then she gives this odd little nod as if she's just confirmed something.

'I was right when I said you take after your mum. She's stunning. And I can see why Griff fell in love with her.' Imogen pauses and stares at the photo. 'Got to believe they'll work things out.'

She prods the phone away and I take it as an indication she's seen enough. I tuck it in my back pocket.

'Yeah,' I say. 'I know Mum wants to.'

'She's told you that?'

'She tells me lots of things. We're pretty close.'

'I never had that with my mum. It was my dad I leaned on for support, but he left years ago.' Imogen's adopted a thoughtful expression. 'That's why it's so wonderful being part of Logan's life again.'

'For fatherly guidance?'

She shrugs. 'I told you I was selfish.'

'You keep saying that, but I don't believe you're helping just so you feel good about yourself. You wouldn't be a herbal healer if you did.'

'Holistic practitioner.' Her arms extend across the table and she wiggles her fingers. She wants me to take her hands. I'm so in the moment, I respond and reach out. Her skin is chilled. 'I'd love to have a daughter like you,' she says. 'You're so kind and caring.'

And there it is. The defining moment. How Imogen views me. I'd clearly been picking up rogue signals. It's a relief, to be honest. I'm happy in the knowledge I'm a normal teenager, with crushes and fantasies just like everyone else. I can't help smiling.

'What is it?'

'What you said. It's a nice compliment.' I'm not returning it, though. I'm happy with the mum I've got. 'Thank you.'

'It's true. It must be wonderful to be part of your family. Mine started disintegrating the day Kieran died.'

I think about this for a minute and compare Imogen's life to mine. The day my dad died, our family started to grow. First in strength and then in numbers. I realise we're the exception.

'I hear Griff talk about you and Dylan, and his love for you both shines through. He's a proud dad. He's part of something special, and it's something I want.'

'It's not wrong to want to belong,' I say, marvelling at the fact Griff spoke about me. 'It's human nature. I'm happiest at home, with Mum and Dylan, even though I'm a bit of a loner by nature. Does that make sense?' Imogen hums her response and I continue. 'We're a little out of shape, but I reckon things will improve with you around.'

I truly believe that. Imogen's input is going to make a huge difference to our lives.

As I look across to her, I notice she's staring down at our arms. My arms. The sleeves have ridden up. I'm quick to withdraw, but I'm trying not to overreact; not to draw attention to my marks.

Imogen's eyes flick up to mine.

Chapter Twenty-Eight

Evie

'I'm so glad you're back.' Evie gave her daughter a quick hug. 'Don't shut the door. I'm off to Logan's. Are you okay to look after Dylan?' She hated passing the responsibility to Tess, but she had no choice. Griff hadn't turned up to look after their son and he wasn't answering his phone, suggesting he was working a day shift until seven, and if Evie took Dylan with her, she wouldn't be able to concentrate on Logan's needs, and he commanded her full attention. As did Dylan.

'It's fine, Mum. Has he had his bath?'

Evie halted, one foot in the hall, the other on the gravel drive. 'I tried, but he screamed blue murder. He was adamant he didn't want one.' She should have stood her ground and insisted, but fighting with Dylan added nothing but anxiety to her already stressful day. It was exhausting and unnecessary. 'I'll bathe him tomorrow. Unlike Logan. He's texting me every two minutes demanding my help with his shower. He's not had dinner yet. I don't know what he's up to.'

'You best go, then.' Tess swatted Evie away. 'I'll see to Dylan.'

'Thank you.' Evie kissed Tess's cheek and then crunched her way to the Mini. 'What would I do without you?' She climbed in and started the engine. 'Did you have a good afternoon?'

'I did, thanks. Which reminds me—'

Logan's red alert tone sirened its way around the drive.

'Sorry. I have to go. Tell me about it later, yes?' Evie

shut the door, waved to Tess, and drove away, fighting to keep her head above the swamp of guilt into which she was sinking – guilt swilling round her ankles because she wasn't at Logan's when he needed her, guilt sucking at her waist because she'd failed to maintain Dylan's boundaries, and guilt engulfing her chest for having to rely on Tess so much.

And for not finding the time to talk to her about her afternoon.

Or Neil.

'Tomorrow,' Evie said to herself, ignoring another blast from her phone. 'We'll go out and we'll talk and we'll start making up for lost time. Before it's too late.'

If Griff would look after Dylan, Evie and Tess could go out for the evening. They could go for a pizza, or to the cinema. Evie couldn't recall the last film she'd seen on the big screen. 'I must have taken Tess,' she muttered.

It wasn't when Neil was around, that was a given. He'd forbidden Evie from setting foot in the place.

'You're not going,' he'd said. 'It's full of dirty pervs in the back row, playing with themselves, waiting for sluts like you to turn up and finish the job.'

So she didn't go. Not for Neil's sake, though. For Tess's. There was no way Evie could have taken her to watch a film without Tess chatting about it afterwards. They'd have been found out on the spot, Neil would have punished them, and Tess would have always associated a pleasurable activity with her father's wrath.

It had been that way for Evie and sex.

Until she met Griff.

Who, at this moment in time, has vanished from the face of the earth.

'Where are you?' Evie said, turning into a side road.

She'd not heard from him all day and she could only imagine his heartache over losing Ozzy. She wanted to see

Griff and hold him and let him know he'd done the right thing, but he wasn't returning her calls or messages, and he hadn't turned up at the cottage, not even for Dylan.

With no time to progress her thoughts, Evie pulled up outside Logan's house and set her mental status from useless wife to able carer.

Having interrogated Evie as to why she hadn't replied to his last three texts, Logan was now showered, in his dressing gown, and eating a late supper of tomato soup and a warmed roll.

'It feels a bit back-to-front,' Evie said, emerging from the kitchen.

'I needed a shower there and then,' Logan retorted. 'Before I had tea. I bet you take one when you want.' He held the spoon as close to his mouth as he was able, and sipped at the soup. A red trickle ran down his chin. He huffed, put his spoon on his tray and wiped his face.

'I promise you, with a two-year-old and a teen sharing the bathroom, I rarely get in there on my terms.' It wasn't a harsh comment or a criticism of Logan's needs, it was a simple comparison to show him how Evie's life sometimes mirrored his. 'And when I do stake my claim, I'm hassled out within ten minutes. I swear the children would be in there with me given the chance.' She stopped. That was a thoughtless thing to say when she'd just assisted Logan in the bathroom. Changing the subject, she took the paper napkin from Logan, and dabbed his chin. 'Have you heard from Griff?'

Logan picked up a piece of buttered roll. 'He came to see me on my birthday. Did you know?'

'Tess mentioned it in passing,' Evie said. 'Was everything okay?' It must have been a shock for Griff to find his father so weak and withered. If it wasn't for Ozzy's tragic accident taking Griff away, he'd have been at the cottage demanding an explanation, Evie was sure.

Logan finished his mouthful, and edged his tray towards his knees. 'Take the plates, will you?'

Evie collected the dishes, deposited them in the kitchen and returned with a handful of grapes. She detached them from the stalk and placed them on the tray. They rolled to the rim.

'Everything was fine until he took Ozzy out,' Logan said, attempting to pick up the largest grape. 'It's sad about Ozzy. He was a lovely dog.' Turning his hand palm up, Logan grasped the fruit between his second and third fingers and transported it to his left hand, which he then lifted to his mouth. The grape fell. Logan's sigh was delivered with an air of defeat. 'Couldn't open my jaws wide enough anyway.'

'I should have cut them. Sorry.' Evie bent to retrieve the remaining fruit, intending to take them back to the kitchen and slice each of them in half. 'You'd think I'd know by now.'

'Throw them,' Logan said. 'Unless you want them. I don't. They're vile reminders I can't do anything for myself. Rheumatoid's a bloody awful disease, Evie. It takes everything away.'

Evie held Logan's face in her palm and kissed the top of his head. 'I know,' she whispered. 'I wish there was more I could do to help.'

'You know what will help, but you've made your choice. I won't push you on it any more.'

'Thank you.' Evie took the tray, sat in the armchair and returned to the previous topic. 'Was it Griff who called you about Ozzy?'

Logan ducked his chin back. 'Good grief, no. He'd used his self-imposed communication time during his visit. He won't be in touch for weeks now.'

'Tess, then?' No one else knew. 'She was so upset. We both were.'

'If you stop talking for a second, I'll tell you.'

Reprimanded, Evie put the tray on the floor, pushed back in her seat, and folded her hands together.

Logan adjusted his position, too, setting his shoulders square and crossing his ankles. 'Griff brought an old friend with him when he came to visit. Imogen. It was a lovely surprise, but that's by the by. It was Imogen who told me about Ozzy. She called me today, shortly before I texted you.'

'Imogen?' It wasn't a name with which Evie was familiar. Was she an ex-girlfriend? 'Why was she with Griff?'

'They bumped into one another a few weeks ago. It was wonderful to see her on my birthday.'

It was apparent Logan was oblivious to Evie's concern. 'But why did Griff bring her here? Are they a couple?' she said, not believing she had to ask the question.

'A couple?' Logan chewed over his reply. 'I didn't ask, but it seems unlikely.'

For want of a distraction, Evie fiddled with the weave of her cuff. Her fingers found a loose fibre. If she pulled it, she thought, the seam would unravel. 'My marriage is hanging on by a thread,' she said, not bothering to hide her indignation, 'and for the first time in months Griff visits you, and he's with *another woman*.'

'She's an old family friend.'

'How old?'

'From when Griff was at school.'

'I meant how old is Imogen?'

'A few years younger than Griff.' Logan fingered the knot in his dressing gown belt. 'Why the interrogation? Can you loosen this?'

'I think I'm entitled to ask questions when my husband

casually turns up with a woman from his past.' Evie left her chair, crouched beside Logan, and slackened the belt. 'I don't know what to think.' That wasn't quite the truth. She was thinking how quickly, now she and Griff were separated, Griff had taken his chance to be with an old flame, and that two nights ago, he had indeed used Evie for sex.

'I'll tell you what I think,' Logan said, brushing Evie's hair away from her face. 'I think having Imogen around will impact your marriage.'

Chapter Twenty-Nine

Griff

Portland Bill belonged to a different realm at five-thirty in the morning to the one it inhabited during the normal working day. In the dark before the dawn, the dusty-grey car park was empty, apart from Griff's old Land Rover; the commanding, red-and-white-striped lighthouse stood tall and peaceful; and the small but popular café with its ice cream parlour on the side was waiting for its owners to arrive and remove its shutters.

Even the sea was tranquil.

Some would consider it eerie, ghostly, but for Griff it was a haven; a little piece of heaven where he was going to scatter Ozzy's ashes. Not today – Ozzy's body was still at the vet's – but soon. And early morning was the right time. It was quiet.

'You know, don't you?' Griff said, speaking to the universe. 'You're waiting for him.'

It was a favourite walk of Ozzy's. He'd jump in the back of the car, thump his tail against the wheel arch non-stop for the thirty-minute journey, bark at his arrival, and run free across the grass and rocks of the peninsular.

Griff regarded the landscape. Apart from their family cottage, this was Ozzy's favourite place. 'I can't take you home, old boy.' By home, Griff didn't mean the flat. That would never be home. 'It wouldn't be fair on Evie and the children. And I wouldn't be able to visit you.' Sniffing, Griff ran his thumb under his nose. 'The garden's tiny, anyway.' The Bill provided all the space Ozzy needed. 'We can come here.'

The associations were strong. Griff could already see the large, lumbering dog galumphing towards the ice cream parlour, willing some poor, unfortunate soul to drop their vanilla scoop on the ground. Ozzy didn't mind a bit of grit.

It was a good image and one that laid the foundations of a smile on Griff's lips. His burgeoning comprehension of his father's desire to connect with Marilyn through him should have built on it further, but a surge of melancholy washed it away.

'I still wish I could've taken you home, Ozzy. Just one more visit to hear Dylan's laugh when you're being daft, or see the settling effect you have on Tess, receive a hug from Evie. One last chance for them to see you. Say their goodbyes.'

Not that it eased the pain, but Griff hadn't made the same promise to Ozzy as he had his mum. There had been no pledge to get him home. He'd not had the time to say much at all.

He had made another vow, though – to do everything possible to save Ozzy – another he was unable to keep.

Awake for two nights on the trot, berating himself, debating whether or not a half-life was worse than death, and questioning the integrity of his judgement, the conclusion Griff reached was that he *might* have prevented Ozzy suffering indignity and pain. It afforded Griff no comfort. Making the decision on Ozzy's behalf and then condemning him to death was awful. God only knows what he'd have done if it had been Dylan or Tess lying on the operating table.

'I never want to be in that position,' Griff said. '*Never.*' The concept was too huge to remain contained in his head, so he let it go, hoping an angel, his mum, Kieran, would hear his prayer. 'We're guided by the experts,' he said, his words drifting on the breeze, his mind returning to Ozzy. 'Is that enough? Should I have explored the options for myself rather than trust their knowledge?' He clamped a hand around the back of his neck and rolled his head. Lack of sleep and weeks in a rickety, single bed were taking their toll. 'What if you could talk, Ozzy? What if you'd told me your future was too bleak to contemplate, and you wanted to die? Would I be more accepting of your fate? Is that why Dad could let Mum go?'

Griff dragged his fingers from his neck to his chin, and gave it a hard rub. It was coarse from two days' stubble. He'd been picked up on it at work. He'd argued they should be grateful he made it in at all, clean-shaven or not. The past few days had been horrendous.

Standing alone, facing Pulpit Rock, he corrected himself: the past few months had been horrendous.

Life was testing his mettle; distracting him, and stealing precious pieces away.

There was nothing on earth that would bring Griff's faithful pal back; no amount of wishing or what ifs or if onlys would change how things stood. His mum, Kieran – they were gone, too. Taken. Never to return. And nothing could or would change the past.

But Griff had the desire and the capability to put right the present.

He shoved his hands in his pockets and strode across the grass to the car.

If his theory about his dad's acceptance was right, he might just have found a way to reconcile their differences.

There was only one way to find out.

Having been to the flat, showered and shaved, Griff pressed the bell on Logan's door, waited, pressed again and entered. It seemed to be the way Logan liked keyholders other than Evie to proceed.

'Hey, Dad. It's me.' He closed the door, stuffed his keys in his pocket and poked his head into the living room.

'Twice in a week. I'm honoured.' Logan waved him in. 'You know where the kettle is.'

Griff traipsed through to the kitchen and set about making two coffees – one white without sugar, and one black with – gazing into the garden until steam fogged his view. 'Nice job with the shrubs,' he said, preparing the drinks.

'That's Evie's handiwork,' Logan said. 'I direct and she does the manual stuff. I'm training Imogen up next. Did you know she's agreed to become my second assistant?'

'Yeah, she told me.' Griff hadn't given it much thought since then. Logan sounded pleased with the idea. 'If you're happy with the arrangement, that's great.'

'I am ecstatic. Not sure what Evie makes of it, though. I think she's feeling a little pushed out. She's arranging to meet Imy.'

Griff carried the mugs through to the living room. 'Evie's looking out for you, that's all. And don't worry, she'll love her, especially if you have Imogen lumping the compost sacks around instead of her.' He put his coffee on the floor next to the armchair and waited for Logan to signify he was ready to receive his. 'That's how it used to be at the cottage. You directing, me doing the donkey work.' So far, so good. Logan nodded. Griff lowered the cup into his hands, not prepared to let go until he was positive his father had a decent grip on the handle.

'I have it,' Logan said, firmly. 'And thank you for not overfilling it.'

'There's some cold water in it, too.' Griff repaired to the armchair, relieved at completing the first task without mishap or complaint. 'I take it Evie's been and gone.' He twisted his watch round and checked the time. 'Is it really only half eight?'

'It is. And someone my age should be tucked up in bed, enjoying a lie-in, not up, dressed and breakfasted. That's an observation,' Logan added, promptly. 'Not a whinge. I know Evie has other responsibilities. I can't deny it would be nice not to have to fit my life into others' schedules, though. I wonder if Imy's a late riser.'

Griff watched as Logan fought to raise the cup to his mouth. With two fingers hooked around the handle and his other hand supporting the base, it was a precarious move, which had Griff on the edge of his seat, ready to dive to his father's aid.

The mug jogged up and down, as Logan laughed. 'At ease, son. I've drunk hundreds of hot drinks this way. It's when I have the steak knife in my hand you should worry.'

Griff kicked back and folded his hands across his stomach. 'Would that be for your Aberdeen Angus fillet steak?'

'Aye. It would.'

'The old vernacular,' Griff said, appreciating his father returning to his Scottish roots. 'I must have been at school the last time I heard you say aye.'

'You probably were. It disappeared. Living in Wales did that. I went all Ivor Emmanuel. It was your mam's fault.'

In one sentence Logan had travelled from the remote Scottish Highlands to the busy Welsh town of Pontypridd.

'Mum never lost her accent, did she?' Griff smiled as he recalled the soft, silken quality of Marilyn's voice.

'We both experienced it full on when she was having a go at us. Do you remember the ticking-off we got when we played cricket with her baby tomatoes?'

'And we used the shed door as a wicket.' Griff's smile strengthened. 'She loved those tomato plants.'

'I loved my shed door.' Logan laid the empty mug down in the valley of his thighs. 'I was told to repaint it that summer.'

'I had to help Mum pot more plants.'

The conversation came to a natural and comfortable end, with Griff cherishing its simplicity and sincerity. It was the first time in years he and his father had shared memories of Marilyn without the volcanic issue of her death erupting.

'I'm very sorry to hear about Ozzy,' Logan said. 'You're not blaming yourself, are you?'

'It was my fault, Dad.' Griff took full responsibility. At the time of the accident, he'd been mulling over his father's words when he should have been concentrating on his two charges.

He opted against a full disclosure; having established a connection with his father, Griff wasn't about to sabotage it by implicating him in the incident.

'I wasn't paying attention,' said Griff. 'I was careless. Stupid. And I know better than that – people depend on me to keep them safe. It's what I do. One mistake, one idiotic slip of the hand ...' He couldn't finish. Anger and sorrow made for a heady mix and he needed a moment to regain his balance.

'So, you're mad with yourself?' Logan stretched his hands over the rounded ends of the chair's arms.

'Furious,' Griff said. 'That's twice my recklessness has led to fatalities.' It was such a formal declaration. Professional. As if he was reporting to his senior officer. 'Two errors, two lives. It's quite a hit rate.' With an unpleasant heat crawling up his back, Griff yanked at his collar. The cool air was quick to soothe his neck. 'I had to make a judgement call about Ozzy. It was bloody difficult.' He breathed. 'The vet was great. I'm sure she should have gone home long before I arrived, but she didn't hassle or rush me. She let me take my time, reach my decision and see it through.' He pursed his lips, his brain sending signals for him to stop. His head was reluctant to relive Ozzy's death. Thank God his heart was committed to the cause. Griff had to show his father how far he'd come. How willing he was to learn from this awful situation.

'I stayed with Ozzy, you know? Until he went. In those final seconds, I held his head and spoke to him. I don't know if he heard. What do you think? He was in a coma. Could he have heard me?'

Marilyn hadn't been in a coma, but she'd been under heavy sedation. To Griff's mind, that was much the same state, and he never truly believed she heard his parting words. What chance did he have with a dog?

Logan gave no reply.

Griff continued. 'He had a drip going into his paw, and he seemed half his size, lying on the huge black table, and when he took his last breath, I couldn't help thinking how familiar it was. There were so many parallels with Mum's passing, even down to the decision to end a life.'

'Not this again.' Logan fumbled for the chair's remote control, pulling the sprung cord inch by inch until the handset was within his reach. As he manoeuvred it into a manageable position, it lurched away and bungee-jumped over the arm of the chair. 'Bloody remote control.'

What should have been an easy undertaking had the potential of turning into a major incident. Logan's physical difficulties had not gone unnoticed.

'Shall I get that for you?' On Logan's signal, Griff vacated his seat, recovered the controller, and stretched out the cord. 'That should loosen it.' He handed the unit to Logan. 'It doesn't seem very remote.'

'Unlike the chances of you and I locking horns over your mother.'

Griff took up residence on the sofa. 'But that's the thing,' he said, leaning forward. 'This business with Ozzy has made me view things differently.'

That the loss of his dog should affect Griff's spiritual understanding sounded ridiculous, but it was the only way he could explain his change of heart.

'I've always thought you gave up on Mum. I believed that with our love and support and the great medical care she was receiving, she'd pull through. And we'd keep doing that until the next new drug arrived or the cancer had gone. I couldn't see her sickness, the damage inside, or appreciate how ill she was feeling. She never complained, not to me. She'd sit in my garden, watching you potter, she'd smile at me whenever I joined you on the lawn, she'd tell me she was all right, and I believed her, because I had a major problem with the alternative. And she knew that.' He paused to take breath and review his verbal deluge. He hadn't thought of the words before he'd spoken them; they'd flowed, a babbling brook of surprises, streaming into perfect, logical sentences.

'That's why it was a shock. From my perspective, she went from my mum who was managing, to a woman ready to die. It came without warning.' This was as much a revelation to Griff as he expected it to be for Logan. 'She was protecting me, I can see that now.' He glanced at his father, whose head was bowed. 'You knew how ill she was. She didn't hide anything from you and when she told you she'd had enough, you understood and you did the most selfless thing a person can do. You let her go.'

Leaving the sofa, Griff knelt at his father's feet. He removed the mug from Logan's lap, and tenderly took a bony hand in his. 'I'm sorry, Dad. I was wrong. You hadn't given up. Mum asked you to stand by her, and that's what you did.'

Logan wrapped his free hand over Griff's, the tiniest tap from his thumb offering the utmost reassurance. 'Son, it's simple. When the person you love lies next to you in bed, crying in agony, telling you this is no life, you listen. When she says there's pain worse than that of separation by death, you listen, even though she whispers she knows how much it will hurt you because it breaks her heart, too. And when she can no longer ask for your help, you watch, and you anticipate, and you do whatever is necessary to fulfil her wishes. Then, when it's time for her to go, you kiss her, you hold her a little longer than you have before, and you tell her how much joy she has brought to your life. You make it clear you understand, and she's not to worry. You tell her you love her, you always have and you always will, and she's to go on her way, to a place where she'll be free of illness and delivered from pain. Then you reassure her there's nothing to be scared of, and you let her go.'

The profundity of Logan's soliloquy hit Griff at the back of his throat, and the ache prevented him from talking. Not that a reply was needed.

The men sat in the same position for a good five minutes before Logan gave Griff's hand a gentle nudge. 'Thank you for listening to me.'

Griff pulled a face. 'It took me long enough.'

'Only six years. We'll call it satellite delay.' Logan produced a weary smile. 'I think I'd like to take a nap now. Are you working today?'

'Not until this evening.' With his legs numb from kneeling, Griff dragged himself onto the sofa and gave his calves a slap. 'I should get some sleep, too.' He rubbed the back of his neck, recalling the earlier stiffness. 'It's impossible, though. Every time I settle, I see Ozzy or Mum.'

'Difficult times.' Logan closed his eyes. 'You can try sleeping upstairs if you like. Just for today. You have a perfectly decent bed at the cottage.'

Where lay the next apology, Griff thought. 'Thanks. It's a tempting offer, but I'm planning on seeing Evie.'

'Oh. She didn't say.' Logan's volume faded to a breath, and his head tipped forward until his chin was resting on his chest.

Ensuring the blood had returned to his legs and they could support his solid frame, Griff rose from the sofa. His left toes still tingled. 'Start on the right foot,' he murmured, repeating Imogen's advice.

Logan stirred, his eyebrows momentarily lifting, his eyes remaining sealed. 'Are you off?' A big sigh.

'Yeah, but I'll see you soon,' Griff whispered, pulling the living room door to.

As he left the house he heard Logan say, 'You will keep listening, won't you?'

Chapter Thirty

Evie

Rolling the Happiness jar from one hand to the other, Evie reached a decision. The note concerning her and Griff's brief reconciliation had to come out. In its place would be one that read: *The children and I are being spontaneous: we're going on a mystery tour.*

Ten minutes into their journey, Dylan was fast asleep. The raw noise and bone-shaker motion of the Mini was the best sleep cure known to Evie. She checked him in the rear-view mirror. His head was turned to the side, and his cheek was cushioned against his car seat.

'He's going to get a bear hug from Griff when he sees him.'

'Did he say when he'd be over?' Tess flipped down the visor mirror and toyed with her brow ring. 'Do you think he'd object to me getting a piercing in Ozzy's honour?'

'I'm not sure he'd notice just now. And no, I don't know when he'll be over. He's not been in touch.' Evie paused as she negotiated a small roundabout. 'I expect he'll come tonight, if he's not working. He rarely forgoes putting Dylan to bed.'

'I'd like to see him.'

Evie glanced at Tess. 'I know. So would I, but I imagine he has a few things to work through.' She accelerated away, making hard work of shifting through the gears. 'Logan told me about Imogen. I gather you've met her.'

'I tried to tell you yesterday, but you were in a hurry to go out.'

'We are the proverbial ships,' Evie said.

A silence followed as they rattled their way along the main road and came to a halt at a junction.

'Which way?' Evie asked. 'The choice is yours, but be quick, there are cars behind.'

'Go right,' Tess said. 'We'll go to Portland.'

Flicking down the indicator, Evie edged into the filter lane and waited for a break in the traffic. 'I haven't been there for a while.'

'We can go and see Olivia.'

The suggestion surprised Evie and she nearly missed her chance to turn. 'We could,' she said, willing the Mini across the road, 'but she's more Griff's friend than mine. Why don't we pop Dylan in his buggy and walk up to the café? It has a new owner. You can try out their hot chocolate.'

'No, no, no. You said it's my choice. Olivia's my friend, too. We'll see her first and then we'll go to the café.' Tess propped her feet up on the dashboard.

'If I crashed right now, your knees would go straight through your head.'

'Then don't crash.'

'Legs down.' Evie batted Tess's thigh. 'You want them in good working order for the walk to the café.'

'I need my head, too.' There was no anger in the exchange, and Tess did as she was asked. 'This is good, Mum. Taking off on the spur of the moment.'

Evie agreed. 'I wish we'd done it more often. Is it too late to start now?'

'Why would it be?'

'You're nearly sixteen. I'm not sure how much longer you'd want to hang out with me.'

At sixteen, Evie worked a full-time job, spent her evenings helping out at a youth club, and weekends at her best friend's house. Her mother was single – not widowed because she'd never married Evie's dad – thirty-six and living it up, entertaining a continuous stream of men of dubious natures and greasy hair.

Spending time with her mum was not something Evie did by choice. At sixteen, she had very firm ideas of what she wanted from life. As Tess would.

'Firstly, Mum, don't say stuff like *hang out* or this will be the shortest mother–daughter spontaneity plan ever, and secondly ...' Tess turned in Evie's direction. 'I can't see me not wanting to be with you.'

The beautiful sentiment lifted Evie's heart, but she knew it was only a matter of time before Tess fell madly in love with someone and wanted to spend every minute with them. Perhaps she already had. Evie recalled Tess talking about Rick, an American lad some months ago. And a French girl. She said she liked her accent. Considered it cute.

Another roundabout gave Evie a few seconds to allow the thought to filter through.

Stephanie. That was her name. Was that a conversation she should have with Tess? At thirteen, Tess had a boyfriend, Evie remembered. He was a cocky so-and-so who'd pushed Tess too far. He got what he deserved, but it wasn't a good experience for a first love.

Evie pressed the accelerator to the floor and urged the Mini to hit fifty miles an hour. The Ferry Bridge linking Weymouth to Portland gave her a long, straight stretch on which to build up power. 'It will come,' she said. 'You'll meet a special person and they'll turn your world upside down and for every minute you're not with them, you'll be thinking about them, or texting them or wishing you were together.'

'Is that how it was with Dad?'

For once a question from Tess about Neil hadn't caught Evie off-guard. 'At the beginning. I was eighteen when I met him. He was a friend of a friend. We were introduced at a party. It was fancy dress.' Evie had viewed Neil as her knight in shining armour. He was charming, handsome, and confident.

'What did he go as?'

'Your dad? He was in a shirt and tie. A red one. Quite flamboyant as it happens. He said he'd come straight from work. Turned out he always went to parties like that. He hated dressing up. Thought it was demeaning.'

'Sounds right. What did you wear?'

'Ah.' Evie's had been the skimpiest outfit of them all. She fixed her sight on the road, not daring to catch Tess's eye. 'I was dressed as a French maid. It consisted of a little black dress, a white apron and a feather duster.'

'And Dad didn't think that demeaning?'

That wasn't the reaction Evie expected. She thought Tess would be laughing and joking at the ridiculousness of it all. 'He seemed to like it.'

Evie's relationship with Neil had been physical from day one – a coming together of the flesh, rather than a meeting of minds. He was Evie's intellectual superior, and both parties knew it. At ten years her senior, he had a deeper understanding of the ways of the world. He'd said as much to Evie, but at the time it had bypassed her as a put-down.

At eighteen she was flattered to have a man like Neil showing an interest in her and taking care of her. He was hot, intense, professional. He was a qualified architect. He told her he was set for life.

Within months of getting together, he'd moved her into his house and insisted she'd give up work. Evie was thrilled. Not only could she care for the man of her dreams, but she no longer had to endure her mother's questionable morals or listen to the lewd, suggestive comments from the succession of greasy-haired boyfriends.

He wasn't Evie's first, but he was her first love, and she

was happy to do whatever Neil asked. She was completely and utterly devoted to him.

That made his future betrayal sinful and unforgiveable.

It was true. Love was blind. And Evie had allowed it to make her a victim.

Having suffered at the hands of Neil, sex was a minefield for her. It had gone from an amazing, intimate expression of love to a vicious, poisonous demonstration of hate.

Thank God for Griff, the kindest, most patient, protective man on the planet. He'd restored Evie's faith and shown her love was a healthy, honest human condition.

'Griff's nothing like Neil,' Evie said.

'I guess not.' Tess flipped shut the visor, settled back, and folded her arms. 'I can't imagine Dad in Santa swimwear.'

Evie laughed. 'You remember the first time you saw Griff, then?'

'Mum, the image was burned onto the back of my eyeballs.' Tess performed a dramatic shudder. 'I'm surprised I wasn't scarred for life.' She held up her hand, her palm facing the windscreen. 'And don't even mention the baubles.'

Evie had, on the day she'd met Griff. There was something that tickled her about the man who'd shimmied past the gathering crowd ignoring jokes about his *gay apparel*. His strategically placed Christmas decorations inspired a rousing chorus of 'Deck The Balls', as the vast number of people singing, slapping his back, and cheering him on assured Evie he was a well-known and well-liked man. It gave her the confidence to speak with him.

'Nice baubles,' she said, before they dived into the harbour.

It was one of her favourite memories.

Unlike her experience with Neil, her first sexual encounter with Griff happened weeks rather than days after they met. He hadn't pushed her or demanded anything from her, putting her in charge of where and when; leaving her to choose. And she had.

There was no singular reason that led Evie to that moment. It was organic. She appreciated Griff's enthusiasm for life, and his kind nature – how he'd call during the day to see if she needed anything picked up from the shops, make hot drinks for everyone, display an endless patience for an inimical Tess.

Evie enjoyed his easy company, his fierce passion for the sea, and the way his gentle hold was strong and protective. And he made her laugh so much, with daft jokes, self-deprecating humour, and slapstick comedy, especially when he was with Ozzy. They were quite the double act.

It was when Evie was kissing Griff one cold February evening that his tender touch caressed away her burden of doubt and caution. From that moment, making love with him was not a conscious decision.

Evie often thought of her first time with Griff as the true moment she lost her virginity. Sometimes she wished it was. He'd been so caring, so gentle, watching her, making her laugh, waiting until she was ready. She remembered crying at being shown how delicate and beautiful love could be.

Cracks of light appeared in the world Evie had condemned to darkness. Griff had brought her back to life.

And he'd brought her new life.

Early in their relationship, Evie had to break the news she was pregnant. The prospect terrified her. The dramatic point of change between her and Neil had been the arrival of Tess.

This time, it was Tess she told first, who, although shocked at the speed and Evie's recklessness, was delighted. 'You have to tell Griff,' she'd said. 'He might surprise you.'

And he had. He was stunned, thrilled and excited. He and Evie celebrated on the spot, in Evie's living room, and again a few hours later in Griff's.

Ozzy missed out on his walk that evening.

Poor Ozzy.

Poor Griff.

'Mum? Are you okay? Your face went from sickly dreamy to sad.'

'It did?' Relieved to make it across the causeway, Evie navigated the one-way system and parked the car alongside the craft centre. 'I was thinking about your dad, and then Griff and Ozzy ...' She trailed off. The afternoon was meant to be about Tess.

Evie returned to the topic in hand. 'So, has that put you off hanging ... spending time with me?'

'What? You dressing up?' Tess laughed. 'Maybe if you went out like it now, but not when you were young.'

Evie joined in with the laughter. It was good to release the tensions of the last few days. 'I *was* young. And naïve. Made plenty of mistakes.' She switched off the engine, twisted in her seat and studied Tess. 'I didn't have anyone to turn to, not really. You have me. You know that, right? Any worries, questions, problems – you can come to me.' She noticed how Tess kept her hands tucked in her lap. For a girl who'd been adored and hugged from the moment she was born, she was not at all tactile. Not a revelation. Not when through a child's eyes she'd seen the horrific consequences of falling in love with the wrong person. 'I will never judge you,' Evie said, refraining from reaching out.

'Mum, I'm fine.' Tess yanked at the door handle, swung round and put her feet on the kerb. 'This has been fun.'

'It's not over yet.' Evie followed suit, knocking her seat forward so she could retrieve Dylan. 'And from now on, I promise I'll make time for us to spend together. If this Imogen woman works out, things can only get better.' *As long as she stays away from Griff.*

Tess stood and pushed shut her door. 'She's all right,

and Logan really likes her. As far as he's concerned, it's sorted.'

'Sorted?' Lifting a floppy, sleepy Dylan from his chair, Evie covered his head with her hand and brought him into the open. 'Maybe, but I still want to meet her.' She passed Dylan to Tess, let down the boot of the Mini and hauled out a small, green and blue buggy, which she flipped open and locked in position. 'When your father-in-law tells you a woman is going to impact your marriage, I think it's time for concern.'

'Logan said that?' Tess lowered Dylan into the pushchair. 'She's an old family friend. A sister of Griff's schoolmate or something. There's nothing funny going on.'

Evie secured the car and took control of the buggy. 'Logan says the same. He says he meant her involvement would give me time to work things out with Griff.'

'He has a point.'

Evie stared at her daughter. 'Are you on his payroll or something?'

Tess laughed. 'No. I like Imogen. She's got a way about her. She's instantly likeable.'

'Go on.' Evie was data collecting. Logan hadn't been at all forthcoming with information on the new woman, but Tess seemed happy to chat about her. 'Did she turn up on Logan's birthday?'

'Yes. Griff took her over.'

'And they what? Came up with this carer plan between them?' Evie grabbed the plastic handles of Dylan's transport and aimed them in the direction of Olivia's shop.

'I guess so.' Tess marched ahead. 'It's a business arrangement, Mum. No different to if Logan had hired an outside firm. I think it's great. It's a good thing. You'll get more time to do the things you love. Not that you don't love looking after Logan.' Tess peered over her shoulder.

'It's all right,' Evie said. 'You don't need to make excuses for me or Logan. It's just a bit sudden.'

And wounding. This wasn't a business proposition at all. Evie was in no doubt her refusal to assist Logan with dying had caused the abrupt change of heart. This was about him finding someone who would bend to his will. All those times he'd insisted on Evie being his sole carer, all the times guilt had split her in two, knowing she should have been with Tess, or feeding Dylan his tea, or enjoying a lazy Sunday morning in bed with Griff – all those times she'd never get back – meant nothing to Logan.

Evie was to be replaced. Discarded.

'You're wondering what you've done wrong, aren't you?' Tess doubled back and walked alongside Evie. 'It's not like that. Imogen's keen to help and I think Logan's realised he's been unfair on you.'

'Did Griff ask her to help?' He must have done. He'd taken her to see Logan. Evie scratched her head. There was something wrong with that line of thought. Until Logan's birthday, Griff had no clue as to his father's deteriorated state. Unless he really was just trying to help Evie.

It was quite the conundrum.

Visiting his father was a step in the right direction, at least Griff would understand why Evie had to devote so much time to him. It was taking Imogen with him that concerned her. 'Is Imogen—'

'Don't sweat it, Mum. Her and Griff are just friends. I grilled her about it and I believe her. They go back a long way. Family friends. That's all.' As Tess held open the door to the craft centre, a ding alerted the owner to their entrance. Dylan's pale eyelids breached and he looked up at the old-fashioned brass bell. Within seconds, he was nodding off again. 'And she's a holistic healer.'

'Tess. How lovely to see you. And Evie, too.' Olivia

DeVere, dressed in her trademark ankle-length skirt, floral blouse and paisley waistcoat, bent over Dylan and stroked his cheek. 'My goodness, you've grown since I last saw you.' She straightened up. 'To what do I owe the pleasure?'

Her smile and the warmth of her greeting provided reassurance to Evie.

'We're on a mystery tour,' she said. 'Although we know where we are now, obviously.' She glanced around the shop, taking in the polished shells on the racks, the coastal watercolours displayed on the walls, and the driftwood art filling the majority of the floor space, and settled on a youth standing behind the counter. He was concentrating on Tess, hailing her like a long lost friend.

'You've an admirer,' Evie said.

'That's not an admirer. That's Rick.' Tess acknowledged him with a half salute before wandering across to chat.

'He's my American grandson,' Olivia said. 'He's helping me out during the holidays. I have an English grandson too, Seth, but he's only six. I haven't put him to work yet. We're possibly the most cosmopolitan family on the island.' She grinned as she ushered Evie and the buggy further inside. 'Unless we count the new family at the café, but they're not local.'

'We're heading up there later,' Evie said, smiling. 'I'll report back.'

'Excellent. I'd go myself, but we've been so busy. The sea's provided me with lots of materials to work on, and Frank's in demand, organising regular beach clean-ups. Rick and Tess met at one of the early clean-ups.' She broke off and spent a moment studying Evie.

'What is it?' Evie said, inspecting her clothes for dirt.

'In case you're wondering, they're just friends.'

'That's the second time I've heard that today.' Evie arched her brows.

'And the second time you've doubted it?'

'No. I believe it of these two.' There was nothing in Tess's manner to suggest otherwise. The pair were relaxed and chatting with no obvious awkwardness or embarrassment. 'Tess has mentioned Rick a few times. *Cool* comes up a lot.'

'Ah. His favourite word.' Olivia nodded in the teens' direction and then turned her attention on Evie. 'So, a mystery tour. How exciting.' She took responsibility of the buggy and rocked it back and forth. 'Rick, pass the stool over, please.'

From behind the counter, the gangly youth produced a tall, wooden seat. He delivered it to Evie, then returned to his post.

'Sit,' Olivia said, stooping to check on Dylan. 'The little angel. He's dead to the world.'

Like Ozzy, Evie thought, a wave of sadness breaking on her eyes.

A shielding and comforting arm was thrown around her shoulders. 'I'd invite you through to the stock room,' Olivia said, 'but a dingy, claustrophobic space isn't what you need right now.'

'It's okay. I'll be fine, thank you.' Evie used the backs of her fingertips to wipe away the tears. 'We've had some bad news and it's just hit me.'

'The perils of taking a break.' Olivia maintained her hold. 'And visiting me. I touched a nerve.'

Evie reached up and patted Olivia's hand. 'Really, it's okay. It's a relief. I know what I'm dealing with now.' She let both her and Olivia's arms drop. No longer under the older woman's protection, she slipped off the stool, straightened out her clothes and readied herself to fill Olivia in on the details. 'It's Ozzy,' she said, holding back the tears. 'He was hurt in an accident ...' She broke off, intending to continue once she'd recovered her poise, but Olivia was already on the case.

'Oh, no. When?'

'The accident was a couple of days ago. We ... ' Evie reviewed, then revised what she was going to say. 'Griff had to let him go.'

'A difficult few days. No wonder you're frazzled.' Olivia perched on a carved stone block near to the back wall of the shop. She was observing Evie. 'I don't believe in fighting grief.'

'I'm trying to keep a lid on it.' Evie couldn't afford to let her tears for Ozzy escalate into her grieving for Griff. Preferring not to dwell on the matter, she peered over at Tess and Rick. They were engrossed in conversation. 'What do you suppose teenagers talk about?'

'On this occasion I expect Tess is telling Rick about Ozzy.'

Evie continued watching as Tess pulled down her sleeve, clutched the end in her fist, and dragged her arm across her face. 'It affected her more than I expected.'

'She's a sensitive girl with a big heart.'

'She is.' Evie retook her seat, hooked her feet on the bar, and relaxed. Olivia was good company. Perceptive. Honest. She was a straight talker – one of the reasons Griff respected her.

The ladies exchanged a smile.

'This is Portland stone, from the quarry up the road. Isn't it beautiful?' Olivia smoothed a palm over the surface of the rock she was sitting on. 'Not quite white, not grey. It has such majesty. St Paul's Cathedral is built almost entirely from it. Imagine that. Our tiny island producing a rock of such significance. I applaud those who worked out the logistics of transporting tonnes of it to London. It was challenging enough getting this one in here.'

'How did you get it in?' Evie scanned the craft centre for clues, but nothing was screaming out the answer. 'Did you take out a window?'

'There was more to it, but yes, I did.' Olivia slid off the rock, marched across the shop floor and stopped at a large pair of sliding patio doors. 'Well, not me, personally. There are some things even I need help with.' She grinned. 'My very own rock, Frank, had the answer. If I'd not asked him, that beautiful piece of stone would have been shut outside, facing all sorts of inclement weather. Imagine being left to the storms when what you really needed was shelter.'

The shop fell silent as both ladies regarded the ornamental limestone.

Griff was Evie's rock and she'd shut him out. She'd left him to weather the storm, when he deserved her care and attention as much as he deserved to know the truth, regardless of how vulnerable that made Evie. That meant there could be no more excuses and no further procrastination. Everything, every last detail had to be shared. Divulged. Exposed. If they were to start again, she wanted a clean slate. No secrets, no hidden baggage, and everything up for discussion – their fears, their fantasies, their desires. And they had to work as one unit, a family unit, with no resentment or jealousy as to how each spent their time, and with the freedom and security to know they could turn to each other in times of trouble – not just her and Griff, but Tess and Dylan, too.

The prospect terrified Evie, but the dark was a lonely, forbidding place and her past, and Logan's secret, had languished there too long. Bringing them into the open was the only way she and Griff would be able to see things clearly.

After that, if Griff walked away, he was doing it from choice.

'Frank sounds like a lovely man,' she said, easing herself back to the topic in hand. 'So what else did you do to get the rock in?'

'We removed the window and the wall below. Such a simple solution. The rock was brought in and these beautiful patio doors were installed.' Olivia gestured towards the glass as if she was presenting the prizes on a quiz show, her arms and hands splayed wide. 'And isn't the light in here wonderful? Frank didn't just want to patch things up. He remodelled and renewed.'

Evie gained the distinct impression she was being taught a life lesson. She wouldn't have expected Griff to have spoken with Olivia about his marriage, but he could have. He was extremely fond of the old woman. How much did she know?

'It wasn't cheap,' said Olivia, 'but that's the price one pays for the love of art.' She returned to Evie and resumed her position on the rock.

'Love's running up quite a bill.'

'But it's worth it.'

'Depends what value you place on it.' Evie had paid dearly for her early investment in Neil. She'd come through with Griff though. The cost of true love was well worth the price. 'But, yes,' she conceded. 'It is.' She closed her eyes to the possibility she'd already lost her finest return. 'It's worth every penny.' Restoring her vision, she expected to see Olivia studying her, but the older woman was watching Rick and Tess.

'So, who don't you believe are *just friends*?'

Evie was aware Olivia had a method of removing the spotlight from the person centre stage. It was a way to nurture openness. Griff had told her. 'Don't let her pottering fool you,' he'd said, laughing. 'She's listening and taking on board everything you say and do.'

So it seemed. Olivia's attention was on the teens, but Evie was in no doubt the wise woman next to her would hear and process her every word.

'Does it have something to do with the holistic healer Tess mentioned?' Olivia pushed up from the ornate stone and tinkered with a selection of framed prints hanging on the back wall.

'What makes you say that?' Evie narrowed her eyes. Either Griff had confided in Olivia, or, as he'd once said, the lady possessed a sixth sense. She was alarmingly accurate at reading people and situations. Griff had concluded her years as a schoolteacher had graced her with that particular gift.

'No mystery,' Olivia said, swapping one print for another. 'It was the last thing mentioned before we mulled over people being *just friends*.'

That was true. Evie sighed with relief and alighted from the stool. 'Her name's Imogen. She's Griff's new friend. Well, not new, they're old friends, family friends—' Evie stopped herself. 'I don't actually know what they are, but I do know she's entwining herself into our life and I'm not sure I like it.'

Olivia whirled round. She had a small-framed picture in her hand. 'Imogen?'

The tone of recognition was unexpected, causing Evie to frown. 'Do you know her?'

'We're acquainted,' Olivia said. 'She and Griff met by chance in here a few weeks ago. The breeze blows all sorts in.' Olivia offered the print to Evie. 'Hold this, please.'

Evie examined the painting. 'Pulpit Rock. It's beautiful.'

The ancient stack, like a giant's boot stamped into the sea, stood tall, each layer of rock a different hue to the one below; from the blue of the sea to corn, to green, to black, to grey. The artist had picked out the copper veins and rust-coloured stains, drawing the eye to the top, leaving the viewer in no doubt the rock was an object to be revered. It was nature in all her magnificence.

'It is.' Olivia spun on her heels and removed a large watercolour from the wall. 'I'm going to put it here.'

Falling in next to her, Evie swapped her painting for Olivia's, and leaned the discarded one against the nearest set of shelves. 'What's Imogen like?'

'She's like this painting of Pulpit Rock. Beautiful and dangerous. But I didn't take to her.' Olivia stretched to loop the picture wire over a hook embedded in the wall. 'I trust Griff, but she's a whole different matter.'

'Sounds ominous. Tell me more.'

'I've seen her type before,' Olivia said, turning to face Evie. 'Duplicitous, manipulative. She'll wow you with wondrous magic with one hand, while performing dirty tricks with the other.' She collected the large print and headed for the stock room. 'I warned Griff to keep an eye on her. You should, too.'

Making their way up to the café, Evie had plenty of thoughts to occupy her. The ones concerning Griff and Imogen disturbed her most. 'Rick's nice,' she said, directing her energies at Tess. 'Were you talking about Ozzy?'

'To start with, then Rick told me about his mum and brother. They were killed in a motorbike accident a few years ago. His brother was his twin. I think he said his name was Todd. Isn't it awful?' Tess peered down at Dylan, who was wide awake and pointing to every gull within his vision. 'I don't know how he copes.'

'Is he the Frampton lad?' Evie halted, applied the brake on the buggy, and set Dylan free. He ran across to a low-level wall that overlooked the beach, and became transfixed by whatever was below.

'His dad was a Hollywood stunt actor,' Tess said, following Dylan's lead. She tempted the fascinated two-year-old away with the reminder an ice cream was waiting for him at the top of the hill. 'Rick said they moved to England shortly after the accident. Something to do with his dad being born on Portland.'

Curious to see what had caught Dylan's attention, Evie pushed the empty buggy towards the wall, and peeked over. There was a couple in an intimate hold, lying on the pebbles, kissing and canoodling. 'Oh, they've got to be uncomfortable,' she said to herself.

Undeterred, Tess carried on with her story. 'Apparently it was all over the news.'

'It was.' Evie continued on her journey. 'I remember seeing the reports. So tragic. It was about the time your dad died.'

'Yeah. I didn't mention that. Figured we had enough going on with Ozzy and Rick's family.'

As they reached the peak of the incline, the ground levelled out into a tarmacked square. It was graced with wooden benches attached to tables with closed parasols speared through their middles. There was a set of concrete steps to the rear leading to a stony footpath, and to the left was the flat-roofed café with the 'Sold' board attached to its wall. Ahead was a clear view across to the pale rocks of Preacher's Cove.

Evie parked the buggy at the nearest table, reached into her pocket and produced a purse. 'Here's a tenner,' she said, passing a brown note to Tess. 'I'll have a tea, and you and Dylan can choose for yourselves. But I want change.'

Tess grinned. 'I'll see what I can do.'

As Dylan dragged Tess towards the café entrance, Evie took a seat, stared out to sea and let her mind return to thoughts of Imogen. With conflicting reports from Logan, Tess and Olivia, it was impossible to form an opinion of the woman. The sooner she met with her the better.

'Mum?'

Evie turned to find Tess at her side, and Dylan at her knee. A dark-haired waitress from the café was approaching the table. She was carrying a tub of ice cream and two mugs. Evie's eyes strayed to the barrels of bangles on the girl's arms.

'Mum? Guess who's bought the café?' Tess was buzzing with excitement. She replied to her own question. 'Stephanie's mum. I can't believe it. I walked in and there she was.'

'Stephanie's mother?'

'Stephanie.'

The waitress smiled and put the mugs on the table, handing the ice cream tub to Evie. 'For your little boy,' she said, her French accent immediately giving her away. She held out her hand, which Evie took. 'I'm Stephanie Dubois. A friend of Tess.'

The bangles jingled and jangled as Evie shook her hand. 'I'm Evie Hendry, Tess's mum, and this is Dylan. Tess has spoken of you. Pleased to meet you. How do you like Portland?'

Stephanie glanced at Tess. 'Very much, Madame Hendry, thank you. It was a lovely surprise to see Tess.'

'Isn't it amazing?' Tess's eyes were wide with pleasure. 'Madame Dubois plans to change this place into a bistro.' She turned to Stephanie. 'That's right, isn't it?'

'She wants to run it as a café during the day, but can see the potential for evening business, yes.' Stephanie put her arms behind her back. 'I'm helping during the weekends and holidays, but after summer, I'll be at college.'

'Studying for A-levels?' Evie lifted Dylan on to a chair, ripped off the thin, card lid from his ice cream, and handed him a bright pink plastic spoon. 'Did you bring napkins, Tess?'

She received no response; Tess's attention was devoted

to Stephanie. 'Tess.' Evie gave her daughter a playful prod. 'Napkins. For your brother.'

'Oh. Yeah. Sorry.' Tess yanked a bunch of paper serviettes from the back pocket of her jeans and put them on the table. 'Will you be taking A-levels?'

'No, I'm going to enrol in a catering course. I'm planning ahead. I'd like to own a restaurant in my name. What about you? What ambitions do you have?'

Tess linked her fingers behind her back, taking an almost identical stance to Stephanie. 'I have my GCSEs to pass first. I'm taking them next year.'

'We have an equivalent in France.' Stephanie was addressing Evie now. 'But we sit them when we're fifteen. I did mine last year.'

'You're sixteen?'

Evie detected a hint of surprise in her daughter's voice.

It appeared to catch Stephanie's ear, too, making her simultaneously frown and grin as she looked at Tess. 'Is that okay?'

'I ... When we met in January, you seemed ... I thought ... Well, I thought you were older, maybe eighteen.'

Tess's sudden awkwardness showed itself not only in her speech but in her cheeks. They produced a vibrant shade of crimson. It was the most colour Evie had seen in them for weeks.

Conscious her presence could embarrass Tess further, Evie made a point of chatting with Dylan, drawing his attention to the sound of the waves as they washed onto the pebbles.

'I'll be sixteen in October,' she heard Tess say. 'I'm one of the older ones in my year.'

'You should have a party to celebrate.' Stephanie's suggestion.

Evie wiped Dylan's mouth clean of melted ice cream. From

the corner of her eye, she saw Stephanie put a hand on Tess's forearm, a touch from which Tess would normally recoil.

'A party?' Tess looked from Stephanie to Evie and back to Stephanie. 'I hadn't given it any thought. I'm not sure many people would come. I could ask Rick, I suppose.'

'And me.' Stephanie withdrew her hand. 'I'd come.'

'You would?'

'*Mais oui.* Of course. We could ask my mother if you could have it here. Would you like that? I'll be back by then.'

'Back? From where? I thought you were here to stay.'

Evie continued to observe the interaction, noting Tess's disappointment.

Stephanie waved towards the café. 'I've come to help my mother during the holidays. My father's job brings him here in August, so for now he is still in France. Since I am not able to start my catering course until September, I have to go back to Dijon to finish my year at college. I will be back here in July.'

Tess's downturned expression told Evie everything she needed to know. Her teenage daughter, so wise and mature in many ways, was experiencing her first flush of romance and was preparing to invest her trust, and her heart, in Stephanie. As far as Evie could see, the attraction was mutual. She was no expert in body language, but there was mirroring, eye contact, and the occasional touch between them. And they were standing very close to each other.

'We could Skype, maybe? While I'm in France.' Stephanie dipped her head, her dark eyes now level with Tess's moonstone greys. 'By the time I come back, we'll know everything about one another.' She hesitated, uncertainty making a vocal appearance. 'If you would like that.'

Still keeping a discreet watch on the girls, Evie saw Tess hold her eyes shut for a fraction longer than a blink, take a deep, calming breath, and smile.

'I have to go now,' Stephanie said. 'But it's my lunch break soon. Perhaps you would like to join me. All of you.' She turned to Evie. 'I'm sure my mother would be very happy to make your acquaintance, Madame Hendry. She speaks excellent English.'

'That's a kind offer, Stephanie, but I promised I'd take Dylan to see the lighthouse.' Evie congratulated herself on her quick thinking. She had no desire to play gooseberry. 'I'm hoping it's open to the public today.'

'Does Tess have to go?'

'Tess is old enough to make her own choices.' Wasn't that the truth? 'I'll be gone about an hour, but I will have to get back for my father-in-law after that. I'm his carer.' She stopped talking as Tess edged nearer to her.

'I don't want to spoil our morning,' Tess whispered. 'It's meant to be about you and me.'

Resisting the urge to hug her, Evie gazed at her beautiful, sensitive, responsible daughter. 'This has been more about you and me than you could possibly imagine,' she said, her heart providing the words.

'So, you're okay with it?'

Whether Tess meant abandoning her plans with Evie, or her obvious interest in another girl, Evie was fine. More than fine. Happiness, kindness, respect and friendship were what mattered in a relationship. Any relationship. Every relationship. Love was love was love. The right and wrongs lay in the abuse and misuse of that love, not in the question of gender.

'Yes. I'm okay with it. In every conceivable way.' Evie popped Dylan into the pushchair, locked the belt buckles in place, and kissed Tess on her cheek. 'July's not that far off. She'll be back before you know it.'

Chapter Thirty-One

Griff

Griff stared a little way down the road at the corrugated asbestos-lined roof of the garages. As much as he despised them, he missed seeing them every day. They were a marker he was home.

At the moment they were taunting him, reminding him he was scrunched up in his car, on the drive of his cottage, waiting for Evie to appear. He could have used his key and made himself comfortable inside, but he didn't want to frighten Evie by emerging from the living room; he had enough explaining to do without adding another crime to his list.

He rotated his watch so he could read the time. Two o'clock. No wonder his stomach was growling. It was surviving on one cup of coffee.

Ten more minutes, Griff thought, and then he'd have to go. He was on the second of his two nights on shift that evening and as strong as his reserves were, he doubted he could last twelve hours of work without sleep or food first. Exhaustion had already prevented him from showing up at the cottage the day before.

Stifling a yawn, he opened his window and reintroduced his lungs to the fresh, country air, and his ears to the peace of the hillside. Bleating lambs beat the drone of town traffic hands down.

Curious to learn if he could tune into Evie's car, he closed his eyes and listened.

'Hey.'

Jolted from his dream, Griff opened his eyes wide and

turned in the direction of the voice. He sat upright and cleared his throat. 'Hey, Evie.' He ruffled a hand through his hair. 'I must've dropped off.'

'Have you been waiting long?'

'No,' he lied. 'I can fall asleep at the drop of a hat, you know that.' He tested the situation with a smile. Evie's features softened. 'I think we need to talk about the other day,' he said. 'And about my father.'

Evie stepped away from the Land Rover. 'Dylan's inside.'

'How is he?'

'Excited to see you.'

'And Tess?'

'She's with Logan. I'm going to collect her this evening.' Evie paused, the exact reason not revealed to Griff, then she skirted the front of the car and disappeared into the cottage.

'It could have gone worse,' Griff muttered to himself, relieved to escape the confines of the front seat. 'How long have you been home?' he said as he entered the hall.

'Fifteen minutes. I thought I'd get Dylan settled before I woke you.' Evie's voice travelled the length of the corridor. 'You looked like you needed the sleep.'

That was true enough.

'We're in the kitchen.'

Taking that as his cue to proceed, Griff closed the front door and headed to the rear of the property. He was greeted with a huge, milky smile and outstretched arms from a booster-seated Dylan.

'Hey, my boy. How are you?' Griff released the safety belt and hoisted Dylan onto his hip, holding one of his tiny hands in his. 'I've missed you.' He planted a kiss on Dylan's head. 'I hope you've been good for your mum and sister.' His reward was a giggle and a nuzzle to his chest. 'Have you had your lunch?' Reminded of his own hunger, Griff's stomach rumbled, which prompted Dylan to swing his legs and throw his head back, laughing. 'Did you feel that?' Griff blew a noisy raspberry onto the exposed underside of Dylan's chin, generating more giggles and wriggles from the two-year-old. 'You'd power Dorset with your energy.'

'We've eaten,' Evie said, leaning against the edge of the sink. 'But I can make you something. Cheese on toast or a sandwich.' She pushed away from the counter and reached for the bread bin. 'I think we have pastrami in the fridge.'

'That would be great, thank you.'

'We only have white bread,' Evie said, holding up a slice as evidence.

'Honestly, anything.' In Griff's eyes, Evie's peace offering was symbolic of her willingness to talk. He'd eat worms with mustard if he had to, and he hated mustard. 'Is it okay to give Dylan a yogurt?'

Evie's brow puckered. 'Of course it is. You know where they are.'

He threaded Dylan's legs either side of the chair strap and secured it to Dylan's waist. 'Strawberry?'

As Evie buttered the bread, Griff collected the yogurt and meat from the fridge. He handed Evie the pastrami. 'Thanks for doing this. The sandwich and seeing me.' He bowed his head. 'I wasn't sure where I stood after the other day.'

'Daddy. Ta?'

Dylan's large, expectant eyes and high-pitched voice brought a touch of much-needed humour and normality to the moment. Griff prepared the dessert, appropriated a spoon from the cutlery drawer and carried both items across to the table. 'There you go.' He leaned over and brushed his finger on Dylan's cheek. 'You're a good boy.'

A warm, delicate hand filled the hollow in Griff's back.

'Your lunch is on the table,' Evie said, her mouth close to his ear.

Shivers infiltrated his weakened defence, corrupting his

flesh and mind, but as soon as Evie had spoken, she moved away. The sensation of her touch lingered far longer.

'Thank you,' Griff said, aware his gratitude was vague and open to interpretation. It was up to Evie to determine the root.

'How are you holding up?' she asked.

Griff straightened his posture, circled round and watched as she filled the kettle. 'It's tough.' He cast his eyes to the corner of the kitchen, to the space that was Ozzy's safe spot. 'I still have all of his things out at the flat. How about you?'

'It's early days.' Evie opened the wall cupboard ahead of her and took down a jar of coffee. She held it up for inspection. 'Decaf, I'm afraid.'

'I'll take it.' Griff traipsed across to the sink, washed and dried his hands, and relocated to the table. 'The vet asked me what I'd like to do with Ozzy. I thought it best to have him cremated. Was that okay? I should be able to collect his ashes tomorrow.' Griff picked up a triangle of sandwich, put it to his mouth, and faltered. Thinking of and talking about Ozzy had vanquished his appetite. He returned the food to the plate. 'I'm sorry.'

Evie was there in an instant, replacing the plate with a mug of strong, white coffee. 'I'll wrap them up and you can take them to work. Perhaps you'll fancy them later.' She set about her business.

Griff acknowledged her kindness with a fragile smile. If he allowed himself to think it, he could believe none of the last four months had happened. The scene of domesticity they were enacting was one he'd been part of many times.

The clatter of Dylan's spoon landing on the tiled floor broke his fantasy. He reached round, secured the spoon between his thumb and finger, and looked at his son. 'Do you still need this?'

Dylan turned his palms up. 'All gone.' A strawberry grin broke through the yogurt plastered across his chin and mouth.

'Good job, young man. I predict a career in construction.' Griff left his seat, tore off a strip of kitchen roll from a holder near the kettle, and wiped Dylan clean. 'You've filled in all the cracks.'

'Unlike us,' Evie said, storing the packed sandwiches in the fridge.

'Yeah.' Griff screwed up the dirty paper, disposed of it, then rinsed out the dishcloth. He cleared the table, wiped its surface, and when he was satisfied he'd flooded all the remains of the yogurt away, gave the table one more swipe with the cloth.

If all that was separating him and Evie were cracks, they could be filled. His fear was they'd deteriorated into something worse.

Lifting Dylan clear of his chair, he hugged him, set him on the floor and pointed him in the direction of the living room. 'Go and find your favourite book, bring it here, and I'll read it to you.' He sent him on his way.

Retaking his chair, Griff invited Evie to sit down. He leaned his elbows on the table and clasped his hands together, aware the next five minutes and his choice of words could make or destroy the remnants of their marriage.

'I'm sorry I left in a hurry the other day. I was in a state about Ozzy, and I was anxious I'd already missed him. It wasn't a reflection on you, or my feelings for you, or connected in any way to what we did.' He unlinked his fingers and wrapped them around the coffee mug. 'To have you back in my life just for those short hours gave me the strength to get through the long ones that followed, but that wasn't the reason I came. I came because I'd promised Dylan I'd see him, and because you needed to know about

Ozzy.' He sipped at his drink, while keeping his eyes on Evie.

'I thought you'd used me.'

Griff set aside the mug, leaving his arm outstretched, his fingers mere inches away from Evie's.

'It wasn't until I was thinking clearly I realised you might see it that way. I'm sorry. I would never do that to you.'

That Evie could think him capable of such a violation hurt – it choked and twisted his stomach – but he'd provided no evidence to the contrary.

'I should have called you. Explained. But my head—' He closed his mouth. There were no excuses. What he'd done ... No, the way he'd gone about it, the way he'd left it was wrong, no matter what the reason.

Evie scraped back her chair and perched on the end, as if she was about to rise. 'Tell me about Imogen.'

'Imogen?' Griff tried to make the connection between Evie's forgiveness and his relationship with Imogen. 'She's an old friend.'

'So I keep hearing. How do you know her?'

'She was my best mate's sister. She used to hang around us. She'd mastered the art of winding up teenage boys.' Griff reclined, retreating to a safe distance, thankful the chair had his back, as that was the only support he was getting.

'Imogen is Kieran's sister?'

Wow. That shocked Griff. He'd only spoken of Kieran once to Evie. 'You remembered his name?'

'Of course. He was important to you, and what happened to him shaped you, but I don't understand Imogen's involvement or why she's suddenly back in your life.'

There was nothing sudden about Imogen's appearance. She'd been with Griff for years, trapped in his conscience. He thrust his fingers around the back of his neck, his shoulder protesting at the stretch. It was nothing. There was worse pain to endure.

Leaning into the table, Evie said, 'Are you sleeping with her?'

As if the seat had burnt him, Griff leapt up. 'No! I wouldn't.' He paced the floor, coming to a halt at the rear door. Evie's reflection bounced off the glass. She was standing. 'Where are you going?'

'To check on Dylan. I need to make sure he's settled.' Evie marched out of the kitchen and out of sight.

This wasn't what Griff had come here for. He'd come to apologise for his hasty exit and to determine a way forward for him and Evie. This was the second time his attempt to put things right had gone awry. The old saying *the road to hell is paved with good intentions* was proving far too accurate for his liking.

'Shit.' He trudged across to the sink, splashed icy water on his face, and waited for Evie.

'Dylan's fallen asleep,' she said as she resumed her place in the kitchen. 'I've covered him with the throw.'

'Why don't I take him up?' said Griff. 'Pop him in bed. It will give us the chance to talk properly.'

With no objection from Evie, Griff carried out his task, taking a quiet moment to appreciate both his gorgeous boy and the break from the tension in the kitchen. He tucked Dylan under the duvet, kissed his forehead and trotted downstairs, bracing himself for the proper and honest talk he'd just suggested.

As he swung round the stair post into the hall, he heard movement in the living room. Pushing open the door, he saw Evie bent over the open window box seat, packing away Dylan's books and toys.

'He didn't bat an eyelid,' Griff said, retrieving the fleecy throw from the floor. He passed it to Evie.

'Busy day.' Evie flipped down the lid of the wooden box, turned, and folded her arms.

Despite her tiny frame, her stance projected strength.

'Can we sit?' Griff invited her to take a corner of the sofa, and when she was seated, he took the other. 'Imogen's not a threat. I have no intention of being with someone else, any more than you do.' He shuffled forward. 'The fact you're angered by the thought tells me there's hope for us.' Griff transferred to the middle seat and took Evie's hand. It was as chilled as the water he'd poured from the tap. 'I need to know what's going on,' he said, 'because I'm making wild guesses and I haven't a clue if I'm on the right track.'

They sat for a moment, inches apart, both gazing at their linked fingers, Evie's gaining warmth with every second.

'I think life got in our way,' Griff continued. 'I've been wrapped up in work, and Dad needs more care.' He stopped and looked at Evie, seeking clues from her green eyes. They were cast down. 'I've been to see him, like you asked.'

'I didn't ask, I suggested. It was something you had to do of your own free will, Logan was clear about that.' Evie's fingers twitched, but she wasn't pulling away.

'He issued instructions?' Griff edged closer. 'My father told you *not* to insist I visit?' That went some way to explaining Evie's reticence to discuss Logan, but what possible reason was there for him to behave that way? It had put Evie in a difficult position. This was something to do with the mysterious and abrupt breakdown of their marriage, Griff was positive. 'Talk to me, Evie. Make me understand.'

As she lowered her head, a swath of glossy hair fell forward. With his free hand, Griff gathered it and laid it over her shoulder, the red of the strands contrasting with the cream of her neck.

'It was important you went because you wanted to,' Evie

said. 'Not because you felt it your duty. Love isn't about duty.'

And there was Evie's first reason for abiding by Logan's rules. Unconditional love. Her second was her unwavering loyalty.

Still holding her hand, Griff placed it on his chest and pressed it to his heart. 'Do you know how much I love you? How much I've missed being a part of your life? Our life?'

Of her own volition, she laid her other hand on top of Griff's. She'd feel his heart beating, he was certain. It was thumping so fast and with such great force, it was vibrating in his head.

'I couldn't betray him, Griff. And I couldn't betray you. I didn't know what to do.'

He hushed her with a finger to her lips. 'I've been incredibly stupid,' he said. 'I should have been there with you, giving my support, doing my bit, being a decent son. I've seen how dependent my father is now, and if I'd been to visit him sooner, I'd have understood the pressure you've been under.' He fell silent, not knowing where to take the conversation. Eventually, he said, 'I'm sorry. I should have listened to what you were saying. Asked when I didn't understand. Thanked you for taking such good care of my father.' He let down his hand. 'I've spent a lifetime saving all and sundry, but when it came to you ... I don't know ... I should've put up more of a fight.'

'You're here, aren't you?' Evie recovered his hand and cradled it in her lap. 'I'd say you fought long and hard. More than I deserved. I was the one who pushed you away.'

'And I shouldn't have gone.' Griff stooped to meet Evie's eyes. 'I thought I'd lost you. Have I?'

Evie laid her palm against his cheek. Her touch was both comforting and consoling, instilling in Griff an overall sense of foreboding. He left her hand to rest there while he waited for her verdict.

'I don't want to be lost,' she said. 'But what if I've gone too far? What if there's no way back?' She withdrew, pressed herself into the corner of the sofa, and pulled her knees to her chin. 'I don't want to keep hurting you.'

That was all Griff needed to hear. Evie wanted the same as him. 'Then let's work out a way forward. Together.' He crouched on the floor at Evie's side, and swept her hair away from her face. 'I miss you,' he said. 'I'm miserable without you, and I'm a better man for having you in my life. I'm not prepared to sacrifice all of that when I know we can make it right. We've had three great years. We have Tess and Dylan, and shared memories, the same goals and ideals. And dreams. We have all these wonderful things connecting us. Things linking you to me. Things that will bring us together. And they'll help us find our way back.' He offered a smile. 'And we will. This is the beginning. A chance to get things right, and I'm going to start with telling you about Imogen.'

Evie compressed her tightly bundled body into an even smaller package, as her shoulders curved in and her hands clasped her opposite elbows.

'There's not much more to the story than you already know,' Griff said. 'But I'm not continuing until you take a breath.'

As Evie exhaled, her structure loosened. She put her feet on the floor, her back square to the sofa, and she invited Griff to sit beside her.

'Okay,' he said, once he was seated. 'It's like I said before. I felt Kieran's death was my fault. I knew tombstoning was a bad idea, and I should have done more to stop him from jumping, but I didn't.'

Evie turned to look at Griff. 'I thought he pushed you away.'

'Yeah, he did, but the fact remains I couldn't save him, and Imogen, who loved the bones of him, lost the brother she idolised. Since then, I've wanted to look out for her. I cared for her. She was the nearest I had to a little sister. I was prepared to do what I could to help, but her parents warned me to stay away. Even Imogen made it clear she wasn't interested in anything I had to say. More than that, seeing me upset her and her parents. I guess I was a reminder of what they'd lost. I hadn't seen Imogen in years. Not until I ran into her on Chesil.'

Evie leaned into Griff's shoulder. 'Surely the family didn't resent you for surviving?'

'Why wouldn't they? They'd lost their son, and although they never said it to me, I've always thought they blamed me for Kieran's death. I've been desperate to save lives ever since.'

Strands of Evie's hair tickled Griff's neck. He stroked them into place, and laid his head on top of hers. A hint of apple brought him vivid recollections of he and Evie showering together, washing each other's body, shampooing each other's hair. He'd had to kneel so Evie could reach.

'Do you still feel you owe Imogen?'

With a deep breath, Griff directed his senses back to the living room. 'Not owe. It was never about paying back a debt, but I'm pleased we've reconnected. It's good to know she's not alone, and I think she could be a real friend to the family. We can all help each other.'

'Logan and Tess are certainly taken with her.' Evie's tone was a little left of acerbic.

'She's not a patch on you.' Griff sat erect, tilted Evie's chin up and smiled. 'She's going to be great for my father, though, and that can only be good for us. It gives us a chance to spend time together, and I'd really like that.'

'So would I.' Evie surprised him by stretching up for a kiss.

It was nothing like the kiss from the other night. That had been driven by need and passion. It had been done with intent. It had been a promise of what was to follow. This was full of hope. It tasted of new beginnings, and it answered questions, rather than asked.

'You think it could work?' Evie snuggled into Griff's side.

'I think it's meant to be.' The fact Imogen had surfaced at this difficult time in Griff's life was all the evidence he required. 'I'm sorry I didn't tell you about her before.' The reason for his nondisclosure seemed ridiculous now. 'I didn't think it was an important part of my history where you and I are concerned. It didn't affect our relationship.' He held up his hands. 'In hindsight, I should've been open and honest from the start like you, but from this moment, I have no more secrets, no hidden past, and no other skeletons lurking in the cupboard.' The relief of coming clean lifted Griff's soul. 'You know as much about me now as I do you. Everything.'

Evie sat upright. 'Not everything,' she said.

Chapter Thirty-Two

Evie

Evie removed herself from the sofa. She rubbed her arm as the cold air replaced Griff's body heat. 'There's something I need to tell you.' Griff had laid his heart on the line, and in the spirit of true love, she needed to provide full disclosure, too. It was now or never.

She had Griff's full attention.

Giving herself time to consider her phrasing, she walked to the other side of the room. The coffee table stood between her and Griff – a boundary not to be crossed.

There was no way of sugar-coating what she had to say, and the sooner it was out there, she reasoned, the sooner she'd know the true state of her marriage.

She folded back her cuffs, pulled her sleeves tidy and stared at Griff. 'My first husband died.'

Her delivery was more succinct than she'd planned.

'I thought he left you.' Griff's forehead creased – rows of questions lining up to be asked. 'You told me he'd left you and you haven't seen him since.' The lines deepened. 'Tess told me the same thing.'

Challenging herself to continue, Evie took a shaky breath and replied. 'That wasn't a lie. He committed suicide. There was no note, but it was suicide.' Did those details matter here? They mattered to the police and to the coroner. She had the answers perfected. 'He left me. And Tess. And we haven't seen him since that day.'

Griff pushed his fingers along the grave furrows above his eyes. 'Semantics, Evie, but okay, I can see why you would phrase it that way, especially for Tess's sake, but why did you keep it from me?'

She scratched at her arm, anxiety presenting as intense itches. She'd seen her daughter do the same under pressure. 'I do put it like that for Tess's sake because it isn't straight-forward.' Evie steepled her hands together and put them to her mouth in silent prayer. 'Tess found him.'

'Dead?'

Evie licked her lips. What she'd give for a cold glass of water right now. 'Not quite.'

'Not quite as in I've got it wrong, or not quite dead?' Griff was on his feet, his hands anchored around the back of his neck.

'Not quite dead.' The itch had moved to Evie's shoulder. 'He was on her bed. He'd cut down his arm and was bleeding out. Tess was petrified. She couldn't move. By the time I got upstairs, it was all over.'

Griff's arms were outstretched now, begging to hold Evie. 'She watched him die?'

Evie gave the slightest of nods as her reply. 'He had to do it, didn't he? One last attack, one last attempt to show he meant business. One last hurrah to hurt Tess and get to me. The evil bastard.'

'What do you mean?' Griff's jaw set and his fingers balled into tight fists.

'After years of abuse, I'd finally found the strength to divorce him.' Evie reversed a step. It wasn't Griff she feared; it was the dread of the approaching darkness. 'It wasn't the first time he'd threatened to top himself if I went through with it. His choice of words. I was weak before and believed him when he told me I wouldn't be able to live with his death on my conscience, so I always backed down, but every time he won the round, his assaults became more violent, less selective—' She wanted to spit the words out. 'Listen to me, making excuses. He was a vile, wicked man who hated his daughter and who beat and raped me, and he deserved to die.'

Griff skirted round the table, opened his arms wide and closed in around Evie.

She shut her eyes and fell into his body, safe, protected. 'I'm sorry Tess was there. I wish it had been me who'd found him.' She wished a million things where Neil was concerned. She wished she'd been stronger. She wished she'd had the courage to leave him sooner. She wished Tess had never been put through a living hell.

With her eyes now open, Evie looked at Griff. 'We told the police it was me. I couldn't have Tess implicated. I didn't know the law. Did she have a duty of care? Should she have intervened? The fact she couldn't didn't matter. The fact I wouldn't threw a whole different light on the subject.' She breathed in Griff's warmth. 'So when the police arrived, I said I'd found Neil. I lied. I made Tess lie. And then I made her swear to never talk about it to anyone. Not even me. God knows what damage I've done.'

'No, no, no. Don't go there. You did the right thing.'

She was hugged tighter than she thought possible.

'Did he ever ...'

'Tess?' Evie saved Griff the pain of asking. 'No. Not physically, but he was brutal with his words.' She pulled away from the embrace. 'This has to remain between us.'

'Of course.' Griff invited her in for another hug, but Evie stayed where she was.

'It was Tess who thought I should tell you about him. She wants to talk about it. The thing is, she doesn't know the whole story.' Evie glanced at the floor, and she fixated on a squashy juggling ball she'd not put away. 'Her father was jealous of her. He resented her and the time I spent with her, and that's what led to the violence. How can I tell her that?' Evie trapped the ball under her foot. 'Shadows and echoes already haunt her. He haunts us both. In here.' She flattened her fingertips to her temple. 'Tess said something the other day about how it was worth trying to talk him out of her system because the alternative was much worse. She didn't say what that was.'

'Jeez.' Griff's head was jogging left to right. 'On top of me being an arse, you've had all of this going on. I should have been here for you.'

'You didn't know. I kept it from you. I thought I was coping. Managing.' She looked at Griff and presented a feeble smile. 'Like you and Imogen, it's a part of my history that had no direct bearing on us.'

Griff ducked his chin back. 'Seriously? Evie, it's totally relevant.'

'So, if you'd known, you'd have treated me differently? Made your kisses softer? Never undressed me? Not touched my breasts? I didn't want that. I fell in love with you and I wanted to be with you, and that first time we made love, you took this seething, malicious monster from within me and changed it into a beautiful, delicate butterfly. Why would I not want that?'

Her throat dry, and her words exhausted, Evie excused herself and escaped to the kitchen. She gulped down a glass of water, put the tumbler upside down in the sink, and collapsed onto a dining chair.

She'd done it. She'd told Griff. Not only that, he'd supported her and offered her understanding.

And he was still with her.

'I'm going to call in sick.' He padded in from the hall. 'I can't leave you like this.' Standing behind Evie, he arched over her and wrapped his arms around her chest. 'And if I had known, I would have loved you how I always do and always will. And I will never force you into something you don't want to do. Never.' He kissed the side of her neck. 'I just found myself thinking about the coastguard rescues.

I'm wondering if we've saved anyone like Neil. Have we ever saved someone who's gone home and taken out their frustrations on their family?'

Evie grasped at his hand. 'You mustn't think like that. I don't. If I did, I wouldn't have met you.' Griff was in danger of falling prey to Neil, and she couldn't let that happen. The beast had two of them in his claws already.

She had to press home her point. 'There are times when you have to step outside and see the world differently, accept there are other perspectives. Don't let one bad experience shut the door to new possibilities, or new understanding. Challenge yourself, and challenge your beliefs.' She tugged his arm to incite a response.

'I've done that,' he said. 'In the last few days.' Leaving his fingers in hers, Griff swivelled to the front of the chair and kneeled down. 'Letting Ozzy go was one of the biggest challenges I've faced. But it's nothing compared to what you've been through.'

Evie stroked his hair, brushing the waves over his ear. He pushed against her palm. 'You mustn't compare,' she said. 'What you've been through was difficult, too.'

He turned his face into Evie's hand. 'What have I done to deserve you?'

'You've loved me,' was Evie's honest reply. 'And that's not always easy.' She smiled as Griff rose to his full height, and once he was sitting on a chair, she migrated to his lap, put an arm round his neck, and a hand on his chest. 'Tell me about Ozzy.'

He took a deep breath. Evie's fingers moved with his expanding ribs. 'It was difficult,' he said. 'But seeing Ozzy lying on the big, black table, I realised he wasn't coming back, and even if by some miracle he did wake, he couldn't have lived life the way he enjoyed.' Griff nuzzled the skin below Evie's ear. 'The funny thing is, in the midst of all the upset and pain, I suddenly got why Mum wanted to go.'

'You did?' This was another huge step forward for Griff, and it provided Evie with a natural segue into Logan's situation, but that conversation was never going to be a stroll in the park. Yes, they'd opened up the channels of communication and they were being honest and forthright, but with everything that had passed that afternoon, it would have been too much.

For now she'd settle for the path being laid and the journey looking less bumpy.

'I'm proud of you,' she said. 'And I wonder what I did to deserve you.'

The morning sun streamed in through the window, bringing to the kitchen a warmth and brilliance Evie thought lost months ago. Even her breakfast knife sparkled.

'Imogen was there yesterday afternoon.' Tess cut a slice of toast into fingers and put them on Dylan's plate. He picked one up and stabbed at the boiled egg in front of him. Yolk oozed out.

'Yes, you told me last night when I picked you up from Logan's. I'm sorry I missed her.'

'I did tell her you'd be there later, but she said she'd arranged to meet Griff at the Harbour Inn.'

'Griff? He was working last night.' That's what he'd said. He'd offered to call in sick so he could stay with Evie, but she'd convinced him she was fine and he shouldn't let his crew down.

A rush of excitement stirred her insides.

She and Griff had been making love for the second time when Dylan had woken from his nap. It was shortly after that Griff had left.

'Perhaps you misheard.'

'Nope. They were going to take Honey for a walk along Chesil and then stop at the pub for something to eat.' Tess picked at the marmalade label.

'I swear to you, Griff was on night shift.' Evie swatted Tess's hand away from the jar. 'He left from here.'

That gained her daughter's immediate interest and she looked up. 'Well, someone's lying, and it isn't me.'

'I didn't think you were.' There was only one suspect. Imogen. 'Why would she tell you that?'

Tess huffed. 'I don't know. She probably got her days muddled. It happens, especially with Griff's weird working patterns.'

'They're easy, Tess. Two days on, followed by two nights, followed by four days off. Yesterday was his second night shift.'

'You've been with him for three years. It's imprinted on your brain. Imogen's not his wife.'

'As far as I'm aware, she's not anyone's wife.' And that bothered Evie. 'Has she been married?'

'I doubt it. She says she's too selfish to be in a relationship.' Having helped Dylan with his drink, Tess finished her breakfast and carried her dishes to the sink. 'Is Logan having a lie-in this morning?'

Evie's eyes flicked to the clock on the wall. She had five minutes before she had to leave. 'He asked if I could be half an hour late. I wonder if we're working towards a later start and later finish.' Both ends of the day were difficult for Evie. 'Not sure how that's going to pan out.'

'Then, thank goodness for Imogen.' Smiling, Tess liberated Dylan from the confines of his seat, took his hand and led him from the kitchen. 'I'm in today doing homework. Dylan can keep me company.'

The morning visit to Logan's was a perfunctory affair, with

Evie just about finding the time to perform the basics before she was chased out of the house.

'I won't be needing you at lunchtime,' Logan said. 'I'll see you tonight. Can you get here for six?'

'Six? I'll be giving the children their tea, Logan. Why not five as per usual?'

'Because I've arranged for you to meet Imogen. She couldn't make it until then. You'll have to arrange for an early dinner.'

So, having worried about Logan's welfare throughout the day, and leaving Tess to dish up her and Dylan's tea, Evie was back in Burton Bradstock, preparing dinner for Logan and awaiting the arrival of the new wonder woman.

'Did you have a nice lunch?' she called out to Logan in the living room.

'We did, thank you. Imogen took me out to a café in West Bay.'

Evie looked up from the cucumber she was slicing. 'You went out?' Logan never went out to eat. He'd told Evie he found the whole experience degrading and embarrassing. He couldn't cut up food, he couldn't get it cleanly to his mouth, and he hated everyone watching him.

'She has a bigger car than you.'

A bigger car? 'The car was not your primary concern.' Evie marched from the kitchen into the living room and halted in front of Logan. 'I'd have taken you out in Griff's Land Rover.'

Logan shot her a scowl. 'I'm not going out in that thing. I'd have no joints left.'

They stared at one another for a few seconds.

'What car does Imogen have?' Evie folded her arms. 'And does it have leather seats?'

'It has heated seats.' Logan's stony expression broke. His mouth took charge of the smile, and his eyes followed. 'You have a beautiful soul, Evie. Have I ever told you that?'

'I'd remember if you had.'

Projecting an air of innocence, Logan blinked several times and then folded his hands onto his lap. 'It was just lunch and a chat.'

Playing along, Evie dipped her head and peered from under her brow. 'That's how these things start. The flash cars and posh restaurants reel you in and before you know it, she's leaving her toothbrush in your bathroom and her shoes in your wardrobe. Is that how it is? Are you trading me in for a younger model?'

Logan was laughing now, his virtuousness all but vanished. 'I'm training her up, like you suggested we should do with an outside carer. It was a lovely drive, the sandwich was good and the company was excellent. We talked about everything, and I do mean *everything*, but I've had enough excitement to last the rest of my life.'

'The rest of your life?' Logan's insensitivity niggled Evie, and finding the room stifling with the fun sucked out of it, she returned to the kitchen. Bloody Imogen. She was like the new girl at school – fresh and shiny; exotic. Interesting. Whereas Evie ... well, what Logan knew about her was what she wanted him to know, which, when analysed, consisted of the bog-standard details one would expect to find in an uninspired, suburban housewife's diary. 'I'm so boring,' Evie muttered into the salad bowl. 'And ordinary. I bet Imogen's not ordinary. I bet she's fascinating, and intelligent and stunning.' No wonder the others were falling at her feet. Olivia was the only person to take a dislike to her.

'What are you doing? Come back in here.'

'I have to dish up your tea.'

'Is that with a side order of arsenic?'

Evie shook her head. She wasn't mad at Logan. Mad at the circumstances, yes, but not Logan. 'I thought I'd go with ham and a green salad tonight.'

She served up the food, put the small plate on the handy wooden tray Griff had bought from Chiswell Craft Centre, and carried everything through to Logan. 'I'm pleased you had a good day.' She retired to the armchair and gazed out of the window. The streetlamps had turned the outside world orange. 'I thought Imogen was coming.'

'She is. She was late back to work after lunch, so she's had to catch up. Is there somewhere else you have to be?'

Evie bit down on her tongue. The question was typical of Logan, asked as if Evie didn't have a life of her own to lead. 'No. It's fine,' she said, extracting the sting before releasing the words. 'Griff should be there now.'

They'd sent each other two or three texts over the course of the day, Griff confirming he was now on four days' rest, which meant he could help with Dylan, if that was what Evie wanted. Her reply hinted that wasn't the only thing she wanted and he promised to be at the cottage for half six.

Evie hadn't raised the subject of Griff and Imogen having dinner at the Harbour Inn. It was obvious Imogen had lied. It was the reason that eluded Evie.

She squinted at the brass clock in the oak wall cabinet next to Logan. It was nearly seven. Griff would be kissing Dylan on the forehead and wishing him goodnight, and Tess would be watching anime on YouTube or Skyping with Stephanie. And Evie? Normally, she'd be heading home, but here she was, waiting for Supergirl to pitch up.

In your own time, she thought.

A beep of a car alarm being set was the first indication Imogen had arrived. The next was a quick ding of the bell and the rattle of a key in the lock.

'She has a key?' Evie took to her feet, then realising she was standing to attention, sat down again. *Keep it casual.*

'Logan. It's Imy. Sorry I'm late.'

The door banged shut, shoes clacked along the hall and

a rush of air carried the scent of oranges into the room as Imogen entered. Immediately, she thrust a hand towards Evie.

'I'm Imogen. You must be Evie. At last we meet.' The friendly gesture was supported with a smile. 'I'm so sorry to have kept you. I know you have to get back to your family.'

Evie stood again and shook Imogen's hand. Her earlier assessment had been correct. Imogen was stunning. Petite, blonde and blue-eyed. Her charisma was attractive, too. It was almost a person in its own right. 'Can I get you a drink?'

Imogen disrobed and threw her pink mac onto the sofa, before giving Logan a peck on the cheek. 'I'm fine, thanks. I thought we could get straight down to business. The sooner we're done, the sooner you can get home to that beautiful daughter and baby boy. I can stay and help Logan.' She sat next to her coat, crossing her legs and spreading her arms over the tops of the cushions. 'I'm exhausted. Did Logan tell you we went out for lunch?'

Nodding, Evie retook her seat. She was reserving judgement as to Imogen's character. If this whirlwind of energy reflected her true personality, it was easy to see why people were drawn to her. Or was it that they were sucked in?

Choosing to watch, listen and learn, Evie sat back, and studied Imogen. If she was a fake, as Olivia suspected, she'd slip up eventually.

'Wow. Logan can talk for England, can't you?' Imogen switched her attention to the old man. 'We must have covered religion and politics, law, belief systems – everything from birth to death. The last person I could talk like that with was my dad, and he left a long time ago. We had a lovely day, didn't we?' Again, she addressed Logan.

'We covered a lot of ground.' Logan dropped his fork

onto his plate. 'And we found we share similar views on many subjects.'

'Seems as if you're going to be a great asset to the team,' Evie said, aware she should have sounded happier. 'I assume you'll have to fit Logan's care around your work schedule.'

'That's where being your own boss comes in handy.' Imogen brought her hands together and leaned forward. 'I'll fit my appointments around Logan's schedule. He's my number one priority, now.'

That was a dig with a big, fat, metal shovel. So, Imogen didn't do subtlety. That was something to watch for.

Evie sidestepped the freshly dug hole. 'That is so good to hear, Imogen. Both Logan and I had concerns about bringing in outside carers. No one can provide the same love and care as family, but from what I've been told, you're almost as good as family.'

'I've known this one since she was knee-high to a grasshopper,' Logan said. 'We've missed a few years between then and now, but we're catching up.' He asked for the tray to be removed. Imogen was up in a flash.

'Is that all you're having?' Evie had only dished up a small portion, no bigger than she'd have given a six-year-old Tess, but Logan had left the majority of the ham and all of the salad.

'Lunch was filling, wasn't it?' Imogen swiped away the items and came back with a glass of water. She handed it to Logan. 'Now, Evie, you must be itching to get home, so let's thrash out a plan.' Imogen perched on the sofa arm, adjacent to Logan, and in a proprietorial move, extended her arm along the top of his chair. 'Please join in, Logan. I'd hate to do this without your input. After all, you're the important person here.'

An hour later, a new care regime was in place, the washing

up was done, and Imogen was upstairs helping Logan prepare for bed. Evie was waiting for her in the living room.

She didn't deny having Imogen as a second carer was going to make a huge difference to her family life, but she couldn't see what Imogen was getting from the deal. It wasn't for financial benefit. Yes, they'd agreed to a figure per hour, but it was nothing like the cost quoted in the carer brochures. Imogen's assertion she was simply happy to be part of Logan's world again and share stories of her family with him had weight to it, just not enough.

And what of the lie she told Tess about meeting up with Griff? Then there was Olivia's mistrust of her when the others swore she was the answer to their prayers.

Now, that was an interesting notion. Griff's desire was for Logan to be less dependent on Evie. Imogen could fulfil that. Tess needed time with Evie to talk through their difficult past. Imogen's presence would present them with that opportunity. Logan …

Evie wandered over to the gold-edged mirror hanging by the hall door. She stared into her reflection. The only prayer Logan wanted answered was his call to be with Marilyn.

'Oh. You're still here.' Imogen brushed past as she carried an empty mug into the lifeless kitchen. 'Are you checking up on me?'

There was a distinct frost in the air.

She's brought her own weather front, Evie thought. She moved away from the entrance and took a tactical position in the corner of the room, protecting herself on three sides. 'You've dropped the sweetness and light routine already.'

'Routine?' Emerging from the dark, Imogen folded her arms and lounged against the doorframe. 'You don't like me very much, do you? I'm surprised. From everything your family said about you, I thought we were going to hit it off. We seem to have so much in common.'

Evie held her breath in an effort to supress the anxiety stabbing at her stomach. She trusted Griff and Tess not to discuss her personal business, and Logan was a man who valued discretion, but if, as Olivia had warned, Imogen weaved wondrous magic with one hand, while performing dirty tricks with the other, she could be party to a smorgasbord of information. Evie exhaled to a silent count of five, and then spoke in a controlled and self-assured manner. 'We do?'

'Of course.' Imogen's head inclined, and the faint beginning of a smile lifted her features. 'We both want what's best for Logan, don't we? And doesn't helping others give you a real sense of purpose?' She used her shoulder to shove herself away from the doorjamb. 'You must feel the same. You're so dedicated.'

It was concern over what the others had told Imogen that prevented Evie from nodding in agreement. For having never met, Imogen's accurate assessment of her was disturbing.

'You value privacy.' Imogen swung round and stared into the mirror. 'Nobody's told me that. It's something in you I recognise.' The reflection of her eyes levelled with Evie's. 'It's awful to think the people you love have betrayed you. Given away your secrets. It hurts right here.' She clenched a fist and held it to her chest. 'It's happened to me.' Turning back, she gazed directly at Evie. 'I can't stomach disloyalty. Something else I suspect we have in common.'

She was right on all counts. 'You're perceptive,' Evie said. 'I'll give you that. Is this how you won Tess over?'

'Won her over?' Imogen's expression was one of perfect innocence. Maybe too perfect. 'She's a credit to you and her dad.'

Evie froze. The mention of Neil agitated her thoughts, sending them scurrying into every crack in her mind they could find. Try as she might, she couldn't recall if Tess had met Imogen before or after she'd asked Evie to talk about Neil.

'So sad she lost him at such an early age,' said Imogen.

'Tess told you about that?'

'We were ... sharing. We understand the damage caused by losing someone you love. I was eleven when my brother died.' Imogen took a step forward. 'You know about Kieran, right? And Griff's part in it?'

Evie widened her stance, readying herself for battle. 'I know he feels a responsibility towards you.'

'Is that what you think?' Imogen pouted. 'I'd say there's a lot more to me and Griff than a duty of obligation.'

Ignoring the obvious implication, Evie ran with the veiled reference. 'Well, since you brought the subject up, I'm intrigued to know why you told Tess you were meeting with my husband last night.'

Imogen closed her eyes. 'She said that?' A grimace, another pout, and she was back, looking at Evie. 'Griff and I are free to see who we want, and men like him need to be with a woman. You're the one who decided your marriage certificate was worthless.' Her brow rose.

Evie flinched. Not because she believed Imogen, but because Imogen was right; Evie was the one who'd pushed Griff away.

'I've known him a long time,' Imogen continued. 'We have a shared history. I don't suppose he told you we were an item. Together. A couple, doing all those things people in love do – holding hands, kissing. Having sex.' She held Evie's gaze. 'He's very good at it, isn't he? Irresistible in his uniform. Unstoppable out of it.' Imogen slinked past the green chair, trailing a finger up and over its form. 'He's full of surprises, isn't he?'

'And you're full of yourself.' Evie derided Imogen's

claims with a scornful laugh. 'You're too selfish to be in a relationship.'

'Oh. The pretty little teenager told you that, too.' Imogen slipped onto the arm of the sofa, crossed her legs, and hitched her skirt to just above her knees. 'I did say that, but I didn't want her worrying about things that shouldn't concern her. I mean, Griff's not even her father, is he? Why should she care what he gets up to?' She scraped her hair back, amassed it in one hand, and coiled it around her neck. It came to rest on her breast, and she made a play of flattening down the loose strands. 'I like Tess. She's spirited yet vulnerable. It's an attractive combination. I was flattered when she flirted with me. It was sweet.' She smiled at Evie. 'Did you know she has a thing for girls?'

Evie couldn't determine if the woman was fishing for clues, or if Tess had confided in her. It hurt to think the latter; that her own daughter felt able to talk to a stranger – a predator – before her. She pushed the thought aside and maintained a dispassionate exterior. 'That's Tess's business.'

'Logan worries about her.' Imogen plaited and unplaited her hair, her fingers constantly twining and snaking between wisps of blonde. 'He's of the opinion still waters run deep. I agree. I've offered to keep an eye on her after he's gone.'

'You what?' Evie snorted. 'No way.' This was getting out of hand. It was time to shut down the conversation and find out exactly what Imogen was playing at. 'What is it you want, Imogen? Griff? Dream on. He's not interested in you. And he was at work last night, so you can drop your lies about spending the evening with him.' Ha. That knocked Imogen off balance. 'Or perhaps you fancy your chances with Logan. Are you going to seduce your way into his will, bump him off and claim your inheritance?'

Imogen cocked her head. 'We've had some very

interesting chats about death and how you've refused to help him.'

Now they were getting somewhere. Logan had confided in Imogen. Of course he had. Along with Griff and Tess, he'd fallen for her charm.

Evie scoffed at her analysis. It wasn't charm, it was sex. 'Was this before or after you came up with your crazy care plan?'

Pointing to the door, Imogen locked eyes with Evie. 'I'm offering you a lifeline. A way out. You don't seem very grateful.'

'Grateful?' With their exchange taking a sinister twist, Evie lowered her voice to a whisper. 'You're talking about *murder*.'

Imogen threw a hand in the air and laughed. 'What a vivid imagination you have. In your mind I'm a what? Femme fatale? Assassin?' She stood, smoothed down her skirt, and advanced upon Evie. 'As much as I'm enjoying your little fantasy of me, I was simply talking about helping your father-in-law. Taking care of him properly. Paying him the attention he deserves. Murder?' She tutted and exhaled noisily. 'If I were you, I'd think very carefully before judging me. From what I've seen, you're a terrible carer, an unloving wife, and a useless mother. If it wasn't for Logan insisting you still play a part, I'd have replaced you already.'

It was evident to Evie the threat of replacement extended to other areas of her life. Immune to her charm, she could deal with Imogen; the woman was a liar and a manipulator, who used sex – or at least, the promise of sex – to get what she wanted. In that way, Evie was reminded of Neil. Imogen was a baby in comparison.

She pushed her away. 'Get over yourself. I've dealt with far worse than you.' She made a beeline for the hall, willing Imogen to respond. Evie was up for the fight.

'I try to help, and this is the thanks I get. You're impossible to like, Evie. I can see why Tess comes to me with her problems.'

Evie reeled. 'You played on her weakness and you turned her head, but it won't last. You're a novelty. She's an impressionable teen.'

'An impressionable teen with issues.' Imogen pulled up a sleeve and motioned several criss-cross patterns over her skin. 'I've seen her arms.'

Although almost certain this was another lie constructed to divide and conquer the Hendrys, Evie faltered as an image of Tess tugging at her cuffs bore its way into her head. She'd thought of it as a habit; a nervous action of a self-conscious girl, not a means of hiding evidence. Perhaps that was what Imogen had seen too, and was twisting it to add weight to her silly mind games. If it wasn't for the fact Evie could access a number of memories where Tess covered up, she'd dismiss the claim without a second thought.

For now, determined not to show her concern, she recovered her poise. It was time to draw an end to the debacle, and show Imogen she had met her match.

'I don't have time for this,' Evie said. 'So I'm going to leave you playing house, and when you've decided what it is you want, come and find me.'

Imogen closed in on her. 'Oh, I want lots of things.' Taking another stride nearer, she slid her thumb and finger down one edge of Evie's collar. 'And I always get what I want.'

'Is that so?' Evie remained deadpan. 'Well, now you're just sounding like a spoiled brat.' She shook her head, removed Imogen's hand from her jacket, and left the building.

Where did the woman get off interfering in others' lives?

Chapter Thirty-Three

Griff

Clutching his chest, as his heart thumped out a salsa, Griff rolled over and snatched at his phone. It flew off the top of the bedside unit and thudded to the floor.

'Man.' He threw back the duvet, swung his legs over the edge of the bed and found the mobile with his foot. Bending to pick it up, he stopped halfway through to stretch and yawn. It was his first full day off, and he'd not had nearly enough sleep. 'Who the ...?' He scrabbled around for a few seconds and finally got hold of his phone. There was no point looking at its screen – his eyes hadn't joined the party yet. 'Hendry.'

'You look wrecked.' Tess invited Griff into the cottage.

'Interrupted night. What's your excuse?' He licked his finger and drew an imaginary number one in the air.

'Your humour's not affected by lack of sleep, then?' Tess smiled and leaned round the bottom stair post, her neck craned. 'Mum! Griff's here. And he has flowers, the old romantic.' She grinned, as Griff gawped at his empty hands. 'Pick some daffs from the front,' she said as she sauntered into the living room. 'They'll cheer Mum up. She seems a bit low.'

Evie's voice travelled down from above. 'I'm just changing Dylan. Come on up.'

'Two minutes.' Griff ducked through the front door onto the drive, and round to the side of the cottage. He picked seven of the largest daffodils, gathered them together and returned to the hall, all the time wondering what had

315

brought Evie's mood down. The other day with its intense revelations had been tiring and emotional, but Evie had been relaxed and content by the time Griff left. He'd missed her last night, leaving the cottage before she'd returned. Perhaps that was the problem. 'You don't mind me popping round like this, do you?' He took the stairs two by two, his long stride coping effortlessly.

'Of course not,' Evie said. 'This is your home.'

That sounded good. And promising.

He hopped over Dylan's safety gate and checked Evie's eyes. 'Are you okay?' Her sparkle wasn't as bright as before. 'You look done in.'

'How to woo your wife. Thanks.' What looked like the start of a smile was hijacked by a yawn. 'Sorry. Late night. I'll tell you about it later. I'm better now you're here.'

'Good. I'm glad.' That's all Griff wanted – to be there for his family. 'How far through changing Dylan are you? Shall I take over?' The odour of a full and well-fibred nappy reached him a fraction later. 'Can I retract my offer?' Griff laughed as Evie shook her head and passed him the baby wipes. He tendered the flowers in exchange.

'I grow a good daff, don't I?' Evie pressed the gift to her breast. 'Remind me to thank Tess later.' For a brief moment, she held Griff's hand. 'I know they come from your heart. Thank you.'

'There are seven,' he said. 'One for each member of our family – you, me, Tess, Dylan and my dad. And one for Ozzy.'

'That's six,' Evie said, separating the tallest one and showing it to Griff. 'Who's this for?'

'Ah.' He hesitated, debating whether or not to speak the line he'd thought of when he was in the garden. He didn't understand the language of flowers, but daffodils bloomed in the spring, and that signified rebirth; another chance to get life right. 'That one is for love,' he said. 'And the promise of new beginnings.'

'I like that.' Evie drew close. 'New beginnings.' After a tender kiss on Griff's lips, she released a sigh, tapped the packet of wipes in his possession, and directed his attention to their son. 'It's an end you have to deal with now.'

'Daddy.' A pair of chubby legs and two arms waved from the changing mat as Griff attended to his parental duties.

He wafted his hand in front of his nose and pulled a face. 'Phew! Dylan! That's disgusting.' His exaggerated expression sent Dylan into a fit of giggles. 'What's Mum been feeding you? Cabbage? Brussels sprouts? Beans?' He pinched his nostrils together. 'Please. Not beans.'

The clown act produced delightful belly laughter from Dylan, which in turn produced a not-so-delightful bout of wind, and the possibility of a perpetual circle of toilet humour, grimaces and giggles.

'Boys,' Griff heard Evie say. He stiffened his jaw, and widened his eyes.

'Let's get you sorted,' he said, taking pleasure from the joy on Dylan's face. 'Do you have plans today?' He peered over his shoulder at Evie. She had the tiniest of smiles playing on her lips. 'Once you've fixed Dad's lunch.'

'I'm not going in today.' Her tone changed. 'It's the first day of the new *care* system.'

Griff didn't miss the pointed emphasis. He raised his brows at his son. 'It's bound to feel strange to start with. Are you working a rota?' He threw a dirty wipe in the nappy sack.

'Yes. It was Imogen's idea. She has a lot of those. We're taking alternative weekends, but she's taken Wednesday evenings and everything on Thursdays and Fridays.'

'So you have two whole days off?' Having dried and dressed Dylan, Griff scooped him into his arms, squeezed him and then set him down on the floor. 'You know, now Dad and I are heading in the right direction, perhaps I could add my name to your schedule.' He didn't look at Evie. She had every reason to read him the Riot Act and accuse him of only stepping in now that Logan's care was divided. Instead, he tidied away the nappy paraphernalia and trotted out of the bedroom into the bathroom.

Evie was close on his tail. 'You'd do that?' She perched on the closed toilet seat, her face a picture of wonder.

The Riot Act would have caused less guilt.

Griff washed and dried his hands, and propped himself against the basin. 'I should have been doing it already. I've been pig-headed and stupid, and I misread my dad's situation. Now I'd like the chance to do something right. I'd have to work around my shifts, but that won't be a problem.'

He fell quiet, giving Evie the opportunity to consider the logistics of adding his name to the rota. He tilted the mirror on the windowsill and inspected his chin for bristles. After his early morning phone call, he'd shaved in a hurry. It was debatable whether or not he'd been awake enough to wield a razor, but he'd heard somewhere people should do one thing each day that scared the living daylights out of them.

'I think Logan would love for you to help.' Evie's reflection joined Griff's and it mimicked his moves. 'I find a wet shave's the only way to go.' She smiled as she transferred her finger from her jawline to his.

'I agree,' he said. 'About that and Dad. I should have been here for you and him before.'

His face was gently angled towards Evie's.

'You're here now, and that's what matters. Where you and I are concerned, what's past is past. We've already established that.' Her eyes creased at the corners; fine, delicate maps guiding those she'd taught to read them to a world of brilliance and intensity.

Griff pressed his lips to her forehead. 'If I wasn't already in love with you, I'd fall, right here, right now.' He stepped behind her, bringing their bodies together, acutely aware she'd feel how much he wanted her. 'We've never made love in here.' He arched to kiss behind her ear and at first she yielded, rolling her head onto his shoulder, but as he swept her hair into his hand, she quickly reclaimed it and recoiled. He released her immediately.

'Not here,' she said. 'Not the bathroom.' She held her flower-free hand in the air and backed onto the landing. 'Neil ... It's not a good place.'

Out of sight, it was the clunk of a safety gate that gave away her bolthole. She'd retreated into Dylan's room.

Griff waited outside.

Clearly where Neil was concerned, some things weren't past.

'Evie?' Griff knocked on the door. 'Are you okay?'

'I'm fine. I'll see you downstairs.'

Her voice was steady and calm. If she was crying, Griff determined, it would be breathy and stilted. That had to be a positive sign. 'Would you like me to take Dylan?'

Silence.

'Evie?'

'He's not in here. Tess must have got him when we were talking.'

Griff swished the toe of his shoe over the carpet, watching the loose pile form into a thin sausage. 'So ... Don't you think you should come out?'

His gentle persuasion was rewarded. As the door opened, he released the gate handle, and Evie stepped through.

Relieving her of the daffodils, he took her hand and led her to the stairs. With the top gate already open, they descended the first few steps.

'It's not that I didn't want to, you know ...?' Evie cast her eyes towards the bathroom. 'I did. I do. Just not there.' She rubbed Griff's arm. 'Sorry.'

'Hey. No more. We need to get ready to go out, anyway.' She'd talk to him when she was ready. For now Griff was satisfied Evie was handling things her way.

'We're going out?'

'I'm off, *you're* off, Tess is on holiday and Dylan's clean, what's stopping us? It's a little breezy, but we can wrap up.' He tipped Tess's hat off the coat stand on the way past, catching it before it hit the floor. 'And I could use a little support when I collect Ozzy's ashes.' He halted and looked at Evie. 'The vet called this morning.'

'If you don't mind me saying, Griff, I'd have expected the urn to be bigger.' Sitting at a picnic table at Portland Bill, Tess lifted the rectangular, maple box, and tested the weight. 'And it's not really an urn, is it? I expected it to be like a vase.' She put it back down on the slatted surface. 'Is that really Ozzy inside?'

Evie draped a protective hand over the box. 'Perhaps you should take Dylan over to the swings, Tess?' Dylan's face lit up and he wriggled excitedly on the bench.

With their legs already touching, Griff nudged Evie's knee. 'It's okay. Tess is right. The size surprised me, too.' He slid the box from under her hand. 'Yep. It's Ozzy.' For a large dog with a huge character, Griff had expected the container to be bigger. 'There were these great, elaborate, ornamental urns, but it started to get a bit *Aladdin*. And what would we have done with it once we'd scattered the ashes?'

Tess hauled a fidgeting Dylan onto her lap. 'Plant a shrub in it, in Ozzy's memory.'

'Nice idea. Perhaps we could do something similar with the box.' Griff had considered launching it out to sea – a vessel to sail Ozzy safely to his next adventure – but it went against Griff's principles and his love of the ocean. 'I don't think we should keep it inside though.' He found the custom of having an urn on display a little macabre. 'And there's no garden where I'm living.'

'The corner with the white roses was a favourite spot,' Evie said, her hand disappearing under the table. 'We could plant a second bush there in his honour.'

'At the cottage?' Griff's thigh was instantly warmed as Evie laid her hand on top.

'Of course,' she said, a quizzical frown overshadowing her smile. 'It's your home.'

The statement was ambiguous – it lay somewhere between a fact and an open invitation to return. Before Griff had time to pursue it, Tess diverted his attention.

'Mum said I could have a piercing in Ozzy's honour.'

Griff lifted an eyebrow. 'That's ... sweet.'

'You don't mind?'

This was new – Tess seeking Griff's say-so. 'Well, as you know I'm not a huge fan of body art,' he began, cautious not to annihilate Tess's enthusiasm, 'but it's not my body and it's not my art.' He hesitated, reviewing his answer. 'You were asking for my blessing, right? And that was nothing like a blessing, was it?' No wonder Tess was giving him the death stare. He held up an index finger, indicating he had more to say. 'But I do understand it's a form of self-expression and it's a touching gesture, so if your mum says it's okay, then ...' He paused, searching for the right words. 'I thank you for loving Ozzy so much that you'd like to mark his time with us.' He nodded in a self-confident manner, smiled, and waited for Tess to reply.

The death stare had morphed into a gape of sympathy. 'Do you get how truly tragic you are?' Tess lifted Dylan off her lap, took his hand and then grinned at Griff. 'That's exactly how a step-dad should be.' She blew him a cheeky kiss, showed Dylan how to do the same, and then they took off, racing towards the swings.

'I do believe she's given you *her* blessing.' Evie squeezed Griff's leg.

He reached under the table and gripped her hand. For three years he'd hoped Tess would accept him as part of her family. There were no words for such an incredible moment.

He pinched and cuffed his nose, rubbed his fingers over his mouth, and rested his chin in the crook of his palm, watching his children ... *his children* run across the grass. 'She's a good kid,' he said, once he felt his voice wasn't going to crack.

'She is.'

Pulling their hands up from under the table, Griff straddled the bench and looked at Evie. 'Why am I sensing a *but*?'

'It's not a but.' She stopped, giving Griff even more cause for concern, then she released a rapid breath, picked up Ozzy's urn and skimmed a thumb over his name. 'Where would you like to scatter his ashes?'

She'd changed the subject. That didn't bode well.

'I was thinking here,' said Griff. 'On The Bill. What do you think?'

'I don't know. Are you allowed to?'

'I hadn't given it any thought.' It wasn't a concern of Griff's. Ozzy's dusty remains weren't going to hurt the ecosystem. Ashes to ashes and all that. 'Who's going to know, except us?'

Evie surveyed the land and pointed to a group of people posing for photographs next to the lighthouse. 'They'd know.' She turned towards the café. 'And the man coming out of there – he'd know.' She twisted to see behind and nodded to a lone elderly man, sitting on a bench looking out to sea. 'And he'd know, too. It's pretty busy, Griff.'

'I wasn't planning on doing it right now.' He enclosed

Evie's hand in his and settled it on her lap. 'We could do it tomorrow morning, before the world awakes.'

'We?'

'Of course *we*. Tess and Dylan too.'

Evie's eyes enlarged. Their brightness would save ships, Griff thought.

'I guarantee Dylan will be awake,' she said. 'But Tess won't stir before the birds. She's a teen, she's on school holidays and she's already had a couple of early starts helping your dad with his breakfast.' She restored Ozzy's urn to the table.

'Still, I'd like to ask.' Griff's intuition was telling him Tess would want to be involved. 'And I'd like to ask Dad, too. He was fond of Ozzy. Do you think he'd come?'

'Your father's a law unto himself. He went out to lunch with Imogen, so anything is possible.' Evie swung her legs round the end of the bench so she was facing out, leaned back, and propped herself up with her elbows.

The pose gave definition to her breasts.

Lost for a moment in a wild fantasy of taking Evie right there, Griff inhaled a fresh, purifying breath, and redistributed his energy. 'Do you think she'd mind if we stole him away on her second day on the job?'

'She's his carer, not his wife.' Evie thrust forward. If she'd had any weight to her, the entire unit of the table and benches would have rocked with the force. 'She's not even related.'

Griff backed away and held up both hands. 'Steady on.' It took intense pressure for Evie to work up a head of steam. It was rare to see her angry. 'Why's Imogen got you rattled?'

Evie sighed, left her seat and extended a hand to Griff. 'Can we walk? I need to talk to you about something ... about lots of things, really, and I realise this isn't the best time or the most appropriate place, but if I don't tell you now, and there are consequences, I wouldn't be able to live with myself.'

This was serious. Griff was on his feet in an instant. He grabbed the urn and dropped it into his pocket. 'Walk,' he said, forging a course to Tess and Dylan. 'We'll talk.'

Twenty minutes later, his head spinning with Imogen's lies, insinuations and veiled threats, Griff sunk onto the swing next to Tess. Practising discretion, he monitored her arms as she pushed forward and fell back. Her coat was doing its job of keeping her covered.

Evie had given him plenty to think about, his main concern being Tess, and the intimation she was harming herself. Evie was equally as shocked, but she'd had the benefit of an evening's online research. Not that it had reassured her.

'There are so many sites,' she'd said. 'And there are all these people posting messages and questions, desperate to reach out, desperate for someone to hear them, and I'm thinking, is that what Tess is doing? Has her past damaged her ... have I damaged her so much she's had to reach out to someone distinctly unconnected to Neil? Is that why she's confided in Imogen?'

Griff had no answers and the questions crashing through his head would only add to Evie's anxiety.

He kick-started his swing and set a rhythm to fall in with Tess.

'I'm surprised your hips fit,' she said, propelling her legs in front.

'It's snug,' Griff conceded, trying to catch up, the frame complaining and creaking in time with his efforts.

'I'm not sure it can take your weight.' Tess's voice advanced and retreated as she shot past and flew back.

'I'm not sure, either.' Griff forced out a smile, and ran his feet along the black, spongy floor, bringing his swing to an abrupt halt. 'Maybe I'll just sit.'

He saluted Dylan and Evie, who were taking a placid approach to the roundabout.

She'd said there was more to tell, but having reached the playground, the conversation had stopped. What more could there be? Griff had learned of Tess's issues, heard of Imogen's strange, and whacky plan to cut Evie out of the new care schedule, and rightly or wrongly, been amused by Imogen's story of her and Griff being a couple. His laugh, though derisory, had scored him a reproachful scowl from Evie.

'Oh, come on,' he'd said, finding himself walking alone. 'I know you don't believe her. She's winding you up. Having a little fun at your expense.'

The fleeting attraction towards Imogen he experienced in the Harbour Inn counted for nothing. He was the only person aware of it and it had faded as rapidly as it had developed. It hadn't crossed his mind since. It was an aberration and one he had no desire to repeat.

'Evie,' he'd pleaded. 'It's cold without you.' He'd opened his arms and she'd relented, cuddling into his body. 'I don't know what Imogen's game is,' he'd said, 'but she's not the malicious sort. Perhaps she thinks she's helping you by being a friend to Tess. And to be fair, if she's right about Tess harming herself, we should be thanking her for telling us.'

He was with Evie on the topic of Tess's sexuality, however. It was no one's business but Tess's and he was upset Imogen had taken it upon herself to out her, even though Evie said she wasn't surprised by the news.

'How are you getting on with Imogen?' he asked as Tess brought her swing to a gentle stop.

'She's a bit full-on, but I like her. And she gets muddled easily, which I find funny.'

'Muddled?'

'Yeah. Says one thing one minute and contradicts it the next. I reckon it's all those aroma stick things she uses at work. Fogged her brain.' Tess climbed off the swing. 'I'm going to push the roundabout for Dylan. I'll send Mum over.'

Tess baffled him. She was chilled and happy, engaging with him, chatting about Ozzy, enquiring, inquisitive. Was it all a front? If she did self-harm, where did she do it and with what?

Her bedroom was the likely answer to where, and she did spend a lot of time there, but that was part and parcel of being a teenager. They liked their own company, especially Tess. When they'd first met she'd made that clear, impressing upon Griff that her room was private and he was to keep out. He'd have fixed that squeaky floorboard by now if it wasn't for the fact its repaired state of silence would inform Tess of his unlawful entry.

She had panicked the other day when he'd knocked on her door. It was the day she'd come home from school upset. What was that about?

'Hey.' Evie took Tess's vacated swing. 'What are you thinking?'

'If it's true, she hides it well.'

'She does.' Evie wrapped her arms around the metal chains and linked her fingers together. 'My understanding is it's not about attention seeking otherwise she wouldn't cover up. She'd make it obvious, like Neil did. Is it possible finding him with his arm slashed has embedded the idea in her brain? It says on the web, cutting's a symptom of an underlying issue, and Tess has been carrying all this unresolved stuff around in her head for years.'

'I don't know. I'm as lost as you. But we'll work it out. As a family.' Griff reached across the divide and brushed his hand on Evie's cheek. 'Don't start blaming yourself.' She was doing that already, it was obvious. 'I think the first thing is not to overreact. We can carry on researching, we can speak to the doctor and we can learn how to help.' It was all he had, but it was constructive and it was positive. 'In the meantime, we should establish whether or not Imogen is telling the truth.'

His instinct was spurring him into questioning Imogen's integrity, and his opinion of the woman he'd known since childhood was shifting. He'd believed everything Evie had said about her, but he'd been certain there was an explanation for Imogen's actions. Now, with Tess using the words *muddled* and *contradicts* in her description, he was having second thoughts. 'I've a funny suspicion Imogen could be playing us for a pair of fools,' he said. 'I just wish I knew why.'

Up until then, Evie had been swaying as if blown by a gentle breeze. 'I might be able to answer that.' Still holding the chains within her arms, she bowed her head and let it drop onto her hands.

'Go on.' It was unlike Evie not to look at Griff while speaking with him. She hadn't averted her eyes when she'd told him about Neil, or half an hour ago when they were discussing Imogen and Tess, and they were difficult conversations. 'Evie? You have to tell me now, whatever it is.'

'I know.' Her sleeves muffled her voice. 'Are the children okay?'

Griff gave Tess a thumbs-up, which she returned once she'd popped Dylan on the end of the playground see-saw. She was lifting him up and down, telling him to jump every time his feet touched the floor. She was laughing and Dylan was giggling. 'They're good,' Griff said. 'Now, look at me and tell me what you know.'

Raising her head and freeing her arms of the chains, Evie straightened her back and began. 'This is something I've wanted to tell you from the start.'

'Okay.' Griff maintained an open posture, his feet as wide apart as the swing allowed, and his hands resting on his knees – anything to ease Evie's journey. 'The start of what?'

'The start of our troubles.' She bit down on her lip. 'I've never stopped loving you, and I never wanted us to be apart, you knew that, didn't you? Despite the curve balls I threw.'

'We covered that the other day.' Griff dipped his head and smiled. He wanted Evie to keep going until everything, whatever that turned out to be, was out there. 'Nothing can be worse than what you've already told me.'

'This isn't about me, though. This is about Logan.' Evie paused and filled her lungs. 'And you.'

Chapter Thirty-Four

Evie

She'd promised herself she'd follow Griff's lead on the matter of Logan and his request, but Imogen had forced her hand and they were indeed being played for fools.

The risk of telling Griff was colossal. He and Evie had taken significant steps in reconciling, but it was early days and the weight of the truth could destroy them more completely and more conclusively than the deceit of keeping the secret.

She toyed with the last button on her coat. Its cool, smooth surface provided a calming sensation. Drawing strength from the feeling, Evie composed herself and proceeded.

'Before Christmas, Logan asked me to consider a proposal. He asked if I would be a witness for his Advance Decision.'

'He has a directive? Like ... a living will?' Griff's knees closed together and he clutched his hands across his chest.

'He has, and I signed it.' Evie took another steadying breath. 'We've lodged a copy with Logan's solicitor, there's one in his medical files, Logan has a copy, and so do I. Should it come into play, I've promised to ensure his instructions are followed by the health care professionals.' She was aware her words had fallen faster and heavier than a rainstorm and she and Griff would need shelter. 'This is wrong,' she said. 'It's selfish of me to do this now. We should go home. I'll get the children.' This was a conversation to be had in private, not in the middle of a park.

'No.' Griff indicated for her to stay where she was. 'What are my father's instructions?'

Evie scored a finger around the inside of one of the chain links while she considered the pros and cons of finishing what she'd started.

'Evie. Tell me.'

The stern plea pushed her into replying.

'No invasive tubes, no life support, no resuscitation.' There was more detail to the document, but nothing that would make a difference to its overall meaning. Giving Griff time to absorb the information, Evie constructed the next part of her confession. When Griff had finished massaging his forehead, she continued. 'Logan asked me to keep the information to myself.'

'Because he knew I'd raise objections.'

'In his defence, it was his decision to make and his private business. He'd thought long and hard who to ask to be a witness. My name wasn't top of the list.'

Griff's hands unlocked. 'Mine was?'

Evie nodded. 'He said his greatest wish was to have his son at his side when it was time to go, but with your views on keeping the living alive, he assumed you would, as you said, voice your objections. Things were already strained between you and he didn't want to risk another massive falling-out, so he asked me.' Every word was true, but Evie feared every pause between was taking her a breath nearer to losing Griff.

His head was in his hands now, and he was ruffling his fingers through his hair. 'He said that? His greatest wish was to have me beside him when he dies?'

That wasn't the part Evie thought he'd pick up on. And there was no anger in his tone. There was genuine esteem. 'He's never given up on you.'

Still bent double, Griff looked up. 'Why didn't you tell me this the other day?'

Evie alighted from the swing, glanced across to the

children who had moved onto a small climbing structure, then knelt at Griff's feet. 'I felt our souls had searched enough for one afternoon.'

'Is there more?'

'Yes.' If she didn't get through this quickly, there was the danger she'd not get through it at all. 'I need to just tell you straight, Griff. Let me speak, let me explain myself and if you walk away, I'll understand. It's not what I want, but I promise, I will understand.'

He held her face, brought her lips to his and kissed her, long and deep, and with intent, his mouth, his hands, his passion sending the message he loved her and always would.

Evie knew his kiss was given to provide her with courage, but as they broke away, she had a disquieting notion it would be the last they'd share.

She closed her eyes and prepared for the worse.

'Separate to his living will, your father asked something else of me.' She heard Griff draw breath. She opened her eyes, and gently shook her head, cutting him off before he said anything. 'Since he lost your mum, he's not been happy. Not really. Marilyn was the love of his life, we both know that.' She swallowed. 'He's going through the motions of daily living, but with his body failing, he's struggling to find a purpose in being here. He asked me that when he decides to go ...' She rubbed her hands together and took a shuddering breath. 'He asked if I would be there and ...' She looked at Griff and saw her sorry state reflecting in his sad, brown eyes. It wasn't fright stealing her words.

She tried again. 'He asked if I would be there ... and make sure he ...' She clasped a hand to her mouth. 'I can't. I can't tell you.' Her throat ached with raw emotion, and her chest compacted with pain and a grief she knew was to come. She stopped speaking and started shaking.

Griff leapt off his swing, heaved her into his arms, and pressed her head into his body.

His embrace stitched every fibre of her being together.

'I get it,' he said. 'I understand.'

'Please don't hate your father.'

'I don't hate him.'

'Don't hate me,' she whispered. She was hugged tighter still. 'I thought about it, Griff. I thought about helping him. I know what true unhappiness is. I know what it is to wake up to fear, to loneliness. I had days when I wished I wasn't here. But I had a baby. I had Tess. And her survival was my priority. Your dad ...'

'You were carrying this on your shoulders?' Griff laid his cheek on Evie's head.

'I couldn't tell anyone. It was too risky. And I couldn't tell you for all sorts of reasons, but I didn't want to lie to you either. The guilt ... every time I looked at you ... I couldn't deal with it, so I thought it best to create some distance between us, just until I'd decided what to do.' She remained in his hold, comforted by the protection it afforded and the reassurance it provided. 'I didn't know why you and Logan fought, not then, but I knew how proud he was ... is of you. How much he loves you. I'd got it into my head that if I told you about his plan, you'd be so completely devastated, it would finish you, and you'd want nothing more to do with him. I couldn't let that happen. You're too important to each other.'

'You're the most important person to me. I can't live without you.'

Griff's voice vibrated right through Evie.

'And your dad doesn't feel he can live without Marilyn. If I was a braver person, I'd have said yes to helping him, but in the end I told him I wouldn't do it. I don't know why it took me so long to reach a decision. Maybe it was more to do with my inability to say no.'

Neil had conditioned that into her.

'And because you've lived it, Evie. You have empathy. It's one of the reasons I love you. I wish I'd known. I'd never have left. We'd have worked something out together.'

'If we'd have told you, you'd have gone ballistic.'

'Maybe, but you and I wouldn't have spent months apart.'

'But you and your father would. There'd have been two rifts to repair, and Logan was so desperate to make his peace with you, he wasn't going to involve you.' Evie felt Griff bend to look at her.

'Do you know how much I love you?' He kissed her forehead. 'You have such an immense capacity to care. It scares me sometimes.'

'It does?'

'You put everyone's needs above yours. If you can help someone, you will, but it's often at your expense. I hate seeing people use you, Evie. No has as much power as yes.' He tucked her head under his chin. 'I'm not happy about Dad putting all the responsibility onto you.'

'He doesn't see it like that,' Evie said. 'In his mind, he's a burden to us. He said it was clear his needs were creating conflict, that he was taking me away from my family, from you, from our children ...' Hot and thirsty, and suddenly aware she was still in a playground with her children running towards her, Evie moved away from Griff, dried her eyes and forced herself to switch to mother mode. 'I said we could sort that, we could find him other care, we'd hire professionals. He said it wasn't another carer he needed. It was another accomplice.'

'Imogen?' Griff whispered.

Smoothing her coat down behind her legs, Evie crouched as Dylan hurtled into her arms. 'According to her, she and Logan had a long chat about life and death. I think he's asked for her help.'

Griff made a face at his son, while he addressed Evie. 'Why didn't you mention this first thing?'

This had to be one of the most bizarre moments in Evie's history. Her life was in chaos, yet everything around her was normal. Children were playing in the park, paper kites were flying in the sky, and Dylan was blowing raspberries at his dad.

'It was a bit like now,' she said. 'Surreal. I thought I must have got the wrong end of the stick, but the more I think about Imogen, the more I'm convinced she's up to no good.'

Griff relieved Evie of Dylan, tickled his tummy and held him up high above his head. After a brief flight around the swings, he seated him on his hip, and turned to Evie. 'Do you think she's after Dad's money?'

Evie pursed her lips. 'Honestly? I think she's after you.'

Chapter Thirty-Five

Tess

The drive home from Portland was quiet. I don't think Mum and Griff had rowed, but there was a difficult, stilted atmosphere in the car.

We've eaten a late lunch and Griff's gone out. I don't know where, but he's a man on a mission. His jaw was square and tight and his brow was low. Broody. Can a forty-year-old man be broody? I thought that was reserved for my age group. Anyway, someone's got him riled and they're going to experience the Griff Hendry whirlwind at full force.

The fresh air's wiped out Dylan. He almost fell asleep at the table. I had my mobile ready to film him in case he nodded off and face-planted in to his cheese on toast, but Mum took pity on him and told me to put the phone away. Before Griff left, he took Dylan up to bed.

Now it's just Mum and me in the living room, and she keeps giving me sideways looks.

'You're sorting things out with Griff, then?' I say, wondering if that's the subject she's hoping to broach. 'You're both a lot happier.' I'm not mentioning how tired they look, because, quite frankly, I have no desire to know the reason behind their black circles and jaded appearance. I don't think Griff needs any more of my help in the chocolates and flowers department.

'I think we will be,' Mum says. 'Happier.'

What an odd response. 'Have you told him about Dad?'

Mum's nodding.

'Everything?'

She's shifted round on the sofa we're sharing. 'I had to, Tess. I couldn't give him half an explanation.'

'So he knows about what Dad did and what happened to him. And what I did?'

'Everything.'

Griff's sudden exit after lunch has me worried now. 'Is this what you were talking about at the park?' I saw them, close one minute, apart the next. And whenever I was within earshot, they fell silent. 'I knew something was going on,' I say. 'Is this storming out his reaction?'

'You have nothing to worry about, I promise. And he didn't storm out. He's gone to see Logan.' Mum settles back and taps the seat beside her. 'Huddle up.' I'm a little reluctant to take up her offer as my warning signals are still flashing. 'Please,' she says. 'Indulge me.'

'Is this about Stephanie?'

'Would you like it to be?'

I approach Mum's side of the sofa with caution, just in case she's laid a trap. 'I'm not sure.' I reverse into her and she loops an arm over my shoulder. She's the same height as me when we're sitting down. I tug my sleeves to their full length. 'What do you think of her?'

'I think she's charming.'

'Pretty?'

'Yes. Attractive.'

'Girlfriend material?' Our game of word ping-pong falters and I'm wishing I'd just come right out and told Mum how much I like Stephanie. Seeing her at the café set my mind at rest. My feelings are genuine, and she likes me. There's definitely something going on with us.

I haven't seen her in what feels like forever. It was agonising being on Portland this morning and driving straight through Chiswell. I waved at her mum's café.

We're going to get together as often as we can before she goes back to France.

We Skyped last night. Talked non-stop for nearly three hours. I told her I went out with a boy, but it ended badly, and she said she's had one long-term girlfriend, but is single now. She came out to her parents two years ago. I was curious about their reaction – were they shocked? Did they tell her she was wrong? That she hadn't met the right boy yet? Stephanie looked directly down the camera, smiled, and said, 'You'll be okay.' It blew me away. It knocked the air out of my lungs, and I could feel my heart pulsing. Banging. I had an internal bass drum kicking out my rhythm. It was the best rush ever and I thought, I've got to hold onto this feeling, because until last night, cutting was the only thing that gave me that sort of release.

I've been clean a whole week and that's good. It's not that I haven't felt the urge, or thought about cutting, but I've managed to control it by occupying my hands and distracting myself. I went online, too, and got back to the girl from Manchester. She said the urge will decrease in time, and it might even go away completely. Wouldn't that be great? But until I deal with the cause, I may never lose the compulsion. She said I sounded as if I was serious about stopping and if I could find the courage to tell someone, their support would mean the world.

There was a point last night, when Stephanie and I were sharing all this personal stuff, when just for a second, I thought about telling her. But then I had this picture whizz through my mind of a poster with my photo on it and the words *Crackpot Girlfriend* stamped across the front in big, bold Playbill type, and I realised it would be a mistake. It's way too soon to reveal that side of me.

Manchester girl said the thing that's made the biggest difference for her is attending counselling. She said that could be a way forward for me, and I think she could be right. I've already told Mum I need to talk Dad out of my system.

'Tess? Are you back in the room?'

Oh. Yeah. I was about to come out to Mum. She'll be cool, but I'm still nervous. 'I was talking about girlfriend material, wasn't I?'

'We were discussing Stephanie,' Mum says. 'And I suspect that's who you were with just then. You had the smile going on.' Mum uses both hands to exaggerate the upward arc of her mouth.

'Yeah. I was. I can't stop thinking about her.' I guess this is me coming out. I'm going to run with it. 'So ... what do you think? Good girlfriend material? For me, I mean.'

'I didn't think you meant for me.'

I'm craning my neck to see Mum's face. She's smiling. Stephanie was right. I am okay. I've not fainted. Nor has Mum, and the fact we're still upright and conscious will make the conversation even easier.

'I hope she's good girlfriend material,' Mum says. 'But that's for you to find out.' She kisses my temple. 'And you have all the time in the world to get to know her. If she's kind and treats people with respect, and you're the first person she Skypes when she gets back to France, what more could you ask for?'

'And you're okay with this?'

'Of course. Why wouldn't I be?'

'It makes me different.'

I'm pulled in to a tight hug. It's nice. I decide we should do this more often and then remember why we don't. I sneak a peek at my arms. They remain covered.

'We're all different,' Mum says. 'If we weren't we'd all fancy the same person. Can you imagine the stampedes that'd cause? It would be a bloodbath. It came close at school when my friend and I lusted after the music teacher.'

'But he was a man, right?'

'Yep. The music teacher was too.'

It's taking me a moment to work out what Mum's implying, but I've got there and I can't help laughing. She's made her point well.

She's released me from her clutches and has wriggled into a position where she can see me. It occurs to me she might be going to talk about Dad, but she seems to be assessing me. I'm not sure I'm keen on my mother *assessing* me. I go to challenge her, but she speaks first.

'From the day you were born, you've amazed me with your courage, and your wit, and your love, and I thank God for sending you to me. You're the one thing Neil and I got right.'

I disagree. 'He didn't care about me, Mum. He was nothing more than a sperm donor. A violent, sadistic, controlling one, but a donor all the same.'

'Is that how you see him?'

Mum's pushed back into the sofa, as if the force of my statement drove her there. When she gets up, I'll expect to see an imprint of her body.

'Yeah.' I shrug. 'You've done all the nurturing and teaching and loving. You need to take credit where it's due.' I pause. Mum's lost in her own world. I imagine it's the one Neil MacDonald inhabits. I've ventured there a lot lately, especially when I've been thinking about Stephanie. Last night, once I'd decided not to tell her about my cutting, I avoided talking about Dad, because I realise the two are linked. But I can't do that forever. 'You don't think people will judge me because of what Dad did, do you?'

Mum blinks and returns to the safety of our bubble. 'Judge you? What is there to judge?'

My hands are sticky and clammy, and I blow on them. It doesn't help – they're still hot, and now I'm light-headed. And my arm itches. I huff and carry on. 'It's not the case as far as I'm concerned, but it crossed my mind people might assume I've chosen to like girls because my dad's behaviour towards you put me off boys.'

'If by people you mean the person you're with, then you're with the wrong person. If they question your motives and can't accept you for who you are, they need to go, regardless of gender or orientation.'

Mum's moved to the edge of the sofa, her knees are together and her arms are on her thighs. She's totally focused on me. It's intense, but that's okay. I can do intense. Besides, I started this particular bout.

'They're suggesting you've *chosen* to like girls.' Mum's frowning. 'Was it a conscious decision? Because I know I didn't *choose* to like men. It just happened. And you know what? It's nobody else's business anyway.' She's shaking her head. 'You deserve to be safe, Tess, and happy and loved, and though it breaks my heart to say it, you've seen enough atrocities to know what's wrong.'

I'm not sure why, perhaps it's a subtle change in Mum's tone, but I get the feeling I've been steered in a different direction.

She sighs and bites her lip. 'If I ask you to do something, will you promise to try?'

There it is. The handbrake turn. 'I'll do my best,' I say. 'But I need a drink first.' I have a bitter taste on my tongue and my mouth's dry.

It's a relief to feel the cool kitchen air on my face.

As I'm downing a glass of water, Mum comes in and sits on the table.

'Okay?'

'I'll let you know in a minute,' I say. I believe we've left Stephanie in the living room, so I'm thinking this is about Dad. I hop up onto the worktop and lean into my hands. I've braced myself physically and mentally. 'Go on.'

'A short while ago, you spoke about scars left by your dad. Do you remember?'

I nod. That was an easy question to answer, but my insides are fluttering. 'He left his mark,' I say, pointing to my forehead.

'For which I'm partly responsible.' Mum's eyes are flicking left to right. She's accessing her memory banks. 'I made a mistake, Tess. I made the wrong call about keeping our past between us. You're right to want to talk about it, and I promise to tell you what I can, but I'm not the person who can help you heal those wounds. I can't be objective. My entire being is screaming at me to protect you, and that means I'd want to keep stuff from you. That's not going to work. It's not going to help you.'

Wow. I wasn't expecting that.

'We'll find a way forward, a way to talk about this in a manner which won't cause more harm, because it's too important to ignore. The truth needs to be uncovered.'

She's holding her wrist but I don't know if she's seeing Dad bleeding to death or if her subconscious is giving away what I'm beginning to think she knows. She's using keywords – scars, harm, wounds – and I wish she wouldn't. They're acting as triggers and all I can see is my blade and all I want is to feel the cold metal cut through my skin so I can release the pressure in my head.

'Tess?'

It's her quiet, gentle, understanding voice and I don't want to hear it because I know I'll do whatever she asks. And I know she's going to ask to see my arms. Then what will happen? She'll be upset. Disappointed. Sad. I don't want to make her sad, because sadness is complete. Whole. It consumes every part of your being, every inch, gap and space in your brain. And it makes every breath heavy.

I don't want to make her sad. I want to make her proud, but how can I when I'm pathetic and weak and embarrassed. She'll see the real me. The Tess who tries to cut her dad out of her life.

I'm tugging at my sleeves, hooking the cuffs over my thumbs, and folding my arms.

Mum's off the table now and walking towards me. I'm staring at my feet, but she's giving me no option but to look at her. She's lifted my chin and the full weight of her concern is crushing me.

'Tess,' she says, her breath falling on my face. 'I learnt something recently. I say yes to others because Neil taught me that turning someone down would lead to the loss of their love. I've lived with that state of mind for years. He took away my right to say no. Then Logan asked me to help him die and I didn't want to do it. I want him to live. But I risked losing his love if I said no.'

She's pausing to take in air and although she's looking me in the eye, I don't think it's me she's seeing.

'It took me a while to work things out, but I realised I had to take charge of my life, and I had to say no. I had to take back the control Neil had beaten from me. And do you know who gave me the strength to do that?'

She's sweeping my fringe from my face. I give no reply.

'You and Griff and Logan. You've shown me I can say no and still be loved.'

She smiles and kisses my cheek and I can feel she's on the cusp of asking me her question. My heart's gone crazy and I'm dizzy. I'm either going to be sick or pass out.

Mum's hand is on my forehead. It's soothing and my breathing slows down.

'I'll do whatever it takes to put things right for you,' she says, 'but it's down to you to set the pace, to tell me what you want, and to show me how I can help. All I'm asking is that you take control. Claim back the power stolen from you. Do you understand?'

I do.

She wasn't going to ask to see my scars. She wasn't even going to ask if I cut. Not because she doesn't care, but because she does.

And because she believes in me.

She trusts me to take charge of my destiny.

And I love her so much for that.

I roll up my sleeve and show her all the other places Dad left his mark.

Chapter Thirty-Six

Griff

'Griff. Come in.' Imogen retreated from the door. 'We weren't expecting you.'

'I'm sorry. I wasn't aware I had to make an appointment to see my father.' Griff strode past her and into the living room. The green chair was empty. 'Where's Dad?' He doubled back into the hall to find Imogen with a foot on the first stair.

'He's in his bedroom. I was giving him a treatment.'

'What sort of treatment?'

Imogen laughed. 'You're serious today. I was giving him a massage if you must know. Would you like one? You seem tense.'

Griff relaxed his jaw and studied Imogen, trying to determine whether or not she was flirting with him. He'd assumed her tactile nature was part of who she was, but in the conversation he'd had with Evie, it became apparent Imogen used all the artillery in her arsenal to win her battles.

In hindsight, it was obvious he'd been played a little – the kiss to the mouth, the leg brushes, the hand rub – and Imogen had admitted to having a schoolgirl crush on him, but no harm had been done. What Griff didn't understand was why Imogen resorted to such tactics to secure his friendship. Unless, as Evie had said, Imogen thought they could be something more. 'When you're done, can we talk?'

'Of course.' Imogen climbed three steps, stopped and peered at Griff through the open balustrades. She smiled. 'I'll look forward to it.'

He waited for her to leave before spinning round and making his way through the living room to the kitchen.

'That didn't go to plan,' he said, opening the rear door. He shrugged off his jacket, threw it on the counter, and loosened his shirt collar.

He wasn't looking forward to their talk one bit.

He breathed in the soothing scents of his father's garden. Lavender. It was known for its relaxing properties. It was one of Marilyn's favourite plants. She'd dry out the flowers and make potpourri, or stitch them into palm-sized sachets to put in her clothes drawers. No wonder Logan kept the plant in his garden. He'd enjoy having sweet memories of his wife blown to him on a breeze.

Griff rolled back his sleeves. The south-facing garden was quite the suntrap, and the afternoon April sun was making no effort to escape.

Stepping over the door bar, he unreeled a foot of hose from its rack and gave it a tug. It didn't yield. 'Something else to fix.' This was exactly the sort of problem he needed to get on top of. These were the jobs he could do that would help Evie to help his dad. Using brute force, Griff freed enough pipe to reach the shrubs at the back of the garden. 'Someone's got to take care of you,' he said, thinking how thirsty the ground was. 'It's not like you can ask for help.'

Logan had. He'd asked for Evie's help, but such was the gravity of the question, she'd not been at liberty to discuss it with Griff. By rights, Griff should have been furious with Logan, but Evie asked him to be kind and to understand his father's reasons for privacy.

He did understand, but that wasn't going to stop him trying to talk his father round. There was a chance, now he was on board with the care plan, and with him and Evie working on getting back together, that his father would think differently about life. By pitching in and supporting one another, they'd prove to Logan he wasn't a burden; that looking after him was a privilege. They'd take trips out as a family of five; organise late days, when Logan could have lazy, lie-in mornings; spend whole days with him, rather than just mealtimes, and always show they've listened to him. If after that he still insisted he'd had enough of this world, then ... Then what?

Griff jumped as from behind a hand touched his bicep.

'I love to see a man working.' Imogen used Griff's arm as a pole and swung round to stand in front of him. 'There's something very primal about it.'

'I'm watering lavender, Imogen, not hunting stag.'

'Still.' She let go and stepped back, making a show of admiring his efforts. 'A girl's got to get her kicks where she can.'

There was no mistaking that flirt. Completing his task, Griff tidied away the hose, wiped a cobweb from the seat of the nearest of four metal chairs, and sat down. 'What's my father up to?'

Imogen repeated Griff's actions with the chair next to his. 'He's sleeping. What can I say? I'm good at my job. You should let me work on you.'

Interesting choice of words. 'Evie thinks you already have. Why did you tell her we've slept together?'

'She said that?'

Imogen's sheer indignation might have fooled Griff if his faith in Evie was anything but absolute.

She continued: 'I have no idea. Unless ...' She covered her mouth with her hand. 'No. Ignore me.'

He'd bite. Keep her talking. Braid a rope from her string of lies. 'What?'

'Well, with me helping here, she can't use this as a convenient bolthole any more. Perhaps she's finding other ways of keeping you at arm's length.'

'I don't play games, Imogen. You should know that by now.'

'I'm not playing games.' She sat forward, bowed her head, and put a hand on Griff's knee. 'Evie and I had a long chat yesterday and she doesn't want you in her life.' She looked up, her too-blue eyes doing a fair job of imitating sincerity. 'Don't you think it's time you faced facts? Your marriage is over.'

'Excuse me?' This was laughable. And shocking. Griff was astonished at the blatant nature of Imogen's lies, but until he understood her act, he'd refrain from applauding. 'Why are you here, Imogen? The real reason.'

She reclined, crossed her legs, leaving her high-heeled foot touching Griff's ankle, and folded her arms. 'To take care of your father.'

'No. Not that.' Griff waved an index finger at her. 'You have to stop lying now.'

She dropped her shoulders, sighed and bounced her foot up and down. It knocked the end of Griff's trouser leg. He tucked his feet under his chair.

'Okay.' Keeping one arm across her body, she unhooked the other and rubbed her cheek. 'When I saw you that day in that mad woman's craft shop, I was thrown back into my old life – a life of love and family and friendship. A life I lost and would give anything to have back.' She settled both arms on her stomach. 'And then you and I got chatting in the pub, and I realised we'd both had a rough ride. Kieran's death has left us both damaged.'

Her words sounded genuine, but her body was telling a different story. She was compact, tight, holding everything in. Griff remained silent, listening and observing.

'We were two lost souls,' she said. 'I was searching for closure and you were looking for forgiveness. It seemed to me we were each other's solution.' She returned to her bowed head pose. 'When I met Logan and he started talking about my father, I felt like I'd come home. It was so wonderful being part of something again. But it's not just that.' She looked up. 'I'm here for you.'

So Evie was right. 'Look, Imogen—'

'Don't say anything.' She was off her chair, leaning over Griff, with a hand on each of his arms. 'Evie doesn't love you. Don't be fooled by those innocent, green eyes. You talk about me playing games, but she's a master. She's toying with you. Keeping you hanging on until she finds something better.'

Griff scraped his chair back over the slabs, thinking Imogen would let go, but she lost her balance, toppled and fell further into him. Her orange perfume, once provocative, now sickly and toxic, permeated his pores and coated his tongue.

Imogen's mouth brushed his ear. 'She told me how you feel about me.'

'Will you stop with the lies, Imogen?' Griff flicked his arms away from his body, and Imogen lost her grip.

She stood up and withdrew to the lawn.

'What lies, Griff? The one about your self-harming daughter, or the one about your suicidal father? Or maybe you meant the big fat lie about how I lost everything after my brother died. How about the lie, *Griff Hendry, the hero*?'

'I've *never* thought of myself as that.' It wasn't a title Griff felt he deserved. It was the media's doing. They'd given him the label the day he'd pulled a drunken man from the harbour. 'I don't understand what's going on,' he said, vacating his seat and pacing the breadth of the garden. 'Tell me what this is about.' He came to a standstill at the garage wall, scrunched his eyes shut, and pressed his fingers into his temples.

'This is about you having everything, and me having nothing,' Imogen said, her voice travelling through the air. 'How unfair life is. How easy it is to destroy a person.'

As Griff spun round, he opened his eyes and immediately squinted. It took a moment for his eyes to adjust.

Imogen had crossed to the patio and was standing in front of the rear door.

'Kieran's death destroyed me,' she said. 'I thought, given time, I could forgive you. That if I spent long enough away from you, the hate would stop gnawing at my insides, and I could live a half-normal life. Moving to Glastonbury with Mum helped for a while, but then the selfish woman wrapped her car around a tree and I was alone, left covering a mortgage I couldn't afford, on a house that held no real memories. There was nothing of Kieran there. Everything I knew about him was back here. That's when I decided to come home. It took me two years to sell that awful house. I used the equity to put a month's money down on a flat, and secure a business premises in Dorchester. It was my new start.' She shook her head.

'But on my opening day, it wasn't my story the local press was covering. It was yours. You and your heroic record with the coastguard.' She turned her back to Griff and spread out her arms. 'And smack bang in the middle of the paper, staring out at me, was your smug face.' She swung round and glared at him. 'I knew then the gnawing wouldn't stop. At least, not until you understood what it was to lose everything. So I set out to find you.'

'To what? Wreck my life?' With his head pounding from the verbal hammering, Griff returned to the security of a garden chair. He clamped his hands behind his neck, closed his eyes, and focused on his breathing. If he remained quiet, perhaps Imogen would do the same.

'It didn't take me long to track you down, not with your celebrity status,' she said. 'It was just a matter of time before we ran into one another on the beach.'

Griff's eyes burst open and he threw himself upright. 'You engineered that meeting?'

Imogen laughed. 'Honey's not even my dog. Can't stand

the creature. I borrow her from a woman who rents space at my clinic. Did you like how I'd etched my number onto the dirty mutt's tag? It's all in the detail. It certainly sucked you in.' She laughed again, and then joined Griff at the seats, positioning hers inches away from his feet. 'You're lucky it was only your dog injured in the accident.'

'Don't you dare bring Ozzy into this.' Griff leapt up and stormed towards the kitchen. His chair crashed to the floor. 'If it hadn't been for Honey, he'd still be here.'

He regretted his words as soon as they'd been aired.

'And if it hadn't been for you, Kieran would still be here.' Imogen was right behind, poking his back.

The soles of Griff's shoes scratched on the stone as he reeled and grabbed Imogen's hand. 'This has gone far enough.'

She yanked herself free. 'I'm nowhere near done. I'm going to make sure you have nothing left. No job, no home, no family. The dog dying was a bonus and you've already lost your home. I thought breaking you and Evie up would prove easier, but I can deal with that. Tess ... I could turn her against you with not much more than a wink, and as for Logan ... He's begging me to put him out of his misery.'

Griff slammed his fist on the kitchen window ledge. 'Enough!' In less than five minutes since being exposed for lying, Imogen was a seething mass of hatred, jealousy and revenge. Her spiteful words upset Griff, and her wicked threats unnerved him, but there was no way he'd let her hurt his family. 'You stay away from Tess, you don't talk to Evie, and you don't as much as look at my father. When we go inside, you'll give me your key for this house, gather your belongings, and leave.' Griff stood clear of the doorway.

'No. That's not going to happen. Your father wants me here. I can do the one thing for him the rest of you won't.' Imogen folded her arms and refused to move. 'How does it feel to know you can't save your own father?'

She was pressing all of Griff's buttons, riling him, provoking him into biting back, but recent events had taught him there were times when you had to let things go. 'Give it up, Imogen,' he said, tired with her games. 'Go home.'

He headed indoors, and Imogen followed.

'Do you think you can talk your father round? That he'll listen to you? I wouldn't count on it,' she said. 'Experience has taught me Hendry men never listen to anyone but themselves. You didn't listen to Kieran when he begged you not to jump off that bloody rock, did you?'

'When he begged me not to jump? Oh, Imogen.' She'd hit a new low with that statement. 'I get how angry you are, how much you miss Kieran and your parents, I even accept I'm the person you want to lash out at, but don't twist the facts to justify your actions.' Crossing from the kitchen to the living room, Griff indicated for Imogen to enter the hall.

'I'm not twisting anything,' she said, shoving the door shut, and barring Griff's exit.

'Fine. Reinventing them.' Griff perched on the green chair. 'If it helps you sleep at night, I can live with that, but I won't lie if I'm asked what happened. I bear the guilt of not stopping Kieran. Of not saving him. I won't add the weight of deceit, too.'

'Saving him?' Imogen shook her head. 'He saved you. He lost his life doing so. He begged you not to jump, but you didn't listen. You went ahead anyway, and you got into trouble—'

'No. That's not what happened.' Although Griff had interrupted, he spoke softly. Confusion was forming in Imogen's eyes, and it seemed to be questioning what she was saying. 'Who told you this?' Griff asked, leading her to the sofa and sitting her down.

'My mum. She said Kieran had been a true hero that day.'

No wonder the Joliffes had insisted on Griff staying away. He was the only one who would have set Imogen straight. 'Look, I don't know why she said that, maybe because you were so young, maybe because she didn't want you thinking badly of Kieran, I don't know, but it's wrong. I could show you the newspaper reports from the time if that would help. I have them at home.' They were packed in a plastic bag and hidden away in a storage box that had been pushed to the furthest corner of the loft. 'Kieran was going to jump regardless of anything I said to him. And while I live my life convinced I could have done more, I don't actually know what would have stopped him. I went in after him, but ...' Keeping a close eye on Imogen, Griff stepped back and sat on the edge of the coffee table. It was now clear to him she'd lived most of her life believing he was the cause of her brother's death. In her mind, that made Griff responsible for the breakdown of her parents' marriage, and the loss of her mother. He couldn't excuse Imogen's behaviour – she'd set out to play God with his world – but he could understand it.

'Why should I believe you?' she said, her voice barely a whisper. 'You could be saying that just to get me out of your life.'

'Until you started wielding threats, I didn't want you out of my life. I've spent twenty-four years hoping you'd be a part of it.' Griff scraped his fingers through his hair, sighed and looked at Imogen. 'Like I said, I have press cuttings at home if you'd like to see them.'

His offer was not acknowledged, so Griff said nothing more. He was thankful for the break in the storm. A lot of information had been exchanged, which he and Imogen had to absorb. She had a huge task ahead of her, coming to terms with the truth. That was not to be underestimated.

After a few minutes of silent contemplation, she stirred.

'So it really was the other way round?' She clasped a cushion to her breast. 'Kieran went in first and you tried to save him?'

'Yeah.' Griff rubbed at the ache in his ankle. 'I've spent my life trying to save him.'

'He wasn't the hero?'

'He was a sixteen-year-old lad, Imy, doing what lads do.'

'But he wasn't a hero.' With great care, she returned the cushion to its proper place, teased it into position, and laid her palm flat on the sofa. 'Logan likes them just so.'

Without another word, she picked up her handbag from the floor, reached inside and pulled out a key.

She passed it to Griff on her way to the hall.

'I'll walk you out,' he said.

He watched as she climbed into her car, leaned on the steering wheel and buried her head in her arms. Her shoulders jogged up and down.

'Oh, Imogen,' Griff said as the click of the door latch echoed round the hall. 'I hope you find what you're looking for.'

He waited at the bottom of the stairs while the dust settled and while he worked out what to say to Logan, then, after a deliberate, slow, step by step journey, he arrived on the landing and tapped on his father's door. 'Hey, Dad. Are you awake?' He crept in.

Logan, propped up with the head end of his bed raised, opened his eyes. 'Griff. I was hoping you'd call in.' He smiled. There was genuine warmth behind it, but its energy level was low. 'Sit.'

Griff pulled the white wicker chair next to the bed and did as he was told. 'Dad, we need to talk.' He steepled his fingers together and put the tips to his mouth. 'I'll get straight to the point. I know everything. I know about your living will and I know you have an exit plan.'

'An exit plan. I like that name.' Logan looked at Griff. 'You're not angry?'

'No. I'm ashamed of myself for not being the one you or Evie could turn to.' He pulled Logan's duvet tidy. 'I wish I was a better person. I'm working on it. I'm learning to listen.' Something Griff had failed to do with Marilyn and was desperate to rectify with his father.

Logan's trembling hand slid out from under the duvet, and Griff covered it with his. How large his hands were now compared to his father's.

'If I could have gone with your mother, I would have,' Logan said. 'She was the love of my life. But I was destined to remain, and there are many reasons I'm glad I did. I've been part of a wonderful family, I've become a granddad twice, I've come to know Evie, a beautiful, caring woman who'd move the earth if you asked her, and you've come back to me.'

'I never stopped loving you.' Griff closed his eyes and squeezed the bridge of his nose. Water dispersed across his fingertips. 'I should have shown you.'

'You're showing me now.'

Griff blinked open his eyes, and nodded. 'But I wasted six years. Years we'll never get back.'

'I can't deny I've had better.' The skin around Logan's mouth crinkled. 'But I had faith in you. I knew we'd be all right.'

'But you're not, are you, Dad?' Griff cast his gaze over Logan's diminutive frame. 'There's nothing of you.' There'd been nothing left of Marilyn in her final days. No flesh on her bones.

'I live with pain,' said Logan. 'It's what it does to a person. It burns from the inside, and stops me breathing, and walking, and talking. Day in, day out, I'm stuck in that wretched green chair waiting for someone to come to the house. Anyone. I pray the postman will stop with a large parcel just so I can speak to a human being. I can go weeks without seeing anyone other than Evie, and while I love her with all my heart, she's your wife, not mine.' He laid back and closed his eyes. 'I'm sorry for the pressure I put on your marriage. She loves you very much. Don't blow it.'

'I promise.' This was beginning to sound like the last farewell. Griff held his father's hand a little tighter.

Logan opened his eyes and smiled. There was more strength to it than the last. 'Do you understand why I can't be here any more? Why it's time to go?'

Griff swallowed down the rising ball of emotion. 'I've only just got you back.'

'And that's why I can go. You don't need me any more. It's time for me to be with Marilyn.' Logan tugged at Griff's hand, and Griff leaned in. 'And you don't need to worry. Everything is in order. Imogen knows what to do.'

'Dad?' Griff hesitated, hating the fact he was the bearer of bad news. He looked at his father, small, fragile, full of anticipation. 'Imogen's not going to help you.'

'She's not? But she agreed. She said she understands.' Logan retracted his hand, and rallied himself into a sitting position. 'Imogen,' he shouted.

'She's not here. She's gone.'

'Gone where? What did you say to her?'

'Nothing. I promise.' As far as Griff was concerned, there was no value in providing an explanation of Imogen's conduct. Logan believed she was the answer to his prayers, and that she'd consented to helping him for his benefit. Only hurt would come from revealing her true purpose. 'I think the reality of the situation hit home.' It wasn't a lie. 'I don't believe we'll see her again.'

Logan collapsed onto his pillow, his head shaking and his eyes brimming with tears. 'Who will save me now?'

Chapter Thirty-Seven

Evie

The hot summer sun glinted off the Happiness jar, sending starbursts all over the kitchen. Evie was drawn to it the way Alice was drawn to the Wonderland bottle that read 'Drink me'.

'Read me,' the jar said. 'Read me.'

Alone in the house, Evie decided she could fish the first few notes out, take a peek, then pop them back in. The jar was so full, no one would know it had been tampered with. It wasn't like she was drinking from the expensive brandy bottle and refilling it with vinegar.

She'd been found out on that occasion.

As she lifted the container down from the windowsill, her mobile buzzed. She managed to retain her grasp of the jar despite the rapid heartbeat and sweaty palms the sudden noise had caused.

She swiped the phone into life and activated Griff's message.

Hi. Dropped Tess at the café. We're with Olivia on Chesil collecting sea treasure. Dylan's having great fun with Aila. We've got her walking to heel already. She's one smart dog. I'll assume you're making the most of your quiet time. Love you. Xxx

Evie settled at the table, unscrewed the lid of the jar and tipped out the entire contents. If she was going to read them, she was going to read them all. She could act coy and innocent come the traditional New Year's Eve reveal. It wouldn't be the first time.

'There are loads,' she said, revelling at the mountain of

notes. 'I'll be here for hours. Perhaps I best stick to reading a handful.'

She pondered on how the Happiness jar reflected her life. During bad times, it stayed stagnant, but in good times, it became full to overflowing. Since April, the number of tickets the family had added had tripled.

'Right then.' She rubbed her hands together, and picked up a yellow sticky note – one of Tess's.

I've been clean for two whole weeks!

That was an older ticket. Evie knew precisely how long Tess had remained clean, and it far exceeded two weeks.

Next, Evie went for the neat-edged, stark white paper. Bound to be Griff's, she thought.

I fixed the squeaky floorboard in Tess's room.

That was a big deal. Tess had opened her room to Griff.

Evie sighed. She chose one of her own notes next, written on lined paper.

After four long months, the cottage is full again. Griff is home.

There was so much more she could have added to those few lines, but nothing suitable for a family reading. The day Griff moved back home had been incredible. The thought alone was enough to send Evie's insides cartwheeling.

She abandoned her station to open the back door, grateful of the smallest breeze. July was turning into one of the hottest on record.

Back at the table, and in the spirit of fairness, she chose another of Tess's tickets.

Finally! Griff fixed that annoying squeaky floorboard in my room. One less trigger. Thanks, Griff ☺ Talking of triggers, Mum got the bully from my sports class expelled. Result. (Count this note as two, Mum. Ps: You're awesome.)

'I'd debate that,' Evie said. 'If I was that awesome you wouldn't have suffered for as long as you did.' When she'd found out what had been happening to Tess at school, she'd gone into full attack mode, emailing, phoning and visiting the principal until he had the bully removed. 'But I love you for saying that.' She kissed the piece of paper. 'Who's next?' She checked the open notes. 'Griff. What have you been up to?'

I turned 40 today. (Should this be in the Happiness jar?)

Laughing out loud, Evie set the ticket aside. They'd had an intimate gathering to celebrate that milestone, with a menu consisting of jelly, Marmite sandwiches, and orange squash. Dylan had a fantastic time. They all did.

'My turn, again.' As she opened her note, a second fell out. 'Bonus. I get to read both of you.'

I was assertive. I said no to helping out at next week's Mums and Toddlers group. (It's Griff's birthday and Dylan wants to make jelly.)

It was only a couple of months ago, but it was so lovely to have the memory in black and white. Evie didn't make a habit of turning people down, but she was learning the art of saying no at the appropriate time.

She retrieved the bonus ticket. 'And what little joy do you hold?'

Tess encouraged me to take singing lessons. I had my first one today. I loved it!

'You have the time now, Mum,' Tess had told her. 'And it's healthy to do something just for you.'

She wasn't wrong. Singing lifted Evie's spirit.

'I shall practice my Italian vowels later,' she said, dabbing her finger on the sticky strip of one of Tess's sheets.

As of now (this will be read on New Year's Eve, right?) I would like to be known as Tess Hendry. Is that all right with you and Griff, Mum?

'Wow!' Evie reread the comment for the sheer pleasure it gave. 'You kept that quiet, Tess. What a lovely surprise.'

She could already imagine the look of pride on Griff's face as he introduced his daughter as Tess Hendry. 'You never cease to amaze me.'

Evie hid the note in the middle of the heap, extracting one that had Griff's modus operandi.

I tuned my guitar today. First time in years I've picked it up. I taught Tess how to play the intro to 'Smoke On The Water'. She's a natural. Dylan's already her groupie.

The two-and-a-half-year-old had rocked his little socks off. Literally. Evie found them three days later, packed away in the toy box.

These were great memories.

A couple more each, she thought, pinching a yellow sticky note between her fingers, and then I'll put you away.

Started counselling today. I really think this is going to help.

Tess was doing magnificently well, and Evie was so proud of her. She'd taken control and was dealing with her demons. Somewhere in the pile was a note of Tess's that read she'd been clean for two months. Evie had been with her when she'd written it. They'd high-fived at the time.

Next, another precise, ninety-degree piece of paper from Griff. Evie unfolded it and smiled at the words.

We welcomed a new member to the family – Aila – a three-year-old female Siberian Husky, rehomed from the rescue centre. Aila is a Scottish name meaning 'from a strong place.' She is gorgeous.

Griff was a man who needed a dog. It was as simple as that. A month after they'd scattered Ozzy's ashes at The Bill, Evie broached the subject. Two weeks later, they'd fallen in love with Aila.

'My turn again.' She nudged a couple of notes out of the way, and went for one she knew she'd only recently written.

I read an announcement in the paper today. Imogen

Joliffe is engaged to be married. I hope she's found peace and true love, I really do.

One last round. Evie went for a thick wodge of sticky notes. It appeared Tess had written a tome.

Stephanie is back! And I told her the stuff about Dad and she's cool. After that, though, we had our first disagreement – we argued over what to do tonight. Stupid. (Wait, Mum! This is a Happiness note, after all!) Even though we fell out, I didn't feel the urge to cut! And S and I made up. (See? Told you it was a good one.)

'My beautiful, intelligent girl.' Things were certainly on the up. And it turned out Stephanie was excellent girlfriend material.

'Last one for you, Griff.'

*Dad's cremation. We miss you, Dad, but you deserve a place in our jar because you brought us much happiness, and because I know **you** are finally happy. Give our love to Mum.*

Logan had died on April the fourth; a date Evie had branded on her mind.

After years of fearing she'd be the one to find him dead, by a cruel and unkind twist of fate, it had been Griff who'd played out the scene.

'I'll go this morning,' he said. 'You had a tough day yesterday.'

It had been tough. It had been the day on Portland Bill when Evie had disclosed the secrets surrounding Logan's request for help. And, among other revelations, the day she'd expressed her suspicion Imogen was not all she purported to be. It had left Evie exhausted and emotional.

'But it was no walk in the park for you,' she said, reminding Griff he'd been to Logan's to challenge Imogen that same afternoon. 'That can't have been easy, judging by the hour you got home.' She'd invited him back that night, but was in bed asleep before he'd returned. She'd been aware of him pulling back the duvet and climbing in beside her, but she hadn't been able to properly wake to ask him how things had gone.

And then he was dashing out again.

'It was fine,' he said. 'I'll tell you about it when I get back.'

He called her thirty minutes later. He'd discovered his father in bed, cold and still, but serene, a drained bottle of whiskey in his hand and his red tin beside him, emptied of his cocktail of pills.

Logan had executed his exit plan.

Wiping away a tear, Evie scooped up the Happiness tickets and tipped them back into their makeshift home. Griff's note was right. Logan was where he wanted to be, and that needed to be celebrated, not mourned.

She reached behind her and retrieved a pen and her notebook from the worktop. Tearing off a strip of lined paper, she smiled.

I read some of these notes in July. They made me happy.

Chapter Thirty-Eight

Griff

The welcome sea breeze tamed the hot August sun as Griff and Evie strolled the length of Chesil Beach from Olivia's craft centre to Madame Dubois' café bistro.

Two paces ahead, Dylan tiptoed in and out of the gentle waves, giggling as the water and shingle washed over his feet.

At Griff's heel, Aila was keeping an attentive eye on the youngster.

Griff checked his watch. His father's watch.

Hours before he'd died, Logan had passed it to him, saying he could no longer wind it or change the hands, and it would fit Griff 'far better than that stupid one that's always slipping around your wrist.'

He was right. It did. And wearing it gave Griff the sense his father was still close by.

'We'll collect the girls and head off,' he said, his arm relaxed and loose around Evie's waist.

'Are you sure you're okay?' Her fingers were looped through his belt. She gave it a tug and Griff looked down at her.

'I'm fine. Stop worrying. It's a relief. One more thing to tick off the list.'

The sale on Logan's house had completed that morning. They'd accepted a lower offer than the asking price, as the buyer had an issue with it being a house where someone had died. It had been impossible keeping that fact from any of the prospective purchasers.

Griff had kept the details to the minimum, though, as he had with Evie about his father's death.

The picture he'd painted for her was less colourful than the real thing.

Logan had taken his cocktail of drugs, he had consumed a large bottle of whiskey, and they had knocked him out, but in the state of unconsciousness, he'd thrown up and suffocated.

It was enough that Griff knew. His family didn't need to imagine what he saw.

'Thanks for helping me sort through his things.' He pulled Evie's hand to his mouth and gave it a kiss. 'It was tougher than I expected, especially when I found those letters.'

In among Logan's private papers, Griff had found a bundle of handwritten letters addressed to Marilyn. Each envelope was marked with a month and year in the top left-hand corner.

They were all dated after Marilyn's death.

'Have you read them?' Evie looked at Griff.

He shook his head. 'No. I'm going to burn them.' It was fitting to give the love letters the same send-off as Logan. 'It sounds daft, but I feel like the ashes would be carried up into the clouds and they'd reach Dad. It's up to him what he does with them, then.'

'It doesn't sound daft at all.' Evie rubbed his back. 'It's a lovely thought.'

They walked the rest of the journey in a contemplative silence, stopping outside the café to exchange a full-on kiss.

'I have to get the girls,' Evie said, her reluctance to part making Griff smile.

Dylan scrambled up the bistro steps after her, leaving his dad and Aila to enjoy the hush of the water and the shushing of the pebbles.

'I used to bring Ozzy here,' Griff said, rumpling Aila's neck. 'I couldn't keep him out of the sea.'

'Well, look who it is, the only Welsh Highlander in the village.'

Instantly recognising Frank's voice, Griff smiled and waved without turning. 'How are you, old man?'

As Frank pulled alongside, Aila's tail switched from idling to overdrive. 'I'm good, thanks. Haven't seen you in a while. Everything okay?' He made a fuss of the dog.

'Everything's great, thanks. We're taking the time to regroup. Learning to live as a family of four.'

'Five,' Frank said, pointing to Aila.

'Five. As much as I loved my dad, it's been wonderful having Evie around.' With more time to spend together, Griff and Evie had rediscovered the joys of cuddling on the sofa watching soaps, eating dinner at the kitchen table, and sharing a shower in the morning. Their love had deepened; matured. Grown stronger. 'I think we've all benefitted.'

'Sounds as if you're getting sorted. Don't rush yourself, though, Griff. Logan was a big part of your life. And Evie's. Well, all of you. I hear Tess was an absolute star with him.'

'Yeah. She's pretty special.'

'Did you ever get to chat to Olivia about teens? Do you remember? That freezing day at the start of the year when we were doing a beach clean-up and you squelched your way out of the Harbour Inn?'

Griff nodded, then laughed as he recalled the day. 'I never got round to asking Olivia's advice. I'll drop by when Dylan turns thirteen.' He commanded an excitable Aila to sit. 'I did squelch that day. My jeans were wet. I'd been at The Bill and ended up sprawled on the grass stopping a young lad from being swept into the sea.'

'I win the bet.' Frank clapped his hands.

'What bet?'

'Olivia and I had a tenner each riding on why your trousers were wet. I won.'

'Do I want to know why Olivia thought I was soaked through?'

Frank sealed his lips and shook his head.

Laughing again, Griff slapped the older man on the back, wished him well, and sent him on his way. 'Say hi to Olivia and tell her we'll be in soon,' he said.

Frank saluted.

'Hey. How's my girl?' Tess ran to greet Aila, sending her into another frenzy of ramped-up tail wagging. 'All right, Griff? Stephanie's mum's holding a *soiree* this evening and she's asked me to invite you and Mum. Stephanie's dad will be here. I'm quite nervous about meeting him. Do you think he'll be all right with me being the G word? Ginger?' She beamed at Griff and pointed a finger. 'Got you.'

'Bonjour, Monsieur Hendry.' Stephanie slipped in beside Tess. 'Will you be coming tonight? I'd love for you to meet my father. He's a marine scientist. I think you will have plenty to talk about.'

'We'll be there, won't we?' Evie joined the gathering, with Dylan bringing up the rear. 'Dylan's had his very own invite. He's very excited.' She picked him up and plonked him on her hip as he brandished a small French flag at Aila.

'We'll be there.' Griff waved to Madame Dubois, who was standing in the café doorway. 'We'll see you later. Right, Portland Bill here we come.'

To Griff's delight, the lighthouse was open to the public. It was a glorious day, perfect for taking in the view.

With Tess and Stephanie taking Aila for an ice cream, Griff, Evie and Dylan made their way into the building.

'I've never been in here,' Evie said. 'I brought Dylan at Easter, but it was closed. I always seem to choose the days it's closed.'

'You'll love it, especially the view from the top. Come

on.' Taking charge of Dylan, Griff motioned for Evie to go ahead, and the trio started to climb the black, metal steps. They stopped at each landing point to allow Dylan to rest his legs and peek through a window.

Every other flight saw the toddler hitching a ride with his dad.

'Round and round we go,' Griff said, keeping Dylan's energy high. 'There are about a hundred and fifty steps. And there's this huge bulb at the top. I bet Mum can get there before you.'

'I bet Mum can't.' Evie put her hand to her chest and feigned panting.

'I bet you can if I do this.' Griff patted her bottom and she picked up the pace.

The final set of steps was trickier to negotiate. It was narrow and vertical, more like a ladder than stairs. Evie climbed up first and waited for Dylan, who was protected from falling backwards by Griff.

Once all three were safely at the top, Griff lifted Dylan into the crook of one arm, and pulled Evie into the other. They stood, looking out over the Bill.

Below them to their left was the busy little café and ice cream parlour, and further back was a cluster of multi-coloured huts, which always reminded Griff of shoe boxes. Further still was the white tower of the bird observatory.

'Stephie!' Dylan wriggled and pointed to where Stephanie, Tess and Aila were queuing for ice cream. Aila was fidgeting as much as Dylan.

'Tess is doing well, isn't she?' Griff said. 'I'm proud of her.'

'Me, too. I think she's going to be fine.' Evie nestled into Griff's shoulder. 'And I know they're still young and finding their way, but she and Stephanie seem really happy.'

'They take good care of each other. And have you noticed

how when one is talking, the other is completely tuned in? They're great listeners.' A skill Griff had taken forty years to learn. He drew Dylan's attention to a string of kayakers straight ahead, then said to Evie, 'Tell me if I don't listen. It's important to me that you know you've been heard.'

'I promise,' Evie said, inclining her head until her cheek touched Griff's chin. 'And you tell me when things get too much. You don't have to save the world, just be in ours.'

Lowering Dylan to the floor, Griff directed his son's interest towards the large lenses and huge bulb, then he wrapped his arms around Evie.

Over her shoulder and through the lighthouse windows, Pulpit Rock challenged him.

For years, Griff tortured himself by staring at the ancient stack, blaming himself for Kieran's death. Its existence and what it stood for had forced him to confront his own mortality, but he'd spent enough years tormented by ghosts. It was time to concentrate on the living.

'I'm not dead yet,' he said, breathing Evie in.

She glanced up, her eyes liquid emerald.

Always starts with the eyes, Griff thought, losing himself in the moment. He stroked her hair away from her face, trailed his fingers down her neck, and kissed a path from one ear to the other. Her breath quickened, each blow landing legions of shivers on his skin. 'It's not been easy,' he said, his mouth finding hers, the bold playfulness of her lips making his curl. 'And I never want us to go through anything like the past few months again. But you know what?' He took her face in his hands, skimmed the pads of his thumbs over her flawless cheeks, and marvelled at the raw power of the love and desire raging behind her eyes. 'I wouldn't have thought it possible, but we are stronger.'

Holding his breath, he ran his hands down Evie's sides, stopped at her hips and pulled her into him. As he slid his fingers round the back of her thighs, a smaller, more youthful set of fingers grabbed his.

His sense of place brought back to him by Dylan, Griff laughed, kissed Evie, whispering, 'Later,' to her, and swept their child into his arms. 'I think we could all use an ice cream,' he said, fanning the air. 'What do you think, Evie?'

Evie opened her eyes, adjusted her T-shirt and dabbed her lips. 'I think I was just saved by my son.'

Her smile lit up her face, illuminated the building, and radiated out across the Bill.

And Griffith Hendry saw the world in a whole new light.

Chapter Thirty-Nine

Logan

April 3rd

Dearest Griff,

Take comfort from knowing I am happy.

I want to look down and see you laughing and loving, and dancing and singing. Get that old guitar out and serenade your beautiful wife. Shock the unshockable, delightful Tess and get a tattoo; teach that handsome Dylan to swim.

Spend as much time as you can with your family.

It's time for you to live your life.

I'm proud of you and I want to say thank you.

You listened and you saved me.

Dad.

Book Club Questions

What would you do in Evie's position? Would you go along with Logan's request? What factors would influence your decision? Would you tell Griff?

Was Logan being fair to ask Evie?

Do you think a person has the right to choose when to die? What are the arguments for and against?

What would you do if you suspected your child of self-harming?

Thank you

Thank you for reading *What Doesn't Kill You*, the third, standalone book in the Chesil Beach series, and the first under Choc Lit's Dark imprint.

Why the Dark imprint? Well, my characters have a habit of straying from the main road and ducking into shady alleys, and Griff, Evie, Tess and Logan are no exception, although, to help them find their way, I've tried to ensure they each carry a metaphorical torch which they can shine into the blackest corners. The issues raised in the novel are hard-hitting and emotional, both to write and read about, so I thank you for keeping the faith and walking the challenging paths side-by-side with the Hendrys.

I hope you enjoyed the beautiful and dramatic setting of the Jurassic Coast. The initial idea for *What Doesn't Kill You* was sparked by the wild storms of early 2014, where England's exposed south west coastline suffered horrendous damage. There were waves of epic proportion, debris and marine life washed ashore, and parts of the Dorset landscape completely destroyed, but the communities pulled together as beach clean-up parties were organised and the residents of Weymouth and Portland set to work. I have lived in Dorset for many years and consider it my home. I feel blessed to have such wonderful people, stunning scenery and incredible inspiration on my doorstep, not to mention the friendly, comfortable, beachside cafés on hand, that serve up spectacular views and amazing hot chocolate.

Before I go, I'd like to thank everyone who takes the time to read and review books. Reader feedback is invaluable as it provides encouragement to authors to keep learning and writing, and recommendations to fellow readers. If you enjoyed *What Doesn't Kill You*, reviews of any length, from two words to several lines or paragraphs, are always welcomed and very much appreciated. If you'd like to get in touch with me, or find out more about the Chesil Beach books, my details are under my author profile.

Many thanks and happy reading.

Laura xx

About the Author

Laura is married and has two children. She lives in Dorset, but spent her formative years in Watford, a brief train ride away from the bright lights of London. Here she indulged her love of live music, and, following a spectacular Stevie Nicks gig, decided to take up singing, a passion that scored her second place in a national competition.

Laura is a graduate of the Romantic Novelists' Association's New Writers' Scheme, a member of her local writing group, Off The Cuff, and an editor of the popular Romaniacs blog.

Laura was runner-up twice in the Choc Lit Short Story competitions. Her story *Bitter Sweet* appears in the Romantic Novelists' Association's Anthology. *Truth or Dare?*, Laura's debut novel, was shortlisted for the 2014 Joan Hessayon New Writers' Award. *What Doesn't Kill You* is the third novel in Laura's Chesil Beach series.

www.lauraejames.co.uk
www.twitter.com/Laura_E_James
www.facebook.com/LauraE.JamesWriter

More Choc Lit

From Laura E. James

Truth or Dare?

Book 1 in the Chesil Beach series

The path to love …

Kate Blair's sick of unrequited love. She's quietly waited for Mickey for the past six years and finding a compass-carved heart, with their initials scratched through the middle, only strengthens her resolve: no more Mickey and no more playing it safe.

It's time to take a chance on real love and Declan O'Brien's the perfect risk. He's handsome, kind and crazy about her so it's not long before all thoughts of Mickey come few and far between.

But old habits die-hard. Kate may have started to forget … but has Mickey?

Visit www.choc-lit.com for more details, or simply scan barcode using your mobile phone QR reader.

Follow me follow you

Book 2 in the Chesil Beach series

You save me and I'll save you

Victoria Noble has pulled the plug on romance. As director of the number one social networking site, EweSpeak, and single mother to four-year-old Seth, she wrestles with the work–life balance.

Enter Chris Frampton, Hollywood action hero and Victoria's first love. His return from LA has sparked a powder keg of media attention, and with secrets threatening to fuel the fire, he's desperate to escape. But finding a way forward is never simple. Although his connection with Victoria has lasted the test of time, has he been adrift too long to know how to move on?

With the risk of them breaking, will either #follow their heart?

Visit www.choc-lit.com for more details, or simply scan barcode using your mobile phone QR reader.

Introducing Choc Lit

We're an independent publisher creating
a delicious selection of fiction.
Where heroes are like chocolate – irresistible!
Quality stories with a romance at the heart.

See our selection here:
www.choc-lit.com

We'd love to hear how you enjoyed *What Doesn't Kill
You*. Please leave a review where you purchased the novel
or visit: **www.choc-lit.com** and give your feedback.

Choc Lit novels are selected by genuine readers like yourself.
We only publish stories our Choc Lit Tasting Panel want to
see in print. Our reviews and awards speak for themselves.

**Could you be a Star Selector
and join our Tasting Panel?**
Would you like to play a role in choosing which novels we
decide to publish? Do you enjoy reading romance novels?
Then you could be perfect for our Choc Lit Tasting Panel.

Visit here for more details...

Keep in touch:
Sign up for our monthly newsletter Choc Lit Spread for
all the latest news and offers: www.spread.choc-lit.com.
Follow us on Twitter: @ChocLituk and Facebook: Choc Lit.

Where heroes are like chocolate – irresistible!